when
i fall

Alabama
Summer
Series,
Book Three

New York Times bestselling author
J. DANIELS

To Beth Cranford, for loving Reed since he joked about fingering Mia underneath the table.

This is for you.

when

Alabama
Summer
Series,
Book Three

i fall

beth

NEVER THOUGHT a phone call could change my life.

Clothes are flying everywhere as I ransack the bedroom, grabbing everything I own and stuffing it into the open duffle bag on the bed. I don't care how messy I pack right now. I don't care if every article of clothing is wrinkled beyond recognition. I don't want to stay here another second, and now, I don't have to.

"What are you doin', baby?"

I look up at Rocco, standing in the doorway of the bedroom, self-righteous smirk in place.

"What does it look like I'm doing?"

"It looks like you're boltin'."

Genius.

"Yeah, I'm boltin'. I should've never come here in the first place."

He grins and leans his shoulder against the doorframe. "Where you gonna go, huh? Back to sleepin' in your car? You ain't got nobody, Beth. No family . . ."

"I *do* have family," I bite out as my bottom lip begins to tremble. It ceases with the sharp breath I take in. "Turns out my momma has a sister, and she told me I can live with her. *That's* where I'm going."

He shakes his head slowly through a laugh and I look away, grabbing my Kindle off the dresser and lying it on top of my balled up T-shirts.

"You takin' that with you?"

I freeze with my hand on the zipper, slowly lifting my head to meet his icy-blue stare.

I'd never beg for anything from this man. But this, this I might just beg for.

"Go ahead," he says, pushing off the frame and straightening up. "What the fuck would I do with it?"

"Thank you," I reply sincerely, as he turns and heads back down the hallway.

I am grateful for a lot of things Rocco has given me. Food, shelter, money when I wanted a nice headstone for my momma. But there are other things he's given me that I wish I could give back. Things I wish I could leave behind.

Zipping up the duffle and securing it over my shoulder, I step into my old, tattered Dr. Martens, grab my keys off the dresser, and tuck my cell phone into my back pocket.

I'm almost to the front door when Rocco puts his body in between me and the only family I have left.

"Where you goin'?"

"None of your business."

His chest shakes with silent laughter. Mocking. Always mocking me. He tilts his head. "It doesn't matter. You'll be walking back through this door eventually."

I reach up and adjust the strap on my shoulder, just as the whore Rocco picked up from God knows where giggles from her spot on the couch. I don't need to look to know she's naked. Rocco is, so why wouldn't she be?

"I'm never coming back here," I say through a clenched jaw, swallowing down my emotions. "You said you would never keep me here, Rocco. You said once I had a place to go . . ."

"Beth," he says in the softest voice I've ever heard him

use, "I ain't keepin' you here. I don't need to, baby. Fact is, it'll be real sweet when you come crawlin' back to me. I'm lookin' real forward to that." His smile hits me, the same smile that lured me in three months ago, and I fight against my heart's automatic response to this side of him. But it beats wildly in my chest, desperate for this type of connection with someone.

I don't want it with you.

His hands mold to my face, and I brace myself for his next words. I know this mind-game he works on me. I've heard countless versions of it. It's his way of keeping me here, because he would never force me to stay against my will. He's never forced me to do anything.

Rocco gets off on your need for him. Not the other way around.

"No one will ever love you the way I do. No one, you hear me?"

I don't respond. I don't give him anything except my cold stare.

"Those fake pricks you read about on that fucking tablet of yours don't exist. I've told you that. If they did, do you know what they would do?" He leans closer, brushing his nose against my temple.

I close my eyes to shut him out, to keep these words from staying with me.

"They'd fuck you cause you got a hot pussy, then they'd toss you out 'cause they wouldn't want you. No one will want you, baby."

No. I don't believe that. I've never believed that.

I jerk my head out of his hands and move past him, swinging the door open with enough force, the hinges shriek.

His laughter fades in the distance behind me, and I pray I never hear it again. It's almost as bad as the words he uses to break me down with. But I'm not broken, and someone will want me. He's wrong. He has to be wrong.

I slip my phone out of my pocket and dial the number I programmed a few hours ago. The one I didn't know about until today.

"Hello?" A sleepy voice answers on the second ring.

"Aunt Hattie. It's Beth."

I hear movement, covers rustling, then a soft, "Sweetie, it's Beth," before she speaks into the receiver. "Are you coming, darlin'?"

I smile, my first real smile in months.

"I'm coming."

reed

WAS IN love once.

Once. One time too many.

I don't remember what it feels like. I won't let myself remember it. I've burned that part of me, stepped away from the ashes so that I don't have this constant reminder of how pathetic I'd let myself become. That's what love did to me nine years ago. It made me pathetic.

Vulnerable.

Blind.

So *fucking* blind.

I know what kind of man I am. I know exactly what happens when I allow some piece of ass to become anything more than what I need them to be, and I won't make that same mistake again. I fell fast and hard with her, but that shit was something I couldn't control. What's worse was I didn't even want control.

I wanted it desperate. Thoughtless.

But that's how I am. It's how I still fucking am, and it's what makes anything other than mindless, detached fucking out of the question now. I won't leave myself helpless for someone again, not when I know how it'll end for me.

So, I keep my heart out of it. I have to.

I'm a smart guy when I'm thinking with my dick, but when I allow the weakest part of me to get involved, I'm the dumbest motherfucker on the planet.

My heart isn't mixed up in this. It's not even in the damn state right now.

"I won't fuck you again after tonight." I drop my head and my voice, speaking against her hair. The scent of berries and cigarettes invade my senses. Not the most appealing combination, but my dick got past it enough to be interested.

She shifts her attention off the bar and looks up at me from her stool. Waiting.

"This is it. And it's not a date. I don't do that shit either," I continue, needing to clarify this before I take her out of here. "Do you get where I'm going with this, baby?"

I never used to have this speech rehearsed. I figured most women were keen to have casual sex, but unfortunately, I've brought one too many of them home who seemed okay with this arrangement, only to have them clinging to me like damn Saran Wrap the next morning, begging to hang out for the day.

Hang out? No. Fuck. No.

She nods, keeping her lips firmly, seductively, teasingly wrapped around her straw, which I'm pretty sure is only sucking up air now that she's been at it for a good ten minutes.

"One night. Just sex," she affirms, leaning closer to give me a better advantage of her cleavage. I take notice, and she smiles. Her thumb and finger begin stroking up and down the length of the straw. My cock appreciates the innuendo.

"I can do that. I'll even promise I won't fall in love with you."

I stand, dropping a twenty dollar bill on the bar top. "That's not what I'm worried about," I say, staring down into her eyes. The corner of her mouth twists into a smile as I stop her from jerking off the straw. "I hope you don't think that's anywhere near what you're going to be feeling." I flick my head in the direction of my hand as it wraps around hers, forcing all her fingers to grip the straw with enough pressure, it begins to bend in her palm.

She watches me out of the corner of her eye.

"This is how I like it." I stroke her hand up and down, slowly, pressing against her skin. "Firm. You got it?"

She laughs, and it's a nervous one, but I prefer that to some chick who thinks she knows what she's in for. I don't like it to feel familiar, not for me, or whoever it is I'm taking home. We're not going to be getting acquainted. This will never be more than just meaningless sex to me. An empty connection, one that gets my dick wet, but keeps this shit as impersonal as possible.

"Ready?" I ask.

She grabs her clutch off the bar, and spins on her stool to face me. "Ready," she echoes, tugging at the bottom of her skirt as she stands. Her lips go for mine, but I tilt my head and let her full mouth graze my jaw.

"No kissing," I tell her, watching the curiosity spread across her face.

An eyebrow raises as she waits for an explanation.

"I don't do that. Sorry. I'll fuck you until you have trouble walking, but I won't kiss you. That's not part of it."

"I've never had sex with someone and not kissed them. Isn't that weird?"

"No," I answer flatly. I lead her out of the bar to the parking lot, releasing my grip from around her waist when I get close to my truck. "Follow me. I don't mind if you stay the night, but you have to leave first thing in the morning. I have shit to do tomorrow."

I don't. I have absolutely zero plans tomorrow.

She gives me a quirky look as she walks backwards toward

a vehicle. "Have you always been this way when it comes to sex?"

"Yeah," I answer, dropping my head into a nod as I open my driver's side door. I watch her from over my shoulder, catching the limp shrug she gives me in response to my answer before she turns to get into her vehicle.

I climb up into my truck, my head now throbbing along with my dick.

This better be the extent of her questions tonight. The only other response I plan on giving her is "no, you don't have to swallow."

This is just sex, and the only thing this chick needs to know is how I fuck, not why I fuck the way I do. I'm not getting personal. My dick is. End of discussion.

"HEY. YOU GOTTA get up."

I kick the edge of the mattress, jarring the lifeless body slumped across it. She doesn't move, not even a slight stir to let me know she's heard me. I move the coffee cup I'm holding to my other hand and reach down to pinch her bare ass. She squeals.

"Ow!"

"Sorry," I say as her head slowly turns, her eyes peering through the dark hair that's covering her face. "Remember . . . shit to do today? You need to get dressed."

She makes a protesting growl in the back of her throat. "What time is it?" she asks, rolling onto her back and stretching her limbs out around her. Her tits threaten to break free from the rest of her body as they protrude unnaturally high off her bony sternum with the arch of her back.

Christ, she's skinny as fuck. I shouldn't be able to see the outline of every damn rib, but this chick doesn't have any fat on her. Instead of fucking her last night, I should've force-fed her some carbs.

I look down at my dick.

Standards. Let's re-think those.

In the morning light, she's doing nothing for me. Nothing. I prefer soft women with hips and shape, who look like they eat more than a piece of lettuce for a meal. I'm also partial to real tits, as opposed to the cement filled ones I had in my mouth last night. I get it. It's their bodies, and women can do whatever they want to them. But I don't know a man who doesn't have a preference. Mine just doesn't happen to be hers. Even as this chick turns on her side, propping her head on her hand and gesturing at me with a crook of her finger, her tits dart out in the most unnatural way possible. Like they can defy gravity, or the opposite, sink her to the bottom of an ocean.

"Come here. Play with me," her throaty morning voice attempts to bait me.

I shake my head, taking a step back to evade the hand she's holding out for me. "Were you not present during our conversation last night? I told you, you gotta go first thing. Get up."

She drops her hand to the bed. "Really? You're going to kick me out right now instead of sliding between my legs?"

"I'd never kick a woman."

"But you will spank her."

I cock an eyebrow, staring down at the proud gleam sparking back to life in her eyes.

She thinks she has me as she waits expectantly for me to pounce, twirling a strand of hair around her finger.

She never had me. I made sure of that.

I bend down, pick her pile of clothes off the floor, and

toss them onto the bed, covering most of her body up. "Like I said, I'd never kick a woman, but I will carefully, but very efficiently, remove you from my house in ten seconds if you're not out of here. Clothed or not." I raise my wrist in front of my face, staring at my nonexistent watch. "Time starts now. I'd get moving if I were you."

"Shit! What's wrong with you?" she grumbles as she throws her body out of bed, fisting her clothing in her hands. "You'd do it, too, wouldn't you? Throw me out half naked."

"Obviously. I'm counting."

She frantically slides into her skirt, fastens two of the buttons on her blouse, and clutches her panties and bra in her hand as she steps into her heels.

"Nice hustle. You might make it."

"You're a dick," she scolds as she grabs her clutch off my nightstand and heads out of the bedroom. "What the hell kind of guy passes on morning sex?"

"The kind that specifically said you weren't getting any last night. Two seconds."

And the kind who no longer has any desire to fuck a skeleton.

She flings the front door open with a loud grunt, cranks her head around to glare at me, and flips me off.

I smile behind my coffee mug. "See, now this is why I didn't fuck you this morning. My cock only gets hard for ladies." I lean out onto the porch and watch her storm across the grass, fury in each step.

She hates me. Most of them do after our one night together. I don't fucking get it. I'm clear, really fucking clear about not wanting anything to do with them the next day, and in the moment, they are more than willing to agree to those terms. But shit happens the next day with women. They forget all about our little pre-fuck chat, and I'm left throwing their asses out, looking like the bad guy.

I'm not a bad guy. I just can't give them anything more than this.

This is how my Saturday mornings usually start. Sundays too.

Stripping the bed after I get whoever-the-hell out of it, taking a hot shower to remove any trace of sex, sweat, and pussy off my body, and hovering over my Keurig like a strung-out junkie, consuming cup after cup of caffeine until I feel alert.

I can't do this shit during the week. My job requires my ass to be out of bed by 5:00 a.m., and after a night of fucking, I'm usually dragging until noon. More importantly, I need to be focused while I'm at work. My job isn't dangerous, not in the same way as Ben or Luke's, buddies of mine who are both cops, but if I'm not paying attention to what I'm doing, someone could get seriously fucked up.

I've been working construction since I was eighteen years old, but I knew how to operate a backhoe long before that. In fact, I knew how to work almost every piece of heavy machinery on the site before I could drive a car. That's what happens when you're forced to spend every summer at the shop from the time you can take an order to go fetch a tool. I didn't complain. I wanted to be there. While my friends were swimming at Rocky Point, I was following my father and grandfather around, soaking up as much knowledge from them as possible.

I loved it. The smell of grease, sweat, and earth. The calluses hardening my skin after lugging around equipment.

Being outside, getting my hands dirty, climbing on all the machinery. I knew I wanted to learn the trade by the time I was thirteen. After getting a taste of working outside all day, the feel of the sun beating down on my back, I knew I'd never be satisfied with a nine-to-five desk job. If I had to wear a suit every day, I'd punch someone. I'd go fucking stir crazy in an office building, and I'd probably end up being admitted into some psych ward somewhere if I had to work in one of those fucking cubicles.

It's hard work. Really fucking hard work sometimes, but I can't imagine ever doing anything else.

I roll my shoulders as I flip through the newspaper at my table, sipping on my third cup of coffee. My muscles are a little sore, but it's nothing I'm not used to. Giving that skinny pussy the hardest fuck of her life warrants a few aches here and there.

The front door opens in the distance, and seconds later, Riley comes walking into the kitchen, hands full of bags and some paper towels stuffed under her arm.

"Morning," she sings, dropping the bags on the other end of the table.

"You could knock, you know. I could've had somebody in here."

I don't need to glance up from the paper to know my sister is smiling, but I do anyway.

She looks down at the watch on her wrist. "Please. It's after ten. You and I both know whoever you had over last night has been long gone for hours." She drops her hand to her side. "Do you even let the sun come up before you're shoving them out the door?"

"Sometimes." I survey the bags in front of me as she lifts out a few items. I set the paper down and lean back in my chair. "What's all that?"

"I went to Costco last night and picked up some stuff for the soup kitchen. You're always running low on sandwich bags and coffee creamer, so I bought you some." She puts some of the items she bought away in the cabinets, and sets the roll of paper towels next to the microwave. "I had coupons and made out like a bandit."

"Thanks, Mom," I tease behind my mug. "If you feel like doing some of my laundry for me while you're here, or vacuuming, I won't stop you."

She glares at me over her shoulder as her hand closes another cabinet. "Haha. If I was Mom, I'd be lecturing you on your disgusting habit of sleeping with random chicks every night, and hounding you about not settling down with one already." She walks over and slides out the chair across from me, slumping down in it.

"They aren't random. I'm actually very picky when I go about it."

"It's still disgusting, Reed. I almost tossed one of those 500 packs of condoms into my cart when I was shopping. But then I thought, no, I'm just encouraging his habit if I do that."

I let out a slow breath as I set my cup down. My sister and her fucking lectures. "I've got plenty of condoms, Riley. Okay? Please, don't buy me any."

She shrugs, dropping her gaze to the table. "They were actually a really good deal."

"Stop." *Christ. Get me the fuck off this topic.*

"Do you even bother using them?" she snaps, her pale-blue eyes reaching mine with judgment. "That's the important part. You could have a million kids running around Ruxton by now. Little baby Reed Tennyson's everywhere."

Baby Reed Tennyson's? What the fuck?

"Don't think I won't throw your ass out of here too. You're not exempt just 'cause we're related."

"Funny." She smiles. "Just let me know if you find out I have any nieces or nephews. You know how I like to do my

Christmas shopping early."

"Is there a reason why you're still sitting here?" I ask, tilting my head with a glare. "Shouldn't you be at home . . . with Dick?"

She scowls, wrapping her blonde hair up into a messy knot on top of her head. "His name is Richard."

"Which is another name for Dick."

"Why don't you like him? Is it because we're dating?"

I stand, carrying my cup over to the sink.

Not only is my sister constantly in my non-existent love life, she's also always trying to involve me in hers somehow. I couldn't care less who she dates, just as long as they treat her good.

"He's a shit worker. That's why I don't like him," I reply with my back to her as I wash out my cup. "He knows damn well he needs to get his ass to the job site by 6:00 a.m., and he's always late. Then when he does finally show up, he's walking around like a fucking zombie."

"A zombie?"

"Yeah," I reply, turning around after drying my hands with the towel hanging on the stove. I brace myself with my hands gripping the counter. "A love-sick zombie. He looks like an idiot."

My sister blinks rapidly, and reaches up to adjust her glasses. "Really?" she asks quietly with a trembling lip.

Oh, Christ.

"He's never actually told me he loves me. Do you really think he does?"

I lean back, grimacing. "How the hell should I know how he feels about you?"

"Don't you guys talk while you're at the shop? Or when you're on your lunch break?"

"No," I answer, flatly. "The only thing I say to Dick is *why the fuck are you late?* and *go do something.* He's lucky I'm desperate for laborers right now, or I would've fired his ass already."

She gives me a cunning smile, and I know exactly what she's silently suggesting.

"I'm not asking him."

Her head falls back with a loud grunt. "You suck as a big brother. If this situation were reversed, I would totally find out how some chick felt about you."

"I know exactly how chicks feel about me. They're usually pretty damn vocal when I'm . . ."

She holds her hand up. "Okay. Thanks. That's . . ." She shakes her head. "I don't want to know."

I laugh as the heat burns across her cheeks.

Riley is always quick to embarrass. Since we're related, and she bugs the shit outta me about stuff, I push her buttons any chance I get.

She stands, sliding her chair back under the table.

"You leaving?"

Her head drops into quick nods, her eyes casted to the floor. She doesn't move, doesn't make any attempts to leave the spot she's suddenly glued to. She's nervous about something. Going as far as to avoid eye-contact.

"What?" I ask, folding my arms across my chest. "Did that asshole say something to you about asking me for another raise? He's not getting one. Tell him to start showing up on time and maybe I'll consider it."

Her eyes slowly reach mine, and she winces before saying, "I ran into Molly at Costco."

My stomach drops to the floor.

I don't want to react to that name. Nine fucking years should've made it so I don't give a damn about any woman named Molly, but every muscle in my body tenses. My fore-arms begin to burn as my arms lock, tightening against my body.

Fucking shit.

Riley frowns, takes in the reaction I'm doing a shit job at hiding, and lets out a loud, brusque exhale. "I know. If it makes you feel any better, I contemplated ramming into her with my grocery cart. But, I had eggs in there."

"She's not back here, is she?"

Last I heard, four years ago from some asshole I went to high school with who decided I wanted to know this infor-mation, Molly graduated from Virginia Tech but decided to stay there instead of moving back home. I like her being ten hours away. I'd like a greater distance if I could get it.

China. Australia. Fucking Mars would be awesome.

"I have no idea," Riley answers, taking a step forward. "But, she was shopping at a store where you buy items in bulk. I don't think people do that if they're just here for a visit."

"You didn't talk to her?"

Her eyes widen in shock. "No way. Why would I? As soon as I saw her, I turned and went down another aisle. I don't have anything to say to her."

I close my eyes, raking both hands down my face.

This fucking sucks for several reasons. One, we're talking about Molly, and I don't fucking talk about Molly to anyone. I don't like thinking about that bitch, and talking about her makes that a problem. Two, my sister knows this shit affects me, and I hate that. She's practically rubbing my back, telling me everything is going to be okay with the sympathetic look she's giving me. Fuck that. This shouldn't bother me! She knew, even before she said it, this would get to me, and that pisses me off. I shouldn't care. My sister shouldn't know this will affect me. I should be over this.

What. The. Fuck.

I do what I have to do to save any shred of manhood I have left. I lie.

"Who the fuck cares if she's back? That bitch could move in next door, fuck every guy in the neighborhood except me on her porch, and I wouldn't give a shit. I don't care what she does or where the fuck she lives." I grab my car keys off the hook hanging on the wall and stride past Riley out of the kitchen.

I need to get out of here. Riley likes to talk, and I'm not talking about this. Not with her.

"Hey! Where are you going?" she shouts behind me.

"Out. Lock up when you leave."

I pull the front door shut behind me as my other hand reaches for the phone in my pocket. As I'm backing out of the driveway, the call connects.

"This better be important, dick. She's asleep."

I ignore the half-joking, half-I'll-kick-your-ass tone in Luke's voice. Any other day I'd have some smart-ass rebuttal, but my mind is too busy trying to wrap around the information that was just dumped on me.

"Wake her up," I reply, shifting the truck into drive. "I'm on my way over."

beth

OPEN MY eyes and for the briefest moment, forget where I am.

Normal people might panic waking up in a strange room. The unknown is always frightening compared to the familiar, but I guess I'm not normal. I don't feel anything besides a happiness I haven't felt in a really long time, maybe ever, as I piece together why I'm in this bedroom, and not in Rocco's.

The phone call I made yesterday to an aunt I never knew existed. The eight hour drive from Louisville to Ruxton, which left me too exhausted to do anything besides pass out face-down on this beautiful, quilted comforter.

I smile against my pillow as the memory of my arrival in Alabama plays out in my mind.

My aunt's contained excitement, the tears in her eyes as she welcomed me into her home very early this morning. Very, very early. I think she knew I needed sleep, because she didn't try and rope me into twenty-two years of missed conversation. I would've talked if she wanted it. I would've given her every last word to show my gratitude for what she's giving me, but she didn't press for it. Instead, she showed me to this delicately decorated bedroom, with light purple walls and girly accents, and then, darkness.

The unknown is always frightening compared to the familiar.

Not in this case. Not with my familiar.

A knock on the door has me sitting up, hugging my knees against my chest.

"Come in," I call out through my hoarse morning voice, seconds before my aunt's face peers through the small opening.

She smiles, her dark hair pinned back into a high bun. "Hey, darlin'. I was just checking to see if you were up yet."

I nod, shifting on the mattress. "I just woke up." My eyes fall to the foot of the bed, where the boots I didn't bother taking off have left a trail of dried up mud crumbles, streaking across the lavender quilt.

My heart suddenly grows too heavy in my chest.

"Oh my God. I'm so, so sorry."

I swing my legs off the bed and stand, leaning over the quilt and gathering up the tiny pellets. The comforter isn't stained, thank God, but that doesn't make me feel any better.

My aunt joins my side, holding out her hand. "Here," she says with the softest voice, taking the balls of mud from me and picking up the rest on the comforter.

I rub my hand over the quilt as she drops the dirt into the trashcan by the dresser.

"Are you hungry? I made some pancakes earlier. I'd be more than happy to heat you up some."

I look over at the alarm clock on the dresser, noting the time.

"Or," she continues through a small laugh. "Since it is three in the afternoon and not breakfast, I can make you a sandwich or something."

I shake my head, smiling. "No, pancakes sound great. I love breakfast food."

"Me too," she replies. "I'll see you downstairs then. Your Uncle Danny is dying to meet you. He's been going a little stir crazy waiting for you to wake up."

Regret churns in my gut. "Oh, I shouldn't have slept so long. I didn't mean to make him wait."

She frowns, standing in the doorway. "Darlin', you don't need to apologize for anything. Okay? We're so happy you're here. You have no idea."

My shoulders lower a few inches as I let out a slow breath. "I'm happy I'm here too."

"You come down when you're ready."

She shuts the door behind her, and I take a seat on the edge of the bed, pulling at the laces of my boots. I carry them over to the trashcan and knock off any remaining dirt, cursing myself.

I know I must've tracked mud into the house when I arrived.

I set them by the door and pull an old Rolling Stones T-shirt out of my duffle, slipping it on and tossing the one I was wearing onto the chair in the corner of the room. I could put my dirty clothes in the laundry basket, but I don't want my aunt thinking she has to do my laundry. In fact, I'd rather do all of their laundry, just to show my appreciation somehow.

After brushing my teeth, taming my wild bed-head hair, and washing my face in the hallway bathroom, I head down the stairs, following the sound of voices in the kitchen.

Hattie is standing at the island, setting silverware and a bottle of syrup next to the plate that's stacked high with pancakes. She looks up and taps the shoulder of the man standing next to her, getting his attention off the magazine he's flipping through.

He's tall, his thin frame towering over Hattie, who

resembles my mother and me in size. His dark hair is tucked behind his ears, hanging down to his shoulders, which makes him look younger than I imagine he is. His features are prominent, a thin nose and strong jaw, and his skin has a light tan to it.

Hattie smiles as I step up to the island. "Beth, darlin', this is your Uncle Danny."

He sets the magazine down in front of him and extends his hand to me, the sleeve of his flannel sliding up higher to reveal the ink on his arm. It's colorful, bright purples and blues, and my eyes appreciate it for several seconds, trying to decipher the design before I finally settle on his face. His thin lips spread into a smile.

"Nice to meet you, Beth."

"You too. It's so nice to meet you." His large hand encloses around mine, giving it a gentle squeeze. "Thank you both so much for opening your home to me."

"Oh, sweetheart," he says, letting go of my hand. A deep frown line sets into his forehead as he tucks both hands into the pockets of his jeans. "You don't ever need to thank us. You're family. Our home is yours for as long as you need it."

I blink away my tears as I take a seat at the island.

Family. I have a family.

"Beth, I know you just got here, and I don't want to bombard you with questions . . ."

"It's okay," I interrupt, smiling at Hattie. "You can ask me anything you want."

I figured this was coming. Our two conversations on the phone had been brief, and I know I'd be filled with questions if I was her.

She blinks several times, folding her hands in front of her on the island. "What was she like?"

I reach up and tuck my long hair behind my ears, clearing

my throat before I begin.

"I'm sorry," she adds, before I have a chance to speak. "It's just . . . it's been twenty-seven years since I talked to my sister. I know the kind of person she was when she ran off, and I'm really hoping you're about to tell me she was at least a good mom to you. I don't think I could bare to hear it if she wasn't."

"She was," I reply, nodding my head quickly. "She loved me, I know she did. I have some really great memories with my mom."

"Have you always lived in Kentucky?"

"I think so. I don't really remember where we lived before we moved into the trailer. I was six when we got that place."

Danny opens the refrigerator and pours three glasses of iced tea, handing one to me and then one to Hattie. I take a sip, quenching my thirst while Hattie does the same. It's sweet, with a hint of lemon.

"So, she had a job?" she asks after setting her glass down.

"No." I look between the two of them, wrapping both hands around the chilled glass in front of me. "I . . . I'm not sure how my momma got money. I didn't want to know, so I didn't ask. We got food stamps, and the bills always got paid. I wanted to get a job to make some money on my own, but she didn't want me to do that. She said she was the parent, and she would provide for me." I take another sip of my drink, licking the tea off my lips. "She was very adamant about that."

"What about your dad?" she asks, timidly. "Was he around?"

"No," I answer. "I've never met him. I don't even know who he is."

Hattie looks over at Danny, and I drop my head, feeling slightly ashamed from that admission.

"You said you found a picture your mom kept of the two

of us," she says after a few moments of silence. I look up, and she gives me a weak smile. "You wouldn't happen to have it with you, would you?"

I reach into the back pocket of my jeans, sliding out the old photo I stuck in there before I left Kentucky, and hand it over to her.

She brings the photo up to her face, her eyes instantly welling up with tears. One hand presses against her mouth. "Oh my God. I remember this. This was taken a few months before your Mom took off."

She shows it to Danny, and he wraps his arm around her waist while they both study it.

"I found it in this old shoe box my mom kept our photos in. It was the only thing I took with me besides clothes when I got evicted from the trailer, but I never really looked through it until a couple days ago when I was missing her. I found that and . . ." I pause, gaining Hattie and Danny's attention off the photo. "You two looked so much alike. Growing up, Momma never talked about her family. I figured if she had any siblings, she would've mentioned them. So, I thought maybe you were a distant cousin or something."

"How did you know my name to search for me?"

I lean over the island, running my finger along the back of the photo. "Your names are on the back." She turns it over, and smiles. "I got lucky. I really didn't think I would find you on Facebook, but I had to try." I look over at Danny. "What's your last name?"

"McGill," he answers, dropping a kiss to Hattie's head. "This stubborn woman never would take my name."

"And thank God I didn't," she teases, pushing playfully against his chest. "Beth never would've found me if I wasn't still Hattie Davis." Her smile fades when she gazes back at the picture in her hand. She stares at it longingly.

"Annie was always troubled. Even when we were little, she just never quite fit in. Not with us, anyway. She found other people, the wrong kind of people to fit in with. She took off when she was fifteen, and at that point, my mother was too tired to care where she went. I figured she would come back, maybe after a few months, but she never came home." Her eyes reach mine, the sadness blistering behind them. "It was drugs, wasn't it? It was drugs that killed her."

I swallow heavily, dropping my gaze to my lap. "The paramedics said she had a heart attack, most likely brought on by whatever she took. I don't know if it was too much, or maybe it had something in it." I shake my head. "I don't know. I'm sorry, I don't really have any details. I couldn't afford an autopsy to find out what exactly happened."

Arms wrap around me from behind, squeezing me gently. "Oh, darlin', I'm so sorry you had to go through that alone. All of it. Please know, if we had known about you, we would've been there," Hattie says against my hair. "I can't imagine how hard your life has been."

"It really wasn't too bad until after she died."

Hattie claims the stool next to me, covering my hand with hers. "Do you want to talk about it?"

I look from her to Danny, who seems just as interested in the life that lead me here as my blood relative. He's focused, his eyes dilated in concentration as they remain trained on me.

I give him a thankful smile before looking away.

"There's not a lot to talk about, really," I begin, letting my eyes lose focus on the island. "I couldn't afford to stay in the trailer after she died, so I started living out of my car."

I take in a deep breath, thinking back to the first night I crawled into my back seat and tried to close my eyes. The noises in the dark. The utter loneliness that awakened a fear inside me I've never experienced before.

My chest tightens with emotion, but I mask it and continue.

"That was scary. I've never been alone before. Even though she stayed high most of the time, Momma was still always around, and we always had a home. Not having anybody to talk to was probably the hardest thing." I look over at Hattie, watching the tears stream down her cheeks. I don't want to cry, so I quickly avert my gaze back to the island. "I would've gone crazy if I sat in that car all day, so I wandered around a lot. I cleaned myself up in gas station bathrooms, and I kept moving my car to different parking lots so no one called the cops on me. I didn't have a lot of money, just a wad of cash I found in the trailer before I got evicted. I tried to get a job but apparently, having an address is vital when it comes to employment." I shake my head, remembering the looks on the manager's faces when I told them my address was a McDonald's parking lot.

Hattie squeezes my hand gently.

"I'm sure that's not the only reason why they didn't hire me. I know I didn't look that great after not having a real shower in several days, and I probably smelled worse. I really tried to stretch my money, but I was . . . I was just *so* hungry."

Danny slides the pancakes closer to me, and a laugh bubbles in the back of my throat.

"Danny, let her finish," Hattie scolds with a soft voice.

He leans back against the counter, crossing his arms over his chest. "I don't like thinking about my niece starving, or the fact that she had to go through all that hard life shit by herself. It shouldn't have happened. Hearing about it makes me want to go have a smoke."

"You better not! You're going on three weeks without one."

"It's okay. I only went a few days without any food."

My words don't seem to ease his discomfort whatsoever. If anything, he seems to become even more uneasy, running both hands down his face and blowing out a harsh exhale.

"Go ahead, Beth." Hattie gives me a gentle smile, removing her hand from mine and placing it into her lap. "What happened after that?"

"Rocco happened," I reply, the words spilling from my lips.

Danny clenches his jaw tight and begins pacing back and forth between the counter and the island. Over and over, his heavy boots stomping against the wood. I'm not sure what has him so worked up. I haven't told my aunt hardly anything about Rocco, but it's almost as if he knows, or suspects I've endured worse things than going days without a meal.

I decide to get through this last part as quickly as possible.

"He found me, crying in my car after I'd gone several days without any food. I was kinda defeated at that point. I guess he saw how hungry I was, or maybe I just looked homeless. I was trying to sleep, trying to take my mind off my stomach cramps when he came up to my window with one of every item from the Burger King menu. I normally wouldn't take anything from a stranger. I'm not stupid, but I was desperate, and very hungry. And he was . . ." I close my eyes for a moment, almost ashamed to admit this next part. "He was really handsome. No girl in their right mind would say no to a hot guy holding a bag of free food."

I shake my head at myself as Hattie laughs softly next to me.

Danny continues to pace, not finding my humor at all funny.

"Anyway, he sat with me and talked to me while I ate. I was so happy to have someone to talk to. I didn't want him to leave. I actually panicked when I thought he was getting out of the car. I just . . . I hated being alone, and I didn't want to be alone anymore. Plus, what was going to happen to me? I was going to have to start stealing food, or finding ways to get money. I didn't know if I would ever see him again, and no one else had ever stopped to offer me help."

I picture the look on Rocco's face when I reached for him, begging him not to leave me. The smile that twisted across his lips as I wrapped my hand around his arm. Now I know, he got off on that.

He saw my vulnerability, and he took advantage of it.

"I almost couldn't believe it when he asked me if I wanted a place to stay. He offered me his home, food, and money for as long as I needed. He didn't ask for anything in return, and he was so nice to me. I know I had a choice, but I felt like I couldn't say no. I was scared to be alone, and I liked him." I feel every muscle in my body tense at the memory. My voice softens. "I really liked him. I moved in that day, and everything seemed pretty close to perfect for a little while." I look over at Hattie, her eyes still glistening with unshed tears. "I never would've stayed with him if I had somewhere else to go, but I couldn't . . . Aunt Hattie, I couldn't go back to living out of my car."

Danny halts his pacing, and moves to stand directly across from me. "I'm gonna ask you somethin', and I want you to be straight with me."

Hattie flattens her hands on the island, leaning forward. "Danny."

He looks over at her. "No, I'm askin'. She's our niece, and if I have to go handle some asshole in Kentucky for puttin' his hands on her, I'm doin' it."

"Oh, no. He didn't . . . he never hit me." I look between the two of them, Hattie's eyes regarding me with suspicion. She doesn't believe me, and by the rough exhale coming from Danny, I'm doubting he does either.

"Rocco never touched me unless I let him," I admit, dropping my head to avoid the judgment in their eyes. "Our relationship, or whatever it was, it was more about me needing him for things, and him knowing I needed him. He talked down to me a lot, but he never hit me." I look at Hattie, then at Danny. "Never. I swear."

"He sounds like a real charmer," Hattie says through a tight jaw. "So, he verbally abused you? Is that what you're saying?"

I shrug, and Danny pounds his fist on the island, startling Hattie and myself.

"I need a goddamn smoke."

"No, you don't." Hattie stands and walks around the island, placing a hand to his chest. "Beth is fine. She's here, with us. She's not with that man anymore."

"He won't come after you?" Danny asks me, his chest heaving with each breath he takes.

I shake my head, adamantly. "No. I know him. He'd never do that."

"You're sure? 'Cause if you think you're in danger, I need to know about it."

"I'm sure," I vow, my voice steady. "Rocco would never come after me. I promise, Uncle Danny. I would never bring danger here. If I thought he'd do something, I'd leave."

"You need to get that thought outta your head, 'cause you're not goin' anywhere," he corrects me, his tone final and sounding how I imagine a father would sound, talking to his daughter.

He grabs the plate of neglected pancakes and sticks them into the microwave, hitting a few buttons.

I look over at Hattie, waiting for her to soften his words somehow with her own version of them, but the only thing she gives me is a limp shrug.

You're on your own, darlin'.

The microwave beeps, and he grabs the plate of pancakes and sets them back down in front of me. He flips open the cap on the syrup, holds it over the top of the tall stack, and waits for me to nod before he begins to pour.

"If you think that asshole is plannin' on doin' somethin', you tell me. I got a couple cop buddies I can call up." He flips the cap closed and sets the bottle down, his other hand sliding the knife and fork in front of me. "You hear me, sweetheart?"

"Yes," I answer, avoiding his eyes like a child who's just been scolded.

"Any man who talks down to a woman, who puts his hands on her or does anything to make her feel inferior to him, ain't a man in my book."

I lift my head, meeting his gaze that has gentled considerably.

"I'll have no problem teachin' him some manners. You just let me know." He holds his hand out to me, and the second I place mine in his, he slides his grip to the back of my hand and presses my palm against the silverware. "Eat. No more starvin' for you."

I love this man.

Danny walks over to Hattie and kisses her temple. "I'll see ya in a few hours, babe."

"Hold off the crazies for me."

Danny gives me a rough pat on my head before he exits

the kitchen, heading in the direction of the front door.

After fixing the mess he just made of my hair, I cut into the top two pancakes and shove a massive bite in my mouth. Hattie moves to stand across from me.

"Good?" she asks through a proud smile, as if she already knows the answer.

Sweet Mother of Bisquick.

I close my eyes through a moan as the buttermilk deliciousness bursts against my tongue. "Mm mmm. Sooo, so good," I say through my mouthful, wiping the back of my hand across my chin when I feel the syrup running down my face.

I don't care in the least that I probably look like a savage right now as I open my eyes and shovel another huge bite into my mouth. I've never been a modest eater. Besides, I think the greatest compliment you can give someone who cooked for you is showing them just how much you're enjoying their food. And that's exactly what I'm doing. Enjoying the hell out of my food.

I animatedly chew my mouthful as Hattie watches me, amused grin in place.

She drinks the last of her tea and deposits the glass into the sink behind her. Her hands smooth down the front of her white blouse that's tucked into her jeans. Looking at Hattie is like looking at a healthy version of my momma. Her frame isn't rail thin from the years of drug use. Her teeth aren't decayed, or chipped, or missing. She's beautiful. She's what my momma should've been to the world, even though I always saw it.

"I'm going to be heading to work in a few hours. Everything in this house, the TV, the computer, all of it is yours to use. You don't need to ask permission." Hattie moves around the island and stops next to me, pushing in the stool she was occupying during my trip down memory lane.

"Where do you work?" I ask, licking the syrup off my lips.

"Danny and I own a pub in town. It's this sweet little honky tonk bar."

I smile, swinging my legs so that I'm facing her. "Oh really? Like line dancing and stuff?"

"Sometimes. There's a bit of a rock crowd there too, so not too much line dancing." She runs the back of her hand along my cheek, a gentle smile warming her face. "Are you gonna be okay by yourself?"

I want to say yes. The word is right there, on the tip of my tongue, but it won't come out. It's ridiculous, I know. I won't be alone for that long, but for some reason, I can't force myself to be okay with being alone for even a few minutes.

She cups my face with both hands. "You're coming with me."

I open my mouth to protest, because I don't want her to feel like I'm some burden she has to babysit, but she speaks before I get a chance to so much as take in a breath.

"Anytime you want to tag along with me and Danny, you just let us know. You're always welcome with us, Beth. Always, okay?"

She wants me there. I'm not a burden.

"Okay."

"You better eat up," she says, nodding toward the plate in front of me as she drops her hands to her side. "You're gonna be subjected to bar food tonight."

I smile at the thought of greasy burgers and fries covered in cheese as her footsteps trail off behind me.

Hell yes. Bring on the bar food.

reed

"**C**OFFEE?"

I look up from the counter I'm sitting at, peering over at Tessa as she stands at the Keurig. The dark blue, four sizes too big T-shirt she's wearing has Ruxton Police Department in bold yellow letters displayed on the back. It's tied in a knot at her waist, meeting the rolled up sweats she's swimming in. I'm guessing everything on her belongs to Luke. There's no way in hell Tessa owns any clothing that doesn't show off her body one way or the other. I've known her since high school, and even though I've never seen her naked, I've gotten pretty damn close with some of that skimpy shit she wears.

She meets my gaze over her shoulder, holding up a mug. "You want some?"

"No, I already had several cups, thanks."

I look around the kitchen as she goes about making her cup. It's so homey in here, lived in, and warm. The whole house is. The wood on the cabinets is weathered with little nicks in it, the wall has one of those growth charts etched onto the paint with pencil, depicting Luke's growth spurts, and one recent measurement of Tessa. If someone would've told me this was where hard-ass Luke Evans grew up, I wouldn't have believed them. I always pictured him living in the Alabama backwoods like a savage, eating squirrels and small children.

But with Tessa living here with him, it fits. Maybe it's because they're together, I don't know. But it works.

"So, what's up, and why aren't you in bed with one of your whores?" She gives me a playful look over her shoulder, softening the blow of her dig.

I clasp my hands in front of me. "*One of my whores?* For your information, the woman I brought home last night was in law school."

"Oh, perfect. She'll know how to properly sue your ass for sexual harassment." She giggles at her crack up, reaching across the island to mess up my hair. "Kidding. Sorry, but you pretty much set that one up perfectly."

I bat her hand away with a glare. "Can we be serious for a second? Please?"

She brings her coffee mug up to her mouth, hiding her smile. "Yes. Very serious."

I take a minute to calm my nerves, rolling my shoulders to ease the tension that's beginning to settle between them. "Molly is back in town." Our eyes connect, hers doubling in size. "My sister saw her at Costco yesterday. I don't know if she's back for good, 'cause Riley didn't talk to her, but she was buying food, so . . . what the fuck?"

Tessa leans against the counter, her finger steadily tapping her mug while she stares at a spot on the floor. "Really?"

I nod, causing her to look over at me when I don't give her a verbal response.

"And this is bothering you because . . ."

I bring my hands to my lap, keeping them folded together. "Gee, I don't know. Maybe the fact that this town is too fucking small to avoid her."

"So what. You're over her, right?"

I squeeze my hands together in my lap. "Yeah," I reply,

my voice hardening.

Tessa sets the mug down on the island and drums the counter with her fingers. "You're such a shit liar, Reed. You wouldn't be here, stressing the fuck out, if you were over her."

"I'm not stressing out!" I clamp my eyes shut, taking in a deep breath while the one person I thought I could talk to about this laughs quietly across from me.

I need new fucking friends.

"I'm actually happy about this."

I slowly open my eyes. "What?" I ask, dragging out the word.

Tessa piles her long, red hair on top of her head and secures it with the band around her wrist. "You said it. This is a small town, which means, the chances of me having the amazing opportunity of running her bitch-ass over with my car is actually looking really good right now. With her living in another state, that probably would never happen. And, I'm sleeping with a cop, so . . . that's like an automatic get-out-of-jail-free card." She shrugs her shoulders before picking up her mug. "I can pretty much get away with murder here."

I snort. "Who are you kidding? Luke would stick your ass in jail for a few days and get off on it."

A wicked smile spreads across her lips. "The gorgeous bastard would do that, wouldn't he?"

I lean my elbows on the counter, digging the tips of my fingers into my temples. It feels like my heart is now lodged in my skull, and with every beat, my head throbs with a pain unlike anything I've ever felt. A slow pressure builds behind my eyes, filling my vision with blotches of indiscernible color. If this is what a fucking migraine is like, I'll start having sympathy for the people who complain about them, because this shit sucks.

"Reed."

"Yeah?"

She leans down, bringing her face to my level. All trace of Tessa's typical smart-ass demeanor is gone, replaced with the same look of concern my sister gave me, standing in my kitchen.

"Don't," I warn, because I know what she's about to say. "I'm not hung up on her. That's not what this is about."

Her eyebrows pinch together in doubt. "Then what is it about? Because right now, I'm two seconds away from offering you the pint of Ben & Jerry's I have in my freezer."

I straighten up, letting my hands fall to the counter. "I don't know what the hell that means, but I'm not hungry."

Tessa lets out an exhaustive sigh, mumbling the word "men" under her breath before taking a sip of her coffee.

"Look," I begin, reaching down to pat Max when he nudges against my leg. "I don't need a walking reminder of the pussy-whipped asshole I used to be nine years ago coming back into my life. The fact that I ever let some chick get to me like that isn't something I like thinking about, and having Molly in Ruxton is going to make that a problem. Ow! What the fuck, Max?" I push him away, rubbing my hand along the side of my leg that's just been mauled. "Jesus Christ. You need your nails clipped."

"He just got them clipped. That's why they're so sharp." Tessa walks over to the container of dog treats on the counter and pops the lid off. As soon as she does that, Max goes flying at her, leaping off the floor to get to the treat she's holding in the air.

"So, you're telling me that you're over her."

"Yes."

"Completely over her."

"*Yes.*"

"Good. So when you see her, not if, because it's bound to happen, and she tells you she's made a huge mistake and wants you to give her another chance, what are you going to say?"

She drops the treat into Max's awaiting mouth, brushes her hands off, and recaps the container, pushing it against the backsplash. Max crawls underneath the kitchen table, cracking into his treat, while Tessa holds her hands out, waiting expectantly for my response.

"Well?"

I stare at her. "Do you think I'd actually take her back?"

"I don't know," she answers, moving back to stand across from me. Her fingers play with the knot in her T-shirt. "This girl affected you, Reed, and not just in your typical break-up sort of way. You were straight-up devastated after what she did to you."

"I was sad," I correct her.

"No, you weren't just sad." She points a finger at her chest. "I know how it feels to be way past the point of being sad, and that's exactly what you were. For a long time." She drops her hand, bringing both of them in front of her to wrap around her coffee mug. "And now look at you. You're completely different when it comes to women."

"Yeah, I am," I agree, raising my eyebrows. "What's your point?"

She narrows her eyes at me across the top of her mug. "My point is that this chick did a number on you, and when someone who affects you like that comes back into your life, old feelings resurface, whether you want them to or not." She pauses, her eyes losing focus before she says quietly, "Trust me."

I pinch my eyes shut with a heavy sigh.

Old feelings? No, fuck that. If I do run into Molly, I sure as hell won't be feeling anything toward her besides the ongoing hate I have streaming through me now. That bitch isn't getting anything else from me, and Tessa is out of her mind if she thinks I'll be tempted to take her back. I don't care if Molly's sorry. Fuck her and her sorry.

A damp cloth hits me on the side of the face. I reach up, pulling the towel off my head and catching Luke's guilty smirk.

"Ass," I spit, dropping the towel onto the counter in front of me.

"Dick," he replies through a laugh. He turns his head. "Babe, where's my shampoo?"

Tessa leans her hip against the counter. "Uh . . . oh, it's in the other bathroom. Max needed a bath yesterday, and he was out of his doggie shampoo." She smiles behind her mug. "Now he smells all yummy like you."

"You used my shampoo on Max?"

"I didn't have anything else to use. Mine's too expensive."

Luke pulls her against his chest and kisses the top of her head. She wraps her arms around him, holding her mug behind his back. He nods in my direction. "What's up with broody over there? Someone piss in his cereal this morning?"

Tessa looks at me, smiling against him. "Nah, he's just upset because his ex-girlfriend's back in town. She's the skank who made Reed the glorious man-whore we know and love today."

Luke looks at me, frowning. "You gotta be able to get pussy to be a man-whore, babe. Reed's too busy trying to figure out how to suck his own dick."

I flip him off, which only stirs his amusement.

"Hmm, you know," Tessa says, smiling coyly at me as she peels away from Luke. She drops her gaze to the lowest part of my shirt she can visibly see above the counter, then brings her eyes back up to mine, gleaming with mischief. "Some guys can do that, and they even finish in their own mouths. I've seen it online and it's . . . surprisingly hot."

"I'm out." I push off from my stool, hearing Tessa laugh quietly as I exit the kitchen.

This conversation just went from pointless to fucking disturbing, and I don't need to stick around and listen to Luke weigh in with his opinion on Molly moving back to Ruxton. He'll just give me shit about it.

Luke Evans likes to act like he isn't affected by stuff the way normal people are, but that motherfucker would've done anything to avoid running into Tessa after their break-up. I'm just not stupid enough to remind him of that.

He has a gun somewhere in this house. I'd rather not get shot at.

"UNCLE WEED! WHAT arwe you doing herwe?"

I look over my shoulder as I grab some tools out of the bed of my truck. Nolan is running down the driveway toward me, carrying a styrofoam airplane over his head. The damn thing is almost as big as he is.

"What's up, little man? Where's your brother?"

He stops at my side, watching me closely. "He's with Mommy. He pooped everwywhere."

I smile down at him while he catches his breath, clutching the airplane in both hands against his chest. He has to crane his neck to the side to see around it, which he does so he can look up at me.

"Whoa!" His eyes double in size as I lift a large tool out of the truck. "What is that?"

I set the machine at my feet before grabbing a few more items out of the bed. "That's an auger. Looks pretty cool, huh?"

"It's all twisty. Like a big corwk scrwew." His smile spreads, showing the gap in the front of his mouth where a tooth fell out a few weeks ago. Mia told me he was so pumped to get money from the tooth fairy, he's obsessed with trying to loosen the rest of his teeth now.

He's asked me several times to pull a few out.

He drops his airplane into the dirt and runs his finger along the smooth edge of the bit. "Can I play with dis?"

"No way, dude. Your mommy would kill me. Do you want to see her chase Uncle Reed around with one of your swords?"

He nods animatedly. "Oh yeah! She could chop yourw head off! That would be sooooo awesome!"

I shake my head through a quiet laugh. "Jeez. What TV shows are you watching where people are getting their heads chopped off? Game of Thrones?"

He looks down at the dirt. "I wasn't watching it, Uncle Weed. Daddy was watching it." Keeping his head down, he looks up at me from under his lashes. "Mommy got weal mad I got outta bed."

Oh shit. That show is definitely not for five year olds. I'd ask him what all he saw, but I'm almost afraid to stay on this subject. Mia will freak the fuck out on me if she finds out I'm talking about graphic violence with Nolan, and I'd very much like to keep my balls.

"Here," I say, holding out my tool belt to distract him. Nolan lifts his head. "Carry this for me, will ya? I'll get the big cork screw."

Nolan grabs the belt so fast a few of the tools fall to the dirt.

He's always this excited with stuff, no matter what he's

doing. I think I could hand him a bucket of rocks and he'd take it with the same enthusiasm that's lighting up his face right now. He's such a cool kid. I never thought about having any, but I'd take Nolan. He's pretty fucking awesome.

I wait for him to stuff the tools back into the belt and walk behind him as he leads me up the drive.

Ben walks out the front door with Chase in his arms as Nolan carries the tool belt toward the back of the house.

"What's up, man? You getting started today?" Ben asks, looking down at the machine in my hands as I come to a stop in front of him.

I'm about to answer when Mia walks out the door, her face flushed a bright red and her hair disheveled. She takes a rag and wipes down the front of her neck as she comes up to stand beside Ben.

She smiles at me, and it's that genuine, make-any-guy-do-just-about-anything smile I'm used to seeing from her. Mia returned to Ruxton two years ago after moving away nine years before that. I didn't know her when she lived here before, since I didn't attend the same Elementary or Middle School as Tessa and her. Back then, Ben and Mia wanted nothing to do with each other. He tormented the hell out of her, and she was his sister's annoying best friend. But when she came to visit for the summer two years ago, there wasn't anything that would've kept the two of them apart. Not even a bitter past. Ben staked his claim, and everyone got that message, loud and clear. Mia was his. I couldn't blame the guy for being drawn to her. It is really fucking easy to like Mia. Everybody likes her. She's the kindest person I know, and she'll do anything for anybody. Plus, she took on the role of Nolan's mom after his real one turned out to be a worthless piece of shit. You'd never know that kid wasn't hers.

She's always belonged in Ruxton. She doesn't just make Ben better. She makes us all better.

"Why is your face all red?" I ask, studying the red blotches on her skin.

Mia bunches up the cloth in her hand. "Chase puked on me. Thank God I had my mouth closed."

I look from her to Ben, who seems as casual as if this shit happens daily, then I drop my eyes back to her, my face pinched in disgust. "He threw up on your face?" I turn to Chase, who's hiding his guilt well. "What the hell, dude?"

"He's a baby, asshole," Ben replies, sounding annoyed. "They throw up. It's not like he was aiming for Mia."

"Does he like give you a warning or something?" I ask.

A valid question on my part. I hold that kid a good bit.

Ben stares at me for long seconds of silence. "Yeah. He usually tells you what's about to happen with his extensive vocabulary."

Mia laughs quietly, looking at Chase and grabbing his little arm. She forces him to wave at me. "Can you say what's up to Uncle Reed?"

Chase chews on his other fist, smiling around it at Mia while I go completely unnoticed.

Mia looks back at me and studies the machine in my hand with a curious frown. "What is that thing?"

I motion with my head for them to walk with me around the side of the house. I need to get back there before Nolan hides all my tools in places he can't remember.

"It's gonna help me dig the holes for your deck. I'm at least going to put the posts in today."

Mia's mouth drops open, and she looks up at Ben as she tucks the washcloth into her front jeans pocket. "What deck?"

Ben smiles at her as we get to the back of the house. "The

deck Reed's building for you, Angel. You keep saying you want one. It looks like he's starting on it today."

"But I thought we were going to wait until we saved up a little more money. I didn't think we'd get one built this year."

"Reed's only charging us for materials. We have plenty of money."

"I don't know why you two are insisting on giving me anything. You know I don't feel right about charging you. I can do this for free. It's not a big deal." I set the auger down in the grass and scan the backyard for Nolan. He's up on the wooden landing of the swing set, sending each tool one-by-one down the sliding board and laughing hysterically when they hit the bottom. I take a mental inventory of the tools in that belt to make sure there's nothing in there that could be dangerous to him.

"We're paying you something," Ben corrects me, gaining my attention.

We've gone over this a dozen times, but I still don't feel right about it.

"You're not doing this shit for free."

Mia lifts her hand and rubs it against Chase's back when he stirs against Ben. "How long do you think it will take?" she asks me.

I look at the house, squinting as I run through the plans I have in my head. "Depending on the weather, if I can get over here every weekend, I should be able to have it done by the end of the month. You might not have the stairs ready, but you'll at least be able to use it while I'm finishing up with that."

Mia grins so big, I think her face might actually split in half. "Oh my gosh! This is so exciting! We'll be able to sit out on the deck and eat under the stars." She links her hands around Ben's neck, kissing all over the side of his face. "I love you so so soooo much."

"You better." He turns his face and kisses her.

I choose that moment to look back at Nolan. He's at the bottom of the slide now, picking up the tools.

"Hey, little man. You gonna help me or what?"

His dimpled grin hits me, suddenly fueled to gather the tools faster. I turn back around, regretting it the second I see Ben's tongue slide into Mia's mouth.

"Really?" I ask, and they break apart from each other, panting. Their eyes reach mine, and the blinding lust in both pairs has me thinking of other things that will most likely be happening on this deck once it's built.

I look at Chase as he continues to chew on his fist. "You better never puke in your mommy's mouth. That man holding you spends way too much time in there."

I realize how that sounds a second after it comes out.

Mia cracks up laughing, covering her mouth with her hand as I look to Ben for his reaction.

My first mistake was painting an image of Mia sucking his dick. My second was thinking Ben would find it funny.

He doesn't.

"I'm going to go ahead and get started."

"Yeah, you do that," Ben replies, shifting Chase to his left arm and wrapping his right around Mia's shoulders. "I gotta head into work. If Nolan doesn't listen to you, send him inside."

I nod, bending down and picking up the cord on the auger. "Yeah, all right. I'm sure it won't be a problem though."

"I'm taking Chase inside for his nap. Let me know if you need something to drink or anything." Mia gets Chase from Ben and kisses his cheeks. "Come on, baby. Let's go lay down," she says quietly against his skin.

Nolan scampers up to me, eyes wide and wild with excitement. My tool belt in his hands. "I'm weady, Uncle Weed."

I smile down at him.

I originally didn't have plans today, but that changed the second Riley stepped into my kitchen. Staying busy this afternoon will keep my mind off shit I don't want to think about, and having Nolan around will just make this entertaining. He's always saying the craziest stuff.

He slaps the hand I hold out for him with all his strength. "Let's do it."

EVEN IF I didn't go out every Saturday night looking for someone to take home, I would've still gone to grab a drink after I finished up for the day at Ben and Mia's. There's nothing like a cold beer after a hard day working in the sun, and I plan on tossing back a few before I get to my usual reason for walking into McGill's Pub.

The crowd is heavy, which is typical for a Saturday night. All the pool tables are taken, and there's a line forming to play darts at the other end of the bar. Some girls are line dancing in the middle of the room, all of them wearing short jean skirts and cowboy boots. I give the group of them a smile and they move closer together, swaying their hips a little more now that I've noticed. I fucking love that. Any of them will do tonight, and if they don't want to separate from each other, that's fine. There's no crowd limit in my bed.

Hattie, one of the owners and the sweetest bartender in this town, comes to stand across from me as I grab a stool at the bar.

She gives me a wink and a smile, her friendly face never giving me anything different. "How are you doing, darlin'?"

I lean in, playing up my game. "I'll be great once you

leave Danny and run away with me."

I'm just messing with her, and Hattie knows it. Even if I didn't think highly of her husband, I despise cheating, and the people who do it. I don't care if you are in a shit marriage. Get the fuck out of it before you fuck someone over.

A laugh falls past her lips. "You want a beer?"

"Yeah, that sounds good. Whatever's on tap."

She places the glass in front of me and disappears into the back for a moment, reemerging with a plate of food. I take a sip of my beer and watch her walk out from behind the bar and carry the plate over to one of the booths lined along the wall. She sets it down in front of a woman whose back is to me, her dark hair pulled up to reveal the delicate pale skin of her neck. The woman looks up from the tablet she's holding in front of her, and I catch her profile.

I no longer give a damn about the chicks line dancing, or any other woman in this bar.

Hattie bends down and plants a kiss to the top of her head, obviously knowing the young woman. The two of them exchange a few words, and then Hattie comes back behind the bar.

I wave her over, setting my glass down.

"Who's that you were just talking to?"

Her smile softens and her eyes grow distant, as if she's thinking of a fond memory. "That's my niece. She's just the sweetest thing," she answers, glancing over at the woman in the booth. "Didn't even know I had her until yesterday. She just moved in with Danny and me."

"Huh." I follow Hattie's eyes, wishing the woman was sitting on the other side so I could see all of her face. But I'm not going to lie. What I have seen has got me way the hell interested.

"No."

I turn back to Hattie, confused by her response. "No, what?"

That gentle smile of hers is gone, replaced with lips tightly pursed together. She wipes the counter down with a white rag but keeps her eyes on me. "Don't even think about it, Reed. I know how you operate, and that girl over there is off limits. Find someone else to take home tonight."

I tilt my head with interest, unable to contain my grin. "Hattie, darlin'." I flatten my hand against my chest. "Keeper of my heart. Don't you know making someone forbidden to me only fuels my need to walk over there and talk to her? I can't stop myself now."

Her hand stills on the rag. "Reed," she warns as I stand from my stool and drop some cash on the bar for the beer I won't be drinking.

"This is all your fault," I call out behind me, making sure Hattie sees the smile on my face before I focus all my attention on the woman I'm walking toward.

This isn't Hattie's fault. Not at all. I'd be walking over here no matter what she just told me.

So much for throwing back a few beers.

beth

H IS LARGE HAND *grabs my thigh and hooks it around
his waist, anchoring us together. We're both panting and
we haven't done anything more than kiss each other a little,
but this is Ryan Miller. The Ryan Miller. I start having difficulty
breathing the second he walks into the room. If he looks at me, I'm
digging into my back pocket for the pair of spare panties I keep on
me when we work shifts together. And if he talks to me, I never know
what the hell he's saying because I'm too busy staring obsessively at
his full, gorgeous mouth. It's my body's natural reaction to his, so
there's no helping me right now.*

*"What do you want, Jodi?" he asks, so close to my mouth I
inhale his air to keep myself from passing out. "Jodi." He moves
closer, nipping at my bottom lip. "Give me something, babe. Tell me
where all I can touch you."*

"Are you reading porn?"

The low voice in my ear has me pulling my Kindle so
hard against my chest, I fear I may crack the screen. I drop
my chin, inspecting the front for any signs of damage while
the man behind me breathes an amused laugh.

No cracks. *Oh, thank God.*

I settle my nerves before replying blindly, "I don't think
you can read porn. You watch porn."

I turn my head as the man who just startled me moves
to stand next to the booth. Given my position in reference

to his, my eyes land on his body first, and stay on his body. I know I should do the polite thing and lift my gaze to his face, but my eyes don't want to be polite right now.

Besides, he almost made me break my favorite thing in the entire world. The least he can do is stand there and let me gawk for a moment.

He's dressed in a light T-shirt and distressed jeans, looking casual and comfortable, which I'd find sexy even if I couldn't see the outline of muscles through his shirt. The material stretches to fit him, forming to his chest, his shoulders. Oh God, he's got that build I love, long and lean, not bulky like some 'roided up gym rat. His one hand rests on the back of the booth, the muscles in his forearm tense, and I know I stare for a good fifteen seconds at a body part I never paid too much attention to before on men. I mean, who cares about forearms?

I do. Now, I definitely do.

I decide not to make my new obsession so painfully obvious and slowly lift my head. When my eyes finally reach his jaw, his lips, his eyes, I do what might be the dumbest thing I've ever done in my entire life.

I smile. Really, obnoxiously big. Like a kid on Christmas day kind of smile.

Oh man. This guy wearing nothing but a bow would be exactly what I'd ask Santa for.

I don't know why I'm reacting this way. I've been around hot guys before, and usually I can keep my cool long enough to at least get through introductions. Maybe it's because this guy caught me reading smut in public, and I'm smiling to hide my embarrassment, or maybe it's because he's the first guy who's paid any attention to me since Rocco. I don't know. But I'm grinning like a full-blown idiot over here, and there's nothing I can do about it.

My reaction throws him off. I see it, the way his mouth relaxes, forgetting whatever it was he had locked and loaded on the tip of his tongue. I'm sure it was something witty. He looks witty, but now he seems unsure of how to approach me. He blinks several times, his eyes shifting across my features, and I take his silence as my chance to really study him. But not before I relax my face a bit.

Let's not scare him off, Beth.

His blonde hair is messy, long enough to fall into his eyes and tuck behind his ear. His eyebrows are thick, a shade darker than his hair, and his cheekbones sit high on his face, etched into skin that's seen the sun. He reminds me of a surfer, or someone who should be modeling surfboards, but he's got this rugged thing going on that toughens up his features. There's nothing pretty about him, but in the same breath, I know I'd use that word if someone asked me to describe him.

He looks down at my mouth, and his lips twist into a stunning smile. One that makes my heart shudder against my ribs. His eyes reach mine, a crystal shade of blue, so light they appear translucent.

"Hi," he says, breaking the silence between us. His voice is low, and smooth. "Mind if I join you?"

I shake my head and set my Kindle down next to my plate. "No, not at all."

I'm expecting him to move to the seat across from me and claim that side of the booth. I'm prepared for that. What I'm not ready for is him sliding in to join me on my side, but that's exactly what he does.

I shift over a few inches to put some space between us, to give us both a little room, but he just slides closer until his leg touches mine.

He doesn't want space. I have a feeling if I keep backing

away from him, he'll just move with me. Like we're tied to the same rope, forced to mirror each other. I won't test that theory, because I don't want to back away. There's something about this man that has me leaning closer, pressing my weight against his, wanting his contact. He keeps one arm behind me on the back of the booth and brings his other hand up to rest on the table, keeping his body angled toward me.

His eyes drop to my mouth, stay there for several seconds, then meet mine with a heat I feel spike the temperature in my blood.

"So," he begins, a dangerously wicked smile playing on his lips. "Where all does he touch her?"

"Uh . . . what? Who?" Confusion pinches my eyebrows together, until he nods at the Kindle on the table in front of me. I look back into his eyes. "No idea. I've never read this story before, and someone interrupted me before I got to any of the touching."

"You could read it now. Out loud, preferably."

"You want me to read you a sweet love story?" I ask.

He points a finger at my Kindle. "If that's your idea of a sweet love story then hell, yes I do. I fucking insist you read it out loud."

I grab the cherry floating in my drink and pop it into my mouth, keeping hold of the stem. I chew before saying, "It is a love story. Jodi's crazy about this guy, Ryan, and he's slowly falling for her. Just because there's a bunch of filthy sex in it, doesn't make it any less sweet." I drop my stem onto the side of my plate of fries. "Stories should feel real. Wanting something wild and romantic at the same time feels real to me. I think relationships need both. And it's not porn." Our eyes meet. "Porn doesn't make me cry."

He leans closer, dropping his head next to mine. "I could

disagree with you on that. There are people out there who are into some really fucked up shit. I've almost cried watching some of it."

I fall into a laugh, letting my head tilt back against the booth. "Oh my God, I know what you mean. I accidentally stumbled on this video one time . . ."

"You accidentally stumbled on it?" he interrupts, the corner of his mouth lifting. "You mean, you were searching for porn, which is extremely hot to hear, and you came across a certain video."

"I was not searching for porn."

"That might be true, but if you don't mind, I'm just going to keep imagining you were. I like that version of this story." He lifts his hand off the table, sweeping it in front of him. "Please continue. I'm dying to hear all about your porn preferences."

I shake my head through a laugh. "I've never searched for porn. Ever. If Google decides to throw in a few websites based on what I'm looking for, that's not my fault. And I usually don't click on them, but this one had a catchy title."

"What was it?"

"Edward Penis Hands."

He raises his eyebrows in surprise. "What the hell were you searching for that gave you *that* as a result?"

I shrug. "I heard they were remaking that movie, and I wanted to see if they had already started casting people. My search was very innocent. And in case you're interested, the actor who played in that version was Johnny Dildo." I smile. "I think it got the same ratings as the original movie."

He laughs, low and soft in my ear. It's husky, and deep, and so purely male.

I don't know when he slid closer, but his entire side is

formed against mine now. I don't object to it. It feels good being with him like this. Hard versus soft.

I'm the soft one. In case there was any confusion.

The tight ridges of his stomach are pressing against my arm, while his toned leg keeps firm contact with mine. He smells fresh, a light clean scent that I'm thinking must be the soap he uses. He's not wearing any cologne, and I love that. This is him. His natural smell mixed with the slightest fragrance. It's not overpowering or offensive. If anything, I want to rub him all over me and absorb him into my skin.

'Cause that wouldn't be weird at all.

"What's your name, sweetheart?" he asks, and my cheeks burn up at the sentiment. I almost don't want to tell him my name just so he'll call me that instead. But I'm curious what my name sounds like coming out of that mouth. Really curious.

"Beth."

"Beth," he echoes, his tongue lingering on the *th* sound.

My God. This should be his job. Just saying words that end in *th*.

He runs his tongue along his lips, wetting them, as if he's tasting the trace my name left on his mouth. I suddenly feel drugged at the idea of him doing just that. Savoring me.

His tongue. My skin.

"Beth Davis, right?"

Confusion creases my brow. I'm snapped out of my lustful thoughts with his question. "How do you know that?"

"I know Hattie. She told me you were her niece." He smirks. "Right before she told me to stay away from you."

I stare up at his face, a bit shocked.

Stay away from me? Why would she tell him that? This guy seems harmless. Dangerously charming, but harmless. Maybe she said it because of all the stuff I endured with Rocco.

Maybe what I told Hattie this afternoon painted me as a victim, broken and beaten down, and she doesn't think I'm ready, or strong enough for anything with another man. Not even innocent flirting. But I'm not broken. I've never believed the things Rocco said to me. He tried to crush my spirit, but he failed. Hattie doesn't need to protect me. I'm ready. I'm more than ready for this.

The man lifts his hand off the table and uses it to tuck a strand of hair behind my ear. The gesture has me sucking in a breath, but I stop breathing all together when he trails the back of his hand intimately down the side of my neck. Caressing me. Stroking me.

"I couldn't leave you alone," he confesses, his eyes following his hand. "I couldn't sit at the bar, watching you, and only wonder what you felt like against me. I think I would've gone a little mad just staring at you." His eyes meet mine. "You see that, right? You see that I had to come over here."

I nod because I want to believe him. I want to believe he couldn't stop himself from doing this.

There's a good number of women in this bar, most of them dressed in tight, skimpy outfits, while I'm wearing tattered jeans and a T-shirt I cut up to fit me better. I've never had low self-esteem, but I am realistic. I know how I measure up next to the women in this bar. I'm a plain kind of pretty, while they shine in bold, vibrant colors. I'd normally go unnoticed in this crowd, or any crowd, but he notices me. This guy notices me.

He's telling me he couldn't leave me alone, and there's nothing else I'm going to believe.

I whimper uncontrollably when his fingers run over my collarbone. It's the softest sound, but by the way his lips part and his eyes drop to my mouth, I know he hears it. My bones become heavy and I drop my head back against the booth, giving him better access as he works slowly back up my neck. He's barely touching me, just the back of his hand grazing, testing out the feel of my skin, but I'm burning up from the inside out.

My thoughts are all over the place. I imagine his hands kneading my flesh until it's raw. His mouth clamping down on my skin. Teeth, and lips, and tongues.

Dirty, filthy thoughts.

"Don't look at me like that," he says, causing me to blink him into focus. "I'm not a decent guy. I have no problem bending you over this table right now, but I'd rather not do it in front of your family. And the way you're looking at me, like you want me to take it that far," he pauses, shaking his head and dropping his hand back to the table. He lets out a slow breath before continuing, "You have no idea what that's doing to me."

My mouth goes dry, but luckily, the image he just put into my head makes me salivate instantly.

Me.

Bent over this table.

Him.

Doing the bending.

My chest shudders on an exhale.

"How was I looking at you?" I ask, sounding breathless.

His eyes darken, and now, he doesn't even need to answer. I know exactly how I was looking at him while I was envisioning what all we could do together. I think I'm probably staring at that exact look right now.

Commotion comes from the front of the bar near the entrance, gaining his attention before he can reply.

I watch his profile tense considerably.

It's instant, his reaction. His entire body goes rigid, jaw ticking at the sharp angle of it, and his breathing becomes heavy, uneven with panic.

I follow his eyes through the bar and land on a leggy blonde by the jukebox, her eyes scanning the crowd as if she's looking for someone.

I know who she is to him. At least, I think I have a pretty good guess. You only react one way when you see someone you never want to see again. Someone who's burned you. Someone you once loved.

I look back at the man next to me. The one who made me laugh minutes ago. The one who made me smile bigger than I've probably ever smiled. I don't really know him, not at all, but I hate thinking he was hurt by this woman, because that's the vibe I'm getting. He looks ready to bolt, or pass out, or throw up, and I really hope it isn't option three. Especially with what I have planned. He's made me feel special, and I want to do something for him in return.

I wait for the perfect moment, the one I need to confirm she is who I think she is to him. It only takes a few more seconds before her eyes find us, focus on him with that same 'deer in headlights look', and that's when I do what could possibly be the second dumbest thing I've ever done in my entire life.

I grab his face with both hands, turn his head, and form my mouth against his.

I'm expecting fireworks. Stars bursting between our lips. That *fuck yes* feeling you get when you first kiss someone.

I don't get that. I don't get anything close to that.

He's frozen against me, paralyzed with confusion, or fear. I can't tell which. He was tense before, but somehow, I've escalated his panic. He doesn't pull away, but he isn't giving me anything either, and he needs to. For this to look believable, he needs to work with me.

"Kiss me." I press the words against his lips as my one eye peeks at the woman staring at us. "Kiss me, she's looking. Come on."

I force his head to tilt, sealing our mouths together. He gives, leaning against me, dropping his hand to my waist. He understands this game now, and becomes the willing participant I need him to be. His touch becomes firmer, hungry, and desperate. The second my teeth sink into his bottom lip, he opens his mouth with a moan and welcomes my eager tongue.

Now, this is a fucking kiss.

He's all over me, kissing like a man who isn't practiced with this. It's wild and messy, and so unbelievably perfect. He can't decide whether he wants to suck on my tongue or bite it. His sounds are unreal, low and throaty, vibrating against my lips. I'm practically in his lap, swallowing him alive. I don't care how inappropriate I look right now. I don't care if this building goes up in flames. I'm going to continue kissing . . .

My mind draws a blank.

Oh, nice Beth. Way to completely forget to ask the man's name before you find out if he has any fillings.

He doesn't. *Sweet Mother, even his teeth are perfect.*

"Reed?"

We break contact, but only our mouths, as a woman's voice cuts through the air. I'm still clinging to him like we're on the Titanic and that bitch is sinking fast, and he's holding onto me like he wants on that door that we all know would've fit more than one person.

Her word echoes in my head, and I smile, tagging my stranger with a name. I let my hands untangle from his hair and slide down his body, flattening against his chest.

We're both panting, lips wet and swollen, ignoring anyone

and anything around us.

"Reed," the voice repeats, but this time in the form of a command.

To look at her. To give back his attention to her.

He doesn't do either. He's staring at me with a lost look weighing on his features. As if he doesn't know whether to keep kissing me, or whether he should've allowed it to happen in the first place.

Clearly, he liked it. He was definitely kissing me back. So that second possibility is really throwing me off.

Before I give him the chance to screw this whole thing up with his odd behavior, I decide to handle the conversation that apparently needs to happen.

He can sit this one out.

Keeping my hands on his chest, I look up at the blonde, greeting her with a genuine smile. "I'm sorry. I didn't see you standing there. Can I help you with something?"

She looks from me, back to Reed, blowing out a quick breath. "Um, no, I just . . ." She flattens her hand on the table and leans her head down. "Reed, can you at least look at me please?"

He pinches his eyes shut through a swallow, then slowly turns to look at her as his hands fall away from me. "What?" he asks sternly, the hand now in his lap curling into a fist. "I'm looking at you, Molly. What the fuck do you want?"

Her mouth drops open, but she quickly contains herself and rights her jaw. Both hands grip her clutch in front of her, and it's then I take notice of her designer clothing. She's head to toe in stuff I couldn't even dream to afford. Tight pencil skirt, silk blouse. I don't even bother looking at her shoes as I tuck my Dr. Marten's further under my seat.

Her mouth, shiny with lip gloss, curls into a smile. "It's

been a really long time. How are you?"

"*How am I?*" he repeats, angry, livid even, and I decide to cut in before Reed flips the table over.

I hold my hand out to her. "Hi, I'm sorry, I didn't get to introduce myself. I'm Beth. Reed's girlfriend." His eyes are on me before I get that title completely out, boring into my profile. I give him a quick wink, *I got this*, before I shake her hand. "And you are?"

"Molly." She drops my hand all too dismissively, as if she's already bored by my presence. She looks at Reed. "Girlfriend, huh? I heard you didn't do that anymore."

"What, are you keeping tabs on me?"

"Would you like to join us?" I ask before she has a chance to answer him.

I'm not sure who hits me with a more startled look, Reed or this woman.

"Um, no, thanks. I'll pass," she answers, not bothering to hide the humor she finds at my request. "I'm meeting up with some people."

"Are you back?" Reed asks. "My sister said she saw you at Costco."

"For a month. Then I'll be headed back to Virginia."

"Why are you here for a month? You've been gone for nine years. Why come back now?"

She holds her left hand up, palm facing her, and even if I didn't notice the blinding sparkly diamond on her ring finger, I know that universal hand gesture.

Oh, shit.

Reed goes perfectly still next to me. Even his breathing ceases. The music overhead grows distant as I absorb his reaction to her.

He hates her. That I'm sure of. He still loves her. That I

don't know.

I do what any loyal girlfriend would do. I protect him.

"Congratulations." I smile at her as my hand wraps around the fist in his lap, coaxing it to relax. I feel like I'm squeezing a stone. "You'll have to let us know where to send a gift," I add.

She grimaces as if my thoughtfulness distastes her. "Yeah, okay."

"I'm completely serious. Reed and I are very happy. Why shouldn't we celebrate when others find love the way we did?" I look over at Reed, finding his eyes already on me.

Still lost. Still mildly terrified by my actions.

"Well, in that case." Molly's words have me lifting my gaze to her. She opens up her clutch and withdraws a small, light blue envelope. "We're having an engagement party next Saturday. You two should come. Show off your happiness." She throws in that last remark with some sass, and I'm suddenly geared up and ready for this fucking engagement party.

I gladly take the envelope, but Reed snatches it out of my hand and tosses it back at her. It falls to the table.

"I'm not interested."

Molly smirks as if she knows the game, looking between the two of us. "Right. I didn't think so." She snaps her clutch closed and looks down at Reed, ignoring me completely. "It was fun running into you, Reed. You look good."

Her heels click away on the wood floor, and I slump against my seat, letting out a whoosh of air.

"Wow. She was something else."

He looks over at me, dropping his elbows to the table, his hands clasped together inches from his face.

"What the fuck was that?" he asks gruffly.

"What was what?"

"The kissing. The girlfriend bullshit." His head shakes ever so slightly. "What was that?"

"I did you a favor," I answer defensively, my voice tight with emotion. "I saw the way you reacted to her. I knew she was someone who hurt you, and . . ." I almost don't say it, but I've already made this pretty clear to everyone in this bar. My voice softens. "And I like you, okay? I didn't want to see you look like that."

"So you kiss me? What good did that do?"

I suddenly want to slide under this booth and either curl up into a ball or punch this guy right in the nuts. He was clearly hitting on me. I'm sure we would've kissed eventually with or without the audience. So what's the big deal?

Instead of bombarding him with questions, I settle on giving him the same glare he's giving me as I hide the rejection slow burning beneath my surface.

"You know the best way to get back at someone who hurt you? Without risking jail time? Show them how happy you are with someone else. Even if you're over the other person, it can still sting. Not always. It was a risk I was willing to take, and it worked. She clearly got uncomfortable seeing you and me together."

"You shouldn't have done that."

"Why not?"

"I don't do that," he hisses. "I don't . . ." His eyes pinch shut. He turns his head away from me, digging the heel of his hands into his eyes. "*What the fuck?*" he whispers harshly before raking both hands down his face. He looks over at me. "And roping me into that engagement party? Are you out of your mind? Why the fuck would I want to go to that?"

I reach for the card and hold it out for him to see. "*This* was a challenge. She's not convinced we're together. I bet she doesn't think we'll show up to this."

"We won't."

"Maybe you won't," I counter. "I can play your girlfriend with or without you, and that's exactly what I'm going to do. Of course, it'll be a lot more convincing if you're there, which I think you should be. This is the perfect opportunity to stick it to that snobby bitch."

He stares at me in silence, searching my face for reasoning as his taste continues to saturate my mouth.

Watermelon, I think. Maybe the gum he was chewing earlier. It's sweet, and tangy, and *him*. I'd go for seconds, but I honestly don't know what he would do if I attacked him again. I can't handle him pushing me away, so I keep my lips to myself and savor what he's already given me.

"Look," I begin, dropping my hands to my lap. "It might be uncomfortable being around your ex and her fiancé, but it'll be worth seeing that look on her face again when I kiss you. *That* was priceless."

"Why are you doing this? What's in this for you?" he asks, concern flooding his voice.

I set the card down, grab my Kindle off the table, and settle back against the booth. My eyes stay on the screen as it slowly powers on. "I already told you. I didn't like seeing you look like that. I'm not doing this for me."

I like you. I want to spend time with you. How obvious do you want me to be?

"I want to do this for you, so I am. It's that simple."

He stands from the booth, running a rough hand though his hair before looking down at me. Our eyes lock, and I see that my explanation of my actions isn't settling him at all. He's either not buying it, or he's not okay with it, but I made my decision. I'm going to this thing. Maybe I can convince her on my own that we're together.

"I'm not going," he states, his words conclusive. "If you want to go by yourself and pretend we're something we're not, go ahead. Have at it."

His words sting my ears, and something else in my body.

More central, and slightly moronic due to it's tendency to fall for the wrong guy.

Why is he so different with me now? What the hell did I do besides continue what he started?

"You kissed me back," I say, halting his first step as he tries to leave the table. He slowly turns his head to look at me, and I swallow hard before I elaborate. "I didn't imagine that. You could've pushed me off, but you didn't. You really kissed me, and I think you liked it."

You wanted me. I think you still want me.

His lips part to speak, but he says nothing. That lost look is back in his eyes, and that's the only thing he gives me before he disappears through the crowd and walks out the door.

I fall back against the booth, clutching my Kindle to my chest.

reed

THREE DAYS.

Three fucking days, and I still can't shake that damn kiss.

It doesn't help that it's rained every day since Sunday, shutting down the job site and the distraction I desperately need. Work is a really good thing to keep your mind busy, but I don't have it. I have my cock instead, which is reminding me every time I think I'm over that fucking mouth of hers how wrong I am. I've ignored it. I'm not jerking off to a goddamn kiss. Her sexy little body and the image of it tied to my bed while I pound into her, *that* I have jerked off to. But not that kiss.

I won't break over something I didn't even want.

My hand isn't on my cock because she gave me a wild unlike I've ever had.

I'm not stroking myself because she took my mouth and fucking owned it like it never even belonged to me.

And I'm definitely not moaning her name because I liked that kiss.

No, that's not what's happening. Not even close.

I fucking loved that kiss. Loved. It.

Me, a guy who goes out of his way to avoid kissing the women he brings home because I don't give a damn about anything but sex, is ruined from thirty seconds of one chick's mouth. That perfect *fucking* mouth. Full, soft lips, the bottom slightly bigger than the top. That wicked little tongue and the way it sought after mine.

She was right. I could've pushed her off. I could've gotten the hell out of there before completely screwing myself. But I didn't. I wanted her, and that mouth, and I fucking took it. Or she took mine. Or we both just took what we wanted and didn't give a damn about the other person because that's how it felt.

I was greedy and envious of every other man who tasted that mouth before me.

And she was . . . fuck, she was vulgar. Grinding against me, moaning around my lips. Biting and sucking and owning.

Motherfucker. That mouth.

My cock goes limp in my hand the second my thoughts shift to Molly. She had to walk into that fucking bar. It's like the bitch knew I'd be in there, and she couldn't wait to shove that fucking invitation in my face. I gave her everything. Every-fucking-thing. I showed her how fucking serious I was about us before she left. Maybe I was a little desperate. But I would've waited for her. I could've handled four years. I was fucking handling it.

So why . . . fuck, why wasn't I enough?

The cell phone ringing down the hall pulls me out of bed. I toss the covers aside and stretch my back, flexing my right hand so it doesn't hold the grip I've had all morning. I actually feel the loss of fluids as I toss the handful of tissues into the trash bin and attempt to sprint down the hallway in the direction of my ringtone. My body fatigues quickly, slowing my movements.

Shit. I need some electrolytes.

I grab the phone just before it goes to voicemail and hold it between my shoulder and ear.

"Hey, Mia," I answer before taking a swig of the Gatorade I pull out of the fridge.

"Hey, you're off today, right? 'Cause of the rain?"

I wipe my mouth with the back of my hand. "Yeah, why? What's up?"

"Is he comin'? Can I talk to him?"

I smile at Nolan's voice.

"Can I pweaaase?"

"Nolan, shh, wait a minute." Mia mumbles something else away from the phone, then blows out an exhaustive breath. "I'm going to ask you because it's the polite thing to do, but you're coming. I'm not telling him anything different."

"What am I coming to?"

"Sal's. Nolan wants pizza for lunch and he'll only eat it from there now. He says the crust tastes better or something."

I smile. Kid has taste. "He's right. Can't argue with that. Plus their slices are huge. So, you really get more for your money."

"Mommy, tell Uncle Weed about my hat!"

"Nolan, go grab your brother's binky. It's in his crib," Mia directs away from the phone. "Sorry," she says in my ear.

"He sounds excited."

"You have no idea. He's been talking about you non-stop since Saturday. Now he wants to go out and buy his own tool belt so he doesn't have to use yours when you come over."

"Really? That's awesome. I thought maybe he was getting bored holding my tools for me. He couldn't really help out with the digging for the posts. I was worried he'd fall in a hole or something." I take another drink. "I'm glad he had a good time."

"Reed, it's *all* he's talked about. Seriously. You know Nolan. He obsesses over things." She laughs quietly. "Just wait until you see him . . . when you come to lunch, 'cause you're coming. He'll be so disappointed if you don't."

I stick the Gatorade back in the fridge. "What time do you want to meet? I need to take a shower first."

A scalding hot shower. One to hopefully burn away the shame of the past three days.

"That's fine. I gotta feed Chase before we leave anyway. Wanna meet in like forty-five minutes?"

"Yeah, that sounds good."

"Great. Nolan, Uncle Reed is coming!" she yells away from the phone.

"Oh, yeah!"

Mia's laugh breaks up her next words to me. "All right. We'll see ya in a little bit."

"Yeah, see ya."

I disconnect the call and toss my phone next to my truck keys.

A distraction. One in the form of an amusing five year old and one of my best friends. This is good. This is really fucking good.

I PARK NEXT to Mia's red Jeep outside of Sal's, grunting when I see Tessa's Rav4 a few spots down.

Shit. I should've known she'd be here too.

Not that I don't love Tessa, but I know exactly what topic her conversation is going to steer toward, and I'd rather avoid it. But I can't. Because Nolan's smiling face spots me through the restaurant window a second after I shift my truck into reverse to get the hell out of here.

Yes, I was going to bail. I would've found a way to make it up to him. He's not the hardest kid to please.

As soon as I step inside the small, family owned pizza joint, Nolan dives out of the booth they are all sitting at and runs at me, his bright yellow hard hat wobbling on his head. The strangest feeling washing over me, riddling me with guilt for almost leaving.

"Uncle Weed! Look at my new hat!"

I set it straight on his head, tilting it back ever so slightly to see his eyes. I smile down at him. "Looks good on you, little man. Are you wearing that all the time?"

He nods quickly, his one hand clamping down on the hat to steady it. "Do you weawr one too, Uncle Weed?"

"Sometimes."

His face falls, the elated happiness ripped from his expression. I glance up at Mia who is watching us a foot away, her face pinched in distress in response to my answer. Tessa flips me off behind her menu.

Shit.

"Uh, yeah, I wear it all the time," I recover quickly. "I just didn't have it with me on Saturday because I left it at the job site. But I should've had it." I knock a fist against his hat. "Safety first."

He grins, his dimples hollowing out his cheeks. "Cool." He slides into the booth next to Mia who is cradling Chase against her chest. She slowly shakes her head at me.

"Sorry," I mouth.

"It's okay," she mouths back, smiling.

"So," Tessa begins, drumming her nails on the table after dropping her menu. I look over at her, watching the calculating smile spread across her lips. "I've already filled Mia in on your news. She agrees with me and is also interested in pursuing vehicular manslaughter."

"Tessa," Mia scolds in a warning tone. She tilts her head

to the side where Nolan is sitting. "Let's not teach him new phrases to repeat, okay? He's already picked up Ben's favorite word and brought it up in Sunday school last week. Now the whole class is referring to cats by their *other* name."

I drop my head, laughing silently next to Tessa who isn't holding hers back at all. She's falling against me, her loud cackles filling the restaurant.

"I would've loved to have been there when you got scolded by the nuns," Tessa says between her hysterics. She sits up and wipes under her eyes. "Who was it? Sister Francis?"

"I wish. She's not that scary," Mia answers. She shifts Chase against her so he's facing us, his back to her front.

I never know how to acknowledge babies. He's obviously here, and staring at me with those big brown eyes that resemble Mia's, waiting for me to give him something. So I settle on a nod, an informal *what's up.*

Drool falls down his chin and onto his shirt.

He's not amused. I should've went bigger.

Sal, the owner, comes walking up to our table, holding a ball of pizza dough in one hand. He knows all of us well, especially Tessa and myself. We came here all the time back in high school.

"How's it going? We bring our big bellies today?" He smiles down at Nolan and sets the dough on the table in front of him. "You make any shape you like, okay? I bake it for you and you take it home."

"Oh cool!" Nolan starts pounding his fist into the dough to flatten it out.

Sal looks around the table. "What'll it be today?"

"Just cheese for us," Mia replies before looking across the table. "Do you want to do half and half?"

I nod. "Yeah, sounds good." I look over at Tessa. "What

do you want? Everything?"

She turns her hand into a gun, points it at me, and makes a clicking sound in the back of her throat. "Bingo."

"Okay, half cheese, half the works," Sal echoes the order in his thick accent. "And to drink?"

"White milk," Nolan declares as he sits up on his knees and hovers over the dough for leverage.

"White milk?" I ask.

Mia shakes her head through a smile, looking between Sal and myself. "He means plain milk. Not chocolate. It's how he's been saying it lately."

"Daddy says milk will help me get big muscles like him." He looks across the table, tilting his head up to see me underneath his hat. "Do you dwink white milk too, Uncle Weed? For youwr muscles?"

"Yeah, of course." I look up at Sal. "I'll have a root beer."

A foot connects with my shin underneath the table, and I drop my eyes to Mia who's exaggerating her stare and officially confusing the hell out of me.

"*What?*" I silently ask, holding my hands out. It's then I look back to Nolan and see his eyes still on me, wide and unsure.

Ah. Got it.

I look up at Sal. "On second thought, I think I'll do white milk too. I wouldn't dare drink anything else with pizza."

Nolan grins and resumes hitting his tiny fists into the dough.

"I'll have a root beer," Tessa says through a teasing smirk as her fingers poke me in the ribs.

"You're a menace. You don't even like root beer."

She shrugs, her smile growing obnoxiously. "I like it just fine, thank you. Mind yo' business."

"I'll just have a water," Mia orders, sending Sal away from the table. She bounces Chase gently in her lap when he starts fussing. "So, what do you think you'll do if you see Molly? Are you going to talk to her?"

I settle back in the booth while my fingers pull apart the napkin in front of me, tearing it into tiny pieces. "Already saw her."

"What?" Tessa shoves against my shoulder.

Christ, these two are violent when they're hungry.

"What do you mean you already saw her? And you didn't call me? What's wrong with you?"

"Nothing's wrong with me. I just didn't feel like talking about it."

"Girl code, Reed." Tessa crosses her arms with a pout, leaning her back against the window to fully face me. She makes a soft *tsk* sound. "I'm disappointed in you."

The fuck?

"Girl code? Is that what you just said? You realize I have a penis, right? A very large, well-loved penis."

Nolan giggles across the table, and I realize my error, which is only confirmed as I lock onto Mia's tested glare. I risk a glance over at Tessa, who merely rolls her eyes, as if she'll never believe I'm not a fucking chick.

"Well, what happened, Mr. Zero Filter around my children? Where did you see her?"

I dodge Mia's expectant stare, pinch my eyes shut, and let my head fall back as I take in a slow breath.

This is just what I need. On my own, I can't stop thinking about Saturday night. Now I'm going to be forced to re-live it out loud, and I don't think getting an erection right now will play out well for me.

"Hellooo." Tessa snaps her fingers in front of my face,

prompting me to open my eyes and tilt my head down. "I do need to get back to the house sometime today. I have a stack of transcripts waiting for me."

I nod a silent thank you to Sal as he sets our drinks down in front of us. Nolan grabs his milk and brings it up to his lips, his eyes seeking mine and willing me to do the same.

For fuck's sake. I need a beer right now. Not some kiddie drink. But it's Nolan. And he's staring at me, wearing that crazy big hard hat, like I'm his damn idol or something.

I grab the milk, tip it back, and swallow a mouthful. Nolan does the same after I've set my glass back down.

"It was at McGill's on Saturday night," I begin, glancing between the two sets of eyes to make sure they're paying attention. I can't go through this again. This will be the only time they hear this story, and hopefully, the last time I remember it.

"I was talking to this girl, just . . . you know, doing what I usually do when I'm at McGill's." I shift a knowing look between them. They're both familiar with my weekend strategy. "Then out of nowhere, Molly walks in, and I completely freeze up."

"Did you talk to her?" Mia asks, taking a sip of her drink.

I laugh through a slight shake of my head, then pinch the top of my nose as the memory of what happened next stirs wildly inside me. "Yeah," I answer through a strained voice. I decide to skip some parts of the story and get this shit over with. My hand falls to my lap and I look between the two of them. "We talked. She's engaged. I got the hell out of there."

Engaged. Unfuckingbelievable.

Confusion passes between the two of them as I shoot the rest of my milk like it's goddamn whiskey.

Ah, yeah. That's better. Sweet dairy. Really helps take the edge off.

"She's engaged?" Tessa questions doubtfully, with a tinge of jealousy coating her words. "What idiot would want to marry that cumdumpster?"

"Tessa, seriously?" Mia covers Nolan's ears, keeping Chase tucked against her, but I don't think Nolan's heard anything. He's too engrossed in the giant hammer he's trying to form out of the pizza dough.

Nice.

"Could you *fucking* not?" Mia whispers through a clenched jaw.

"Sorry! But what the h, Luke?" Tessa turns to me after exchanging a smile with Mia and pointing at her bare ring finger. "Well, what did you say? You said you two talked. What did you talk about?"

"Honestly? *She* talked. I didn't say much of anything."

I didn't need to. My girlfriend did all the talking.

Shit. Don't call her that. Don't even think about her. Leave her ass out of this story.

"Wait a minute." Tessa voice cuts into my head, a look of disbelief etched on her face. She points a finger at me. "You're leaving something out."

"No, I'm not," I counter, turning my glass over and setting it on the table. I look across the restaurant in the direction of the kitchen.

Where's the fucking pizza? Tessa wouldn't be this chatty if food was involved.

"Yes, you are," Mia agrees, nodding. She pulls something out of the bag sitting next to her and holds it in Chase's mouth for him to suck on. "You're being defensive," she continues. "And you just slammed your milk like we're actually at McGill's. Something else happened."

I shake my head and keep my gaze cast down at the table.

I'm not giving them anything else. I've told them enough. Confiding in them any more will only do more harm than good.

"What happened with the girl?"

Shit. Motherfucking FUCK.

I don't look up at Mia. "What girl?" I ask, coolly. Calmly. Completely in control.

It's at that exact moment I realize the universe hates me. That if there is a God, she must be a chick who I screwed over at some point or another.

The front door chimes, and I glance up, locking onto the stunner who walks in to officially ruin my life.

Wearing a faded Eric Clapton T-shirt, ripped jean shorts hanging low on her hips, and Dr. Martens covered in colorful flowers, I take my first real look at the body I've spanked, sucked, and fucked in my head over the past three days, and my dick hardens so fast, you'd think she was wearing nothing but those fucking boots.

Fuck. Now I just gave myself another image to jerk off to later. Like I needed anymore variety.

"Reed. The girl . . . hello?"

I hear Tessa, but every part of me is focused on Beth as she walks up to the counter, oblivious to my presence.

Christ, what is she wearing and why the fuck is that doing shit to me? I mean the shorts, yeah, I'm fucking loving the shorts. She's tiny, but she's all fucking leg in those things. But Clapton and Dr. Martens? Why the fuck is that so sexy?"

Beth leans further against the counter, tilting her ass into the air. My entire body goes stiff before I drop my head against the table with a barely audible groan.

"What's going on?" Mia asks, sounding confused.

I keep my head down, clamp my eyes shut, and get through this confession as quickly as possible.

"The girl I was talking to at the bar, that's her. At the counter."

I hear movement, no doubt Mia shuffling Chase around to get a good look.

"Are you ducking her? Is she like a clinger or something?" Tessa asks.

"No," I lift my head an inch, then drop it against the table again. "I don't know, I didn't get her out of McGill's to find out. When Molly walked in, that girl grabbed me and kissed the hell out of me. Now Molly thinks we're a couple, because *that* girl told her we are, and I'm supposed to be going to her engagement party this weekend, with my girlfriend." I turn my head to gaze up at Tessa's shocked face. "And I don't mean how I kissed you that one time when you pretended to be my wife. I mean she *fucking* kissed me." I mouth the word 'fucking', and Tessa's eyes widen in alarm, but her shock is short-lived.

Because it's Tessa. Because my misery is amusing to her. And because she sees an opportunity to make this shit unbearable for me, and she's going to take it.

A slow smile spreads across her lips before she turns her head and looks across the table. "Well, I think we need to meet this girlfriend of yours, don't you think, Mia?"

"Absolutely." Mia's voice is practically giddy, reveling in my obvious discomfort.

Male friends. That's what I need.

I slowly sit up, my eyes immediately being drawn to Beth and her ass that's barely covered. I swallow down my moan. "Please don't."

"Oh, relax, Reed. We won't embarrass you." Tessa puts her hand on my shoulder and pushes against me to gain some height in the booth. "Hey, Clapton! Over here!"

Beth immediately turns her head, connects with my eyes that are trained on her like a fucking vulture, and smiles like I've just given her the world or something.

Never been smiled at like that before, besides when she did it Saturday night. There's no shame to her excitement at seeing me. No containment to it either. And fuck if I don't smile right on back.

"Oh, you are such a shit for keeping this from me," Tessa whispers as Beth walks up to the table. "Look how happy she is to see you."

She stops a few inches away, letting her smile soften marginally. "Hey, how are you?" she asks in the sweetest fucking voice I've ever heard.

I've jacked off countless times to you. I've never been this obsessed over pussy I haven't tasted yet.

"Good," I reply, almost harshly. I'm not trying to be an asshole, but reacting any other way to her might result in getting banned from Sal's for public indecency. I can hear Mia now.

"I can't believe you fucked that girl right here on the table! You're paying for Nolan's therapy."

Beth pinches her mouth together through a curt nod, looks down at the floor, then back up at me through her lashes. "Me too, thanks."

Fuck. Don't be a dick. It's not her fault you've rubbed yourself raw.

The fuck it isn't!

Tessa pushes her weight against me to lean closer to Beth. "Hi, I'm Tessa. Please excuse my best friend's behavior. He sometimes gets shy around pretty girls."

Beth smiles as her cheeks flush pink, and follows Tessa hand as she motions across the table.

"That's my sister in-law, Mia, and her two boys, Chase

and Nolan."

Beth lifts her small hand and waves. "It's nice to meet you. I'm Beth." She taps Nolan on the head. "Cool hat, dude."

Nolan turns his face up, hitting her with his toothless grin.

"Do you want to join us for lunch?" Mia asks before dropping her eyes to mine. She smiles at the tortured frown I'm giving her, and I can't help it. I let a quiet laugh slip past my lips, because I can't be mad at Mia for anything. Especially her friendliness to everyone she meets.

Beth takes a quick glance at me, sees the unspoken answer to that question written all over my face, and looks back at Mia, her shoulders sagging. "No, thanks. I'm actually picking up my order. My aunt's waiting for me at home."

"So, when's the engagement party?"

Beth jerks her head toward Tessa, sending a strand of dark hair into her eyes.

I fist my hands in my lap to keep myself from reaching out and doing what I did a few nights ago. I know what that silky hair feels like between my fingers. I know how smooth the skin is behind her ear, and down her neck.

She moves the chunk out of her face before answering. "Saturday night. Six o'clock, I think. I have to check the invitation."

"You're still going?" I ask, leaning forward.

I honestly figured she was baiting me on Saturday, and when I said I wasn't going to that bullshit, she'd toss the invite into the trash. But she's actually going?

She stands taller, letting her hands fall to her sides. "Yes, I told you I was. I want to play this out." Her bottom lip becomes caught between her teeth, and she stares at me for several silent seconds before stating as a fact, "You're not going."

I shake my head, keeping my eyes on her mouth. "No."

"La mia bella, here you go, my dear," Sal calls out from behind the counter, his hands clutching a large pizza box.

Beth nods over her shoulder, avoids me, and smiles at the rest of the table. "It was really nice to meet you. Maybe I'll see you guys around."

Tessa and Mia both tell her goodbye, and Nolan waves behind her back.

My eyes follow Beth out of the restaurant through the glass window to the parking lot.

"What is wrong with you?" Tessa asks with a firm shove to my shoulder. "You should go to that party with her."

"Why would I go to Molly's engagement party?"

"Why would she invite you?"

I stare at Tessa, waiting for her to answer her own question.

She lets out an annoyed sigh, as if this explanation is a waste of her time. "She's trying to make you jealous, obviously. There's no other reason why she would want you there. And showing up with your hot little girlfriend is a good way to shove that jealousy right down her mother effing throat."

I look over at Mia. "You wanna weigh in on this?"

She faintly lifts her shoulders. "I agree with Tessa. If my ex invited me to something like that, I'd grab the hottest guy I could find and take him with me as my date."

Tessa holds her hand out over the table and Mia high-fives it enthusiastically. "Thank youuu," Tessa sings.

I look out the window, spotting Beth closing her passenger door and walking around to the driver's side.

"Do it, Reed," Tessa encourages. "If you're over Molly like you say you are, what's the harm?"

I don't answer her. I can't, because I'm too busy shoving out of the booth and exiting the restaurant, waving down

Beth's car as she backs out of her parking spot. The rain has let up for now, but the clouds are still heavy overhead, threatening another storm. She sees me through the front window and stops half-way out of her spot as I come up to the driver's side.

"All right, I'll go," I tell her as soon as she rolls down her window.

I'm expecting that smile. I want that fucking smile. But her lips pull down in distress as she shifts her grip on the steering wheel.

"I know you don't want to go with me. I get it. It's not a big deal."

I flatten my hand on top of the hood, angling my body down to get closer. "This has nothing to do with you. That bitch thinks I'm still hung up on her, and I'm not. That's why she threw that invite out. She wants to make me jealous or some shit, but you gotta care to get jealous, and I don't care. I stopped caring a long time ago. I said I wasn't going because I don't really like the idea of being around somebody I never wanted to see again. Someone I regret knowing. Not because I still give a shit about her." I take a deep breath, letting it out slowly as she watches me with steel concentration. "Do you get me?"

She nods, hesitantly, her eyes gentle as they gaze up at me. "I get you. I know what that's like."

"If we're doing this, we're fucking doing this. That means we need to spend some time together before Saturday. This isn't going to be believable if I don't even know where you're from."

The corner of her mouth twitches. "How did you know I wasn't from here?"

I drop my gaze directly to the source of that sweet sound. "You've got a little drawl to your voice, and it isn't one I'm used to hearing."

That sexy mouth, all full and soft, curls up slowly. "I'm from Kentucky. Louisville. Lived there most of my life, I think." Her tongue wets her lips, and I lift my gaze before my dick punches straight through her driver's side door and scares the shit out of her. "And you're right," she continues. "We should probably be prepared for questions about each other."

I straighten my spine but keep my hand on the hood. "It's supposed to rain again tomorrow. If that happens, I'll be free, if you are."

"I'll be free. I was just planning on running out to the Verizon store in town to get a new phone plan." She smiles, so fucking big, my heart reacts to it. "Would you come with me? I need to pick out a new phone too and I don't know what I'm doing with any of that stuff. The only tech thing I'm good at is my Kindle."

I give her a nod. "Yeah, all right. I can do that. Is noon okay with you? I can meet you there."

"It's perfect with me."

We stare at each other, her smile growing the longer the silence lingers.

I can't fucking help it. I breathe out a laugh, letting myself feel not just okay with this, but fucking good about it. My hand falls to my side and I take a few steps back.

"Tomorrow, sweetheart. You and me."

"You and me," she echoes.

I turn away, flipping off my two best friends through the window as they enjoy the show.

beth

DON'T THINK I've ever prayed for weather before last night.

Maybe when I was a little girl, and I wanted to wake up to snow on Christmas morning, maybe then I whispered into the dark, hands folded and eyes closed. I can't remember if God ever listened to me then. Not for something as trivial as a weather request, but I'm sure I would've given it a shot anyway if it was something I really wanted. Something I couldn't make happen on my own. And maybe God appreciates those little wishes, the soft voices in the night that aren't calling out for the impossible. Maybe that's why he gave me rain this morning. Amongst all the heavy hearts and tired minds around the world, pleading for miracles before bed, I chose to quietly ask for a day to get to know Reed. A day that apparently needed bad weather to happen. It seems silly, and insignificant, and maybe this has nothing to do with God. I know what causes rain, and I probably just got lucky. But today, as I listen to the soft tapping against my bedroom window, I'm going to choose to believe something greater was behind this.

I take a long look at myself in the bathroom mirror as I secure the hair tie onto the end of my braid that falls over one shoulder.

My cheeks are flushed with excitement, or from the warm shower I took a half hour ago. Or maybe my nerves are on full display, because I definitely am nervous. I have no idea what to expect from this meet up with Reed. Spending time together to get to know each other should seem pretty straight-forward. I'm expecting a lot of questions, a thorough back-and-forth to cover all our bases. But I honestly have no idea what version of Reed I'm going to be getting today. I've witnessed several sides of him already in the two times we've been together, ranging from charming flirt to unapproachable asshole. Yesterday I seemed to get a mix of both, so yeah, I'm nervous.

I want the guy who came up to me at McGill's, not the one who walked away.

Hattie is sitting at the kitchen table, sipping iced tea and flipping through a magazine when I walk into the room. She looks up and gives me a warm smile as her hand lowers the glass down in front of her.

"Well, don't you look pretty," she admires as I fetch my car keys from the small dish on the island.

I look down briefly at the outfit I settled on today, a cream sundress that clings to my body until it hits my waist. There it fans out a bit and falls to mid-thigh. Not too revealing, but definitely an outfit I've gotten attention in before. I've paired it with the only shoes I own, my boots, and they keep it casual, which is how I like to be. This is about as dressy as I get. I've never worn a pair of heels, and I'm not planning on it either.

I'll get married in these boots. Just watch me.

"Doing anything fun today?"

I turn around and walk up to the table, keys in hand. "I'm meeting up with Reed. We're going to hang out and he's going to help me pick out a new cell phone." I grab a few grapes out of the bowl in front of Hattie and pop one in my mouth. "I might be gone for most of the day."

Hattie leans back in her chair, waiting until I look at her to speak. "You're meeting up with Reed?" Her face visibly tenses when I nod. "Beth, darlin', I'm not sure hanging out with Reed Tennyson is the best thing for you. He's a sweetheart, don't get me wrong, but he's not really . . ." she pauses, her eyebrows pinching together before her gaze drops to the table. I can tell she's struggling with her next words, and I know it has to do with my past.

What else could it be?

"Aunt Hattie, I'm fine," I tell her, prompting her to look up with eyes filled with worry. "I love that you're looking out for me. I do, but, I'm really, really good. I promise." I smile, hoping to get a mirrored reaction. Her lips pull up slightly. "Thank you for caring about me. You don't even really know me yet. You don't have to care, but the fact that I have family who does means so much."

She flattens a hand to her chest. "Oh, darlin'. I'm sorry. It's not my place to butt in. Just . . ." she waves her hand dismissively. "Just ignore me. I'm being overprotective."

"That's okay." I pop another grape in my mouth, chewing behind my smile. "Did you and Uncle Danny ever want to have kids?"

She closes her eyes briefly, then nods as she looks up at me. "Yes, we did. Lots and lots of kids. We tried for a few years, but it wasn't in the cards for us. We're okay with it now, but it is wonderful having you here." She reaches out for me and squeezes my hand. "I think your Uncle Danny sees you as the daughter he never had. Talk about overprotective." She lets a quiet laugh slip past her lips, then feigns seriousness with a straight face. "Don't tell him where you're going today."

"Got it," I reply, reaching for a few more grapes. I step away from the table, only to remember something just before I head out of the kitchen. "Do I have a curfew?" I ask in the doorway, watching Hattie lift her glass to her mouth.

"You're twenty-two years old, darlin'. I don't think you should have a curfew." She tips the glass to take a drink, but freezes, lowering it back down a few inches. Her back straightens in her chair, and caution tightens her frown. "I just ask that if you aren't planning on coming home for the night, you give us a head's up, okay? I don't need your Uncle Danny pacing outside with his shotgun."

I pinch my lips together, trying not to smile. "Okay."

Hattie rolls her eyes. "You think I'm joking," she says under her breath before finally taking a drink of her tea.

I can't imagine what that would look like, and I don't have the desire to find out.

Hattie smiles at me, and I wave, quietly slipping out the front door in case Danny is still around.

ON THE WAY to the Verizon store, I stop at a red light just outside the downtown part of Ruxton where all the small businesses and family owned establishments are located. A beautiful church sits just off the main road, its doors open to allow access to the line of people slowly inching forward out of the rain. A white sign is propped against one of the doors. Holy Cross Soup Kitchen is written in bold lettering across it, with other words written below that I can't make out from this distance. I take another look at the people lined up, and see something in common amongst the crowd. Something very familiar to me. The car behind me beeps, and I glance up at the green light before moving through the intersection.

I park out front of the Verizon store, pulling into a spot next to the highest lifted truck I've ever seen. The tires, coated in thick mud, are eye level with the window of my Cavalier.

Eye level.

I'd need a ladder or one hell of a boost to get up in that thing.

As I direct my attention to the floor to ceiling front window of the store, I scan for Reed's face through the light crowd of people, thinking maybe he'll be watching out for me. I don't see him, and I panic that maybe the light drizzle we've had all day wasn't enough for him to be free for me. Maybe he needed a monsoon, or something worthy of an ark.

Don't get down. There's still a chance he'll be here.

I palm the phone I'm about to replace and open up a new text.

> *Me: I just wanted to let you know I'll be mailing this back to you today. Thank you for letting me use it.*

Turn it off. Turn it off and don't give him the chance.
The phone vibrates against my hand. So quick. Too quick.

> *Rocco: Keep it. You'll need it when you move back in.*

"No, I won't," I whisper to the silence of my car.

I won't need it. I won't move back in. My finger moves to the button that shuts Rocco out of my life. It vibrates.

> *Rocco: No one but me.*

Too fucking quick.

I should break this, send it back to him in pieces with a note attached. *Fuck you. I'm never coming back.* Guilt would riddle me, and I don't want that. I don't want anything connecting me to that man. Not even remorse.

The phone is sealed in the envelope lying on my passenger seat. Working. Intact. And still powered on. He can charge the shit himself.

After locking up my car, I dart inside and avoid most of

the rain, catching a few drops on my forearm that's shielding my eyes. I spot Reed at the back of the store as my hand collects the wetness off my skin.

He's talking to a young woman wearing an employee polo shirt and an overplayed smile. My shoulders push back as I watch the two of them, but mainly him.

He's leaning against the counter, keeping his body angled and all of his attention on the woman behind it. His profile lifts into a smile, and she reaches out and places a hand on his arm. Touching. Slowly moving her hand closer to his wrist. I stop breathing when Reed leans in and whispers something to her. I'm sure it has nothing to do with a phone plan, and I'm also positive her salary isn't based on flirting. I decide two things in that moment as I watch the two of them.

One, I'm not going to let this bother me. I've never felt jealousy before, and if that's what I'm feeling right now, if that's what's causing my stomach to tighten into an unforgiving knot, I don't want to feel it.

And two, if anyone in this store is getting commission off my sale, it's definitely not going to be her.

"Hi, welcome to Verizon. How can I help you today?"

I turn my head, meeting the friendly smile of another employee. A woman, but much older, and apparently, not Reed's type. I risk a glance back in his direction, and he either heard the woman address me, or he's finally noticing me on his own.

He straightens, pushing away from the counter without another word to the woman behind it. His eyes run down the length of me, stop at my feet, where I watch something pass over his face. Lips parted, he blinks several times before he finally lifts his head. Slowly.

My mouth goes dry as I *feel* him look at me. I don't know

how that's possible. He isn't touching any part of my body, but if I were to close my eyes right now, I'd swear his hands were moving over me instead of his gaze.

"Hey." His voice cuts through the air as his long strides bring him to me quickly. "Did you just get here?"

I nod through a hard swallow as I will my body to react a little less obviously to him. "A few seconds ago." I glance over his shoulder at the woman he left behind the counter, who looks like she's waiting for Reed to walk back over. "If you need to finish your conversation, it's fine. I can get started without you."

"I'm good." He smiles, reaching up to brush some of his blonde hair off his forehead.

He's wearing a light blue T-shirt that makes his eyes appear more vibrant, khaki shorts, and sneakers. Reed seems like the type of guy who doesn't get dressed up for anything, and I'm oddly grateful for that. I can't imagine how hot my skin would feel if he were standing in front of me in something other than casual wear.

He looks at the woman next to me, the one I've completely forgotten about. "She needs a new phone, and a new plan. Can you help her with that?"

The woman motions with us to follow her. "Of course. Did you have an idea what type of phone you wanted?"

"Cheap," I reply, tearing my eyes from Reed and forcing myself to look at the woman. "Like, the cheapest you have."

She stops in front of a display case. "A lot of our phones, even the newest iPhone, you can get for free when you sign up for a two year contract. It really just depends on what you're looking for."

I let my eyes roam over the choices in front of me as the woman moves to stand behind the case. Reed steps closer until his arm is pressed against mine.

"Do you know what you want?" he asks, his breath hot against my temple.

Do I know what I want? Has there ever been a more loaded question?

"Not really." I look up into his eyes. "What do you suggest?"

"If you can get the new iPhone for free, I'd say go with the iPhone. I have one. I like it."

"Okay." I turn to the woman, my mind made up. "I'll take the new iPhone."

She glances between the two of us, smiling. "Wow. I've been here for thirteen years, and I don't think anyone has ever bought a phone from me without at least holding it first."

I shrug my response, trap my bottom lip between my teeth, and steal a glance at Reed. Our eyes meet instantly, as if he hasn't been looking elsewhere, shifting all over my face with a gentle curiosity.

"What color?"

I look back at the woman, then lower my eyes to the display case. Black or white are my only options, and it really doesn't matter.

"Surprise me," I tell her.

She nods and opens up the glass case, grabs one of the boxes, and sets it on top. Paperwork is laid out in front of me. "Fill this out, and if you want to pick out a case for your phone or any other accessories, they are along the wall behind you."

I grab the pen and look up at Reed. "Can you go pick me out a case?"

"What?"

"A case. Can you grab me one? I don't care what it looks like."

He stares at me in silence, then reaches up and runs a hand along his jaw, raking across the stubble. "Yeah, sure," he says as he walks over to the wall behind us.

I finish the two pages of paperwork before Reed narrows his choice down to one. I'm expecting him to walk over, grab the first case he sets his eyes on, and be done with it. But that's not what happens.

He goes from three cases in his hand, to five, stacking them against his chest as he walks back and forth along the wall. He's putting a lot of thought into this, and that keeps my feet firmly planted where they are.

What guy, who barely knows someone, not only agrees to pick out a phone case for them, but also spends this much time doing it?

He finally settles on one, and the woman rings me up and gives me everything I need for my new phone. I have a little over a month before I should expect to see the first bill, which gives me time to find a job.

As we step outside, I stay under the awning, giving me the shelter from the rain to examine my phone. It's hardly drizzling now, but I don't know what the rules are for iPhones and water. I power it up and turn it over in my hand.

Black, with a floral design. Almost identical to the pattern on my boots.

"I'm hungry. Are you hungry?"

I look up at Reed, keeping my emotional reaction to the case he picked out for me hidden. Clutching my phone against my chest, I smile at the question I will never say no to.

"Starving."

He produces a set of keys from his pocket and motions with his head toward the lifted truck "Come on. Ride with me. I'll bring you back here after we eat." He opens the passenger door, leaning back to look at me when I haven't followed. "What's up?"

"That's your truck?"

"Yeah."

"It's huge!"

He smiles roguishly. "You have no idea how many times a day I'm told that."

I let out a dry, sarcastic laugh as I tuck my phone and the small Verizon bag against my body.

I could react a completely different way to that. I could ask him how many times a day, or tell him until he provides evidence of that question being factually relevant, I won't believe him. But I keep the comments that will surely flush my skin siren red to myself.

After sticking the bag in my car, Reed steps back and allows me room to squeeze between him and the passenger seat. I look up, way up into the truck.

"Uh . . . is there like a ladder or some sort of a lift to get me up there?"

His steps closer until his body is flush against mine. Two hands take hold of my waist. "Put your foot on that bar and grab the handle. I'll do the rest."

His breath is warm, blowing into my hair, and his grip tightens the longer I stand still.

I will my hand to lift, my foot to brace my weight on the bar, but nothing happens. I'm frozen, powerless against the daze his contact puts me under. His thumbs dig into my back, and the pressure shoots up my spine, exploding into a thousand goose bumps at the base of my skull.

"Sweetheart, I'm starting to get wet," he warns against my ear.

You ain't kidding.

"Sorry." I grip the handle with my free hand, my other clutching my phone, and place my right foot on the bar. I glance over my shoulder and nod when I'm ready.

Reed smirks, as if to tell me he doesn't care if I'm ready or not, and lifts me off the ground, taking all my weight with ease and releasing me the second I settle onto the seat.

I should've flailed, squirmed in his arms a little. Anything to prolong that moment.

Really need to plan things out better, Beth.

"Thanks." I smile down at him as I reach back for my seatbelt, only to find my hand grasping something unlike anything I've ever attempted to strap on. "What the . . ." I turn around in my seat, eyes widening at the bright red harness I'm supposed to be fastening.

"Ah, allow me." He steps up on the silver bar below the door, gaining height.

I flatten against the seat when he leans over me to grab the strap beneath my left shoulder.

"Why do I feel like I'm getting ready to go drag racing?"

His quiet laugh rumbles all around me. "Truck's been modified for when I go mudding. I had the other seat belts removed and replaced with these." He brings both straps around my body, loops my arms through, and secures them together in the center of my chest.

"Is it that rough that you need to be strapped in like this?" I look down as his fingers tuck underneath the belt and give it a tug, lurching my body forward. "This seems a bit extreme."

"The truck I had before this one, I flipped it off-roading four years ago. Totaled it. I was fucking lucky wearing only that lap belt. Only ended up with three cracked ribs and a nasty gash on my head."

He leans back a bit, pushing all the hair off his forehead

and exposing a white scar running along his hairline. It's long, close to two inches I'd guess, and about as thick as a line you would draw with a blunt tip marker.

"See? I can't go messing up God's prefect creation any further. Any more damage to this pretty face, and the female population of Alabama would plummet." He drops his hand and steps down out of the truck.

I laugh dryly. "So, you're really just doing a service to your home state by using the latest safety features?"

His cheeks lift with his smile. "Exactly. There'd be nothing left for you women here if I didn't have these looks."

The door shuts and my eyes follow him through the front window.

God, I've never met a man so self-possessed before. Normally, cockiness isn't something I find charming. Men can say too much, act too assertive, and I'm immediately tuning them out and wishing I never looked at them in the first place. But with Reed, his confidence only adds to what makes him appealing. I want him brash and unapologetic of his actions. No other way but this.

He climbs into the driver's seat and starts up the truck. My seat rumbles with the engine, bouncing me ever so slightly against the soft leather.

"So, what are you in the mood for?" he asks, looking over at me as his hand drops to the gear shift. "Burgers? Mexican?"

My mouth waters. "Mexican. I love tacos."

His hand shifts down, backing us out of the parking spot.

I've never ridden in a truck before, but I've seen them. Heard them. None have been this loud. This truck rumbles like there's a fire burning in the engine. With each shift of his hand, it roars to life, the thunder below my seat vibrating against my legs. This isn't just a man's truck. This is Reed's truck. It's as arrogant as he is, commanding attention as we drive down the street and tower over the other vehicles. It smells like dirt and leather and him. Something distinctly Reed. Something I can't quite put my finger on.

The song changes on the radio. A soft tune, one I don't recognize, spills through the speakers and stills me against the seat. The man's voice is gravelly, scratching the air, with an accent that distorts the words filling the car. But not the words falling from Reed's lips.

Oh . . . my . . . God. Are you kidding me?

His perfectly smooth voice has me breathing quieter, but somehow, heavier at the same time. I don't turn my head. I don't look at him for fear he'll stop the second he realizes he has an audience. He's barely singing loud enough to distinguish between him and the voice on the radio, who doesn't hold a candle to Reed, and maybe he knows I'm listening, but I won't risk it. I also won't ask him the millions of questions I'm dying to ask to get to know him better. I can wait until we get to the restaurant, or until this song is over.

I'll stay silent, clutching my phone, while he pulls me under just a little bit more. I can do that. No problem at all.

reed

BETH IS QUIET the entire ten minute drive to La Cocina Mexicana.

I steal glances at her every few minutes, catching her eyes either focused out the passenger window, or cast down at the phone in her lap. Her profile is lifted into a comfortable expression, like she couldn't be more content than she is right now, sitting next to me.

I, on the other hand, can't decide how the hell I should be feeling.

I know today was my idea. I know I suggested we get to know each other to make the situation Beth put us in seem believable, but I was still expecting this shit to feel forced upon me. I was still expecting this to feel like an obligation, something I was cornered into doing because of circumstances I had no control over. Yes, I ultimately agreed to partake in this bullshit on Saturday, but Beth was the one who forced me to have to consider it. Beth was the one who seemed to be on a mission that night to screw me as much as possible with that perfect fucking mouth. Take her and what she did to me out of the equation, and I'd never be preparing myself for a night with my ex.

This was all her doing. My hand was forced, and I'm spending time with this woman to fulfill a requirement. That's it.

So why the hell am I struggling to view any of this as a chore?

I turn the truck off after parking in front of the restaurant. Beth takes a minute to look over at me, and when she does, her head falls back against the seat and a slow, satisfied smile lifts the corners of her mouth.

"Hey," I say before blinking heavily at the absurdity of that greeting.

She didn't just fucking get here, dumbass.

"Hey," she echoes, without the slightest trace of amusement to her voice. I open my eyes, catching her still watching me. "That was so much fun."

"What was?"

"Riding with you."

I tuck my keys into my pocket. "You've never ridden in a truck like this before?"

She shakes her head as her fingers begin unfastening the harness. Her eyes drop to the front of her. "Nope. You're my first."

"Yeah?"

She nods, and I can tell she's still smiling. Even though her braid is now covering some of her face, I can still see the slight lift in her mouth.

I go for my own buckle. "Well, in that case, I hope I was gentle. I've been known to get a little rowdy sometimes."

All of her movement ceases, abruptly stopping my own efforts.

"I'm not a virgin," she says quietly, before letting her shoulders relax against the seat. She lets out a slow breath. "I guess that's probably something we should know about each other, if we're going to be pretending to be a couple. Though I'm not sure why that question would come up." Her head slowly raises until our eyes meet. "Did you think I was?"

I cannot for the life of me get a read on that question. She almost sounds pained, or disappointed that she isn't a virgin, but why the hell would that matter? And fuck! Do we really need to be talking about this? Is she trying to kill me with visuals?

I don't know how the hell to answer that without possibly hurting her feelings, or pissing her off, or doing something that will only make my life more difficult. But she's staring at me with those big doe eyes, filled with curiosity, looking like she'd wait a damn lifetime for what I'm about to say.

"It wouldn't matter," I manage through a thick voice, throwing my arm on the back of the seat so that it's between us.

My fingers brush her soft hair, and she seems to lean closer, giving me more of it. I continue after I force my hand to clamp down on the seat.

"When we're together on Saturday, when you're with me, that won't matter. You understand?" I say my words slowly, hoping they'll sink in and we'll never have to talk about this again.

"It would never matter."

What the fuck did I just say?

She sucks in a sharp breath, nods, and drops her head back down. "It wouldn't matter for me either." Her fingers begin working the harness again.

Well shit.

I get out of the truck before I can say anything else that sounds like a damn confession, and before I let what she just admitted affect me in any way. *Fuck.* Maybe taking her to a restaurant where they serve tequila as a condiment wasn't the best idea. I'm already acting like an open fucking book with this woman. Add in alcohol, and who the fuck knows what all I'm going to say?

She hops down out of the truck without waiting for my assistance. Her face is a bit flushed, and I wonder if it's from the rain that's got a bit of a chill to it, or the conversation we just had.

"I'm so hungry right now, I think I could eat a taco the size of my head." Her voice breaks with a laugh, all cute and soft. She joins me on the sidewalk with her one hand still gripping her phone.

"We could make a game out of this," I reply, opening the door of the restaurant and allowing her to walk ahead of me. Her eyes meet mine over her shoulder, waiting. "Whoever eats the most, gets out of paying. I was going to treat you to lunch, but if you think you're up for a challenge . . ."

"Deal," she says, almost triumphantly. She turns to face me after we get inside. "You're underestimating me because of my size. I may be little, but I can pack away food like a squirrel on a nut hunt."

I look down at her, watching that damn smile grow so big, I know it's matching the one I'm wearing now.

"Nut hunt?"

She giggles as her free hand wipes the water drops off her forehead. "You like that? You can use it if you want."

"Yeah," I answer, lifting one eyebrow. "I'll be sure to let everyone know I go hunting for nuts."

The hostess walks up to the podium we're standing behind and picks up two menus. "Booth or table?"

I motion with my head for Beth to decide. Doesn't matter to me.

"Booth," she replies.

The hostess leads us to the back of the restaurant and

sets the menus on the table. Beth settles into one side of the booth, picking up her menu which I quickly snatch out of her hands. She eyes me curiously as I pick up the other menu and hand them back to the hostess.

"We'll take two of the taco platters with everything on the side. I'll have a root beer with mine." I sit down across from Beth, waiting until she looks at me before I ask, "What do you want to drink?"

"Sweet tea."

"Okay. I'll let your waitress know." The hostess steps away with our order as Beth sets her phone down in front of her. I reach for it, sliding my thumb across the lock screen and opening up her contacts.

"What are you doing?"

"Putting my number in here. In case for some reason after I drop you off, you want to call me and apologize." I enter my phone number and set the phone back down in front of her.

She looks down at the phone, then back up at me. "And why would I do that?"

"For thinking you could beat me in a taco-eating competition."

"I don't *think* I can beat you. I *know* I can beat you."

"You sure about that?"

"Absolutely."

"Okay. Let's make it a little more interesting then."

She leans back, intrigue lifting her eyebrows. "Name your terms."

The waitress returns with our drinks, and we both take a sip, looking at each other over the glasses.

I use this moment to think of something, anything to up the stakes because I honestly didn't think she'd call me out on it. If by some miracle she does beat me, I never had the intention of making her pick up the check. This may not be a date, but I'm not an asshole. The only woman I ever let pay when we're out together is Tessa, and that's only because she likes to remind me she has the bigger dick out of the two of us, and arguing with her is exhausting.

"Well?" Beth asks, licking the tea off her lips. Her one hand tucks some stray hair behind her ear that fell out of her braid, as her other stays wrapped around her glass that's back on the table. "Worried whatever you're about to say, you're going to have to do?"

"No. There's no way in hell you're going to beat me."

"Then what is it?"

"I can't think of anything." I set my glass down and brace my weight on my elbows. My mouth presses against my hands that are folded in front of my face, and I watch her eyes drop to a spot on the table between us.

"Can I ask you something?"

"Isn't that why we're here? To ask each other questions?"

Her shoulders lift into a weak shrug as she continues to avoid my gaze. "Yes, but this wasn't one of the questions I was planning on asking you. I'm not even positive I want to know the answer to this, but if I don't mind your answer, then I could offer a suggestion to make this more interesting."

"Can you do me a favor first?" I ask.

"Okay."

"Can you look at me?"

I can tell she isn't expecting me to say that, but she doesn't hesitate. She lifts her head, looking at me straight on and giving me her full attention.

"This is how I want to talk to you," I tell her. "If I didn't care about seeing your face, I could take you back to your car and we could have this conversation on the phone."

"Would you rather we do that instead?"

"No, I hate talking on the phone. Ask me what you were going to ask me, but keep your head up."

She nods once, then takes a quick drink before she goes for it. "Were you okay with what I did last weekend?"

"Which part?"

"When I kissed you."

My eyes drop to her mouth, and the memory of what those lips are capable of has me slowly hardening underneath the table. Plus, now they're wet.

Wet and fucking perfect.

"That night, before you left, you said I shouldn't have done that, and I've been trying to wrap my head around why. I think maybe I just surprised you, or maybe you like to initiate things, and that's why you said it."

"I haven't kissed anyone in nine years. You did a little more than surprise me," I explain through an even voice, lifting my eyes back up to hers and dropping a hand to my lap.

"You haven't . . ." She leans over the table, letting go of her glass and flattening both hands in front of her. "You haven't been with a woman in nine years?" she asks quietly.

"I've been with a lot of women. I just don't kiss them."

"Why not? That's like . . . sometimes the best part."

I tilt my head with a grin that has her blushing so fast, it's as if I'm showing her exactly what she's doing to me underneath this table. I watch her slowly sit back before I continue.

"If you think kissing is the best part of being with a man, then you've been with the wrong ones."

She pinches her lips together, fighting a smile. After a subtle shake of her head, she replies. "I think kissing is a very important part of it. It connects you to the other person in a way that sex can't, in my opinion. And I'm honestly not sure how you can sleep with someone and not want to kiss them. Isn't that one of the things that draws you to another person? Wanting to see how they kiss?"

I adjust my shorts discreetly, giving my erection room to breathe. *Christ, I've never gotten hard this quickly. I feel like a goddamn teenager.*

"I don't know. I don't pick up women to kiss them. And when I do get them alone, that's the last thing on my mind." I brush my hair out of my eyes and lean against the booth to stretch my back out. Silence looms between us as Beth takes a lot longer than I'd like to respond to me. The smile she was fighting seconds ago is no longer a threat as the corners of her mouth pull down in confusion, tightening her soft features. "Beth."

"Yes?" she asks, never once dropping her head, even though I'd bet money on her wanting to do that right about now. She seems uncomfortable, maybe even a little wounded. I'm not sure if it was hearing that I wouldn't have kissed her had things gone my way that night that's gotten to her, or something else. Maybe it's my announced habit of sleeping around that has her shutting down on me. Either way, I don't like her quiet like this.

"To answer your question," I begin, trying to coax more conversation out of her. "Going that long without kissing someone, and having it be you, and that mouth, and the way you did it, grabbing me like that and not giving me a choice . . . you surprised the hell out of me, sweetheart, but I have never been more okay with something in my entire life. The fact that I know you're going to pull that shit again on Saturday has me fighting off an erection every five minutes."

Her lips slowly part. Shock. I've shocked her? Is my obsession not as obvious as I think it is?

"Wow," she finally says after giving me nothing but silence for thirty-seven seconds.

Yes, I counted.

"I was just expecting a one word answer to that."

"Ask me again."

The corner of her mouth lifts into a smile, and fuck me, if my chest doesn't tighten at the sight of it.

"Were you okay with what I did last weekend?"

"Yes."

"So if I were to suggest whoever wins this competition, gets to do what I did . . . you'd be up for that?"

My brows pinch together. "Do what you did?" I repeat, trying to understand.

She sits taller in her seat, excitement radiating off her in waves. "Kiss the other person, but on their terms. Anytime. Anywhere. Not necessarily on Saturday."

Beth turns her head as the hostess arrives with our food, smiling up at the older woman.

As our platters are set down in front of us, I think about this wager. I think about it really fucking hard.

Winning means I basically get to assault Beth with my mouth whenever I feel like it. I can pull exactly what she did, maybe even catch her off guard. The part of me that usually runs what I do in the bedroom is geared up for this, rolling his shoulders and cracking his neck from side to side. He wants to win. He wants to claim that fucking mouth whenever and wherever. But the other part of me, the part that wants to lie back and let this woman take me anytime she wants is picking up his napkin and waving it in surrender before this shit even gets started.

Fifteen tacos. Can she even eat that many? I sure as hell can, but this little thing across from me can't weigh more than a buck fifteen. If I actually give this my best shot, let fate decide who gets to take who, is there a chance she'll beat me?

"Oh, and one more thing."

Beth breaks into my thoughts with anxious eyes and a hungry tongue, snaking out between her lips as she eyes up her tacos. She finally looks up at me.

"Because I've already kissed you on my terms, it would only be fair that if I *were* to win, I got to do something else instead, if I felt like it."

"Something else?" I ask, my voice suddenly so thick, I nearly choke on my words. I pick up my glass and take several gulps as a slow, sexy smirk twists across her mouth.

Fuck. Me.

I don't know how she does it, but she manages to look this perfect blend of innocent and I'm-about-to-fuck-your-world-up. Images filter through my head, ones of her in all white, looking up at me as she drops down to her knees, ready to worship my cock. Then of her tying me to a bed, my arms and legs bound, unable to touch her, taste her, or fuck her the way I want. She brings me to the brink of orgasm with her hands, her mouth, teeth breaking my skin while I beg for her pussy and she denies me everything but suffering. She won't let me come, but she makes me watch as she moves beside me, fingers sliding in and out of her while she chants my name. My fucking name.

What. The. Fuck. More important question, why am I harder than steel at the thought of option two?

"If I win," she says, "I can choose to kiss you again, or, I can choose to do . . . whatever I want."

Whatever she wants.

Option two. Please, for the love of God, say option two.

I look down at my plate, silently thanking my food for

looking appetizing, because I'm not going to be able to enjoy it the way I had originally intended.

Life is funny like that. One minute, you're ready to show a woman that you never challenge a man to an eating competition. The next minute, you're thinking about all the fast food places you're going to pass on your way home from dropping said woman off at her car. I like to plan ahead. Burgers sound pretty good.

I lift my head, feigning confidence with a smug grin. "Deal."

SHIT. I AM fucking starving.

Beth is sitting across from me, working on taco number nine, and looking like she's nowhere near stopping. Where her food is going, I have no idea. Maybe to those plump tits that are teasing the hell out of me beneath that dress, causing my erection to be a permanent fixture beneath the table. I've almost excused myself twice to go get some fucking relief in the men's room, but honestly, I didn't want to miss a moment of this challenge. I've never seen a woman tackle this much food before, and look this good doing it.

I, on the other hand, have given up at a half-finished sixth with a hand to my stomach and a wince tightening my brow every few minutes. I need to play this up, otherwise she'll never believe I could only handle five and a half tacos. My man-hood is on the line here. I actually wish I did have the stomach ache I'm faking. Maybe then my mouth wouldn't still be watering at the sight left on my platter.

Think of the prize. Remember what's at stake.

Beth wipes her napkin across her mouth and drops it down on the table. "Finished already, rookie?" she asks, victory lifting her voice to a cocky pitch. Her finger points to the food in front of me. "I see a whole lot of tacos left over there. I thought you said there was no way in hell I was going to beat you?"

I force my eyes to close tightly as I let my head hit the back of the booth. "Stomach cramp. I think there was something in my guacamole."

"Or you just can't run with the big dogs. And that's fine. I won't tell anybody." A soft laugh rings out from her direction. "Or, I'll tell everybody."

I open my eyes, glaring at her as the smile on her face calls out to something inside of me. Something that would do more than I'm willing to admit just to see her face light up like that.

"Give up?" she asks, looking down at my platter, then back up at me.

I answer her by sliding my food away from me, and she begins to wiggle in her seat, bopping her head back and forth as her eyes close and her mouth quietly utters the phrase "oh yeah, oh yeah" over and over.

Damn. That's cute as hell.

"Would you like a to-go box?"

I look up at our waitress who has arrived at the table.

Beth dissolves against the booth, halting her victory dance and shaking her head quickly as she acknowledges the woman with a nervous grin.

"No thank you," she tells her, clearly embarrassed for getting caught basking in her win.

I pick up my platter and hand it over to the waitress. "I'm good. We'll just take the check."

If I had gotten anything but tacos, I'd consider taking it with us and devouring it in my truck after I drop Beth off.

But I don't do cold or reheated Mexican food, and it's been decided already. I'm stopping for burgers.

"Finished gloating?" I tease, getting Beth's attention off her lap.

"For now." She smiles, drops her elbow to the table, and rests her chin on her hand. "We need to come up with our history together. How we met, how long we've been dating, all the relationship stuff. I'm pretty sure those are questions that could definitely be asked on Saturday."

"Okay."

"And since I said we're in love, I think we should at least be going on a few months together. Like two or three, which would put us at meeting . . ."

Two or three?

"Wait a minute." I hold my hand up, halting her insane line of thinking. "You've fallen in love with someone that fast before?"

That's not possible. Besides the only two people on the planet who are the giant freak exception to that rule, Ben and Mia, no one falls in love that fast. It took me almost a year to realize I loved Molly.

She slowly drops her hand down to her lap, joining her other one. "I've never fallen in love with anyone. But I think you *can* fall in love that fast. I think sometimes it can happen almost instantly. Like as soon as you see someone. You immediately feel this pull toward that other person."

"Yeah, you want to have sex with them. That's what that pull is. Or in my case, it's usually a firm squeeze, and then a pull."

I grin.

She rolls her eyes.

"No," she says through a shake of her head. "Sex obviously

does play a part in it. But you can also have feelings for somebody right away that you don't understand. Maybe at the time you think it's just a desire to sleep with them, but then weeks, or months later, you think back and it's like, wow. That's what that was. That's why I needed to be with them." She drops her eyes to the table. "That's what I would want," she says through a much softer voice. "Love should be unpredictable. I want it to hit me and like, knock me on my ass. And I don't want it to take me years to realize that's what I was feeling. I think two to three months is plenty of time, if not sooner." She blinks up at me. "But I'm not an expert on this. You probably have more experience on this subject than I do. So, you decide. How long would it take you to fall in love with me?"

This woman. Fuck.

I stare at her as the stomach ache I was faking becomes something very real. Though it's not really an ache. It's more like a fist wrapping around every organ in my body and squeezing it just until it becomes restricting.

I know her question is justified. I know this is something we need to have locked down before Molly or someone else asks us separately about our relationship. Beth is asking me this because she has to, but this feels like something much more important to her. And shit, it's now suddenly important to me. Giving her the answer she wants isn't my only option, but it's the only way I want to respond.

I struggle through a swallow, getting down the last bit of saliva left in my mouth. "Three months sounds good. That'll work for me."

She blinks several times before her nose crinkles with a smile. "Okay. Three months would put us at March. Where would we have met?"

"Can we say McGill's? There's at least some truth to that."

"I was playing pool, and I had no idea what I was doing. You came over and gave me a few pointers."

I smile playfully at her set up, and she reacts by slowly nodding, as if she knows what I'm about to say. *The little minx.*

"I showed you how to handle my pool cue."

"And your balls."

She masks her own amusement with a serious face, and I give her one right back.

It's a stand-off, neither one of us cracking until I see the slightest twitch in the corner of her mouth. I can't hold my reaction in anymore, and we both start laughing at the same time. Hers muffled by the hand clamped over her mouth, and mine echoing out around us.

What the hell is it about this woman that makes me feel lighter?

Sliding her hand down, it settles on her chest as she recovers slowly from her laughing fit. "What do you do anyway? Like for work?"

I let the chilled root beer quench my thirst before I answer. "Construction. I work for my family's company."

"Do you like it?"

"Yeah, I love it. It's all I've ever known, but I don't think I'm missing out on anything. I like hard work, earning that beer at the end of the day. It's really important to me. I'll probably be just like my grandfather and do it until I can't fucking walk anymore."

"When it rains, you don't have to work?" she asks, rubbing her thumb along the condensation that's built up on her glass as the smallest crease pinches her eyebrows together.

"No, it usually shuts everything down. We don't get that much rain here, so it's not too bad. We've never gotten behind on a job."

I down the rest of my drink when Beth picks her glass up, and it's then I realize that I haven't asked her any questions. I don't know anything about her, yet she seems so strangely familiar to me.

"Hattie told me the other night you just moved in with them. Did you leave the rest of your family in Kentucky?" I ask, setting my empty glass at the edge of the table for the waitress to pick up. Maybe she's just visiting with her aunt for the summer.

She shifts in her seat while her hands fall to her lap, pulling at the bottom of her dress. I know this because of the way the material moves against her stomach. She's fidgeting all of a sudden. Why? Isn't this what we're supposed to be doing?

"No, I don't have any other family," she answers anxiously, and I suddenly feel like a dick for causing the change in her demeanor. "My momma died a few months ago. She was all I had."

Shit. "I'm sorry."

The corner of her mouth lifts ever so slightly. "She had some issues, but she was a good mom. When she died, it was really hard not having anybody. I didn't know about my aunt until right before I moved here a few days ago."

I want to ask more about her mom, but I don't want her getting sad. "Your dad?"

"Don't know him. I don't even know if my momma knew who he was." She scrapes her teeth along her bottom lip. "Sorry, there's not much to tell about me. I don't have a job yet. The only family I have are my aunt and uncle. I'm twenty-two, I love to read, and I'm really, really glad I'm here."

Here. Alabama? Or here, here? With me?

I smile, hoping to ease some of the worry that's making her tense up on me. "I think what you've just told me is plenty."

The tension dissolves from her body, and she reaches for the check the waitress dropped off sometime during this conversation. How did I miss that?

"I'll pay half. You put up an impressive fight."

The fuck she will.

I grab the check from her, stand from the booth, and reach for my wallet. After throwing sixty bucks on the table to cover our meal and a generous tip, I tuck my wallet back in my pocket.

"Another thing you should know about me," I tell her, watching those eyes of hers gauge me with blunt intensity. "When we're together, you don't pay. Even if I would've won you wouldn't be paying, and any guy that takes you out like this and expects you to cover any part of the meal, is a dick."

"But this wasn't a date or anything."

I brace one hand on the ledge of the booth behind her, flatten my other hand on the table, and lean down, getting inches from her face. I'm expecting her to back up, or maybe startle a bit at my intrusion, but fuck me if she doesn't tilt her head up, welcoming it.

"It doesn't matter what this was. If you ever go out with a guy and he makes you pay, don't go out with him again. You understand?"

She stares at my mouth. "Is that an Alabama thing? Are all the guys here like you?"

I straighten up, giving her a smirk that brings out that damn smile of hers. I had my cocky response ready, but my face breaks into a grin and wipes my memory of whatever line I was about to give her.

"Shit," I mumble, running my hand over my jaw as she stands from the booth.

How can a fucking smile knock me off my game? It's a

smile. It's not like she's pulling her dress off, and then beaming up at me like that with her tits out. That would definitely prevent me from coming back at her with something. My mouth would be too busy worshipping every part of her.

She looks up at me. "What?"

I form my hand to her lower back and move her with me through the restaurant. "I don't know. Just pretend I said something really witty. And maybe give a guy a warning next time you're planning on smiling like that."

"A warning?" she asks, hesitantly as we step outside. Her eyes cast upward to the sky. "Oh hey, it stopped raining."

I don't even register the change in weather. Just another thing that slips by me when I'm in her presence.

I open up the passenger door and step back, allowing space for her to get in front of me. "Yeah, a warning. Like 'Hey Reed, I'm about to fuck up your chances of forming a complete thought. Just wanted to give you a heads up'."

She climbs into the truck with my assistance, looks down at me after situating her dress, and frowns. "Hey, Reed?" she says more as a question than anything. Her voice suddenly apprehensive.

"Yeah?" I step closer, cranking my neck back to stare up at her. Holding my fucking breath to make sure I don't miss whatever it is she's about to ask me.

Pathetic.

"Fuck," I utter through a rough shake of my head as she does it again. I shut the door, muting her animated laughter. Catching her eyes in the front window as I walk around the truck, she pins me with the happiest face I think I've ever seen.

That smile.

Damn.

beth

I STEP THROUGH the large, rustic doors of the church and descend the staircase to get to the basement. Once I reach the bottom level, the room opens up into a large space. Long tables with bench seating fill the area, reminding me of the cafeteria at my high school back in Kentucky. It's busy in here, but not a lot of noise. Everyone is eating and focused on their food. Tables of families huddled together, talking softly between bites. Other people sit alone, but they don't look lonely. They don't look despaired or destitute. They have a quiet hope about them as they eat their meals and keep to themselves.

I move past the line of people waiting to be served and head for the doorway that leads to the kitchen. A woman looks over at me, pausing with a soup ladle in her hand.

"Hi, can I help you?" she asks, using the back of her free hand to push the brim of her glasses up on her nose. She's young, not much older than me if I had to guess.

Smiling, I step further into the kitchen. "I spoke to someone on the phone yesterday about volunteering. I was told to show up around eleven today."

"Oh, yes!" She pulls her gloves off and drops them into the trash bin on her way over to me. Taking my hand in a firm shake, her light-blue eyes shine with a familiar light, but I can't understand why. We've never met.

"I'm Riley. You spoke to me on the phone."

"Beth, hi, it's nice to meet you." I drop her hand and follow behind as she moves back toward the table covered in hot food, the steam billowing above the containers.

"Thank you so much for coming. We're extremely short-handed lately," she tells me over her shoulder. She stops behind the two other volunteers. "This is Wendy, and Tonya. Ladies, this is Beth. She's going to be helping us out occasionally."

We exchange quick hellos as Riley grabs an apron for me off the wall. After securing it around my waist, I rub my hands together and eagerly step up behind the table. She gives me a quick run-down of the procedure for serving the people who come in. Everyone gets portions of whatever they'd like, and if there are leftovers after they go through the line, people can come up for seconds. Riley tells me most days they have enough for that to happen, except for holidays when the crowd wraps around the building.

"This is so great," I say to Riley as I scoop a generous portion of green beans onto a plate. I hand it to the woman waiting across the other side of the table. "I wish they would've had something like this where I'm from. I could've used it."

She looks over at me, empathy in her eyes, and I see the moment she decides to go a different route with her response. The hesitation forcing her lips to close, then the slight tilt of her head. "Where are you from?" she asks.

"Kentucky. I just moved here a few days ago. I'm staying with my aunt and uncle."

She spoons some soup into a bowl and hands it to the man in front of her. "I would love to travel. I've lived here my whole life. But my family is here, and my boyfriend. He's not much for getting out."

I chuckle when she wrinkles her nose in disgust. "How long have you been together?"

"Few months, I guess," she answers, almost dismissively. "I . . . he's . . ." She huffs. "I don't know. It's complicated, which sounds like such a cliché thing to say."

"Some relationships are."

"Cliché?" she asks.

"Complicated."

Her head drops into a quick nod.

I may have touched on a sore subject, so I decide not to pry any further as I scoop out a hearty serving of green beans onto the next plate and hand it off. Maybe changing the subject would be best.

"Have you ever been to an engagement party?" I ask.

She thinks for a moment, then shakes her head as she hands out another bowl. "No, I don't think so. People have engagement parties?"

"Apparently."

I tap my spoon on the edge of the serving tray, knocking off a few beans. The idea of throwing a party to celebrate locking down a mate seems a bit unnecessary to me. Isn't that the whole purpose of the wedding?

I lean my hip against the table while my hand absent-mindedly stirs the beans. "I'm trying to decide if these parties are usually formal events or not. I own one dress and I'm not sure it's fancy enough. It's pretty plain."

Riley tilts the large pot of clam chowder toward her and peers down into it. "I guess it depends on the couple having it. If they have money, why not throw it around?" She looks up at me as she lifts the pot off the table. "I'm going to get a little bit more before people start coming up for seconds. Are you good?"

I look down into my tray. Not many people stopped for the green beans, although they look and smell delicious.

"I have more than half. I think I'm good."

As she walks to the back of the kitchen with her pot, I slip my phone out of the pocket of my jeans and step away from the table.

I have no idea what Reed's ex-girlfriend's money situation is. She could've blown all her cash on the heavily perfumed invitation sitting on my bedroom dresser. This party could be low-key and informal. It could also be an event that requires Reed to wear a tux.

Shit. I can't handle him in something rented.

Me: Hey, it's me. Is this thing on Saturday going to be really fancy? I don't know if I have anything to wear.

It's not raining today, which means Reed is most likely at work. He might not have his phone on him. I could be stuck making a judgment call on this, but I don't want to buy something I'll only wear once if I don't even need it.

Reed: Who is this?

I stare at the screen, mouth falling open. *Really? Who is this?*

Me: Beth.

Me: Beth Davis.

Me: From McGill's.

Reed: Sweetheart, even if I didn't know who this was, which I did, you could've stopped at Beth. I would've figured it out.

Me: You're hilarious.

If there is a way to text sarcasm, I pray I just nailed it.

Reed: I thought I was funny. So did Connor.

Me: Who is Connor?

Reed: One of my workers. I asked his opinion. He laughed.

Me: He's sucking up to you. You sign his paycheck.

Reed: Technically, my mother signs his paycheck. She runs the office. I just tell him what to do.

Me: Like laugh at your poor attempts to be funny.

Reed: Hold on. I'm programming your number into my phone, Beth Davis from McGill's.

Me: You aren't seriously putting me in like that, are you?

My phone beeps as a photo message comes through, a screen shot of his contacts opened up to my name, Beth Davis from McGill's. I keep my laugh subdued, *okay, that's somewhat funny*, and decide he isn't the only one out of the two of us who can crack a joke.

Me: You could put me in under the nickname I went by in high school.

Reed: What was that?

Me: Beth Deep Throat Davis.

Holy shit. I cannot believe I just typed that.

I have never texted anything that . . . filthy before. Ever. Not even a few words that hinted around to something sexual.

What possessed me to pop my dirty-texting cherry with Reed Tennyson? I was going for funny. Maybe that wasn't his kind of humor. Shit. Shit! My throat suddenly feels tight, my tongue too large for my mouth. What was I thinking? I could've used my actual nickname growing up. It isn't funny, but it's at least a word that wouldn't make my insides feel like they're being held over an open flame.

My thumbs move frantically, trying to undo my error.

> *Me: Sorry. I don't know what made me send that. I've never been called that before. My momma always called me Bethie when I was younger. That's the only nickname I've ever had. If you could erase what I've sent you prior to this message and never speak of it again, I'd appreciate it.*

I've never been the type of person who recovers well from uncomfortable situations. If anything, I'm usually making it worse on myself. Case-in-point.

> *Me: I'd never be called Deep Throat. I have a really sensitive gag reflex. When the doctor does that strep test with the long Q-tip and scratches the back of your throat, I almost throw up.*

> *Me: Luckily, I don't get dick very often.*

I nearly swallow my tongue.

> *Me: OMG. Sick! I meant I don't get sick very often!*

> *Me: Ducking autocorrect!*

> *Me: What the hell is dicking?*

Me: OMG. What is happening?

I'm a second away from hurling my phone against the nearest hard surface, or dropping it into the pot of steaming chowder Riley is carrying my way.

Reed: I think your phone loves dick.

Some of my embarrassment subsides as I read his cavalier response. The hand covering half my face slides down and resumes typing.

Me: I am so sorry if I made this awkward.

Reed: Not awkward for me. You've kept me amused on my break, which is now over. Text me your address. I'll dick you up at 5:30 p.m. on Saturday. (See what I did there?)

I muffle my laugh with my hand. *Good one.*

Me: Oh, wait! You didn't answer my question.

Reed: What was it?

Me: The party. Fancy? Do I need to dress up?

Reed: Probably. Molly's family is loaded. They'll have all the best shit.

Me: Okay. Have a great day constructing.

Have a great day constructing? Good Lord. What is wrong with me? I should not be unsupervised with a cell phone.

I step up next to Riley as the line for second helpings begins to form. The previous conversation circles in my head, heating my skin and lifting the corner of my mouth.

I don't get dick very often.

Forget texting him my address. My whore of an iPhone will have a field day with Balzac Street.

I THINK IN another life, I had to have been a man.

I've never liked shopping. Never. It's one of the reasons almost everything I own is something my momma used to wear that I've altered to fit my body. She was little like me, but had a bigger chest, so most of her shirts hang funny until I take a needle and thread to them. I've gotten pretty good at fixing up stuff to fit me. I still go shopping for some things, but honestly, I've always liked my momma's style better than anything I can ever find at the mall. Being teased in school for wearing torn concert tees and ratty flannels didn't stop me. I didn't care what people had to say. I was me. I have always been me. I'll never change for anyone, and if someone doesn't like it they were never meant for me to know anyway. Life's too short to dress boring and predictable. I don't want to wear things that make me uncomfortable in my own skin. But sometimes, you have to bite the bullet. Sometimes, you have to drag yourself into very overly priced boutiques, searching for something to wear to a party which will apparently have all the best shit.

I'm on dress number eight, and I'm exhausted.

"Mommy, look! Buy dis! It's got a puppy on it!"

The cutest little voice seeps into the small dressing room I'm standing in, bringing the only smile to my face since I stepped into this god-awful strip mall.

"Nolan, put that back and come stand by me, please."

Nolan? Nolan . . . why do I know that name?

I secure the zipper underneath my arm and step out to

view this disaster I'm wearing in a three-way mirror. As I'm turning to gauge how wrong this thing looks from the back, an infectious little laugh comes from somewhere in the store. *God, that's adorable.*

"What's up, Clapton?"

I lean back to look out into the store from the secluded area of the dressing rooms.

The red-head who was sitting next to Reed the other day at the pizza place is standing just outside the doorway, leaning her elbow against a rack of blouses. She tilts her head with a coy smile.

"Fancy seeing you here." Her eyes fall to my dress, then a finger darts directly at the material rejecting my body. She hisses through a grimace. "That dress," she says, her voice tight with judgment. "It's not working for you at all."

I breathe a raspy sigh while running my hands over the satin covering my stomach. "Tell me about it. None of these dresses are working for me."

"It's giving you this double boob thing. Does it have a built-in bra?"

"Yes," I answer, staring down at my chest. *Double boob? That can't be the only issue.*

"Mm mmm. That's it. That's the problem."

"Oh hey! It's you!"

I look up as the other woman from the pizza shop walks over, stopping at the rack of clothes and wearing one of those kangaroo baby carriers on her chest. The little guy against her makes a soft, cooing sound, while the boy I'm certain was responsible for the giggling hides behind her legs, peeking his head around her thigh.

Nolan. That's why I know that name. The cutie with the hardhat.

She looks at me like I'm an old friend. Like I'm someone who already means something to her.

"It's so good to see you. Beth, right?"

"Yes, hi. It's good to see you guys too." I wave at Nolan and he giggles again, ducking behind a leg.

I can't decide how I want to prevent this nightmare I'm wearing from blinding them. I'm fidgeting, but it has nothing to do with nervousness as my arms cross over my chest, then flatten against my stomach, then tug at the material, hoping it'll somehow tear from my body to reveal something perfect underneath.

I look down at the front of me, then back up at them. "I'm sorry. I forgot your names."

"Tessa." The red-head speaks up first.

"Mia."

The little boy reaches up and tugs on Mia's shirt. "Mommy, can I pway with your phone?" She hands it to him and he shifts the Playskool tool belt around his waist before hoping up on the chair just inside the dressing room area. His little feet swing in the air.

"Stay out of the app store, please." Mia tilts the hard hat on his head to see his face. He smiles up at her with the cutest dimples I've ever seen, two massive craters sinking in his cheeks, then drops his attention to the phone in his hands.

"I love his little tool belt," I admire, watching the proud smile spread on Mia's face. "Is he really into building stuff?"

She works a lock of her dark hair out of the tiny fist claiming it. "He is now. Reed's given him a new obsession."

"Speaking of Reed."

I look over at Tessa, who's beaming like she's in on some big secret. Her bright green eyes are wild and knowing, directed solely at me. She pops the gum in her mouth and wiggles her eyebrows before adding, "Ready for Saturday?"

My eyes falls to the front of me. "Not if I can't find something to wear."

Tessa rushes out of the dressing room, barreling past Mia.

"Where are you going?" Mia asks over her shoulder. When Tessa doesn't answer, Mia turns back to me. "So, how are you liking Ruxton? Reed told me you just moved here from Kentucky."

My eyes widen. *He talked about me.*

I softly clear my throat. "I like it. I haven't really explored a whole lot yet, but everyone seems really nice. I like the small town feel. I've never had that."

"Yeah, I've always loved that about living here. Everything is so laid back."

"It's so different from Louisville. I hated the fast-paced city life. I'm too boring for that. Being here, it just feels right, you know?" She smiles when I pause. "I'm really glad this is where I ended up."

Her expression turns tender. "I think I said something very similar to that two years ago."

"You didn't grow up here?"

"No, I did, I just moved away for a few years. Tessa had me up for the summer and I never left." Something flashes in her eyes, a memory that brightens them. "I don't know what it is about this town. Maybe it's the people."

"Yeah," I agree, turning my head when I feel the blood rush in my veins. The dress I'm wearing somehow becomes tighter, more constricting against my ribs. "I think it's the people," I say quietly as I tug the material away from my body.

Her delicate laugh grabs my attention. She could pry, ask me if I'm referring to Reed or anyone else in particular, but she doesn't.

"We should all hang out sometime. Tessa and I could use another girl in our group. We're quickly getting outnumbered." She places a hand on the back of the baby's head and lifts her eyebrows, waiting for my agreement. I say agreement because I doubt anyone has ever said no to Mia. She seems too sweet to let down.

"I'd love to hang out with you guys."

"We have game nights and stuff at my house. It's really a lot of fun. And you need to meet the guys." She begins twisting back and forth, bouncing a little when the baby begins fussing. "Ben, my husband, is Tessa's brother. She's dating Luke who works with Ben. And you already know Reed."

She bites her bottom lip to keep her smile under control. That only fuels mine. Ear to ear, I grin like he's standing directly in front of me. She drops her mouth to the top of the baby's head and lowers her voice.

"CJ comes sometimes. He's really nice too."

I do a quick count of the men, including the two in the room. "You're definitely getting outnumbered," I tell her as Tessa walks back into the dressing area.

"Here we go," she says, marching directly at me.

"Oh, uh, is . . ." I stammer as several garments are shoved against my chest. All black dresses, but different styles.

Tessa guides me into the dressing room I emerged from minutes ago with a hand to my shoulder.

"Any of these dresses will do for Saturday. I guessed a size five-six, was I right?"

Wow. Who can guess someone's size just by looking at them?

"Yeah, that's . . ." I look down at the dresses in my hand, then back up at her. "How did you . . ."

"It's a gift."

She takes one of the dresses and hangs it up on the rod

along the wall, repeating this until I'm left holding one. Her red hair is slightly disheveled, falling out of the loose pony at the base of her neck. We're similar in size, but I have a couple inches on Tessa. Mia towers over us both. The two of them couldn't be more opposite, not in appearance or demeanor.

Turning to face me, Tessa brings her hands to rest on her hips, looking satisfied with herself.

"You need to look slammin' at this thing. You have great tits, so use them. All of these dresses can be worn without a bra, and that's exactly how they should be worn. Don't cage those babies up. You want to leave some things to the imagination, but a bangin' cleavage isn't one of them." She moves past me and closes the door behind her, leaving me alone in the small room.

I hold the dress up in my hands to get a good look at it. It's short, the material form-fitting, and the part that would cover my chest is sheer.

"This would show nipple," I mumble, sticking my hand down the neck of the dress.

"Nothing wrong with that!"

I laugh at Tessa's remark, then turn my head so I'm staring at the door. My arms drop. "Are you two waiting for me to try these on?"

"Yup," both women answer, their voices light with excitement.

"Even if you don't like it, step out and let us see it," Tessa says. "I might be able to tweak it so it'll work."

"Some of these are really short." I pass a hand over the dresses hanging in front of me. I'm not used to wearing anything like this. "And this one . . . who wears a dress that has a slit up this high?"

Forget about the possibility of everyone at this thing

seeing my chest. This one would show vagina.

"I own that one in white."

I pull my hand back into a fist, wincing. My eyes fixate on the door as uncomfortable silence fills the longest seconds of my life.

Shit. Recover, Beth! Say something!

"It's . . . I love it. It's so pretty." My words stick to my tongue, struggling to escape my mouth. I'm insulting my new friends. Awesome. I'm sure they'll be dying to hang out with me now.

As my head drops against the wall, laughter erupts from behind the door.

"Tessa, tell her you're kidding!"

"I am. I'm sorry. I'm sorry. That was too easy." Tessa's voice breaks with a cackle. "Whew. I crack myself up sometimes."

"You're a brat," Mia teases, her voice getting louder as she moves closer to the door. "Beth, we're ready when you are. Take your time."

I like these girls. They make even this torture enjoyable.

Lifting my head, I pull my shoulders back and switch the dress in my hand for another that's hanging up. "Okay, but I'm not doing nipple. I'd like to leave whether or not I have any piercings to the imagination."

I KNOW I shouldn't feel this way.

I know this entire night will all be for show. One giant lie.

I know this isn't going to mean anything, and whatever happens at this party will be done based on the need to make our roles believable.

But I can't help my excitement. Reed has made me feel

more comfortable in the short time we've spent together than any other person I've ever been around. It's easy with him, and not in a chummy friend sort of way. My heartbeat rivals a hummingbird on crack in his presence. I've never had many friends, but the ones I did have never elicited that type of reaction.

And now I can't even hide it.

Now, when it all becomes too much, when the warmth in my blood reaches the surface of my skin, when an unforgiving pressure forms between my hips, and my lungs struggle to keep up with the pace my heart is setting, I can't look away to catch my breath. He forces me to keep my eyes on his. He overloads me with stimuli, and then pins me down, stealing my reaction as if he's earned it, or as if it was his all along and he's taking it back. I'm sure it'll be like this tonight. I'm sure he'll do something, or say something that will provoke my body. Even if it is a night where every touch will be an act, I get to be around someone who makes me smile more than I've ever smiled in my entire life. So, no, I can't help my excitement. I want to be around Reed, and I'm not ashamed to admit that.

Even though I am filled with unrestrained enthusiasm, I hold off getting ready for as long as I can. I read a little, watch The Fault In Our Stars with my aunt, hold ice cubes under my eyes to relieve some of the puffiness brought on from watching The Fault In Our Stars, and read some more. I take a bath instead of a shower, trying to stretch out my minutes. I spend longer than I ever have on my hair and makeup, and still finish with an hour and forty-five minutes to spare before Reed is due to arrive.

It's a habit of mine. I'm an early person, and I always have been. Luckily I'm also stellar at killing time. Being a lover of books has its perks. There's always a story waiting to be read. A hero to fall in love with. A heroine to adore. Sometimes I think I should change genres and actually give the potential men in my life a chance.

My expectations of love are dangerously unrealistic.

Danny is already at the bar, and I know Hattie will be leaving soon to head into work. She mentioned earlier when we were sobbing next to each other on the couch that she wished she had memories of me. She would've loved to have held me when I was a baby, or been there to watch me walk across the stage at my high school graduation. I would've loved that too. I want her to have the time she missed with me. I can't give her that, but I can give her something that might help ease some of the ache of knowing she'll never get those moments. A small thank you for being here for me now.

She's at the kitchen island, sifting through some mail when I walk into the room. Her face turns up and gentles considerably at the sight of me.

"Wow, darlin', you look so beautiful." She grabs her purse and digs out her phone, holding it out to take a picture. "Sorry. I have to do this."

I hold the shoebox behind my back and bend my knee, giving her my best smile. "Good?"

She looks down at her phone, nodding before setting it back in her purse. "Of course it is. Davis genes, honey. We can never take a bad photo."

I step up to the island and pull the shoebox out from behind my back. A crease forms between her eyebrows as I slide it across the counter.

"I wanted you to have this. There's so many pictures of me in here. Ones when I was a baby, up until right before my momma died. I thought you could look through them and live out some of the memories with me."

Hattie attempts to blink away her tears, but a few slip past her lashes and drop to her cheeks. She brushes them away quickly and places a hand on top of the shoebox.

"You are just the sweetest thing, Beth. Thank you. Of course I won't keep this. These are yours, but I would love to look through them."

"There might be a few of me with my mom. I don't think I've ever really looked through the entire box."

She pops off the lid and peers inside. "Would you mind if I scanned them into the computer? I'd love to get copies printed."

"Nope. I don't mind." I grab a mint from the small dish in front of me and pop it into my mouth. When she doesn't say anything more, I think Hattie is flipping through the photos, until I look up and catch her eyes on me.

"Are you sure this isn't a real date?" she asks, lifting a skeptical brow.

Her question has me biting down on the mint, shattering it into pieces. I bring a hand up to my mouth to shield her from bits of peppermint as I respond. "I don't think he sees this as a real date." I chew up the mint quickly, fearing I'll choke if I don't get this down before she asks me anything else.

She tilts her head. "But do you?"

I swallow down the last bite of mint and wipe my fingers along my mouth, removing any trace of it. "I don't know," I answer honestly, watching her expression somber a bit. "I like him. I know that."

The doorbell sounds behind me, causing my chest to pinch. I look over my shoulder as a loud, breathy exhale pushes past my lips. The chill of peppermint cools my mouth while my skin becomes hot with excitement.

He's here. He's here. He's here.

Reed.

"Beth?"

"Hmm?" A gentle touch on my shoulder has me spinning my head back around, meeting the curious stare of my aunt.

She laughs gently, then nods in the direction of the door. "You might want to get that before he starts banging."

Reed. Banging. Banging Reed.

I move quickly through the kitchen, waving a hand over my head at my aunt. "Don't wait up!" I yell, grabbing the small clutch off the table in the entry way.

I pull the door open and pray for a Reed who disappoints. One who didn't dress up for this, because I'd like the use of my vocabulary.

Maybe he's hoping for the same thing as our eyes move over each other. Maybe we're both caught up, struggling to communicate. He's not wearing shorts and a T-shirt. He totally dressed up for this. I open my mouth to speak. He does the same. One word is shared between us.

"Fuck."

And we both say it.

reed

THOSE FUCKING BOOTS.

I don't know what I was expecting. Heels, I guess. Most women wear heels with dresses. But Beth isn't most women. I knew that before I drove over here tonight. Hell, I knew it a week ago. I should've been prepared. Before I got dressed, I jacked off in the shower, but maybe I should've done it more than once. Maybe she knows I've pictured her in nothing but those boots while I live out my dirtiest fantasies, and that's why she's wearing them. Maybe she's trying to kill me slowly. What a fucking way to go though. Looking at her, right now, like this. Alone, there is nothing sexy about those boots. But those legs, in that fucking tiny black dress that's hugging every perfect curve of her body . . .

"Fuck."

She says it too. I imagine her tacking on another word. Me or yes or please. Her ass in my hands while she whispers it against my lips. The word getting stuck in her throat while I fuck her mouth.

Shit. Not helping.

She shuts the door behind her and steps down onto the small porch I'm standing on. Her hand flattens against my tie. "You look nice."

"Nice?" I ask, tilting my head. "That pretty mouth of yours just cursed at the sight of me. We both know I look damn good." Her fingers pinch the material of my tie, then release it all too quickly as she gauges me with uncertainty. "You look damn good too, sweetheart."

She wets her lips. "Thanks. So do you."

A smirk tugs at my mouth. Fuck, I love that I do that to her. Make her forget what she's just said.

I guide her down the steps with a hand on her lower back. "We covered that already. But if you want to continue boosting my ego, you can tell me all night long how amazing I look. No guy minds hearing that."

Her eyes narrow before she swats at me with her purse. "Like your head can afford to get any bigger."

"It can. I'm actually not told that enough." I step up behind her after she opens the passenger door. "Ready?" I ask, hands gripping her waist.

She looks at me over her shoulder, then nods.

I'd draw this moment out if she was wearing anything else. That plump ass is barely covered. I don't need it in my face when I'm parked in her aunt's driveway. Not when I've done some of the filthiest shit to it in my head.

"Reed!" she squeals as I toss her up into the truck. Her body slides across the bench seat to the driver's side with the force of my hands.

Fuck, I forgot she weighs nothing. I could've thrown her clear through the window.

She moves back over where I meant to put her, her mouth fighting a smile. "Eager?" she asks through a subtle laugh. Her fingers rake through her dark hair, untangling it at the ends. It's wavier than it was the other day. Disheveled from the lift I just gave her. I imagine this is what it looks like after she's rolled around in a bed. Or the aftermath of fucking her in the bed of my truck.

Why? Why would you give yourself that image?

"Reed."

"Yeah?" My eyes snap to hers, pulling away from the fingers in her hair.

Her hand reaches blindly for the harness. "I asked if you were eager." She studies me with curiosity.

I probably look like a creep with a hair fetish.

"Yeah," I say, finally giving her an answer before shutting the door.

I am fucking eager. The shoes aren't helping. That fucking dress isn't helping. *Beth* isn't helping.

I climb up into the truck and start it up. I pray she's buckled because I can't handle strapping her in right now. Not when I know how close my hands will be to the parts of her I want to taste.

"You good?" I ask, backing out of the driveway, my eyes on the rear-view mirror.

"Mm. Yeah. A little nervous."

"Why are you nervous?" I shift into first gear and risk a quick look in her direction. Her head is turned away as she stares out the passenger window.

"I know I'm going to kiss you again tonight."

"Right." My knuckle cracks as I squeeze the steering wheel.

"I'm just nervous about it," she adds, her voice growing quiet. "Not because I don't want to kiss you. I just don't want to feel like I have to do it."

I slow to a stop at the end of the street, then look over at her. "If you feel that way, don't kiss me." She turns her head and our eyes lock. "We can be a couple who doesn't do PDA. There's no reason why we have to be all over each other for this to be believable. And you shouldn't be doing anything you don't want to do. Not with me or anybody else."

"I don't think I'll feel that way. I don't feel that way right now." She shifts her gaze to the dashboard. "When I kissed you before, I wanted to do it. If I kissed you right now, it would be because I wanted to do it. But when we walk in there, everything you do is going to be for her to see. If you kiss me, it'll be for her. I don't want to feel like I'm kissing you back because I have to play along."

"If I kiss you, that's going to be for me. Not for some bitch I don't give a shit about."

Her mouth falls open with the softest gasp. "Oh."

I look past her shoulder to clear traffic, then drive forward. My gaze shifts between the road and her profile, lingering on the latter.

"Don't be nervous. Just be how you are with me. And quit looking away when you need to tell me something."

The corner of her mouth lifts slightly. She tucks her hair behind her ear, pulls her shoulders back, and reaches into her small purse.

"Do you know where Swan Harbor is?" she asks, pulling out a teal blue card and studying it.

I grind my jaw. My head falls back against the seat as I inhale through my nose.

If that shit wasn't already printed on that fucking invitation, I'd swear Molly picked this venue just to see if I reacted to it.

"Yeah," I answer, shifting gears as I cut through traffic. I'm suddenly ready to get this night over with. Ready to show up, prove I don't give a damn, and leave with Beth on my arm.

Swan Harbor. What a cunt.

"I know exactly where it is."

BETH LEANS AS close to the dash as her harness allows as I drive down the rocky path. She's straining to see the source of the light and music in the distance, but the packed parking lot isn't making that task easy.

Some asshole in a bowtie signals me with a flashlight in his hand to keep moving.

No, I was planning on parking right fucking here. Block people from getting out.

"Look at this dipshit. We get it. File in behind the car in front of you." I gesture with an open palm at the kid, who indicates for me to pull into a spot. His flashlight illuminates the grass with quick streaks of light.

"You okay over there?"

I pull into the spot and glare at the bowtie wearing douche. "He's probably making more than I do in a day for two hours of shining a damn flashlight."

The kid smiles at me, clearly hearing what I'd just said through my cracked window. He tugs at his bowtie and takes a step back. I lift my chin.

"What time is your mom picking you up?"

Beth smacks my arm. "Reed, relax. Why are you so edgy all of sudden?"

"I'm not edgy."

I'm fucking edgy.

I turn the truck off and step out onto the grass, inhaling the night air as I drop my head back. The sky is clear enough to see all the stars. Not a cloud in sight. It would actually be a nice night to be here with Beth under different circumstances.

A car door shuts, and I drop my head as she rounds the front of the truck.

Fuck. Again? Can't this woman wait until I get over there to help her get down?

"I'm going to leave my purse in the truck. You don't think

I'll need it, do you?"

"You could wait for me, you know," I tell her, stepping forward and ignoring her question. My keys get tucked into the back pocket of my khakis as I reach her side. "If you fell out of my truck, I'd be pissed."

She looks up at me through dark, thick lashes, her eyes almost black in the night. "It's not too high for me to jump down. I just can't get up in it by myself . . . easily. In fact, if I ever fall out of your truck, I probably am the one who's pissed." Her grin stretches across her mouth. "As in drunk."

I tip my chin down. She tilts hers up, shamelessly giving me that damn smile.

"Easy, sweetheart," I warn, stepping closer.

She doesn't budge. Doesn't move back, or ease up on that killer fucking smile that warms the inside of my chest, making me feel like I'm the reason for her happiness.

"One of these times I'm gonna kiss that smile right off your face."

Her eyes double in size, the black irises swelling at my threat. Her lips pull down, then open slightly. The tease of her tongue wetting both like she's getting ready for me.

I shake my head. *Not yet. Not now.*

She pulls her shoulders back and squints. *Fine. Your loss.*

I snort. *Yeah. Don't I fucking know it.*

We share a quiet laugh. Beth turns her head in the direction of the music, looking out across the packed lot. A nearby lamppost illuminates the side of her face and sends streaks of light through her hair.

She looks like she's glowing. Shit, I feel like she should be. No woman has ever stood out to me like this before. Yeah, a lot have caught my eye when I'm out, earned them a spot in my bed, but there's nothing special about them. Nothing that makes them any different from the others. Even talking to them feels like we're both working off a script. But with Beth, I've never felt that way. I've never felt like I could easily swap her out for another and not be able to tell a difference.

I couldn't leave you alone.

I said that to her at McGill's. It was probably more of a line at the time, but now I'm not so sure. Maybe I wasn't spouting bullshit. Maybe I would've gone mad if I hadn't walked over to her.

Walked? Right. I practically sprinted.

I lift my gaze from the exposed skin of her neck the second she looks back at me.

"Ready?" she asks, holding out her hand for me to take.

I guess this is part of it. Couples hold hands.

Beth loses her smile when I hesitate, but it materializes again the second my palm slides against hers. I give her a stiff nod and begin leading her through the parking lot, our fingers slowly interlocking, sealing us together. Nothing about this feels awkward. Not even how small her hand feels in mine, like I could crush it if I'm not careful. She stays quiet, tucked against my side, taking everything in.

Swan Harbor is a popular spot for waterfront weddings in Ruxton. It sits on over five hundred acres of farm land that's been landscaped, with a wildflower garden that's showcased every summer in the local paper. It's open to the public all year round, and people come up here to sit under the gazebo that overlooks the lake, or walk along the garden to take pictures. The restored farmhouse comes into view first as we make our way up the lawn. Caterers filter in and out as they carry trays of tall champagne flutes toward the large white tent in the middle of the field. We file in behind other guests and step under the cover provided.

Beth reacts to the sight by squeezing my hand.

"Wow," she whispers, her head lifted as she looks along the ceiling of the tent.

I follow her entranced gaze.

Strings of lights run along the edge of the white cover, then cut across the top and connect with a large chandelier that is suspended above the dance floor.

"Thank God I went shopping for this." She looks around the room at the other guests.

Everyone is wearing dresses and suits, but none of the women here look close to as good as Beth looks.

Tiny black dress without straps, exposing more of her skin to me than I've seen up until this point. Those fucking boots, looking like she's had them for years, all tattered and scuffed up, but still somehow sexy as hell. She looks like she's ready to enter a damn pageant, then kick the asses of the other women in it after she takes the crown. Beauty and badass rolled into one hot little package. Fuck the chicks here in heels. Fuck Molly, wherever she is, no doubt wearing something worth more than my truck. Nobody is holding my attention like Beth is.

"You wanna get a drink?" I ask her, spotting the bar at the far end of the tent. My eyes land on Mr. McCafferty, Molly's dad, standing by a table talking to a few other guests. I've always liked him.

"Okay." Beth starts walking toward the bar. I let go of her hand and touch the small of her back, guiding her to go on without me.

"I'm going to go talk to someone real quick. I'll meet you over there."

She looks at me like she might protest leaving my side, but it's brief. After a simple nod, she moves fluidly between guests in the direction of the bar.

I turn and make my way across the dance floor to the other side of the tent. Mr. McCafferty meets my eyes briefly as I get closer, then recollection lifts his chin. He says something to the man seated at the table, sets his tumbler down, and steps forward with a hand extended.

"Reed, it's good to see you. How's the construction business going?" He shakes my hand, keeping his gray eyebrows pinched together. Silently asking what the hell I'm doing here.

I give him a look, *I have no fucking idea*, and he breathes a laugh before running a hand over his short beard.

I stick my hands in my front pockets. "It's good. Busy right now. We just started a job over at St. Joseph's putting in that new wing."

"Oh yeah, I read about that in the paper. Cancer center, right?"

I nod as my eyes find Beth across the room. Her back is to me while she stands alone at the bar. Shit. I need to make this quick. I don't want her feeling like I've abandoned her.

"How's your grandfather doing? Is he still working?"

I look back at Mr. McCafferty. "Yeah, he's still working. We can't keep him away from the shop."

"How old is he now? I'm surprised he's not retired."

"He turned eighty-six two months ago. My grandmother keeps begging him to retire, but I don't think that'll ever happen. He doesn't know how to sit still."

He laughs through closed lips, stepping aside to allow a caterer to pass. "You tell him I said hi when you see him." He offers his hand again, concern settling on his face. "I don't need to worry about you breaking up an engagement, do I?"

"No, sir. Your daughter invited me."

I spot Beth in her same spot, but now being engaged into conversation by the bartender. A lot of conversation.

The asshat apparently doesn't have a shit ton of other guests to serve.

Fucker.

I jerk my chin in her direction as I release Mr. McCafferty's hand. "I'm here with someone. It was good talking to you."

He says in return, "you too" or "take care" or something. I'm halfway to Beth before he finishes whatever the hell it is.

She's holding a drink in her hand, sipping through a straw. Asshat behind the bar can't stop looking at her.

"Hey." I get as close to her as I can without knocking her over.

She looks up at me, still tasting her drink. I slide my hand along her back to her hip, pulling her a little so her shoulder hits my chest. I look up at the guy still staring at Beth, not registering my presence at all. My stomach churns with a foreign possessiveness as my fingers flex against her hip.

Can you not fucking see me with her?

Beth makes a noise in the back of her throat that grabs my attention. Her nose wrinkles as she swallows, pulling the drink away from her mouth. She shakes her head. "No, I definitely don't like that. It's a little strong." She sets the drink on the bar and slides it away from her.

"Aw, come on. I pegged you for a girl who liked sex on the beach."

My head snaps in the dead man's direction. "What did you just say?"

He smiles, amused at himself as he picks up the glass. "Sex on the beach. The drink. I thought she'd like it."

"Well, she doesn't. And don't assume she likes anything. You don't know her."

He holds up his free hand, palm out, and takes a step back. The drink Beth didn't like is still in his other hand. "Easy, man.

She didn't know what she wanted. I was just letting her try it."

I feel Beth's hand on my chest. When I look down, she's giving me the most puzzled expression, like she can't understand my reaction. I can't understand it either. I've never wanted to rip someone's arm out of their socket and beat them with it, but I sure as hell want to now.

I pinch my eyes shut, take a deep breath to calm the rage boiling inside me, and open my eyes to look at her.

"What do you like? Fruity stuff? Like strawberries?" A part of me wishes I already knew this answer.

"I like strawberries," she says, tilting her chin up.

I acknowledge her with a nod before looking over top her head. "Make her a daiquiri. And don't make it that strong."

Asshat jerks his head to let me know he's heard me. He grabs a blender, half-filled with a red slushy consistency, and pours it into a glass. Grabbing a small napkin, he sets the drink down on the bar and sticks a straw in it.

"There. It's not strong. There's barely any liquor in it." He steps away to help another guest, not giving Beth another look.

She turns around, moving my hand along her back, and picks up the drink. I watch her take a sip, then another.

"Mm. Wanna try it?" She offers me the straw but I decline with a shake of my head.

I hadn't planned on drinking at all tonight. And if I was drinking, I wouldn't be throwing back anything that looks like a 7-Eleven Slurpee.

The straw slips out of Beth's mouth as her eyes focus in on something, or someone behind me. Shifting her weight on her feet, she stares for a few more seconds before blinking away.

"We should probably go say hi," she says on a rushed exhale. Spinning around, she sets her drink on the bar after taking another sip.

Maybe I should pick that up and down it.

I crane my neck around and spot Molly talking to a group of people across the dance floor. Might as well get this shit over with now. The sooner she sees me here with Beth, happy and not caring about anything besides the woman on my arm, the sooner we can get the hell out of here. I don't want to be here a minute longer than I have to.

"Come on." I take Beth's hand in mine and lead her across the floor. Looking over, I see the nervousness twitch across her face as we move through the crowd. "Ready to be my girlfriend?" I ask, and so quickly I shock her, drawing that smile out I've gone too many minutes without seeing.

She nudges playfully against my side, her profile still lifted as her eyes train ahead of us. "I'm ready."

Molly sees us coming before we get halfway across the dance floor. She slowly lets her mouth fall open, the whites of her eyes growing as she looks down my arm to where I'm holding Beth.

Yeah, take a good fucking look.

She taps the suit behind her who's engaged in conversation at a table, then leans in to say something to the three women surrounding her. They each give her a hug before walking away together.

As we close the gap between us, Molly wipes any telling emotion from her face, keeping her expression stoic. I'm expecting the first words exchanged to be a concealed insult from Molly. But it's Beth who speaks first.

"Congratulations again. And thank you so much for inviting us." She leans into me, tipping her head back until our eyes lock. "We're having the best time."

Nothing but honestly in her voice. In her face, the way the blush creeps up the length of her. She's not saying that for Molly to hear. She's looking at me, making sure I hear it.

Sweetheart, I hear it.

"What's up, babe?"

A man's voice has me looking up at the suit who still has most of his back to Molly, his head partially turned to look down at her.

"Did you need something?" he asks, sounding bored, and I swallow down the laugh that wants to erupt from my throat. If this is the guy she's marrying, he's more interested in whatever conversation she's trying to pull him out of than anything to do with her.

Karma. God, you sweet, sweet bitch. I could fucking kiss you.

She grabs his shoulder, pushing, urging him to spin around. "Yes, *babe*, I wanted to introduce you to some of our guests. Can you give me a few minutes?"

I jerk my head to shake the hair out of my eyes as the man finally obliges her.

He turns while keeping one hand on the front of his suit jacket, throwing the other over her shoulder. Looking like something the two of them practiced for public appearances.

I look to his face, ready to offer my hand so we can get these introductions over with. Recollection hits me like a two-by-four to the gut. My body tenses, squeezing the air from my lungs. Beth hisses next to me when my grip on her becomes painful. I loosen it but can't look at her. I can't look anywhere but at the man staring back at me, ignorant to who I am. Ready to shake my hand like he didn't have his dick in my girlfriend nine years ago.

Fuck.

I should've taken that drink.

beth

R EED GOES PERFECTLY still next to me.
His face pales, a harshness tightening his profile
and removing any trace of the playful man I walked
over here with. His breathing grows louder, seething against
his teeth. I hiss when he bears down against my hand, wiggling
my fingers when the pain dulls out. He has to be reacting to
the man standing with Molly. I'm guessing it's her fiancé. I'm
also guessing based on the swift change in Reed's mood that he
might already know him. A thought stirs in my head, another
possibility. Reed said he was over Molly. He said he stopped
caring a long time ago. But maybe this is the first time he's
seeing her with someone else, and it doesn't matter who it
is standing next to her. He always thought it would be him.

I try to think of something else to keep myself from
paling.

Reed's hand on my hip. His breath against my hair. His
words from earlier.

I'm gonna kiss that smile right off your face.

That does it.

Molly focuses only on Reed, ignoring my presence now
that she's not standing alone. She straightens with pride,
looking up at the man beside her.

"This is Craig, my fiancé. We met back at Virginia Tech
my freshmen year. Craig, this is Reed and . . ." She looks at

me, squinting. "I'm sorry, what was your name again?"

"Beth," I answer, straining to keep any attitude from reaching my voice. I'm sure she remembers my name.

"Right, Beth." A grin twists across her mouth like a snake slithering in the grass. "Sorry. All the excitement of getting married has left my brain a little foggy. I'm sure you can understand."

"Of course," I reply.

What did Reed ever see in you? I don't say.

Reed stays silent. Another squeeze to my hand. This time I don't wince.

Craig takes his cue and tips his chin to Reed. "Hey, how's it going?"

There's no familiarity in his greeting, so maybe they don't know each other.

His dark eyes lower to mine when he doesn't get a response, and he lifts his eyebrows subtly. "Hi."

As soon as he says the word, his eyes wander to his left, bored, looking for something else to engage him. As if trained to do so, his attention pulls back to Molly when she tugs on the front of his suit jacket.

I'm expecting her to slip a treat out of her cleavage and feed it to him.

Molly glares at Reed for long seconds, growing annoyed at his silence. She threads her fingers through the hand on her shoulder and wraps her other arm around Craig's waist.

"Aren't you going to say anything? Did you suddenly go mute or something?"

I look up at Reed, unsure of what to expect.

He's staring directly at Molly, or Craig, I can't tell, but it's as if he doesn't even realize it. He seems stuck in his head, or so intently focused on his own restraint that he can no longer see anything in front of him. I wonder if I pry my hand away from his if he would launch forward and tackle one or both of them to the ground. It's not like I'm holding him back. I doubt I could, but he's gripping me like he needs to be steadied. Like I'm the anchor he's afraid to let go of. His nostrils flare as he forces the air in and out of his lungs. It's the only noticeable reaction on his face. The tell-all to his torment.

The light from the chandelier above us catches in the stubble along his jawline, stubble I hadn't noticed until now. He suddenly appears more rugged. Maybe even larger. I look down at his exposed forearm when he puts stress on my hand—again.

His dress shirt is pushed back close to the elbow, revealing the thick veins threatening to burst under his tan skin. His muscles roll as he adjusts his grip, causing the pressure to burn across my knuckles.

It's not painful anymore, but I feel it. His distress signal. Maybe he can't tell me this is too much, but he's showing me.

Get me out of here, Beth.

All of a sudden I'm the girl in the bar again, needing to protect the man next to me.

I tuck myself against Reed's side, shifting our joined hands to my back. My other hand presses against his hard stomach as I look up at Craig. "It's very nice to meet you. Congratulations on your engagement."

My eyes shift to Molly, and I keep them kind. "I'm sure you have a ton of people to mingle with so we won't keep you. Again, thank you for inviting us."

I push against Reed to turn him around, to get him away from this mess I put him in, but he doesn't budge.

"Reed." I look up at him, but his attention is over my head. Burning like a wildfire. My hand meets resistance again when I urge him to move, and I think this might be the only fight left in him.

Molly snickers behind me, then her tone changes as she demands something of Craig.

I don't care what she has to say, or what's gotten Craig's attention off her. I'm only focused on Reed.

I lay my hand against his cheek, the bristles from his jaw scratching my palm, and at that sudden contact his eyes collide with mine. Through impossibly long lashes, he looks at me with a vulnerability that slams against my chest.

Tomorrow, sweetheart. You and me.

He said those words to me before, when he agreed to do this.

"You and me, right?" I murmur, only for him to hear.

He seems so distant right now, I fear my voice will never reach him. But his lips part, blowing his warm breath against my wrist as soon as I speak.

I take that as a sign and make my third attempt.

This time Reed moves willingly, permitting me to lead him across the dance floor. We make it out of the tent, and I keep walking, following a caterer into the farmhouse where a few guests are mingling around a large table covered in hors d'oeuvres.

I have no idea where I'm going, or what my plan is, but the second I see a staircase leading to a seemingly quiet second level, I take it.

Reed doesn't protest or try and lead me in another direction. He doesn't speak. He keeps his grip tight on my hand while his heavy feet follow me into the first room at the top of the stairs.

I shut the door behind us, running my hand along the wall for the switch. A small lamp turns on in the corner.

"Are you okay?" I ask, wincing at my obvious stupidity

as I turn to face him.

Really, Beth? Clearly he's not okay.

Pacing in front of the window, Reed rakes his hands roughly down his face, scraping his stubble. His shoulders are hunched forward, pulling the dress shirt tight against his back and displaying his lean waist.

"Fuck!" he growls, stopping to look out the window and pointing at something down below. "That fucking bitch. Not only does she pick this venue, here, to throw this shit, but she invites me to it knowing I'd recognize that motherfucker. And then I go and react like that. I couldn't show her I didn't give a shit about her anymore. I stood there, shocked, unable to *do* anything, *say* anything, like a fucking pussy. Fuck!"

Blinking slowly, I try to take in what he's just said, but my mind floods with questions. It doesn't make sense to me.

"You know him?" I take a cautious step forward, stopping when Reed snaps his head in my direction. My hands tangle nervously together against my stomach. "You . . . were you friends? Why did he not recognize you?"

"We weren't friends." He exhales a heavy, depleted sigh, turning around and slumping back against the wall beside the window. He drops his head and his eyes lose focus. "I never knew him. I just recognize him. A few months after Molly went away to college, she started acting different. I didn't know what was going on. She just stopped calling me, stopped coming home to see me, and when I would get her on the phone, she couldn't get rid of me fast enough. I'd visit her when I could and things seemed fine when I was there, but Tessa was convinced something was going on. She told me to drop in on Molly when she wasn't expecting me. So I did."

I inch forward slowly, looking for any sign from him indicating I should stay where I am, but Reed never looks up.

"What happened?" I ask, apprehensive for the answer but too curious not to probe. The toes of my boots knock against his feet, halting my progression.

He tips his chin to his right. "Walked in on her riding his dick."

I bring my hands to my face, my breath hot against my fingers. "Reed."

He doesn't react to my voice, his name, doesn't lift his eyes from where they stay glued to some spot on the floor.

Oh, God. I knew she hurt him somehow. I thought she ended things, blindsiding him and breaking his heart. But this? Walking in on something like that?

Bitch.

I understand now why he froze up, but that still doesn't explain why having the party here is an issue for him.

My one hand circles his wrist while my other falls to my side. "Why does it matter that it's here?"

Now he can't seem to look anywhere but where I'm holding him. He blinks once, turning his arm so my fingers slide to his palm.

"You're about to hear how pathetic I used to be. I'm not sure that's something I want you to know."

"I bet I won't think you were pathetic."

"Sweetheart." He licks his lips, wetting them. "I was the definition." Lifting his head, he drops it back against the wall and stares at me through half-closed lids. His light hair is disheveled, some pieces falling close to his eyes. He looks tired, but God, he's so sexy I almost forget what we're talking about. Reaching up with the hand not occupied with mine, he yanks at the knot in his tie and pops the top button of his collar.

Now he's unkempt. Unruly.

I've been known to get a little rowdy sometimes.

His words to me from our day together. A joke at the time, but now with this visual in front of me I'm finding it difficult to imagine him ever controlled. And strangely, I don't want to imagine it. I want him messy, up against a wall. Clothes partially undone.

Me, completely undone.

The sound of his throat clearing has me searching for his eyes in the soft light. I had been staring at his mouth. His jaw. The cords in his neck. *Did he notice?*

"I was fine with her going away to college. Four years was a long time, but I knew I would be okay. I wanted her to know that. Wanted her to see how serious I was about us." He pauses to scratch the back of his head, then his hand slaps against his thigh. He shakes his head. "I don't know. Maybe at the time I felt desperate. I loved her. Love makes you do stupid shit. And I was definitely a dumb motherfucker back then to ask that bitch to marry me."

I lean closer, sliding my hand up to the crook of his elbow. "You asked Molly to marry you?"

"Yeah, pathetic, right?"

"No, no that's not pathetic. You loved her."

He seems to find my response amusing. His lip curls up, and his chest rumbles with a quiet laugh.

A loud whistle sounds somewhere outside the house and a burst of light flashes behind the window pane. Reed and I lean over to catch the next firework shooting off against the night sky. It's a beautiful distraction from the ugliness below, but my eyes can't enjoy it. Not while my mind is swimming in guilt.

This is all my fault.

"I'm so sorry I put you through all this."

Reed's head slowly turns away from the window. His

eyebrows pull together into a tight pinch, conveying his confusion as he looks down at me.

I explain through a stressed voice, "I just wanted to do something for you. I've never felt immediately comfortable around someone before, but that night at McGill's, you made it easy. You made me smile, and I hadn't smiled in months. Then Molly walked in and it was like she snuffed you out. I hated it. After five minutes of conversation, I became protective of you. I know that probably sounds crazy, but it's how I felt. I thought maybe seeing you happy with someone else would get to her. I wanted her to look how you looked. But I had no idea I'd be dragging you into all this. I shouldn't have done that in the bar. I'm so, so sorry."

I move to back away, to take my hand off the part of his arm I'm still clutching, but Reed reaches out and grabs my other wrist. He flattens his back against the wall, pulling me closer until I have to lift my chin to look at him.

A softness passes over his face, but his eyes, my God, his eyes are electric.

"You didn't drag me into anything. I said I would come to this, didn't I? I'm the one who picked you up and drove us here, and I don't remember you having a gun to my head, forcing me out of the truck." His mouth twitches. "Fuck, Beth. Can a guy have a little credit? This disaster wasn't all *your* doing."

I almost smile. "You wouldn't be here if I hadn't pretended to be your girlfriend that night."

"How do you know?" he asks, losing the smirk. "That woman down there is a fucking bitch. She would've found a way to invite me to this shit with or without you. And I would've been here, proving to her I didn't care anymore, with or without you. You were a bonus in all this."

My skin becomes hot at the base of my neck, and I

suddenly wish I had worn my hair up this evening.

A bonus? Has he actually enjoyed being with me tonight, despite everything?

"Fuck," he says through a groan, drawing my attention back up from where it had wandered. His head hits the wall as he looks over the top of me. "Can't believe I just stood there. Probably still be standing there if it weren't for you dragging me away. I bet that bitch is laughing her ass off knowing she got to me."

"We can leave," I suggest.

I would completely understand if he wanted to get out of here. Reed's discomfort isn't worth proving a point, and I'm not sure I can handle seeing it anymore without hurling a champagne flute in someone's direction.

He dismisses my suggestion with a jerk of his head. Releasing his hold on me, he scrubs his face again with his hands. He's rough about it. His palms harsh against his skin. Trying to remove any trace of emotion before we go back down there.

When he lowers his hands, I falter at the hold his eyes have on me. The desperation in them. The worry that he won't be able to handle this. He's silent again, but my ears hear the words he's not saying.

Please, don't leave my side.

Please, help me through this.

Please, distract me from them.

Our lunch from the other day. The bet.

Distract him.

This man makes me do the craziest things, but I don't feel foolish moving closer. Something comes over me as my body threatens to form against his. A drive, a need to keep him from feeling anything except what I can control.

Distract him.

Time suspends in that room. Everything seems to happen in the longest second of my life. If there was anything to stop me, his rejection would do it, but as I eliminate all space between us, as my hands run up his chest to his neck, my fingers filtering through his hair, he wraps his hands around my waist and welcomes my assault.

"I want to use my advantage now," I say, sounding hurried. Frantic. Desperate.

"I was picking up on that." He stares at my mouth, tilting his head down. "What do you want, sweetheart? You want to kiss me?"

"Mm."

His breath bursts against my hair. "Mm. Is that a yes? A no? If I remember correctly, you get to do anything you want. Winner's choice, right?"

I lift my chin, grinning, and he takes that as my decision.

He inches down, pulls me closer, closes his eyes with the tilt of his head. "Been thinking about your mouth since you first gave it to me. Can't think about anything else."

I suck in a breath at his admission. A pressure builds between my legs, reminding me of what all I've been thinking about. What I specifically thought about when I upped the stakes of the contest.

My head turns and his lips hit my temple.

"Uh . . . okay . . . something else?" he stammers into my hair.

I nod slowly, leaning back to look into his eyes. "Anything I want. This is what I want."

My hands move down his body and take hold of his belt buckle. He groans at the brush of my fingertips against his erection.

He's hard already. From almost kissing me?

Wetness pools between my legs as his breathing grows louder above me, as his grip on my waist threatens to bruise.

"Beth," he moans my name before I even free him. Rousing at the very idea of what's about to happen.

It's so hot, so unexpected that my fingers fumble with the clasp and the belt seems to tighten instead of working lose.

"Shit."

He laughs above me, then his hands leave my waist and take over where mine are failing. I wait, hands fisted against my stomach as he undoes the clasp on his belt and opens his pants. He grabs my wrist, forcing me to reach for him, scratching my knuckles against the zipper.

Hard flesh fills my palm. Smooth and warm.

"Reed?"

He's staring at me through hooded eyes, his hands now back at my waist, fingers pulling at my dress. He tilts his head down. "Yeah?"

"What . . . what do you like? I want to make this good for you." My hand explores him with tentative squeezes. Little pulses as I turn my wrist, sliding down his length.

So hard. My God, he's so hard.

A greedy smile beams down at me. "I'm not going to have any problem with what you're doing. But maybe a little harder?"

Nodding, I tighten around his base and pull back, watching his mouth fall open. My other hand forms to his hip. "Like that?"

"Mm. *Fuck.*" He winces through a moan, teeth scraping his bottom lip. "God, I'm so fucking hard. And your hand . . . *fuck*, Beth."

"I love how you say my name."

He straightens, takes his weight off the wall and stares

down at me. His lips press against my temple. "Beth," he whispers, moving to my cheek. "Beth." His finger lifts my chin, and he groans, squeezing his eyes shut. "God, Beth."

If he didn't have his hands on me, I think I could float away. The rhythm I thought I had becomes clumsy. There's no pattern, nothing predictable to my hand moving on his cock as he continues to work my name with his tongue. It's so erotic how he gives it to me. Through moans, pressing it against my skin, whispering it into my hair. I've never been this turned on by a single word. And it's my name. *My* name. Go figure.

"Gonna kiss you now."

I open my eyes, leaning back to look at him. "But you didn't win."

The corner of his mouth twitches, and he stills my hand with one of his.

"I feel like I did," he says, so close to my lips I can taste his breath.

He doesn't mean because I'm jerking him off. He stops my hand for that reason, to make sure I understand, to eliminate any confusion. He pauses, waiting until I look up into his eyes from where I'm staring at his mouth, like a hungry little fiend.

"This is for me. You understand?"

I know why he tells me that. My fear from earlier.

"It's for me too."

He smiles, shifting us so it's now my back against the wall. "No, this is for you."

A blast of cool air chills my upper thighs. My dress is bunched around my waist, and he groans, either from the sight of me in black panties or from my grip that's now tightened on his cock.

He cups my sex like he owns it, harsh and demanding.

"Reed," I gasp, lifting my head and welcoming his kiss.

It sears against my mouth, his tongue hot and wet, probing, seeking mine. I tilt my head and open for him, swallowing his dirty little noises. My hand begins pumping his cock as he slides his fingers through my slit.

"You're going to drip all down my hand, aren't you?" he asks, kissing along my jaw.

I answer with a whimper as he fucks me slowly. Two fingers inside while his thumb moves over my clit.

"What made you wet, sweetheart? My cock? Was it how hard I was for you? Or did you get wet just thinking about touching me."

"I think it was when you said my name."

"Beth," he moans against my ear. "I say it every time I come. Do you know that? Ever since I met you, I can't say anything else."

My legs begin to shake. "Really? You . . . Reed, you do that?" I ask, breathlessly.

"Mm." He thrusts his hips, fucking my hand as he curls his fingers inside me.

His lips move to my mouth, where he whispers filthy words between the hottest noises. He asks me if I want him wild, and if I'll let him spend his time on me. He tells me he's thought about doing more than this, and that he also thinks he could come just from the way I kiss him. There's moments when it's just the sound of us filling the room. Breathing, moving, stroking. I blush at how loud his fingers are inside me, and he tells me it's the sexiest thing he's ever heard. He kisses my neck, my lips, my jaw. He asks me if I want to feel his teeth, and I gasp when he doesn't wait for me to answer.

I drop my head against his shoulder when the world in front of me begins to blur. When my skin burns up from the inside out and the pressure becomes too much.

He swells in my palm. I'm melting between my legs. A groan tears from my throat as my body locks up.

"Reed, I'm . . ."

He wraps his arm around my waist, holding me up as I tighten around his fingers. Blood rushes in my ears, my free hand fists his shirt.

He growls into my hair.

Because he's close? Because I'm coming? I'm too delirious to question why.

I moan when he slips out of me, and then realize he needs that hand to produce the handkerchief from this back pocket. His other hand is busy keeping me upright.

His body tightens, his breath hitches above me.

"Beth," he pants, pumping into my fist as warm liquid coats my hand. His head falls back with a groan. "Beth. *God,* Beth."

I can't decide where to look. His gorgeous face, tensing through his orgasm. Or his cock as it twitches in my hand. Still hard. Still warm. I go between the two, trying not to miss too much of either one.

He grabs my wrist when I slide along his length once more, stopping me from smearing the come over the tip.

"Don't kill me, woman."

I turn my head up and he gives me a lazy smile.

"Sensitive?" I ask.

He nods slowly, then steps back. His cock falls from my hand. "I didn't get any on your dress, did I?" he asks, squinting through the dim light.

I quickly examine the front of me, then look down into my hand. "Nope. Looks like I caught it all here."

He gives me the handkerchief and I wipe my hand clean, tossing it into the trashcan after he gives me an odd look for offering it back.

I watch him from across the room as he buttons his pants, tucks his shirt in, but leaves his tie undone. I'm glad. I like it like that.

He moves to the window and stares down at the party. His hair is a mess from my fingers. The back of his shirt is wrinkled.

He looks amazing.

"Now what do you want to do?" I ask, staying a few feet away.

He doesn't speak for several seconds. Just stares below, hands in his pockets and shoulders dropped. His head shakes ever-so-slightly, as if to jerk himself out of a trance. After a loud exhale, he turns around and moves toward me, determination weighing down his steps. He grabs my hand and heads for the door.

"I want to drink. Let's go hit up Asshat."

I stare at his profile. "Who?"

ASSHAT, OR THE bartender Reed decided to nickname, keeps the Jim Beam flowing over the next hour. Molly and her bored-to-death looking fiancé are nowhere in sight, so we stay parked at the bar. I decide after watching Reed slam his first drink back that I'll be sticking to water. Someone's going to need to drive home. I ask if he wants to dance, or go for a walk by the lake. He tells me he just wants to sit and talk with me.

So that's what we do. Or it's at least what I do.

Reed drinks while I ramble about living in Kentucky with my mom. I stick to the good parts of my life, because again, I had decided not to drink. Bringing up my mom's death, living in my car, or anything to do with Rocco would have me reaching behind the bar for something besides water.

Reed engages with me the whole time I talk. His hands stay on me somehow, his eyes glued to mine. Focused and intrigued. As the drink count rises, he becomes more shameless with his affection. He pulls me into his lap and kisses my neck, telling me how good I smell. How amazing it felt to be in my hand. He asks me after Asshat walks away if he can make me come right here in front of everyone. When I blush, he tells me I would love every minute of it, then his eyes darken when he goes into details about what those minutes would entail. I decide to cut him off when I begin to worry he'll actually act out these vulgar acts.

He's brave enough to do it. I'm turned on enough to let it happen.

"Come on. Let's go home." I take his arm and loop it over my shoulder, securing my other hand around his waist. We get through the tent and make it down the lawn, slowing when we hear arguing coming from somewhere in the parking lot.

"You are such an asshole! Why do I have to keep coming to find you? This is our engagement party, Craig. You should be by my side the entire night!"

Reed and I both stop and turn our heads in the direction of the yelling.

Molly is standing in front of a parked car, illuminated by the headlights that are turned on and shining on her. Her hands are fisted at her hips as she stares at Craig, who's leaning against the driver's side door, smoking a cigarette.

He blows the smoke above his head. "What do you want from me? I'm here, aren't I? Why do I need to be stuck up your ass all night?"

"Because we're getting married! You should want to be with me all the time!"

"I am with you all the time! Christ! We're always together,

Molly. Give me a fucking breather!"

"Maybe we should keep going." I try and move but Reed keeps his footing, securing us in place.

"Nah. This is good." He looks down at me and grins. "I think I need to hear this."

I shrug, surrendering to this severe invasion of privacy. Maybe Reed does need to hear this. And it's not like they're secluded or keeping themselves isolated from wandering ears. They're right here, out in the open with it, airing their dirty laundry for every guest at the party to hear. This technically falls on them.

"Can you at least do me a favor and keep your hands off my cousin, Ronnie? If I see you hug her one more time . . ."

"She's hugging me! And you know what? If she wants to do more than that, maybe I'll let her. God knows you've completely forgotten how to work a dick."

"Oh shit," I utter under the hushed sound of Reed's laughter.

Molly points a finger at Craig. "When you can get it up for me for longer than a few seconds, I'll show you how I work it. Now put out that fucking cigarette before my daddy finds you smoking out here."

"Fuck him. If I have to put up with your bitching for the next two hours, I'm lighting up. This shit is unbearable."

"Asshole!"

"Bitch!"

Reed and I keep our laughs quiet as Molly stomps across the grass in the direction of the tent. She doesn't see us, which keeps my breathing even. Craig mumbles something as he pushes off from the car, flicks his cigarette, and goes after her. Slowly.

I don't blame him. I wouldn't be in any rush either.

I start walking us toward the truck, and Reed moves willingly now that the show is over. "Wow. That was totally worth the awful feeling I had listening in on them."

"I don't feel awful. I feel fucking great." He tilts his head down and presses his lips to the top of my head. The smell of liquor clings to my nose. "She can't work a dick. You know who *can* work a dick?"

Oh Lord.

I reach into the back pocket of his pants and slip the truck keys out. "Do you need a boost getting in?" I tease, walking him around to the passenger side of the truck.

He breathes a laugh and throws open the door. "Please tell me you know how to drive a stick."

"Yeah, sure. Can't be too hard, right?"

He slowly turns his head, pinning me with alarmed eyes.

I slap his back playfully and urge him to climb in. "I learned how to drive on a stick. Relax, Reed."

He mumbles something I decide to ignore, like the work a dick comment. After getting a running start, I jump up into the truck and secure my harness. The truck rumbles to life, vibrating against my legs. I shift to first gear and stall out on my first try.

"Awesome," Reed utters, slamming his head back against the seat.

Determination surges in my blood. Yes, it's been six years since I've driven a manual, but it's like riding a bike. You never forget. Right?

I give it another go, and the truck launches forward, faster than I intend. I squeal as I barely avoid the vehicle parked across from us.

Reed makes a sound of discomfort next to me.

I wait until I get out of the parking lot and onto the

main road before I speak my confidence. "See?" I look over at Reed, frowning at his rigid frame against the seat. "We're good. I got this."

"Mm." He slowly turns his head to look at me. "Are you driving to my house?"

"Yeah. I figured I can take a cab home. Or," I smile, looking back at the road. "I can drive this bad boy home and bring it back tomorrow."

Reed groans, and I think I see him stroking the dashboard through my peripheral vision. "Cab it is."

I TURN THE truck off and hop out, meeting Reed at the front of the vehicle where he's holding my purse.

"Here." We exchange items, keys for clutch. "Do you need help getting inside?" I ask, half-teasing, half-serious.

Reed tilts his head, staring down at me without saying a word. I watch his eyes roam over my face. Slowly moving about my features as if he's studying them. The scrutiny has me locking my knees and pinching my legs together. When Reed looks at me, I can't help but feel it. My skin warms at the thought of what we did earlier.

What he said to me.

The sounds he made when he came.

A rushed breath pushes past my lips when his hand finds mine in the dark. He squeezes it, just like he did earlier tonight. Showing me what he needs.

"Reed."

He pulls me against him, running his other hand through my hair. Then his lips are on mine and his hold on me tightens.

One hand on my neck, the other squeezing my ass.

I melt into him, moaning as the bitterness of the Jim Beam

coats my mouth. It's dizzying. The alcohol, or maybe just the kiss. I don't realize he's moved us until I hear the sound of a door being pushed open.

We separate, and Reed steps back into the house. He jerks his chin, motioning for me to follow. When I hesitate, not because I don't want to, because I'm too busy running my fingers over my swollen lips, Reed grabs my hand again and urges me inside.

"Don't call a cab."

I drop my clutch in the foyer, seconds before I'm being pinned against the wall.

reed

MY HEAD POUNDS me awake, throbbing with an intensity that has my eyes refusing to open. Timed with the rate of my pulse, the pain burns along my scalp in an unforgiving rhythm.

It feels like my brain is swelling and slowly cracking my skull.

Rolling to my side, I swing my legs out of bed and sit up, face in my hands. My head isn't the only thing hurting. My back is stiff. The muscles in my shoulders ache as I hunch forward. I drop a hand to my cock. Goddamn. Even that feels like it's been put through the ringer. Since when does your entire body suffer from a hangover? Not that I've had many. I'll drink a few beers, some whiskey occasionally, but I don't think I've felt this shitty since I turned twenty-one.

Fuck. How much did I drink?

I stand from the bed and walk into the bathroom directly across from me. My hands feel for the faucet blindly, or partially blind as I keep my eyes squinted. Cool water hits the back of my hand as last night materializes behind my eye lids. I remember . . . most of it. I think.

Beth. Fuck, I remember Beth.

Her greedy little hand on my cock. Her mouth, sweet and hungry for my tongue, giving me those filthy noises I wanted to drown in. How she soaked my fingers while I fucked her against the wall.

Bare. *God, I love a bare pussy.*

I was seconds from dropping to my knees and finishing her with my mouth. But I wanted her spread out when I did that. On a bed, my kitchen table, the hood of my truck. Then we were coming. Her first, drenching my hand as she clung to me. My name falling from her lips, her hand fisting my cock. I came so hard I forgot how to breathe.

Perfect.

She was so fucking perfect.

There was no awkward moment after. We fell right back into us, the us I'm becoming very comfortable with. Maybe a little too comfortable.

Then the bar, Jim Beam, and Beth talking about . . . blank. That's where I lose it. I know we sat there for a while. I think she drove my truck?

Fuck! How did she get home? How did she . . .

A noise coming from outside the bathroom jerks me away from the sink. Not just any noise. A sleepy little moan a woman would make as she stretches against my sheets.

I shut the water off and turn my head to look out into the bedroom.

My eyes widen, my dick jumps against my hand. The headache I was battling is quickly forgotten as I take in the figure in my bed.

Dark hair lays messy against my pillow. Her back is to me, pale, flawless skin, revealed from the sheets bunched just below the soft curve of her hip.

Holy shit. Beth is in my bed. Naked. Why is she in my bed naked?

I bring my wet hands to my head, raking through my hair, pinching my eyes shut as I scramble for a memory.

Beth at the bar. Asshat pouring me another drink. Then . . . fuck! What the fuck happened after that?

She moans again and shifts on the bed, rolling to her back. Her nipples harden against the assault of the cool air. I look down at my dick, now fully hard, the head already dripping with precum.

What did you do?

I move quietly into the bedroom and open the drawer of my nightstand. My new purchase from a few days ago is still sealed. I know for a fact I didn't have any stray condoms lying around in there. Maybe we didn't have sex?

Beth stretches her arms above her, and it's then I notice the faint marks on her wrists, a light dusting of pink against her pale skin.

Fuck. Fuck! I tied her up. I wouldn't tie her up unless I was fucking her.

All at once, the other imperfections on her skin begin to glow, drawing my attention all over her body. Bite marks on her breasts. Red blotches decorating the line of her neck.

Holy shit. I'm all over her.

"Hey."

My eyes dart up her body, locking onto hers. I swallow, then struggle through a nervous "heyyyy, you."

She looks down, eyes widening and a flush blooming across her face.

Shit. I'm hard.

I grab my boxers off the floor and quickly slip them on. "Uh . . . Beth, I need to ask you something."

She gives me a sleepy smile. Her tongue wets her lips. "If you're going to ask me if my ass is sore, the answer is yes, but in a very good way."

Oh, sweet fuck.

"O-Okay, now I have several other questions on top of the one I need to ask." I start to pace, then force myself to stand still when my heartbeat returns to my head and resumes beating against my skull. "Are you on birth control?" I ask, staring down at her, wincing through the pain.

Her eyebrows pull together. She's confused by my question. "Yes. We went over that already. I told you I have an IUD. I've had it for years." Her hands pull the covers up around her, and she shifts up higher on the bed so her back is against the headboard. A mild discomfort washes over her face as her one hand tames her hair.

I give her a curt nod, rubbing a hand along my jaw. "Right. So, last night, did I . . . I'm guessing I didn't pull out."

She stares long and hard at me, dragging out the silence. "Why are you asking me this? You were there. You know what all we did." Her mouth falls open with a sharp intake of breath. Slowly, she sits up and pulls the sheet tighter around her, keeping her body hidden from me. "Reed, please tell me you remember last night. You weren't drunk. You said you weren't drunk."

"I might've been a little drunk."

I was really fucking drunk.

Beth drops her head. "Oh my God." She keeps the sheet wrapped around her as she scrambles out of bed and searches the floor for her clothes. "Oh my God, I can't believe this. I can't believe you don't remember. What we did . . . shit. I'm . . . God, this is so embarrassing. I've never done . . . oh my God, Reed!"

I move to the edge of the bed as she drops the sheet. She keeps her back to me, stepping into her panties, then her dress.

"I'm sorry! I obviously didn't think I was drunk at the time. I normally don't drink like that." My steps to get closer to her are halted when she glares at me over her shoulder.

"Don't apologize. I should've realized how wasted you were. This is on me." She bends down and grabs her boots. "God, do you remember any of it?"

I don't answer her until she peeks up at me. A shake of my head is all I give her, and I regret it immediately.

Her eyes fill with tears, her lip trembles.

God, I'm an asshole.

"Beth."

"Please don't," she begs, brushing her hand over her cheek as she straightens. She looks so fragile right now, so different from the version of her I remember last night. The woman who held me together when I was slowly unraveling.

She faces away from me, reaching back to secure the hair off her neck.

A current runs through my veins as a burst of images flash in front of my eyes.

Beth on her knees. My hand fisting her hair. Her eyes, wild and willing, holding me over her shoulder.

Holy shit.

Her movement snaps me alert.

"Whoawhoawhoa, wait." I reach for her to stop her from leaving, grabbing her wrist before she gets away.

She keeps her head turned toward the wall, but I can see the tears falling freely down her cheek.

I hate this. She shouldn't be crying.

"Wait, I . . ." My next words get stuck in my throat as a wave of nausea rolls through me. My other hand flattens against my stomach. *Oh, fuck.* "Shit, I'm going to be sick." I release her arm and dart for the bathroom, launching myself at the toilet. Bile rises in my throat as my knees hit the tile. I barely lean over before the contents of my stomach are ejected into the bowl. My head throbs. My throat burns.

"Beth! Don't leave!" I yell, seconds before another bout hits me, then another. It's never ending. Sweat pools at the base of my neck, soaking my hair. My forearms burn as I support my weight. I try and stand, but a roll of my stomach hunches me forward again.

Fuck! I need to talk to Beth.

We had sex last night. Unfuckingbelievable sex, if her marked body and that tease of a glimpse I just had are any indication. And that's all I remember?

Are you fucking kidding me, universe?

The woman I've been obsessing over gave herself to me, I have no idea what all we did together, and now she's crying, and my head is stuck in a toilet?

Molly. That stupid bitch is responsible for all of this.

I push off from the floor when the cramp in my gut seems to settle. After rinsing my mouth out in the bathroom sink, I walk back out into the bedroom, expecting to see Beth waiting for me where I left her. The room is empty.

"Beth!"

I check the second floor and then take to the stairs. Pausing at the entrance into the living room, I look around and question whether or not I was too drunk to feel an earthquake last night. Lamps are turned over. Pictures are hanging crooked on the walls. My couch seems to be at a different angle to my TV.

Holy shit. We had sex all over this room. And we really utilized the entire floor plan.

I move in the direction of the kitchen, stepping over my clothes from last night that are scattered about.

"Beth?"

I turn the corner and freeze in the entryway.

The chairs are pushed back away from the table, with one specifically placed in front of the large, antique wall mirror I have hanging. I don't need two guesses as to why it's there. Forcing Beth to watch herself ride me has been a recurring fantasy of mine. I'm sure it was amazing seeing her like that. I imagine it was, since I don't fucking remember it.

I step further into the room and shove the chair aside. Items from the fridge and cabinets litter the counter, and some of the floor. Lids have been left off the honey and chocolate sauce. The whipped cream is warm when I wrap my hand around the tube. My cock hardens at the thought of eating any one of these off Beth. I look down at the lucky bastard, tenting my boxers.

"I'm surprised you don't need a fucking cast."

A car horn sounds, pulling my attention up.

Beth.

It's like a minefield getting down the hallway to the front door. I step between pillows, books, my phone, which I palm as I move past it. The door is pulled open just as a cab pulls away from the house.

"Beth!" I yell, stepping off the porch and onto the small pathway. The car continues down the street.

"Fuck!"

My free hand grips my hair, still slick with sweat and the water from the tap. I take a look around to make sure none of my neighbors are out. I'm usually not chasing women out of my house wearing only a pair of boxers. They're normally getting shoved out the door, and I'm fully clothed.

I head back inside and slam the door. Kicking shit out of the way this time instead of bothering to step over it, I clear a path for the couch and sit down. My shoulders roll forward as I pull up the contact list on my phone. I place it to my ear, while my other hand cradles my head.

"Come on. Pick up."

Two rings, then the call goes to voicemail. That means she forced it to voicemail. I call again, this time it doesn't ring at all. Her soft voice hums against my ear, asking me to leave her a message. I drop my head back against the couch.

"Will you call me, please, so we can talk about this? I don't like that you left here upset."

I disconnect the call and toss the phone.

Keeping my head back, I let my eyes fall closed as I try and put together more pieces of last night. Nothing new appears, and I try harder, squeezing my eyes so damn tight I swear I strain a muscle in my neck. The same images circle in my head. Nothing past Jim Beam, and Beth sitting and talking next to me at the bar. I can't hear anything she's saying to me. I have no idea what we talked about, but in those flashes she's smiling. Always smiling at me, like I'm giving her something amazing just by listening. My eyes open and I stare up at the ceiling.

This is fucking infuriating.

I've had her. My hands know what her body feels like, all that softness underneath my palm.

My mouth has tasted every inch of her skin, that I'm fucking sure of.

My cock has been buried inside a woman bare for the first time in my life, but it's as if it never happened.

None of it, except for what I was lucid for at the party. I could've done shit with Beth I've never done before, and I wouldn't know. I might not ever know it if she refuses to call me back.

I reach for the phone again, but stop myself mid-way.

Shit. I'm losing it. Losing. It.

Maybe not talking to her is a good thing. Maybe not

having all of these images in my head of every way I've experienced her is a good thing. I've already jacked off more in the past week than I have in my entire life. Thinking about Beth's mouth was already an obsession. Now I have that wicked little hand of hers to throw into the mix. Adding anything else and I might have a serious problem.

Right. 'Cause right now, what I have already isn't a serious problem.

Distractions. That's what I need. Distractions and distance.

I push off the couch and grab my phone before heading for the stairs. The call connects as I'm pulling a pair of jeans out of my dresser.

"Hey, man," Ben greets me over the sound of a kid crying in the background. It's too young to be Nolan.

I pinch the phone between my shoulder and ear. "Hey. Is Chase okay?"

"Yeah, he's just hungry and getting impatient waiting for Mia." Ben chuckles. "Can't say I blame him."

I realize Ben's just insinuated he also gets impatient waiting for Mia's tits. Any other day and I might throw that back at him, but I'm too fucked up thinking about my own problems to come back with something clever. I choose to ignore his remark and fasten the button of my jeans.

"Is it a good time to head over and get to work on the deck? I need to stay busy for the rest of my life."

"Yeah, it's a good time. I'm off today. I can give you a hand."

I straighten and take hold of the phone. "All right, cool. I'll be over in ten."

Something on the top of my shoulder catches my eye before I disconnect the call. "Hang on." I reach back to run my fingers over it, and the sticky consistency clings to my skin.

The jar of honey on the counter.

Nice. I'm probably coated it in.

My hands drop to the front of my jeans after securing the phone against my ear again. I lower my zipper. "Give me an hour. I need to take a shower first."

"YOU WANT A beer?" Ben asks, setting the nail gun down and walking over to the cooler.

I wipe the sweat off my forehead with the back of my hand. *More alcohol? Fuck no.* "Nah, I'm good. Do you have any water in there?"

Ben laughs quietly, then tosses me a water. "Pussy. What happened last night?"

Shit.

We've gone two hours without a mention of anything personal. Manual labor tends to keep chatter to a minimum, which I was expecting, and grateful for. I was also pleased to find out when I arrived that Mia had taken the boys to the grocery store. There was no way in Hell she wouldn't ask me about the party. I had no idea if Ben knew about it or not, but I guess married couples talk to each other about shit like that. And now that he's in need of a fucking beverage, he's asking me about it.

My silence spurs him on.

"I know you took some girl to your ex's engagement party. You don't take girls to anything," he pauses, smirking. "Besides the clinic after you've fucked them."

I glare at him, lowering my water bottle. "Fuck you, man. I'm clean. I always wear a condom."

Except for last night, during my marathon sex.

I shake that unwanted thought out of my head before I

continue. This is not the time for a hard-on.

"I've even doubled up on chicks. You don't really get much sensation, but some of them . . . Yeah, I wasn't taking any chances."

Ben leans his back against the support beam and takes a long sip of his beer, staring at me over top of it. His gaze is relentless, baiting me to give him information he can take back to Mia, I'm sure.

Well, not today. As long as I stay busy, my mind stays off of Beth.

I toss my water bottle onto the grass and pick up a piece of lumber, carrying it over to the work bench.

"You know," Ben starts up again behind me.

I hold the saw steady with my one hand, the piece of wood with the other, and try to zone him out as I cut into the wood.

"She's going to ask you when she sees you. You might as well tell me now so I can give her something, which will in turn give *me* something."

I pause, glancing back at him over my shoulder. "What, do you need my help now getting laid?"

He raises an eyebrow, still perched against the beam. "Do I look like I need your help getting laid?"

I turn back around, trying to focus on my cutting while he rambles on behind me.

"Mia asked me to ask you. So, here I am, asking. If I go back to her with details of whatever the fuck you did last night, which is strictly something only my wife gives a shit about, I will be greeted with a very, very grateful Mia. And grateful Mia drives me fucking wild."

I blow across the wood, removing the sawdust. "And regular Mia doesn't drive you wild?"

If he says no, I'm calling major bullshit on that. Ben only

sees Mia. He's only ever seen Mia since she showed up here two years ago, and it wouldn't matter what version of her she was giving him. He'd still only ever see her.

I like to complain that I was pussy-whipped nine years ago. But this motherfucker right here . . .

He makes an amused sound in the back of his throat. "Every version of Mia drives me wild. I just know giving her this information will make her very happy. She wants to know how things went, and she's not here to ask you herself."

"It went fine," I grunt out, my voice suddenly thick. The saw splits the wood into two, and I set the pieces aside. I grab another 2x8 and toss it on the bench, picking up the saw and lining it up at the mark I drew earlier. My hand remains stagnant.

Fuck. Why did he have to play the Mia card?

I let out a heavy sigh. "It was awkward, okay? I didn't know it was going to be at the same place I proposed to Molly at, and it was. On top of that, she's marrying the douche-bag I caught her cheating on me with. Seeing him with her wasn't really something I was prepared for. I'm hung-over as fuck."

"You proposed to her? When?"

I begin sawing, concentrating on the mark. "Before she left for college. I didn't tell anybody."

Great. Now this shit is going to get out. I'm sure Tessa will have a field day with this information, and then bitch at me for an hour for not telling her about it.

"She said no, and you stayed with her?"

My skin begins to tingle, my shoulder burning from the force I'm putting behind my hand. "She didn't really say no. She laughed, told me I was crazy, which I fucking was, and then sucked my dick to distract me. Or to ease the sting of her rejection. Whatever. It wasn't that great from what I can remember."

"What about the girl?"

I break through the wood. Ben breaks through my resistance.

"Are you sure I'm not standing here talking to Mia? Shit!" I throw the saw down and walk over to the water bottle I threw out into the yard.

Goddamn it. I'm losing it. Losing. It.

What the fuck is wrong with me? Okay, so I may or may not have had the best sex of my life last night. Shouldn't that be a good thing?

No. It can't be a good thing. Because it was with Beth.

Beth, the woman I can't stop thinking about.

Beth, the woman who had me reeling from the memory of a goddamn kiss, and who has now completely fucked my world over from a hand-job and whatever the fuck else.

Beth. Beth fucking Davis.

I squeeze my eyes shut, trying to remember, trying not to remember . . .

"Reed," she begs, thrashing about on the bed, grinding her pussy against my hand. "Please, now. Please . . . I can't wait . . . fuck me. I need it. Need you."

My eyes fly open. Jesus Christ. She said she needed me.

I hear Ben's rough laugh from behind me, which has my hand squeezing the empty bottle, smashing it up. I turn around and toss it into the trash. It doesn't matter that I'm ignoring him. I know without even looking into his pussy-whipped face that it's lit up with amusement.

A sharp sting cracks against my shoulder as he slaps my back. He looks down at me, grinning. "You're fucked. You know that, right?"

I shrug him off, watching him walk over to the nail gun.

"I'm fucked because I'm hung-over, and I have a friend who all-of-a-sudden grew a vagina. Can we please go back to not speaking? I don't want to talk about this anymore."

He holds his hands up, backing away slowly.

I turn away and grab my drill and a few screws, stopping to pick up one of the 2x8's I sawed in half. I think I get thirty, maybe forty seconds of silence before I hear Ben's laugh building from a muffled grunt to a full-blown, throwing his head back, all at my expense laugh.

"You're so fucked," he repeats, bracing the nail gun on one of the posts. "I've been waiting for this. Now you can't say shit about me and Luke."

I line up the board where I want it.

"So fucked. I'm excited."

I drill in one screw. *Just stay focused. Ignore him. Don't think about it.*

"Wait until Tessa hears about this."

The drill slips, splitting the wood as the second screw goes in jagged.

"Fuck!" I set the drill down and grab the crowbar, pointing it directly at Ben. "I'm not fucked." *I'm fucked.* "Nothing happened." *A lot happened, just don't ask me what.* "And I don't give a shit if Tessa hears about it." *I'd rather she didn't.* "Are you ready to get back to work, woman, or do you need another break to go change your tampon?"

Ben drops all humor, and I lower the crowbar. He stares at me with the look I'm sure he gives the pieces of shit he arrests every day. Ben's probably got a good ten to fifteen pounds of muscle on me. He's intimidating as fuck. He always has been. I'm sure if we were to start throwing punches, I could keep up for a while, but one of his blows might knock me into next week.

His eyes narrow, then a slow smirk pulls at the corner of his mouth.

Shit.

"So fucked," he taunts.

I look back at the board I'm about to pry off. My shoulders sag, and I almost kick at the dirt on the ground.

"Yeah," I say through a groan. "Yeah, I fucking know."

beth

HAVE NEVER felt so embarrassed in my entire life.

Not even the time I was caught eating lunch in the bathroom at West Oak Middle School, and that was mortifying. I had been trying to avoid a group of girls who were picking on me every day in the cafeteria. But I was caught. Caught by the very girls I was trying to avoid. They made sure the entire school knew I was eating my peanut butter sandwich on the toilet. After that, the tormenting got worse. Word got around school, even reached the teachers, and I was eventually sent to the guidance counselor to talk about my *issues*. Issues? I didn't want to be around mean girls. The classrooms were off limits during lunch hours, and I just wanted somewhere quiet to eat where other kids didn't make fun of me. How is that having an issue?

No, not even seventh grade tops this moment. It can't. Seventh grade was typically embarrassing. No one likes middle school. This, what happened two days ago with Reed, this is in a whole other universe of embarrassment.

I had the best sex of my life, times a million, and I'm the only one who remembers it.

I took advantage of him. There's really no other way of looking at this. Reed was apparently way more intoxicated than he led me to believe, which has left him with zero memory of what we did. I was completely sober, which gives me the painful advantage of remembering every single detail of our night together. Painful because it only adds to my humiliation.

I can't forget what happened. He can't remember. And what we did? Well, that just kicks the embarrassment meter up several thousand notches.

It wasn't just everything I've been imagining us doing in my head since I first looked up into his face. I let him do everything he'd been imagining doing to me since I first smiled at him. No limits. No fear. We did things I've never even thought about doing, things I know, without a doubt, I wouldn't have done with anyone else. But it was Reed. He asks me if I trust him, and my answer is automatic.

"Yes," I whisper, offering him my hands, my fingers threaded together like he showed me. I look up into his eyes, nodding, swallowing down my eager moan. "I trust you."

My body hums at the memory. Eager. Yeah, I was definitely eager.

And he was drunk.

He wouldn't have done what we did if he wasn't drunk. I saw it in his eyes the next morning. The regret, gentled to spare my feelings, but it was there. And now I'm questioning everything that's happened between us. I was nothing more than a distraction for him up in that room at the party. It didn't matter that he was sober at the time, a willing participant in one of the hottest moments of my life. He didn't instigate it. He didn't grab me and kiss me that night at McGill's. Everything, aside from what we did at his house, was initiated by me. Reed needed enough alcohol to make him sick the next morning to touch me on his own. He's probably grateful he has no memory of what we did.

You can't feel shame if you can't remember.

"Will you call me, please, so we can talk about this? I

don't like that you left here upset."

I set the phone on my chest after listening to Reed's voice-mail for the hundredth time. He's called me once since I left his house. No texts, or anything else from him since. I haven't called him back, and I'm guessing since he hasn't reached out to me anymore that it doesn't matter if I do or not. The game is over. We don't have to pretend we're something we never were. He's going back to the life he had that didn't involve me. I need to do the same, it's just . . .

"Beth. God . . . fuck, Beth."

I can't stop thinking about . . .

"I'm so hard. Fuck, I'm so hard for you. All the time. I can't sleep. I can't fucking think straight anymore."

All I can hear is . . .

"You have the tightest pussy. Mm . . . fuck, so good. And you're so wet. God, if you could see my cock right now."

I run my hands over my flushed cheeks. I'm worked up, again. It's no surprise. Just hearing the way he says my name, all breathy and desperate, has me pinching my legs together to ease the throbbing.

"Fuck, Beth. Beth. BETH."

Why couldn't I have been named something that didn't sound so hot coming out of his mouth? Like Mildred. I doubt he says Mildred sexy.

My phone beeps on my chest, and I tilt it up to look at the screen. I don't recognize the number, but I swipe my thumb across it anyway to open up the message.

> Unknown: Hey, it's Mia. Tessa is coming over to have lunch with me. Wanna come?

I sit up and swing my legs off the bed, staring down at the phone in my hand.

I do need to get out of this room. Besides using the bathroom, the only time I've ventured out in the past forty-eight hours was to grab a quick snack from the kitchen. And I really like Tessa and Mia. I meant it when I said I would love to hang out with them. But these are Reed's friends. Won't that be weird?

My phone beeps again. Another unknown number.

Unknown: Come on, Clapton. Get your ass over to Mia's so we can chat. I don't bite.

The notifications begin firing off as text after text rolls in.

Unknown: What are you bringing, Tessa?

Unknown: I'm supposed to bring something? Get your life right! You invited me!

Unknown: I'm making shrimp salad, but I don't have any rolls. Can you bring rolls? And a side? Chips or something.

Unknown: Oh crap. Beth, are you allergic to shrimp?

Unknown: Oooo is it my mom's recipe? I love her shrimp salad! Do you have drinks?

Unknown: Yup. I have sodas and sweet tea. Beth, shrimp? Are you allergic?

Unknown: I think we lost Clapton.

I type quickly.

Me: I am so confused right now. Is this going to both of you?

Unknown: Yes, it's a group text. Haven't you done a group text before? And where are we at on the shrimp allergy?

Unknown: Have you been living under a rock? Who doesn't know what a group text is? CLAPTON, SERIOUSLY?

Me: I need to program your names in here. Hold on.

I think I could get away with not assigning Tessa a name. Her messages are definitely . . . Tessa.

Tessa: Helloooo. . . .

I laugh as I type my response.

Me: Okay. No, I'm not allergic to shrimp.

Mia: Oh, good! Are you coming? You don't have to bring anything.

Tessa: WTF. Fine. I'll bring EVERYTHING.

Mia: HAHA.

Me: I don't mind bringing something. It's not a big deal.

Tessa: You are bringing something. Your chatty little mouth.

Mia: Next time we do lunch you can bring something. Can you come over at 2?

Tessa: Why are we eating at 2? Who the hell eats lunch that late? I'm going to have to eat something before I come over there.

Mia: *The boys will be down for their naps by then. I'm not having girl time with a kid strapped to my boob.*

Tessa: *Nice change from Ben though, huh?*

Mia: *Shut up.*

Me: *I can be there at 2.*

Mia: *Yayyyy! Here's my address: 79 Arrondale Drive. We're the house with the blowup bouncy castle in the front yard.*

Tessa: *Have you and Ben had sex in that thing yet?*

Mia: *What? No! It's in the front yard!*

Tessa: *And . . . I bet it's like fucking on a water bed. That's on my bucket list.*

Mia: *Is everything on your bucket list a different place for you and Luke to have sex?*

Tessa: *No. I also have skydiving on there.*

Tessa: *While having sex.*

Mia: *Nice. Okay, the baby needs me. See you both at 2!*

Tessa: *Don't stand us up, Clapton.*

Me: *I won't. Thank you for inviting me.*

Mia: I just love her. She's so much sweeter to talk than you.

Tessa: Mia, we're still in the group text.

Mia: Oh . . . okayyy, see you soon!

I toss my phone onto the bed and grab some clothes. Even though I already took a shower today, I hopped right back into my pajamas after I dried off.

Pathetic, I know, but why bother getting dressed when you have no intention of leaving your bed?

I step into my boots, grab my keys, tuck my phone into my pocket, and head for the stairs. "Aunt Hattie?" I call out, peeking my head into the kitchen.

"I'm in here, darlin'."

I turn around and walk back down the hallway.

Hattie is sitting at the computer with the shoe box I gave her in her lap, sifting through the pictures. She stops and looks up at me when I walk in.

"I was beginning to worry about you. You haven't come out of that room much since Sunday."

My eyes wander to the floor as I try and think of an excuse.

She can't know the real reason why I've been shut away for two days. I'm embarrassed enough as it is. Informing my sweet aunt that I had face-down, ass-up, hanging from the ceiling, spread across the table, do me faster, harder, has any man ever done you here sex might make this situation worse. But I have to give her something.

A sickness. Of course! I could've easily been sick.

I flatten a hand to my stomach and raise my head. "I think I had a virus or something. My stomach hated me."

She seems convinced, a look of concern pulling together

her eyebrows. "Oh, no. You're okay now?"

"I am. I feel so much better."

"Well, that's good. There was this horrible stomach flu going around right before you arrived. Maybe that's what you caught."

I nod, letting my hand slide down to my side. "Maybe." My eyes flick to the shoebox. "Have you looked through all of the pictures in there?"

She looks down into her lap. "No, but I'm only allowing myself to pick a few a day. Seems silly, I guess. But I want to experience every picture as if I'm living it with you. It might take me a while to go through all of these. I framed one when you were a baby and put it up at the bar." Her deep brown eyes find mine. "I hope that's okay. It's not out in the open or anything. It's back in Danny's office."

"That's okay with me. I actually had a question about the bar."

Stepping further into the small room, I run my finger over a picture frame hanging on the wall. Hattie is much younger, smiling at the camera, dressed in her wedding gown. Danny is smiling down at her, his tie undone.

Reed's tie undone.

Oh no. Don't think about ties being undone. Stick with your question.

Clearing my throat, I look over at Hattie, and my movement draws her attention off the photos again. I put my hand on my hip. "Is there any chance the bar could use a waitress who's willing to work long hours? I really need to get a job."

When I was batting around ideas for employment, one of the first options I thought of was working at McGill's. The food is great, I love the atmosphere, and it would allow me to spend more time with my family. There is one minor problem.

"I've never waitressed before, but I'm a fast learner," I add, hoping I didn't just eliminate my chances. But I don't want her thinking I'm going to walk in there and know how to work a register.

She thinks it over for a few seconds, laughing softly when I fold my hands in front of me and whisper the word "please", over and over.

Leaning back in her chair, she sets the shoebox on the desk and stands. Her hands circle my wrists. She smiles. Then I smile, really big, which causes her to pull me into a hug.

"I think we can work something out," she says, leaning back after our short embrace. "Week nights would probably be better for you to waitress. The weekend is really more of a bar style setting, and I think you'll get a lot more tips when it isn't that type of a crowd. People only come in to drink on the weekends. They come in to eat during the week."

"They should come in to eat all the time. The food is great." Major bonus about working at McGill's. Free bar food. I beam at my aunt. "I'm so excited! When can I start?"

She releases my arms and moves back to her desk chair, smiling at my excitement. "How about tomorrow? It'll give me time to smooth this over with your Uncle Danny."

My heart sinks as I stare at her. "He won't want me working there?" I ask, stepping closer.

Hattie quickly shakes her head, dismissing my concern. "No, it's not that he wouldn't want you working there, darlin'. Danny just knows what kind of men come around the bar sometimes. He's protective of you is all. If he sees some sleazeball getting too close to his favorite niece, he'll take them out back and beat them with something. He'll just worry about you. I know him."

I love how quickly I've fallen into this family. How

naturally it happened, as if I was always here.

I jingle my keys. "I'm going over to my friend's house for lunch. Let me know what he says, okay?"

"Oh, I'm sure he'll let you know what he says. Especially if the answer is yes. Get ready for a lecture, darlin'."

I wave to Hattie, hearing her sweet laugh fade out behind me as I head out the front door.

"HI, COME IN. Tessa is on her way." Mia steps back and ushers me inside her home with a waving hand. "Did you find the house okay?" she asks, closing the door behind me.

"I did. You don't live that far from me."

"Really? Where do you live?"

"Laurel Woods," I answer, following her down the hallway and toward the delicious smells coming from what I assume to be the kitchen.

We pass the living room, which has toys and baby items scattered about. There's a small pack-n-play in the corner next to the window, and a detailed Lego castle that's proudly displayed on the coffee table. If someone were to be sitting on the couch, that castle would completely obstruct their view of the TV.

I really, really love that it's there.

The hallway breaks into the kitchen, and I watch as Mia rounds the table and gestures for me to have a seat.

"What would you like to drink? I have tea, soda, water." She opens the fridge, looking over her shoulder in my direction with raised eyebrows.

I pull out one of the kitchen chairs and take a seat, setting my keys in front of me. "Tea would be great. Thank you."

Mia pours us both a glass and carries them over to the

table. She hands me mine. "I'm so glad you could make it. I was worried you would be tied up already when we texted you."

My eyes widen. Oh, no. No.No.No.No. Don't think about him. Don't think about . . .

"You okay, sweetheart?"

I look up at my hands. Bound, tied to a support beam that's been left exposed in the ceiling. My fingers wrap around the soft fibers of the rope. It doesn't hurt. It doesn't even feel foreign, which it should. I've never been tied to something before. It feels strangely . . . comforting. Like this rope is holding me together, keeping me safe. Or maybe that's Reed. Maybe he's the reason for my harmony.

A hand on my cheek draws my attention back down.

"Beth," Reed whispers against my mouth, biting my lip when I whimper at that single word.

My name. God, it's unfair how sexy he can make it sound.

He threads his fingers through my hair, dropping his forehead to mine. "Tell me you're okay with this. Tell me it's too much. Just say something. I'm about to lose my mind on you."

I stare into his eyes, the palest blue I've ever seen. Like the sky after a snowfall.

I'm about to lose my mind on you.

"Beth?"

I nearly drop my glass. Both hands steady it as I focus my gaze across the table. Mia keeps herself from smiling with tight lips, while I filter through images of Reed's dick for the question Mia asked me before I zoned out.

Tied up. Right. Got it.

I take a quick drink before I answer, hoping to douse the fire I've just ignited beneath my skin. I don't feel the slightest relief.

"No, I was free. Very free. Never tied up. I don't even know what that's like." My words come out in a blur. A very unconvincing blur.

Shit, one word and I'm transported back to Saturday night. My skin feels like it's ready to singe off at any second. My heart is racing, threatening to send me into shock. God help me if she says anything about asses . . .

Mia rests her chin on her hand. Her face is expressionless. "Mm. Okay."

The front door opens, the noise quickly followed by an animated, "I'm here!"

Mia snaps her head to the right at the same moment her hand loudly flattens on the table. "Shh! If you wake up Chase, I'm going to punch you in the throat."

Tessa walks into the kitchen, hands full of grocery bags. She pauses in the doorway and frowns at Mia. "Sorry, boo. I forgot." She raises the bags, smiling as she walks to the counter. "I brought goodies."

Mia gets up and joins her, and I wonder if I should be doing anything besides sitting here, daydreaming about Reed's kink. I scoot my chair out as I stand, but slowly lower myself back in it when Mia motions for me to sit.

"We got it, sweetie. Just relax."

Tessa leans back to look at me, taking the back of her hand and brushing the red hair out of her face. Her smile slowly stretches across her mouth. "Hey, Clapton. You ready for girl time?"

I stare back at her, and the longer I go without answering, the more knowing her smile becomes. She suddenly looks like the Cheshire cat, grinning at Alice who has no idea what the fuck she's getting into.

What exactly happens during girl time?

I know we're eating lunch. I imagine we're going to be talking, getting to know each other better, building a friendship and all. I'm prepared for the mom discussion. I'm also willing to talk about the rough couple of months after she died. Mia and Tessa will probably talk about their husbands or boyfriends. Their families will most likely be brought up. That all seems pretty standard. So, what am I missing? Why the look?

Leaning back in my chair, I finally give Tessa a quick nod and then let my gaze wander to the window I'm sitting near. "You sure I can't help with anything? I really don't mind."

"We got it." Mia carries two plates over to the table. She sets one down in front of me, taking the other one for herself and claiming her seat with it. "If you don't like the shrimp salad, you can blame my mother-in-law. It's her recipe."

I look down at the plate, and saliva fills my mouth. Everything on it looks amazing. The shrimp salad, the bag of chips on the side. Even the pickle. Maybe it's going two days without really eating anything substantial, but I really don't think I'm going to have trouble with this plate.

I give Mia a smile as I pick up my roll. "I'm sure it's delicious. I'm so hungry though, it could taste like garbage and I'd probably still eat it."

"Oh, well, I guess that clears me to cook for us next time," Tessa jokes, joining us and sitting in the chair next to Mia. "I only know how to make garbage."

The three of us share a laugh, and then fall into a comfortable silence as we eat. I take a bite of my sandwich, then another, chewing as I look around the quaint kitchen.

There's drawings covering the refrigerator, ones of dragons and airplanes, and a few of stick-figure people standing in front of a house. It's adorable. I imagine every room having something kid related in it. A toy, or a page ripped out of a coloring book, displayed proudly somewhere.

"Are you married, Tessa?" I ask after noticing the framed

wedding photo on the wall next to the window.

Mia pauses with her sandwich close to her mouth. Her eyes slowly roll to her right, where Tessa is gently hitting her head on the table next to her plate.

"Sore subject?" I ask, regretting my urgent desire to start-up conversation.

Tessa lifts her head, laughing, and bumps her shoulder playfully against Mia's, who resumes eating after situating herself in her chair.

Tessa looks over at me. "No, it's not. I just like being all dramatic about it. I'm hoping it'll kick Luke's ass into gear and make him ask me."

"I can't believe he hasn't already," Mia says, disbelief tightening her jaw.

Tessa tilts her head, glaring. "I know, right? It's been almost six months since he told me he was going to. And I keep thinking he's going to do it, and he doesn't, and then I end up looking like an idiot." She shakes her head with pursed lips, and then glances between the two of us. "The other day he dragged me to Home Depot with him and bent down to tie his shoe right in front of me. I started screaming. I thought, this is it! He's doing it! Everyone was staring at me. Some were clapping. Then I look down and see he's just fixing his laces."

"What did he say?" I ask, leaning forward.

Tessa tries hard to fight her smile, but it breaks through, lifting the corner of her mouth. "He looked up, gave me that cocky smirk he's always wearing, and said 'babe', like come on. In Home Depot?" Her hand flattens on her chest. "I would have been ecstatic to be proposed to in the lumber aisle."

I laugh quietly, as does Mia who dabs her napkin against her mouth.

"I think he's planning something big, and that's why he

hasn't asked you," she says, setting her napkin next to her plate. "Something crazy romantic."

Tessa picks up her sandwich. "Whatever. I don't need anything big, or romantic. It's Luke. I'd say yes to him if he decided to pop the question while he was on the toilet."

"Well, that's romantic for sure," I chuckle. "Babe, will you hand me the toilet paper, and your hand in marriage?"

Tessa and Mia both burst out laughing.

"I like you, Clapton." Tessa points at me, lifting her head off Mia's shoulder. "You're funny."

I look down at my plate as something warm blooms in my chest.

How is it that everyone in this town holds the capability of making me feel like I've known them my entire life? No awkwardness. No forced conversations. I don't have a lifetime of memories with these girls, but I feel like I easily could.

A throat clearing draws my attention up and immediately to Tessa, who is leaning on her hand and staring at me. I shift my gaze to Mia, who is also staring, her arms crossed over her chest as she sits back in her chair.

How long have they been doing that?

"Is there something on my face?" I ask.

Tessa cranes her neck to look at Mia. Mia looks from Tessa, to me. They both smile at the same time, and it hits me.

Girl talk equals boy talk.

Oh, God no.

I sit back in my chair, my shoulders drop, and I glance apprehensively between the two of them, waiting for the first question to be thrown at me. Maybe they won't ask me about the party.

"So, what happened the other night at the party?"

Son of a . . .

My hands tangle together in my lap as I look up at Mia, her eyes expectantly waiting for my response. I'm not a horrible liar. I could attempt to lie my way through this. Save any shred of dignity I have left.

"Mm? Party?" I lift my shoulders. "Nothing. Typical party stuff."

Tessa points a finger at me. "Typical party stuff, my ass. This is girl talk. What is said at this table, stays at this table. And we're not getting shit from Reed, so you're going to tell us everything that happened."

My stomach knots up. "You spoke to Reed?" I ask, watching both of them slowly nod. I suddenly wish I still had an empty stomach. Throwing up all over this kitchen might eliminate my chances of getting another invite to hang out.

Mia sighs, shifting her arms across her body. "He's avoiding me now. The jerk won't answer any of my texts." She looks at Tessa. "When was the last time you spoke to him?"

"Yesterday." She pops a chip into her mouth. "I called him from my mom's cell. I knew he'd answer it 'cause he wouldn't recognize the number. The bastard hung up on me when I started talking." Tessa brushes her hands off over the plate and pushes it away. "This is what we know," she says, narrowing in on me as she braces her elbows on the table.

Air becomes lodged in my throat as I reflexively hold my breath.

She gives me a soft smile. *Relax, Clapton. It's not that bad.*

My lips pull down. *It is though.*

"We know that Molly is marrying the fuckwad she cheated on Reed with. We also know, which this next little nugget of information seriously pissed me the hell off, that Reed proposed to that bitchasaurus before she left for college, and that the party was at the same spot he pulled that stunt at."

Tessa's eyes narrow. "Seriously? I can not believe he kept that shit from me. We've been best friends since ninth grade."

"He was probably embarrassed," Mia says, somberly. "I know I'd be embarrassed if someone rejected me like that."

"He loved her," I add, looking between the two sets of eyes trained on me. I sink a little lower in my chair. "He told me he was stupid for doing it, but I think it really hurt him when she turned him down."

Tessa shakes her head, disagreeing. "Molly is the world's biggest cunt hair. Reed would've been miserable with her. Hell, half the time they were together he was miserable. She did him a *huge* favor by turning him down."

Mia cringes. "Cunt hair? You say the sickest stuff sometimes."

"I waited until you were done eating."

The two of them share a laugh, then Tessa turns back to me. "Anyway, that's all he gave us. I don't need to be a mind reader to know something happened between you two."

I try to focus on anything besides the two eager faces staring at me, but my eyes are all over the place. My lap. The window. The sandwich I want to keep eating, if only to prevent my words from being understood. I'm uneasy, and I'm not hiding it well. My face is burning up, I'm chewing a hole in my bottom lip. I probably look psychotic right now.

"Beth."

I look across the table at Mia, lifting my eyes off the glass vase centerpiece.

"Whatever you're about to say, stays between us. We would never say anything to Reed or anybody else. Okay?"

I take in a deep breath, exhaling it slowly. My eyes fall closed as I drop my head. "We had sex all night and Reed doesn't remember any of it."

Silence. Dead silence, as if both of them have ceased breathing.

I peek up and see two sets of eyes, waiting for further explanation. Groaning, I plant my elbows on the table and let my face fall into my hands.

Just get it over with. Like a band-aid. Rip this shit right off.

"Reed freaked out a little at the party when he saw Molly's fiancé. It's like everything came to a head and he couldn't handle it anymore. I pulled him into the farmhouse and things . . . happened. Just like touching and stuff. He wanted to drink after that so we went to the bar. I knew he was feeling the alcohol, but I didn't think he was completely wasted. When I drove him home, he asked me to stay, and I did. I asked him if he was drunk, he said no." I look at them between my fingers.

"And . . ." Tessa urges.

I pinch my eyes closed. "I've never had sex like that. He was everywhere, all over me, touching me, saying the dirtiest stuff while he held me down. He tied me up and fucked me for what felt like hours. We did it in every room, every position . . ." I swallow hard. "*Everywhere.* He was so turned on and I was so turned on, and it was like we were racing each other to see who could come the most. I think we tied, maybe, I don't know. Honestly, I lost count. It was filthy and perfect and I can't stop thinking about it. I don't know what I was expecting the next morning, but him not remembering what we did wasn't it. It was so, *so* embarrassing. I got out of there while he was puking in the bathroom and I haven't talked to him since."

My breath against my face becomes too much, too thick, too suffocating. I lower my hands to allow the cool air to hit me.

Mia's eyes are brimming with questions, her mouth hanging open in shock. I look at Tessa, and immediately wish I hadn't.

She's grinning like I've just told her I shoved Molly in front of a freight train.

"I knew Reed was a freak!" she squeals, slapping the table. "Damn. I feel like I need a cigarette after hearing that. He tied you up? Like with rope?"

I nod.

"You did it everywhere?" she probes, lifting an eyebrow.

I nod, again. No reason to verbalize this humiliation.

Her smile grows even more. "Hot."

Mia begins fanning her face, and then downs the rest of her iced tea. "Wow. I had no idea Reed was so creative in the bedroom."

"He was *really* creative in the kitchen," I softly add.

Mia's eyebrows hit her hairline. Tessa nods appreciatively.

I take a bite out of my pickle, chew it up, and then elaborate when their eyes encourage me.

"There was a lot of honey involved."

Mia stands with her empty glass in her hand. "I need a refill. I'm having a major hot flash." She heads for the refrigerator, leaving me alone with a very pleased looking Tessa. It's as if she's the one who had the sex of her life two days ago.

She crosses her arms over her chest and settles back in the chair. "No wonder Reed's ducking us. He's probably losing his mind knowing he's been with you and can't remember any of it. I bet he's going crazy."

I lower my eyes. "He regrets it."

"Says who?"

Looking up at Tessa, I see the harsh frown she's giving me. I wait for her to explain. She waits for me to inquire. We both open our mouths at the same time, but our words are halted by the sound of the front door opening.

Several deep voices follow. I look to my left as three men step into the kitchen. Three large men. Three very, very attractive men. All in police uniforms.

Good Lord. If I wasn't already having a difficult time with shit lately, now I get handed the task of not staring at men who look like they could easily be cast in Magic Mike 2? Did I murder a litter of puppies in another life or something?

"Angel." The biggest out of the three makes a direct line for Mia. "Give me that mouth."

Mia blushes instantly. "Hey, babe." She sets her glass on the counter and throws her arms around his neck. They share a brief, but hotter than hell kiss. "Come here. I want you to meet Beth."

I realize then that I'm the only one left at the table. Tessa is shoving one of the other men against the wall by the refrigerator and assaulting him with her body. The other guy is standing in the middle of the floor, hands in his pockets, unsure of where to look with all the affection surrounding him. He settles his eyes on me and smiles.

I smile back.

He smiles bigger.

I quickly blink away before I give him my Reed smile.

Oh, great. Really? My Reed smile?

Mia walks up to the table with the big cop glued to her back. She drops her head back against his chest, then her eyes notice the man standing in the middle of the kitchen.

"Guys, this is Beth. She just moved here from Kentucky. Beth, this is CJ." She tips her head in the direction of the man who was smiling at me, is still smiling at me, then wraps her hand around the bicep nearly crushing her. "And this is Ben, my husband, and Tessa's brother. The one she's got pinned down is Luke."

CJ reaches across the table and takes my hand. He squeezes it gently. "Hi."

"Hi."

His deep auburn hair is cut short, resembling the hairstyle of the other two men. I assume that's a job requirement. He has strong features, a square jaw, wide forehead, and sharp, angular cheekbones. His lips are thin, framing perfect teeth. His eyes are a beautiful shade of blue. He's handsome. Very, very handsome.

Ben offers me his hand, keeping his other arm wrapped around Mia. "Kentucky? What brought you here?"

I bring my hands back to my lap. "My momma passed away. I found out I had family here and moved in with them."

"We met her through Reed," Mia whispers, turning her head into Ben's.

His face tightens, then recollection dawns on him. Two massive dimples dent in his cheeks.

"No shit," he says, grinning wildly. Turning his head, he looks over at the wall covered in Tessa and Luke. "Hey, asshole. Did you meet Beth? She knows our boy Reed."

"Hey." Luke lifts his chin in my direction, but keeps his eyes on Tessa.

Ben straightens. "I said she knows Reed."

"I heard you. Little busy right now," Luke says, then groans against Tessa's mouth, "What's gotten into you?"

Ben bares his teeth. "The fuck? Stop having sex in my kitchen and get over here. You need to meet Beth, the girl Reed *knows*."

I look from Ben, to Luke, to CJ, who hasn't stopped staring at me, to Mia. She gives me a half a smile, then blushes two shades redder than Tessa's hair. *Oh. Ohhhhh.*

Luke grabs Tessa's face, kisses her hard, and then breaks away from her, leaving her whining behind him like he's just denied her an orgasm. He steps up next to CJ and runs a hand over his buzzed hair. "Hey. So you're the girl, huh?"

The girl? What girl? Reed's girl? Is he calling me his girl?

I pinch my lips together through a shrug. I have no idea how to answer this question.

"Are you doing anything tomorrow night?"

All eyes, including mine, dart to CJ. He's staring directly at me with a lazy-smile, which gets knocked off his face when Tessa slaps the back of his head.

"What are you doing?" she angrily demands. "Were you not present during the introductions?"

He rubs the back of his head, then glares at Luke. "Reel your woman in, or I'll toss her outside."

"No, that's a great idea." Mia wiggles free of Ben's arms. He immediately resumes his hold. She turns her head and stares at Tessa for several seconds. Tessa smiles, as if reading Mia's unspoken words, then nods enthusiastically. Mia looks over at me. "We're having game night here tomorrow. You should definitely come."

"Baby," Ben says against her cheek, his eyes burning holes into the side of her face.

CJ wraps his hands around the back of the chair he's standing behind. "Yeah, you should," he adds, nodding. "You should come."

Mia brings her hand behind her and presses it against Ben's mouth. "Really, Beth. Please come. It's so much fun. I promise you'll have the best time."

I look around the room, gauging the faces staring down at me. Three of them smiling. Two of them looking like they have no idea what's going on.

Maybe they aren't in on game night?

"Okay," I answer, watching as the girls high-five each other. I give CJ a quick smile, then turn back to the girls. "But I'm bringing something. I'm not showing up empty handed again."

Tessa laughs, leaning her head against Luke's muscly arm. "Bring whatever you want, Clapton. This is going to be amazing."

"You two are crazy," Luke says, grabbing Tessa and heading for the shrimp salad.

"I hope you know what you're doing," Ben says into Mia's neck.

She shushes him and directs him toward the food. "Eat up, big man. You need your strength for later."

He gives her a stunning grin over his shoulder. "Baby, you have no idea."

I turn to CJ.

He smiles.

I smile.

Grabbing my half-eaten sandwich, I take a massive bite, preventing me from giving him what is *so* not my Reed smile.

reed

IT'S BEEN THREE days since that cab pulled away from my house.

Three long, grueling, hand-stuck-on-my-dick days.

I haven't seen Beth. Haven't spoken to Beth. But that's not stopping me from fucking thinking about her every other minute. New images keep filling my head of our night together, making my dick hard in the worst possible places. The job site. The grocery store. My parent's house. I can't take this shit much longer. It probably isn't helping that my sheets still smell like her. That my house is still a fucking wreck, taunting me every time I walk through it. I've stripped the bed four times, moved furniture back in place. Not even five minutes goes by before I'm putting those same sheets back on and sitting that goddamn chair back in front of the mirror in the kitchen.

Magic pussy, that's what I'm blaming.

Magic fucking pussy.

I know I'm only making shit worse for myself. Burying my face in the pillow, inhaling that faint trace of sweet vanilla she left behind. Staring at that chair while I eat dinner and hoping it'll trigger a memory. It's like I'm in a goddamn trance, under Beth's spell after three days of completely useless distance. I want to remember what we did, but I can't imagine this shit getting any worse. And knowing all of it, every detail of her body, every place I touched her, fucked her, sucked her . . . I will lose my fucking mind with that information.

Grabbing the six-pack off the floor of my truck, I hit the lock on my key ring and head for the front door.

I need this tonight. I need something to break up my routine of getting off work and then getting off at home. Maybe I can convince Mia to have game night tomorrow too. I love my dick. I'd be devastated if I broke that shit off, but that's exactly where I'm headed if I don't find a better way to occupy my time.

I push the door open without bothering to knock. Voices boom from the kitchen, Tessa's standing out over the others, which isn't unusual. Everyone's here already by the sound of it. Good. We can get this much needed distraction started.

I step into the kitchen and set my beers on the table. Ben's the first person I see.

Standing at the end of the counter, he lowers the beer in his hand as his lips pinch together in a thin line. Tessa and Mia are talking behind him, not having noticed me yet. Ben nudges Luke with his elbow, and the two of them share a look before heading in my direction.

"What?" I ask as they step in front of me. I grab one of my beers and pop the top.

Ben speaks first. "This wasn't our idea, man. Don't do anything that'll get your ass into trouble."

I swallow, and turn to Luke, tipping my beer at Ben. "What is he talking about?"

Luke nods at my beer, his face just as tense as Ben's. "You might want to shotgun that. Or put it down and get the hell out of here. We'll cover for you."

I whip my head between the two of them. *What the fuck?* "Is this part of game night? Have Reed try and guess what the hell you two idiots are getting at? Just say it, already. I suck at charades."

The room goes quiet. I look over Ben's shoulder, expecting to see Mia and Tessa looking at me, and they are. Both of them are wearing their biggest smiles, leaning on the counter, waving at me like they know something I don't, which apparently is the running theme of the night.

I open my mouth to ask them what the hell is going on, but it all becomes clear when my eyes are drawn to Beth, standing next to CJ.

Standing *with* CJ. Together. Looking all comfortable and shit.

Beth fucking Davis. Here, in Mia's kitchen, wearing the same dress she wore during our lunch together. The same fucking boots on her feet.

Making my chest tight. My dick hard. My mind a fucking scrambled mess.

What the fuck is she doing here?

A hand slaps me on the back of my head. Ben mumbles something about me being an asshole. I pull my attention off Beth and see the agitated glares being directed at me by everyone else in the room. Tessa is looking particularly murderous.

Fuck. I said that out loud?

I look at Beth, her big, brown eyes expanding and pinning me to the wall. Her lips pinched together in distress.

Fuck, I need to explain.

"I didn't mean . . ." My teeth clench when CJ's hand finds her lower back.

I look at him, ready to throw his ass out the nearest window.

He looks at me, lifting his chin into a friendly nod.

"What's up, man? You know Beth?"

I narrow my eyes.

Do I know Beth?

Yeah, motherfucker. I know her more than you ever will.

"Well, everyone's here. Why don't we get game night started?" Mia grabs Beth's hand, pulling her away from CJ and leading her toward my direction.

I could kiss that woman. Always having my back.

"Do you know how to play hearts, Beth?" Mia asks.

Beth looks at me briefly, then shakes her head as Mia pulls a chair out for her. She sits down at the opposite end of the table I'm standing at. "No, I don't think so," she says timidly.

Mia smiles. "That's okay. CJ can show you."

I have zero friends in this house.

CJ claims one of the chairs next to Beth. Mia takes the other. I debate on getting the hell out of here, but the second I see Beth staring at me across the table, looking just as fragile as she did standing in my bedroom, letting me know just by those eyes of hers that she had no idea I'd be here, I pick up my six-pack and carry it to the fridge.

Fuck it. What's the difference between struggling to keep my hand off my dick at home and battling the same urge at Mia's dinner table?

I take the last remaining seat at the table, putting me directly across from Beth. As Ben stands and deals out the cards, Tessa leans closer to me, chin resting on her hand, looking guilty as shit as the grin spreads across her face.

"Hey, buddy," she whispers. "You doing okay over there?"

I slowly turn my head, my eyes narrowing. "You know something, don't you?"

Tessa leans back, pops her gum through a smile, and picks up her cards.

Ben sits in his chair. "All right, we good? Beth, you know how to play now?"

Beth looks down at her cards, her thumb scraping across her bottom lip. "I think so. If I want to run, do I tell everyone I'm going to do it?"

Collective "no's" fill the room, everyone except me offering their response.

Beth looks across the table, waiting, wanting the answer she hasn't gotten yet. As if mine is the only one that matters to her.

Fuck. Is it? Is it the only one that matters?

Lowering my beer, I keep her gaze and slowly shake my head. She blinks several times, then looks back down at her cards.

I chug half my beer.

CJ laughs, slips his arm behind her, and rests it on the back of her chair. "No, baby. Don't tell anyone what you're planning on doing. Especially if you're trying to run."

Blood runs hot in my veins.

Baby?

"Baby?" I set my beer down and lean forward on my elbows. The room goes quiet. "What, you met her five minutes before I got here and you're already giving her a fucking nickname? Or is the word Beth too difficult for you to remember?"

Confusion tightens CJ's face. "What the hell's up with you?" he asks gruffly, leaning back in his chair, keeping his fucking arm exactly where it is.

I grit my teeth, looking around at the six pairs of eyes on me. One set in particular feeling like they're holding me by the throat and the balls.

You're losing it. Losing. It.

"Nothing. Let's play the damn game." I lean back in the chair and pick up my cards, setting three aside to pass to Ben and taking the ones Tessa hands over to me. I then toss the two of clubs out in the center of the table, starting the game.

Ben takes his turn, then CJ. Beth seems unsure of what she can or can't play, looking between her cards, then at the ones in the center of the table, back and forth repeatedly. She tosses a five of hearts on the stack.

"You can't play that yet," I tell her, reaching across the table and tossing her back the card. "Hearts can't be broken on the first trick."

"Oh. Right, yeah, I knew that." She tucks the card back into her hand. Her eyes slowly lift to mine. "I don't have any clubs."

"You can play anything but a heart on the first trick," Mia says, popping a grape into her mouth. "After hearts are broken you can play as many as you want."

"A trick?" Beth frowns, studying her cards again. "What's that again?"

CJ leans back and looks at her hand. He sets his cards down. "We'll play together, okay? Until you get the hang of it."

I glare at CJ. "I think she can figure it out by herself. It's not that hard."

"Relax, man," Ben mumbles next to me.

"What? We're playing hearts, not bridge. She doesn't need anyone holding her hand and walking her through it like she's a fucking idiot." I look directly into Beth's eyes, the veins in my forehead threatening to burst. "Do you?"

She flinches. Her chin trembles. A hand covers her mouth. Her cards hit the table seconds before she's pushing her chair back. "Excuse me," she whispers, leaving the kitchen in a hurry.

I reach out to stop her, but a sharp sting cracks against my shin. "Ow, fuck." I scowl at Tessa. "Did you just kick me?"

She shoves against my arm. "What is wrong with you?"

"Seriously, Reed," Mia snaps, looking over my shoulder.

"That was really rude. I think you hurt her feelings."

"Because I don't want CJ hanging all over her? Why the fuck is she even here?"

CJ stands from the table. "What is your problem, asshole?" He moves to follow after Beth.

Fuck that.

I get up in his face. "If anyone's going after her, it's going to be me. Sit the fuck back down and make sure everyone else knows what a trick is, since you're so willing to help."

"You know what, Reed? I've never had a problem with you, but right now, I'm real close to knocking your ass out."

Ben's at my back. "CJ, let him go after her. He's the one who needs to apologize."

"Nobody's knocking anyone out." Mia gets up from the table and pulls against CJ's arm. "I just mopped the floor this morning."

"I told you women this was a bad idea," Luke says from his seat at the table. He leans back and takes a swig of his beer, then frowns at Tessa. "You get off on his misery, babe. It's kinda fucked up."

Tessa waves him off. "I do not. I'm helping Reed. He just doesn't realize it yet."

Ben steps back and allows me to pass. I look over at Tessa. "You're helping me? How is this helping me?"

She says something behind my back as I exit the kitchen, but I don't hear it. It probably doesn't make sense anyway. Whatever the hell her and Mia were trying to achieve with this clusterfuck of an evening, I'll never understand.

I'm ready to punch a cop. Beth's hiding somewhere in the house.

I fucking hate game night.

Heading upstairs after checking the first floor, I notice

the light shining underneath the bathroom door at the end of the hallway. I knock on it gently.

"Beth?"

She sniffles, then clears her throat. "Hold on. I'll be out in a second."

Fuck. She's crying. I made her cry—again.

I take a step back and stare at the door, counting to five before my hand forms to the knob. Another five before I'm testing to see if it's locked. It isn't.

"Hey." I step into the bathroom and push the door shut behind me. Her head snaps up from her hands. "Beth, look I'm . . ."

The biggest dickhead on the planet.

Her eyes are glistening with tears, a few wetting her cheeks. She quickly stands from the stool she's sitting on and wipes at her face. "I'm so sorry I'm here. I had no idea you were coming tonight."

I move closer, shaking my head. "Stop. I didn't come in here to get an apology from you. You don't owe me one, okay? I'm the asshole. I'm the one who needs to make this better."

She stares up into my eyes. "Make what better?"

"Us."

"There's an us?"

"I think there *was* an us. Up until you left my house the other day crying, I think we were . . . something. Am I completely off here?"

Her nose wrinkles as she sniffs. She blinks up at me, looking at my mouth, my nose, above my eyes.

I wipe my hand across her cheek, brushing away a tear. "I'm really sorry I couldn't handle that shit downstairs. I've been jealous twice in my entire life and both times have been with you. It's confusing. I don't know how to deal with it. And the past couple days," I force my hand down when I realize it's traveled to her neck. "Fuck, Beth. The past couple days have been really fucking awful. Why didn't you call me back? Did you get my message?"

After a brief hesitation, she nods. "No, I did. I got it." She sniffs again. "I just didn't know what to say. It was really embarrassing when you didn't remember what happened between us. I feel like I took advantage of you."

I smirk.

She fights a smile, then shoves against my chest.

"Stop. It was, Reed. What did you expect me to do? Call you back and go over every detail of what we did?"

"That would've been awesome." I grab her waist and lift her so she's sitting on the edge of the sink. She gasps against my neck.

"What are you doing?"

"Cleaning you up. You have black stuff on your face." I cup her cheeks when she tries to look in the mirror behind her. She stares up at me, lips parting. "I got it. I made you cry. Let me do it."

She relaxes against my hands. "Okay."

Reaching behind her, I grab a few tissues out of the box on the sink. I wipe them along her skin. "And you wouldn't have to tell me every detail. I am remembering some of it."

"You are?"

Our eyes lock. Her breath suddenly blowing out faster against my hand.

Nodding, I move to her other cheek. "Yeah, but not a lot. It's fucking torture, if I'm being honest. I'll get little flashes of us together, and then, nothing. It's gone. Then I'm miserable, waiting for the next image to pop into my head. I hate that I've been with you and I can't just think about it whenever I want.

These little glimpses of what we did are killing me. I don't know how you felt around me, what you sounded like when I made you come with my cock." I tilt my head. "I'm assuming I made you come with my cock. Please confirm that."

Her cheek lifts against my hand. The slightest blush appears. "You did."

I turn and toss the tissues into the trashcan. My hand rubs harshly across my forehead. "I'm just waiting for the image to pop into my head of me eating your pussy. I think I'm miserable now, but seeing that is going to really fuck me up. Because I know I did it. There's no way in hell I didn't have my mouth all over you. And then I'm going to go around breaking shit when I can't remember what you tasted like."

Fucking Jim Beam. I'm never drinking that shit again.

Several seconds go by. I look over at Beth when she doesn't respond. Head tilted down, eyes on me, peeking through her lashes. Hands nervously fidgeting in her lap.

She wets her lips. My chest expands, and I move.

"I remember what one part of you tasted like," I say, cupping her cheek to lift her head. My thumb runs just below her mouth, tugging at her chin to part her lips. "I'd never forget it. So sweet and wet, and greedy. You have the greediest mouth. The way you suck on my tongue when you're coming from my fingers. Biting me. Trying to swallow me whole." I inch closer, slowly moving in. "Those dirty little noises you make against my lips. And your words to me when you're right there. More, faster, harder. God, I get so hard just from kissing you." Her hands fist my T-shirt. I close my eyes. "Beth."

"CJ asked me out."

My eyes flash open. Hers may have never closed.

"What?" I ask, leaning away, blinking her into focus.

What the hell did she just say?

She shakes her head, and my hand falls away. "I . . . he asked me out tonight, and I said yes. We're doing something next weekend." Her voice is timid. Nervous. Unsure.

Why? She agreed to him. She made her decision already.

I take a step back, needing the space. My hands tuck into my front pockets.

Fuck. What am I supposed to do with this?

Beth slides off the sink, her hands smoothing over the bottom of her dress. She steps closer. "I just didn't want to be up here kissing you when I told him . . ."

"No, I get it," I interrupt, halting her words and her movements. I lift my shoulders. "You want to go out with him, go out with him. What the hell does it have to do with me?"

Her lips pull down. "I don't know. Does it have anything to do with you?"

I stare at her.

Are we really playing this game?

"Beth, what do you want me to say? I just tried to kiss you, and you tell me you're going out with another guy."

Something soft hits the door. I turn my attention on it, then look back at Beth when nothing else happens. She's avoiding my eyes now like I hate, her bottom lip trapped between her teeth.

I open my mouth to ask her to look at me. "Are you feeling him?"

The wrong damn question comes out.

Jesus Christ. I don't want to know this. Unless the next words out of her mouth are "No, Reed. I'm feeling you. Now can we please go back to having sex all over this bathroom?" But if she says yes . . .

"He's nice," she answers quietly.

Nice? Well . . . fuck. What does that mean?

I let out an exhaustive sigh. "Look, you know I'm miserable. You know I hate that I can't remember what happened between us. I've told you all that. What else do you want?" The same noise from behind the door happens again. "What the hell?"

I look back at the door. Beth moves in my peripheral vision.

"Reed," she whispers.

The door bursts open, allowing a very sleepy Nolan into the bathroom. He's dancing around on his feet. Pinching his legs together, then crouching down a bit. I'm not a father, but I know that sign. We need to get out of here so he can do his business.

He takes one look at me and throws both hands into the air. "Uncle Weed!" His eyes widen in alarm, the smile vanishing from his face. Both hands fall to the front of his pajamas as his legs pinch together. "Uh oh." He scrunches up his face, then whispers, "Uh oh. I didn't make it."

Shit. Poor kid.

"Oh, no, buddy. It's okay." Beth moves to help Nolan. She bends down and rubs his back. Nolan leans against her and digs his knuckle into his sleepy eye.

I step past the two of them to get out of the bathroom. "Reed?"

I look back at Beth when I get out into the hallway. Her eyes are pleading me not to go, to finish this conversation with her. But what does she expect me to do? She said yes.

I jerk my chin down the hall. "I'll get Ben or Mia, and then I'm going to go."

Her hand stills on Nolan's back. "Oh," she says quietly. "Okay. Well, it was nice seeing you again."

My breath catches. The air in the hallway becomes too

thick to inhale.

Fuck. She's so damn sweet. Too sweet for her own good. How does she do it? How does she make me feel horrible when I'm only doing the right thing here? She said yes. She obviously wants to go out with CJ. Why does she care if I hang around tonight or not?

I stare back at the woman who I really don't want to leave, but need to leave. All long, dark hair, big eyes, the sweetest heart-shaped face. My eyes fall to her boots, and a weak smile tugs at my mouth. I look up at her and let her have it. Whatever. It's fucking hers anyway.

I run a hand through my hair. "Yeah, sweetheart. Yeah, you too."

I inform Ben what happened with Nolan, ignore CJ when he asks about Beth, tell everyone else at the table that Beth is fine and currently helping Nolan, and then walk out to my truck. If they asked me questions about what happened upstairs, I didn't hear them. I didn't hear anything, besides the voice in my head telling me to get the hell out of there.

I STEP THROUGH the door and take a quick sweep of the crowd.

The place is packed solid with women who barely look old enough to vote. Some are shaking their asses on the dance floor, grinding up against each other and loving the attention they're getting. Others are sitting at the booths lined along the walls, giggling and whispering together.

I follow their eyes to the back of the room.

Assholes with stupid looking Greek letters on their shirts are standing by the pool table, fighting over who's buying the next round. Frat guys.

Jesus fuck, it's college night. This is why I don't do this

shit during the week.

I run a rough hand down my face.

Well, pussy is pussy. Legal pussy is all I care about. And after the shit that happened last night with Beth, I fucking need this.

Stepping up to the bar, I take a seat next to three girls huddled together, all of them sipping on something non-alcoholic. No way in hell are any of them twenty-one.

I wave over the bartender. Thank fuck it's Mick and not Hattie.

"Give me a Coors, will ya? And another round for these three beauties."

The one next to me turns her head, her eyes raking down the front of me, slowly taking me in. She's hot enough. Blonde, short hair. Blue eyes. A smile that doesn't make me stupid as shit. In other words, exactly what I fucking need.

Mick hands me my beer and gives the girls refills.

I lean closer to the one brushing up against my arm, doing all she can to press her tits into me. "I'm Reed. What's your name, baby?"

Her eyes widen, she wets her lips nervously, biting and licking them like she can't decide what to do. Her hand falls to my thigh. "Kellie. Thanks for the drink."

"No problem. What brings you girls out tonight?"

I really don't need her to answer this question. The way her nails are clawing at my leg is giving away why she's really here, no matter what her next words are.

She sets her glass down and shifts on her stool. Her leg nudges between mine. "My boyfriend and I just broke up. My friends think I need to forget all about him. So I'm here."

"Lucky me." I grab my beer and take a long sip. "I'm looking to forget about someone too. We can help each other out with that."

"Girlfriend?" she asks, leaning closer, practically crawling into my lap. "Did she break up with you?"

No, but shit if it doesn't feel like she did.

"I just need a distraction."

Smiling, she takes a sip from her straw, then pushes her drink away. Her free hand brushes against my cock. "I can be very distracting. My ex used to say I had the best mouth at Ruxton U."

"Is that right?" I force myself to stay engaged. To seem interested. It's a fucking struggle.

She nods, licking the corner of her mouth, pressing firmly against my flaccid cock. "Yup. Wanna find out for yourself?"

Christ, just do it. You'll get into it once she starts.

I stand and Kellie takes the cue. Tossing two twenties onto the bar, I wrap my arm around her as needy hands tug at the bottom of my shirt, brushing against my lower abs. We get halfway to the exit before she pushes against me.

"Oh, wait! I forgot my purse."

She runs back over to the bar. I stand in the middle of the dance floor, watching Kellie lean in and whisper to her friends. I'm trying to keep my interest on this chick. Problem is, my cock isn't feeling it. I'm not feeling it.

Why the fuck am I here?

This isn't going to work. Kellie's not going to do anything for me. None of the women here would do anything for me. I turn to get the hell out of here and my eyes slam on the figure standing at the end of the bar.

Two plates in her hands. A fucking apron around her waist. Jimi Hendrix clinging to those perfect tits.

The only woman who would ever do something for me.

What the fuck? She's working here? And Hendrix? Why the

fuck is that sexy?

Our eyes lock, my heart joins my dick and reacts to her like I don't want it to, beating erratically against my sternum, making my chest ache. She's beautiful. Crazy, shining at me like a beacon, beautiful. Her hair pinned up off her neck. Her brown eyes lined with makeup, making them pop out even more at me. Those thick lips that still look swollen from our night together.

I want her. Fuck, I want her.

A hand pushes against my chest. Beth breaks eye contact, looking at something else. Or someone else.

I can't think straight. God, I'm so hard. So fucking hard because of Beth. Always because of Beth. I close my eyes.

"Stroke my dick. Ah, yeah, like that. Fuck, look how hard I am. Look what you do to me."

The night air hits me. My back presses against a wall. Something tugs at my belt as a burst of images fill my head.

Beth kneels between my legs, fists my cock, and swallows me whole like she's been starving for it.

"Fuck." My hands thread through her hair. *"Your mouth. Holy shit,"* I moan, lifting my hips off the mattress. *So good. So fucking good. "God, Beth. Ah, fuck, don't stop."*

A soft hand wrapping around my base snaps me into coherence. I look down at Kellie, on her knees outside the bar, hungry eyes staring up at me. The wrong color. Blue, instead of brown. Her lashes not as thick, not fluttering like they should be as her breathing quickens. She leans in to take me into her mouth.

"Fuck, stop." I push her hand off and tuck my cock back into my jeans. I can't do this. I don't want to do this.

Kellie lifts her head and glares up at me with wet lips. "What the hell?"

"This isn't working for me. No offense."

"Isn't working for you?" She sits back on her heels and gestures to my cock. "You're rock hard."

Yeah, and it has nothing to do with you.

"How is this not working for you?" Her mouth falls open, eyes widening. "Oh my God. Are you gay?"

I laugh, zipping up and tightening my belt. Offering her my hand, I help her to her feet. "You have no idea how easy my life would be right now if that were the case. Go back inside to your friends. This isn't going to happen."

She looks up at me, confused, then shrugs her shoulders before turning and walking away. "Your loss," she yells out, just before disappearing to the front of the building.

I palm my erection, rubbing my other hand down my face.

I should go in there. Talk to Beth, explain shit.

No, fuck, I need to get out of here. She said yes to CJ. What the fuck is there to explain?

I dig my keys out of my pocket, my other hand pulls out my phone. I send one message before I get the hell out of here. Why I send it? I have no fucking idea.

Me: Nothing happened.

beth

"HOW ARE YOU doing over there?"

I look up at Riley from across the small kitchen at Holy Cross. It takes a few seconds for my eyes to adjust, for the smile she's fighting to come into focus. "Huh?"

She laughs, setting the baking sheet of dinner rolls on top of the counter. "You've been stirring those instant potatoes for the past ten minutes, which would be fine if the burner was turned on."

"What?" I look down at the knob on the stove. *I never turned it on? Are you kidding me right now?* My hand clutching the spoon stills, my other forming over my eyes.

How am I doing? Not fucking good, apparently.

"Maybe I should switch with Wendy. I don't know how I could screw up refilling the napkin dispenser." I turn the burner on and continue stirring.

"Do you want to talk about it?"

"Talk about what?"

"Oh, I don't know. The current situation in the Middle East? Kanye West's unwavering affection for himself?" She lifts an eyebrow when I finally look up. "Obviously, whatever it is that has you spacing out over there. You can talk to me. My brother says I'm irritatingly perceptive when it comes to stuff."

Riley moves around the kitchen, grabbing the serving

trays and getting everything ready for the crowd we're expecting today.

Maybe I'll feel better talking to somebody about this. I debated on bringing it up to Mia when she called me over the weekend, but after making plans for another girl's lunch, she had to get off the phone. She was at a doctor's appointment and her name had been called. The more I think about it, the more I'm glad I haven't asked her opinion on this. She's friends with both Reed and CJ. I wouldn't want Mia to feel like I'm putting her in between the two of them. Same with Tessa. But Riley could give me an unbiased opinion. And I need an opinion. Bad.

I don't know what I'm supposed to do, what I'm supposed to be thinking, feeling. I've read that last text from Reed more times than I can count. The conversation we had in the bathroom has been playing on loop in my head. He's miserable. He wishes he could remember what happened between us. But he went out the next night and picked up another girl. What am I supposed to do with that?

Is he miserable? Or is his dick miserable?

I whip the potatoes vigorously. "There's this guy," I begin, and Riley is in front of me in seconds.

"I knew it. It's always a guy." She grabs a stool and sits next to the stove. "Go on," she encourages, pushing her glasses back on her nose.

"Well, there's technically two guys."

"Fighting over you? I'm not hearing a problem yet."

I turn off the burner when the potato flakes begin to boil. Laying the spoon down on the counter, I grab the nearest stool and sit down next to Riley. My shoulders roll forward as my elbows hit my legs.

"They're not really fighting over me. I really, really like

the one guy. He's sweet and he's funny. When we were together, it was . . . it was everything." I look down into my lap, remembering what it was like, how easy it was with Reed. "I've never felt like that before with anyone, but now we're not spending any time together. He says he's miserable, but it's not like he's asking me out like the other guy, who seems really nice."

"Are you feeling him?"

Reed's question burns in my ears. He looked conflicted asking it. I felt sick answering him.

"Why aren't you spending time with the first one anymore?" Riley asks. "Did you break up?"

I shake my head, keeping it turned down. "We were never really a couple."

But we were something. Reed said we were something.

God, why didn't I ask him what he meant by that? It's like I turned into a speechless moron when he stepped into that bathroom.

"Ah, yeah, I've had relationships like that. No labels or whatever. So the other guy asked you out, but you're still thinking about the first one. Right?"

I nod.

"If the first one is miserable, why isn't he making a move?"

"He is, just not with me." I look up when Riley groans. "I saw him the other night leaving my work with some other girl."

She crosses her one leg over the other, crosses her arms over her chest, and scowls. "Oh, really? Did he see you?"

"Yes."

"And he still left with her?"

"Yes."

"Ass. I'm no longer team first guy."

My stomach drops at the memory of Reed with that girl.

Her hand on his chest. How he kept his eyes on me while she maneuvered him outside. I couldn't look anywhere else. I was paralyzed, my eyes glued to Reed, my feet glued to the floor. Shaking so badly I nearly dropped the plates I was carrying.

I clear my head and focus on Riley. "They left together, then not even five minutes later I got a text from him saying nothing happened. But why? Why would he text me that? Did he feel guilty because I saw him? Would something have happened with her if I wasn't working that night?"

"Mm." Riley wraps some hair that's fallen from her pony around her finger. She thinks silently for a moment. "Do you really think nothing happened?"

"He wasn't lying. I know he wasn't." I pinch my legs together before my body answers that question for me. "Even if it had been a whole five minutes, Reed lasts a lot longer than that."

Riley makes a noise between a strangled groan, and a choke. "Reed?" Her eyes widen, she leans closer. "As in Reed Tennyson?"

"Yes." I lean back to reclaim some of my personal space. "Why?"

"That's my brother!" she screams, jumping off her stool.

Wait, what? WHAT?

I stand so quickly the room starts to spin. My one hand flattens on the stool, my other presses against the side of my head. "I . . . are you sure?"

Her brother?

Reed is her brother?

Oh my God. I just told her he lasts longer than five minutes.

I cover my face with my hands, groaning, wishing the world would just swallow me up already.

Riley wraps her hand around my arm and shakes me. I

peek at her through my fingers.

"Yes, I'm sure! Beth! You slept with Reed? You really, really like him? Oh my God!" She sucks in a loud, startled breath, releasing her hold on me. Her nostrils flare. "I can't believe that idiot picked up another chick in front of you. I'm calling him."

I grab her wrist as she reaches into her pocket. "No! Please don't. Riley, don't say anything to him about this. I'm embarrassed enough as it is."

She must see my panic. God knows I hear it in my voice.

Looking down at her arm, Riley slowly pulls her hand out of her pocket, empty. She picks up her stool and carries it back over to the counter. "Okay, I won't say anything," she says over her shoulder. "Who's the other guy? Maybe he's my cousin."

"Haha." I slide my stool back underneath the counter. *Christ, how small is this town?* "His name is CJ. I don't know his last name, but he's a cop."

"Ohhh." Our eyes meet, and she smiles playfully. "I know who he is. I've never met him, but I've seen him with Ben Kelly and Luke Evans. The three of them together are like, almost too hot to look at."

I think back to my lunch date with the girls. The guys in their uniforms. How I contemplated committing a felony for the first time in my life.

"Mm mmm," I agree, letting my hair untuck behind my ear to hide my blush.

Riley leans her hip against the serving table. "So, you were hanging out with my brother, now you're not, for whatever reason. CJ asked you out, and now Reed is miserable? Did I get it right?"

I grab the pot of mashed potatoes and carry it over to the serving table. Riley moves down to allow me some room.

"Pretty much." I look into her eyes, the same strange, pale-blue color as Reed's.

Way to miss that gigantic clue, Beth.

"It's not that I don't want to go out with CJ. I wouldn't have said yes if I didn't. But hearing Reed say he wishes . . . certain things, I don't know. I just feel like we're nothing right now, and I don't want to be nothing with Reed. I miss talking to him. I miss hanging out with him."

"It sounds like he misses you too."

I give her a weak smile, letting my arms fall to my sides. "But in what way? What was I to him? He told me we were something. What? Friends? More than that?"

Riley lifts her shoulders, then grabs a few empty serving trays from the shelf below the table.

"If my brother is jealous because you're going out with another guy, which it definitely sounds like he is, I'd say you were in the more-than-that category. But," she pauses with a cautious look. "This is my brother we're talking about, and he doesn't get jealous, or miserable, or anything else over women anymore, so, I don't know. The last woman I ever saw him feel anything for was his stupid ex, and that was nine years ago."

"Yeah, I know. I met her."

She drops the trays on the table and whips her head around. "You met Molly? How? Was Reed with you? Oh my God, he saw her and didn't tell me?"

"Whoa." I hold my hands out in front of me. "Yes, to all of those questions, I think. I'm assuming he didn't tell you."

She gently rolls her eyes. "Unbelievable."

"That's kind of how we started hanging out. I roped the two of us into attending her engagement party last weekend." I swallow hard when she slowly looks at me. "As a couple," I meekly add.

"As a couple?" she questions, her voice reaching a higher pitch. "Reed did the whole boyfriend-girlfriend thing with you?"

I almost take offense to that, until I remember Reed telling me he hasn't kissed anyone in nine years. I'm going to assume he hasn't been a boyfriend in that long either.

Jesus. That witch was his last girlfriend?

I stare into Riley's eyes. "Yes. He did the whole boyfriend-girlfriend thing."

She huffs, dropping her shoulders. "You think you know somebody." Riley shakes her head as her hands curl into fists. "I want to call him so bad right now." She holds a finger up in front of my face, halting my protest. "But I won't. I'll pretend I know nothing about this."

"Thank you."

She grabs the serving trays off the table. "I don't know, Beth, really. Like I said, Reed doesn't get jealous, but he also doesn't usually pretend to be someone's boyfriend so he can spend a night with his ex. I might be just as confused about this now as you are."

She walks away, carrying the trays over to the baking sheet of dinner rolls.

My head feels heavier now, putting strain on the muscles in my neck. It's not even noon and I feel like I could lie down and sleep for days. Maybe Reed isn't jealous, or miserable.

Maybe I've imagined everything.

His words to me in the bathroom, his hand on my neck, his urgent breath against my skin.

"CJ asked me out."

I've never hated the sound of my own voice before, until that moment.

"You want my advice?" Riley calls out, moving around

the kitchen.

I lean back against the wall, nodding when she looks over at me.

She carries over two trays of rolls. "Go out with CJ. If Reed doesn't like it, make him do something about it."

Wendy walks through the doorway and grabs an apron off the wall. "Five minutes until the doors open. Are we ready back here?"

Riley looks at me. I take in a deep breath.

Make him do something about it.

She's right. It's Reed's turn to grab my face and kiss me without giving me a choice in it. It's his turn to reach for my hand, to touch me first. He's miserable? He's jealous? Let me see it. The only thing he's shown me is how easily he can be dragged out of my work.

I reach for two aprons, tossing one to Riley. "We're ready."

I STARE BACK and forth between the two objects tempting me. My gaze lingers on the one, my cell phone.

Don't even think about it.

Forcing my eyes to the left, I size up the plate of freshly baked chocolate chip cookies I've just slaved over for tomorrow.

Nope. You're wasting your time looking.

Back to the phone. I rest both elbows on the counter, leaning my chin on my fists, a heavy sigh rolling past my tongue.

I miss him. So sue me. Sending Reed a simple 'how is your day' text isn't the same thing as forcing him to kiss me. Right?

It's close.

Grunting, I flick my gaze back to the cookies.

Still warm. The perfect golden brown color, with the tiny chocolate morsels instead of the regular sized ones. I only made a dozen. I alone can eat all twelve of these bad boys, which is why I shouldn't eat one right now. One will become seven, seven will lead to me grabbing my car keys and heading back to the store. But then, there's the other temptation in the room. If I'm going to cave and reach for something, shouldn't it be the cookies?

My eyes sweep the counter. I think back to the last text from Reed. The one I never responded to. Is he waiting for me to write back? Is that why he hasn't sent me anything else?

The hardest decision I've faced in a long time just became incredibly simple.

One hand reaches for a cookie, the other grabs my phone. I round the counter and head for the couch, taking a bite of the cookie and unlocking the screen.

Technically, I'm not sending him a regular text. I'm sending him a reply to a text. That is completely different than putting myself out there with an unprovoked message. I'm reacting. Nothing more.

Me: Ok.

There. A simple response. The whatever is in his court now. Ball, or something.

I set the phone down in my lap and take another bite. The chocolate melts against the heat of my mouth, coating my tongue. I lick a tiny bit off my thumb as my phone beeps.

Reed: What's ok?

What's ok? Did he not . . .

I scroll back to his last message. Yup. That was definitely the last thing he sent me.

Me: You said nothing happened. I'm saying ok.

Reed: What the hell, Beth? I sent that 6 days ago. You couldn't text me back sooner?

I read his message twice.

Couldn't text him back sooner?

Really? He's mad about this? Maybe I took 6 days because I was still in shock from what I saw. Maybe I didn't have anything to respond to. It's not like he asked me a question. I don't remember reading 'Did you see that just now?' or 'Any chance you missed that chick dragging me outside?'

I shove the rest of the cookie in my mouth, typing my response. His text comes in before I can finish.

Reed: I'm sorry you saw that.

Holding down the back-arrow, I erase the message I was nearly finished typing.

Okay. This isn't what I miss. I've never felt awkward doing anything with Reed, but if we stay on this topic, I know that's what I'm going to feel. I don't want to think about that night anymore. I've already allowed my mind to run rampant with images of what he did with that woman before he was dragged out of the bar. I know how Reed flirts, and I'm grateful I didn't see it. But that hasn't stopped me from thinking about it.

Constantly thinking about it.

Time for a subject change.

Me: What are you doing right now?

I drop my head back onto the couch after I press send.

Shit. Maybe he doesn't want to talk about anything else. Maybe now that he's made sure I know how regretful he is, there's no other reason to keep this conversation going.

I should've grabbed the entire plate of cookies.

My phone beeps.

Reed: Having a great day constructing.

I smile against my hand. That, right there, that's what I miss. Reed being exactly how he's always been with me. Making me smile when I'm two seconds away from crawling underneath something and hiding out until winter. Easy. Playful. This is the Reed I want. The one who brings out the happiest version of myself.

Me: Didn't I ask you to erase that entire message off your phone?

Reed: No. You asked me to forget you said you don't get dick very often. I didn't, btw.

Me: Awesome! I'm so happy to hear you still have that conversation. That wasn't embarrassing for me or anything.

Reed: It's safe with me. Only I know how deprived you are of dick.

I set the phone down and grab a glass of milk out of the fridge. Deprived of dick? Hardly. Reed made sure of that. *Oh, no. Don't go there right now.*

My ringtone sounds from the couch. After grabbing another cookie and carrying it across the room with my glass, I set it down on the coffee table and pick up my phone.

"Yesss?" I answer, playfully stretching out the word.

"You didn't respond."

His voice is tight. Was he worried I wouldn't?

I dunk my cookie into the milk. "I was getting a drink." I take a bite. "For my cookie. Did you think I was going to make you wait another six days?"

His dry laugh fills my ear. "The thought crossed my mind.

What are you doing?"

"Eating cookies."

"Besides that."

"Nothing." I lean back onto the couch, tucking my feet under my butt. "Are you on break?"

I hear a door close. "Not really. I feel like I fucking need one though. If my sister's asshole boyfriend doesn't stop screwing shit up, I might have to fake an illness and go home. He's getting on my last fucking nerve."

Riley. I completely forgot about that awkward discovery yesterday.

"Even if it had been a whole five minutes, Reed lasts a lot longer than that."

Jesus Christ. Thank God that's all I said.

"Have you talked to her lately?" I ask.

"Who?"

"Your sister. Did she tell you we know each other?"

There is a long pause, then finally, "Uh, no. How do you know Riley?"

Leaning forward, I dunk the other half of the cookie into the milk, then pop the rest of it in my mouth, chewing before saying, "We volunteer together at Holy Cross Soup Kitchen. She's really sweet. I like her."

"You volunteer at the soup kitchen?"

"Yes."

"Why?"

"Because I used to be homeless."

An even longer pause settles between us this time. I shift uncomfortably on the couch, untucking my legs and pulling my knees against my chest. His breath quickens in my ear.

"Are you fucking kidding me? You were homeless?"

"I wouldn't joke about something like that."

"What the fuck, Beth?" he growls, startling me.

I rub the part of my shin I've just dug my nails into. "Jeez, calm down."

"Calm down? Why the hell don't I know about this?"

I wipe my hand off on my shorts and fall back onto the couch, feet at one end, head at the other. "Um, I don't know. I guess it never came up."

And it's not something I usually like to talk about.

He draws out his next breath. "When?" he curtly demands.

I pick at my lip.

"When, Beth?" He sounds pressing, maybe even a little urgent.

Because I didn't tell him? Because he doesn't like the idea of me going through that?

Pinching my eyes shut, I think of how different things would've been if I lived here when my momma died. Maybe I never would've been homeless. Or if I was, maybe it would've been Reed who came up to my window that day, offering me food and some company.

What would he have thought of me?

"Beth," Reed says gently, losing the edge in his voice. "When?"

I stare up at the ceiling. "Right after my momma died. It wasn't for very long."

"And then you found out about your aunt and moved here?"

"No." The bottom of my shirt becomes bunched in my fist. "No, I was living with someone when I found out about my aunt."

Please don't ask me anymore. I don't want to talk about . . .

"Who?"

Shit.

"Nobody. Just this guy I met. It doesn't matter. Look, I'm volunteering because I want to. It's nice to do things for other people. You should try it sometime." I sit up slowly as my heart pounds against my ribs. *Wow. Way to freak out a little.* "I'm sorry. That sounded really bitchy."

"I'm just wondering why you didn't tell me this before. I thought we were getting to know each other."

"We were." I swallow, my voice quieting when I continue. "We are. I just don't like to talk about it. I'm here now. I'm not living in my car anymore. That's all that matters."

What would Reed think of me if he knew I lived with a man who told me daily how worthless I was? Who got off on it? I can't risk him losing respect for me. Living with Rocco was about survival. Doing what I had to do. Not in the beginning, but that's what it became a few weeks after I moved in. But Reed might not understand that. I doubt most people would.

It's hard to imagine how bad things can be when you've never had everything taken away from you.

Reed sighs just as my phone beeps with an incoming call. Mia's name flashes on my screen.

I place the phone back to my ear. "Um, hey, I gotta go. Mia's calling me."

"All right, yeah, I need to get back to work anyway."

"Okay." I suck on my bottom lip. "I guess I'll talk to you later."

"Beth?"

"Mm?"

Another pause has my back rigid against the couch.

God, I hate that I can't see his face through his silence. Is he mad right now? Disappointed that we're having to get off the phone?

These stupid pauses are going to give me a heart attack.

"Nothing," he murmurs. "Forget it. I'll talk to you later."

The call ends. I click over to answer Mia before my head has time to fill with a thousand more questions.

"Hey, how are you?"

A quiet sniffle comes through the phone, and I'm once again stiffening against the cushions.

"Mia?"

"Beth, can you do me a favor?" she asks through a timid voice.

"Are you okay?"

I'm on my feet, carrying my glass over to the sink in case this favor involves leaving.

"No." Her voice breaks with a whimper. "No, that's why I'm calling."

reed

"NOTHING."

Fuck. She has to go. Hang up before you start sounding like a desperate little bitch.

My free hand wraps around the door handle. "Forget it. I'll talk to you later."

Ending the call, I hop out of my truck and tuck my phone back into the front pocket of my safety vest. My back hits the door as I run a rough hand down my face.

Jesus. What the fuck is wrong with me? Beth tells me she used to be homeless, and I act like a fucking psycho and yell at her for not mentioning this to me before? Yeah, I calmed down, but initially . . . shit, I fucking yelled at her. I was frustrated, angry, confused as hell for feeling frustrated and angry. I don't know why. I know how this woman gets to me. I know she's going to make me feel things I don't understand. But it didn't matter. The second those words came out of her mouth, I lost it. The thought of Beth living on the streets had me seconds away from smashing out every window of my goddamn truck. Someone could've grabbed her, could've put their fucking hands on her. Then I got jealous of every other person she's told about this before me. I can't handle not knowing everything about this woman. The good, the bad, the fucking ugly shit she gets quiet about. I want all of it, and I want her to feel like she can give it to me.

I'm sure I've made her feel real comfortable about sharing personal shit with me now.

My phone rings in my vest. Pushing off from the truck, I reach for it as I walk back over to the job site. Mia's name flashes on the screen.

"Hey."

She takes in a shuddering breath. "I know you're working, Reed, but is there any way you can come over? Like right now? Please?"

My footsteps abruptly cut short, kicking up dust out of the gravel. *She's crying. Why is she crying?* "Mia, what's going on?"

"It's Ben," she answers through a whimper. "I don't know what to do. I don't . . ."

"Fuck! Was he shot? I'm at St. Joseph's now. Are they bringing him here?" I start off running toward the entrance to the hospital.

Shit! Motherfucking shit! The boys. Mia. This can't be happening.

"No, no Reed. He's home. I said I need you to come here."

"Oh." I skid on the gravel. "Mia, what . . ."

"Reed!" Tessa yells into the phone.

"Jesus Christ." I rub my ear with my free hand, then raise the phone back up, keeping it at a safe distance from Tessa's mouth.

Why is she yelling at me?

"Get over here! My brother needs you. Mia needs you. Stop asking a million fucking questions and move!"

The call disconnects. I stare at the screen. *What the hell could be going on?*

"Weston!" I yell out to one of my laborers as I take off running back to my truck.

He looks up at me. "Yeah, boss?"

"I need to go. Go find Connor and tell him he can reach me on my cell. And call the shop and let my dad know I'm leaving the site."

He nods and gives me a thumbs up.

My heart is pounding by the time I settle against the leather seat. I strip off my vest, throwing it and my hard hat into the back. Tires spinning, I peel out on the gravel and take off toward the gate. My mind tries to work out possible scenarios, all of them scary as fuck.

The kids could've gotten hurt. I could've left one of my tools out from working on the deck and Nolan could've grabbed it. He's obsessed with watching me. Maybe he was trying to copy what I was doing or something.

My breathing becomes heavier. I tug at the collar on my T-shirt, loosening the choke-hold the material suddenly has on my neck.

Chase.

Fuck, what if Mia had him up on the deck and he got too close to the railings. He's so small. Could he fit through the slats? Did I even secure the railings this past weekend? I told Mia she could walk out on the deck, but fuck! I'll never forgive myself if that shit wasn't one hundred percent safe.

Wait, no, they'd be on their way to St. Joseph's if something happened to one of the kids. That can't be it. So, what the fuck? What would make Mia that upset, or Ben? What the hell is going on?

My fist connects with the steering wheel. This is why I was asking a million fucking questions, Tessa!

I weave in and out of traffic, running two red lights to get to the house as quick as possible. A patrol car is in the driveway, Tessa's Rav4, and another car I recognize as Beth's. I stop beside it after jumping down from my truck.

It's small, a two door beater looking Chevy, with paint chipping everywhere and rust spots covering the roof. Bending down, I look into the backseat. Some blankets, a few T-shirts, and some shit that looks like trash cover the seat and the floor. My neck muscles twitch.

She lived in this.

I straighten up, fingers pinching the top of my nose, chest heaving against my shirt. I can't think about this shit right now. I can't think about her being alone, how scared she might've been. Not with whatever the hell is going on inside.

"Hello?" Pushing the door open, I listen for voices as I look around the entryway. "Mia?"

Nolan comes running down the hallway, holding his stuffed dragon above his head. "Uncle Weed!" He jumps up and down in front of me, the biggest smile lighting up his face. "Arwe we worwking on the deck today? I'll go get my tools!"

I pick Nolan up, squeezing him gently against my chest. *He's okay. I'm sure Chase is okay too.* "No, little man. Not today. Where's your mommy?"

He points in the direction of the kitchen. "She's weally sad. She keeps crwying."

Carrying him with me, I continue down the hallway as he walks his dragon across my shoulder. "It'll be okay," I tell him, seeking comfort in my own words.

Mia, Beth, and Tessa are sitting in the small room just off the kitchen, huddled together on the couch, the two girls on either side of Mia. I watch the three of them slowly lift their heads when I step into view. Mia's face is wet with tears, while Tessa and Beth look like they're trying to keep themselves from breaking down.

I put Nolan on his feet, my chest tightening, every muscle in my body flexed. "Go play, Nolan. I'm going to talk to your mommy for a minute." He runs back down the hallway and I step further into the room. "What the hell is going on?"

Mia stands from the couch. "Thank you so much for coming over. I hope it wasn't a problem leaving work."

"No, it wasn't, but would you please tell me why you three look like that? I'm starting to freak out."

She wipes her fingers across her cheeks, then pushes her dark hair back out of her face. "I found a lump in my breast last week when I was feeding Chase. I went to the doctors and had an ultrasound, and he suggested I get it biopsied because of my family history." She pauses, pinching her lips together.

Beth and Tessa both stand, flanking Mia's side in support, offering her comfort by each of them grabbing a hand.

I stare into Mia's eyes, my stomach twisting, my chest burning. Thoughts of Mia's mom dying from breast cancer two years ago flood my mind with panic.

"Did you?" I ask.

Mia nods. "A few days ago. We didn't tell you guys because we didn't want you to worry if it was nothing. We were supposed to get the results yesterday, but nobody called. Then we woke to a message really early this morning from someone at the office. They said my results were in, and for me to call back, but I can't reach anybody. I've been calling them all day, and it just sends me to voicemail. It could be nothing, it could still be nothing, but I can't get an answer." Her chin trembles.

She pulls free from the girls and steps closer to me.

"Reed, Ben's losing it. He seemed okay yesterday, but he was so angry we missed that call this morning. And then he blew up when they didn't just tell us the results in the message. I told him they can't legally do that, but he won't listen to me. His mind is made up that something's wrong. I can't calm him down, I can't talk to him. I told Luke to take him outside because I was afraid he would start scaring Nolan. I've never seen him like this. I don't know what to do. You know how he is with me."

I reach up, gripping my neck with both hands.

Shit, the whole fucking state knows how Ben is with Mia. He'd kill for her. He threatened to put my ass in the ground several times when I first met her and he thought I was making a play. I've never met anyone that insane over someone before, and it's been like that since the beginning for Ben. If he lost her, I don't know that he'd ever recover from that.

Shit, I don't know if any of us would.

I wrap my arms around Mia, pulling her against my chest. Her tears wet my shirt.

"I'm sure it's nothing. I'm sure the doctor is just busy right now. And I think it's good that they want to give you the results over the phone. If it was bad news, wouldn't they want you to come into the office to discuss it?"

"I don't know. I don't know how my mom got her results."

My stomach sinks. I grip Mia tighter.

"I'm so scared, Reed. What would happen to Ben? And the boys, I can't," she sniffs, her body shaking. "I can't leave them."

My eyes connect with Beth's over the top of Mia's head. She blinks, sending tears down her face as her lips try and give me that sweet smile of hers. They barely lift before she turns away to hide her emotions. Tessa's face is buried in her hands.

Fuck. This can't be happening. Not Mia. Not our Mia.

I press my mouth into Mia's hair. "Nothing's going to happen to you. Ben's going to be fine, those boys are going to be fine because *nothing* is taking you away from them. You're strong, Mia. You need to stay strong right now, okay?"

Her head moves against my chest. Another whimper is muffled.

"I'm going to go outside and try and talk to Ben. Promise

me you'll stop thinking the worst."

She leans back, dropping her arms from around my waist. "I promise." Squeezing my hand, she looks up into my eyes. "Thank you for coming over."

"Damn it, Mia. Stop thanking me. You know I'd do anything for you."

Her lips quiver into a weak smile. Letting go of me, she turns and starts rubbing her hand down Tessa's back, whispering words to her I can't make out. Only Mia would think to comfort other people right now when she's barely keeping herself together. Sometimes I think she's too good for all of us.

I'm almost out the front door when footsteps quicken on the hardwood behind me.

"Reed, wait a second."

Turning my head, my gaze falls on Beth. Her eyes are still threatening tears.

"Yeah?"

She slowly moves toward me, studying my face with rapt attention. "Are you okay?"

Letting out a deep breath, I lift my shoulders, barely raising them. "I don't know. I'm trying to be. It's Mia, though, you know? This is fucking scary."

"I know it is." Reaching her hand out, she wraps it around my forearm and applies the lightest pressure. "You two are really close, huh?"

I look down as her thumb begins moving along my skin. "Yeah. Well, we all are. Everybody loves Mia."

"You were so sweet with her in there. I think you really helped her."

"You're helping her too." I swallow, looking into those big, dark eyes. "It's really nice that you're here for her. I know that means a lot to Mia."

Beth's mouth twitches. "I was really shocked that she wanted me here. I just met you guys. I'm not used to people taking to me so fast."

"Who wouldn't take to you?"

Her hand flinches against my arm, squeezing me, as those perfect lips slowly part. Air rushes into her lungs, her face washes over with color. She's isn't hiding her reaction to me, and for the first time since I met her, I wish she was. This is not what I need to be doing right now. Brushing my hand along her cheek, allowing the heat of her blush to warm my fingers isn't what Mia asked me over here for. I can't see that I still do this to Beth. Not right now.

My hand falls away from her face when she begins to lean into it. "I gotta go outside. See what's going on with Ben."

She wets her lips, looking over my shoulder briefly. "Okay."

Stepping back, I open the door and head outside before all the blood in my veins reaches my cock. It's fucked up, but it's Beth. I'm beginning to realize it doesn't matter where, when, or what the fuck is going on around us. I can't turn it off with her. Hell, I'm not sure I want to.

I walk down the side of the house, unsure of what I'm about to get myself into. I know what's going through my head right now. I can't imagine amplifying that to the extreme the way Ben does with everything involving Mia. He can't control shit when it comes to her. I've seen him pissed off plenty of times. That's threatening enough. But angry and upset?

Luke comes into view first. Standing at the back of the property, he's facing the wooded area that separates Ben's house from the one behind him. I hurry across the yard as a loud cracking sound breaks through the air, then two more, quickening my pace. It's coming from the woods. Luke turns his head when I'm almost at his side.

Arms crossed over his chest, he acknowledges me with a quick jerk of his head. "Sorry, man. He needs to break shit right now, and it was either this or Nolan's swing set."

I stop beside him and look between two trees.

Ben has a stack of 2x4s I brought over for the deck scattered on the ground. Some are split in two already. He drops the splintered piece in his hand and swaps it out for another, mumbling curses under his breath.

"You try talking to him?" I ask, watching Ben take the piece of lumber and strike it repeatedly against a thick tree trunk. Tiny shards of wood break off with each blow.

Luke looks over at me, the one side of his mouth split open. I stare at the dried blood sticking to the wound.

"Yeah, I tried talking to him. He doesn't want to talk. He wants to do this. If you think you can calm him down without taking a fucking punch, go for it."

"Shit." I rub my hand along my chin. *He hit Luke?* "If he starts whaling on me, pull him off, all right?"

"Yeah, sure. No problem."

Ignoring the sarcastic undertone in Luke's response, I walk through the trees and come up to the pile of wood behind Ben.

If it wasn't for Mia, I'd still be standing next to Luke, keeping my fucking distance. I'd rather not bleed out in my best friend's backyard. But Mia's scared. She called me over here because she's worried about Ben. I need to at least try and talk to him.

Ben swings the wood across his body and it breaks against the trunk. He turns around, scowling when he notices me, tossing the wood at my feet.

"Shut the fuck up, Reed."

"I didn't say anything yet."

"Yet," he grumbles, picking up another 2x4 and pointing it at my chest. "I won't have a problem busting your mouth open either, so don't fucking test me. There's nothing to talk about."

I hold both hands out, palms facing him. "You don't know anything yet, Ben. Mia could still be fine. All of this you're doing is just making shit worse for her."

He drops the wood. "What the fuck did you just say?"

I take a step back when he moves forward, keeping space between us. "She's scared. You're fucking scaring her, man, and I know you don't mean it. This shit can't be easy on you. I'd be going crazy if I didn't have any answers yet. But think about Mia. Think about . . ."

"Think about Mia?" he yells, clenching his teeth, moving closer with quick strides. "What the fuck do you think I'm doing, asshole? I'm always thinking about her! She's all I fucking think about!"

He backs me into a tree, fists my shirt with both hands. Every vein in his neck is threatening to burst. His face is boiling, sweat beading beneath his hair line. Nostrils flaring, he looks ready to eat me alive as he gets nose to nose with me.

"Don't ever fucking tell me to think about my wife! You hear me?"

I nod.

"Fucking say it!"

"Ben, ease up." Luke's voice comes from my right. It's close so I know he's moved into the woods.

I hold my hand out, keeping Luke back, my eyes staying glued to Ben's.

"I hear you, man. But are you hearing me? Mia's fucking scared. She called us all over here but she doesn't need any of us. She needs you. And what the fuck are you doing?"

Ben visibly shakes as he takes in a breath. "My entire world is about to be ripped from me."

"You don't know that."

"No?" he challenges. "What the fuck do you know, Reed? Can you tell me my wife is going to be okay? Can you tell me I'm not going to lose her?" Tears well up in his eyes. "I can't fight this. Do you understand that? There's nothing I can do if this shit decides to take her. And what about my boys? How the fuck am I going to explain this to them? You tell me how." He releases me, taking a step back, staring me down for an answer.

I keep my back flat against the tree, letting my hand fall to my side. "I don't know. I don't want to think about that."

"Yeah, well, I have to fucking think about it. I'm going to have to tell my sons their mother is dying."

"Stop saying that! Jesus fuck!" Luke yells, pointing at Ben. "You don't know shit right now! Your woman is in there bawling her eyes out, needing you, and you're out here coming up with the worst possible scenario in that thick as shit skull of yours! Man the fuck up and go to her!"

Ben whips his head around and charges at Luke, getting up in his face, snarling like a caged animal. "Man the fuck up? Who the fuck are you to say that to me? Weren't you the sorry ass motherfucker bailing on my sister last year because you couldn't fucking handle how you felt about her? And you're telling me to man up?"

"I came back!"

"Yeah, after I called you, dickhead. And now look at you. You're still fucking scared to make that shit permanent. If anyone needs to man the fuck up, it's you two idiots." Ben glares in my direction.

"What the fuck did I do?" I ask, moving away from the tree.

Luke pushes against Ben's chest. "Shut the fuck up! When I ask Tessa to marry me is none of your fucking business!"

Ben snorts. "Right. Well, until you do, you ain't got shit to say to me about this." He looks at me. "Neither do you. Are you just going to stand there and do nothing while CJ takes out your girl?"

I grit my teeth. "Leave her out of this."

His jaw ticks with a smile. "Did I hit a nerve, Reed?" He moves closer, tilting his head, that fucking grin stretching across his face. "What are you going to do about it? Huh? Are you going to let him move in on that pussy you're strung-out on? Does she even know how pathetic you are over her yet?"

"Ben," Luke warns. My hands curl into fists.

I help him eliminate the space between us. "I'm pretty sure she's figuring it out. What's your point?"

His smile fades, a distraught frown replacing it as he looks between Luke and myself. His shoulders drop.

"My point is that until you two assholes wise the fuck up and lock down your women for life, neither one of you will know what this shit feels like. I could get a phone call any second telling me Mia, *my Mia* is going to die. I can't fucking handle that. I can't think of my life without her in it, because I don't fucking have one. What am I supposed to do if something happens to her? You're both telling me to go inside and be there for her, and I can't. I can't let her see me like this. I'm supposed to be strong and I'm fucking terrified. I won't let her worry about me when she's the one . . ." Pausing, he wipes at his eyes, then rubs his hand over his face. His head stays tilted down as Luke and I exchange worried looks.

"I have to think that this is it," Ben says, the pain strangling his voice, making it sound like he's been swallowing broken glass. "I have to start thinking she won't be here with me. If I let myself believe anything else, and someone tells me I have to say goodbye to her . . . I told her I would never do that, two years ago after I got shot, I promised her, but I always knew something could happen to me. It's the fucking job. But her being taken from me, leaving my boys without their mom, I've thought about how she would go on without me, but I never thought I'd be the one trying to figure this shit out. I can't do it. If she dies, I die."

A soft gasp cuts through the air.

Everyone's attention is drawn to Mia.

Standing at the tree line, she stares directly at Ben with a hand to her mouth. Her pain is silent, no cries, no whimpers, while Ben just announced his unintentionally in front of her. She heard him say he can't do it. If she dies, he dies. Stuff she doesn't need to be hearing right now.

"Mia," Ben chokes out, but doesn't go to her. Doesn't move an inch.

Paralyzed by his own suffering, he stays glued to the ground as his breathing becomes violent, as the air between the two of them begins to pulsate with his agony. She must see it, his devastation, crippling him and keeping him captive. It strips the discomfort from her eyes.

Slowly lowering her hand, she nods, as if to say she understands, or it's okay, or I love you, then stares at Ben for another long second before turning and walking back to the house.

Ben drops his head, pinching his eyes shut through a groan.

I realize now there's not a fucking thing I can say to help him get through this. Not after that.

He turns and picks up another 2x4. I press my back against the nearest tree, slide to the ground, and rest my forearms on my knees. My head falls back as Ben strikes the trunk. Luke mimics my position a few feet away. Wood splinters in the air.

Another 2x4 is broken, then another. Time passes as the pile of fragmented wood stacks high off the ground. I retrieve more lumber when Ben needs it, but doesn't ask. Above the house, the sky burns in oranges and reds as the sun moves closer to the earth. Tessa walks down to the tree line at one point and asks if we need anything. Ben answers for the group.

"Go back inside, and don't come down here again unless you have news for me."

Luke glares at Ben, knuckles white, but doesn't say shit to him about upsetting Tessa. Just cracks his neck from side to side and resumes looking at the dirt.

Another ten boards are broken before I close my eyes.

I try to think about anything that'll take my mind off this horrible fucking mess, but nothing settles me. Nothing fills my head but images of Nolan and Chase missing their mom, crying over her, getting older and wondering where she is. Or Ben, a ghost of the man he is now, never getting over it, never accepting that she isn't still here with us. He's preparing himself for the worst, and fuck, maybe I should be to. What if this is it? What if Mia dies and we all lose her? What the fuck then?

"Ben."

Mia's voice snaps my eyes open, grabbing all of our attention so fast, it's as if she's shaking each one of us with it. The three women are standing at the edge of the yard where the tree line begins, Tessa and Beth flanking Mia's side.

I get to my feet. Luke does the same. Ben steps forward as I look down at the phone in Mia's hand.

"Ben." Placing a hand on his shoulder, I'm ready to point out what I think brought the women down here, but he must already see it.

"Angel," he whispers, his voice shattered. He moves

through the trees and cups her face in his hands. Luke and I move closer.

Mia stares up at Ben, their foreheads touching. She smiles and he crushes his mouth against hers, lifting her off the ground. I collapse against the nearest tree, my legs ready to fail me as relief surges through my veins.

She's smiling. She wouldn't be smiling if it wasn't good news.

Mia's words are broken up by Ben's frantic assault on her. I manage to pick out something about the lump being nothing, benign or some shit. That's all I need to know.

"Thank fuck," I say, rolling my head to the side. "Did you think he was going to hit me?"

I look over at Luke, expecting a response, an acknowledgement, something. He's staring at Tessa like a man possessed.

Body stretched, eyes fixated on her with a darkening intensity, chest heaving in quick bursts. He moves past Ben and Mia, grabs Tessa's face, and pulls her against him as his mouth drops to her ear. Her body goes still. Slowly lifting her eyes, she stares up at him for a long second, then nods. Luke kisses all over her face.

Beth takes a few steps to her left, blushing at the two of them.

Ben sets Mia down on her feet. "He's sure?" he asks, keeping her in his arms. Mia nods her head. "Where was that fucker yesterday? He was supposed to call us. And why the fuck couldn't we reach anybody all day? Does he know what we've been going through?"

Mia smiles. "He was in surgery all day. He apologized for that."

"Give me the phone."

"Why? So you can threaten his life?"

"Fucking right." He kisses her again. "You're really okay?"

We don't need to worry about anything?"

"I'm really okay."

Ben grabs her face again. "Mia, baby, I'm sorry I couldn't . . ."

"Shh." She silences him with a finger to his lips. "I love you."

He closes his eyes, visibly relaxing, and kisses the top of her head. "I love you. So much."

I push off from the tree. "I need a beer. Anybody else feel like they need one?"

Ben lifts Mia again. She squeals in his arms. "Fuck yeah. You know how close I was to hitting you?"

I smile at Beth as I walk through the trees. "You know how close I was to hitting you? Calling me pathetic, like I don't know."

Ben laughs. "You do need to handle that shit."

I nod, looking from Beth to Tessa and Luke, who are standing a few feet away.

Luke lifts his head when we reach his side. Tessa's climbing all over him like she needs his air to breathe, wrapping her limbs around his body.

"We're going to head out," he says, looking at the group, his hands planted on Tessa's ass. "Really fucking good news, Mia. We're all really happy you're okay."

"Soooo happy," Tessa agrees, kissing Luke. She grabs his face and stares at his lip. "What the hell? Why is your mouth cut?"

"Sorry about that, man."

Tessa glares at Ben after he speaks. "You hit him? Are you serious?"

"Ben, you didn't." Mia leans back to look into Ben's face.

"It's fine, babe. Your brother punches like a little bitch."

Ben shifts Mia against him, flipping off Luke.

"Come on," Tessa urges, pressing her lips against Luke's neck. "We need to go," she whispers.

The group of us head across the yard toward the house. I fall in next to Beth.

"Hey."

She lifts her head, smiling gently. "Hey."

"Wanna have a beer with me? Or do you need to go?"

Her lips pull down. "I would love to stay and have a beer with you, but I've missed several calls from the bar and one from my aunt's house. The messages just tell me to call them, but I can't reach anybody at either number. The answering machine at the bar keeps picking up."

"Were you supposed to work tonight?"

"No, but maybe they need me to come in. That might be why they were calling me." She looks ahead of us, smiling when Mia giggles against Ben. "I'm so glad everything's going to be okay. She told us about what she overhead. About him not being able to live without her. That broke my heart."

I turn my head, watching Ben carry Mia into the house, her hands threading through his hair while she kisses him. Beth and I continue down the driveway as Tessa and Luke get into their separate cars.

I look over at her. "Yeah, I realized I didn't have shit to say to him after that. Not that anything I had already said to him did much of anything, besides piss him off more. I should've just stood there and offered myself up as a punching bag."

Beth opens her car door, lifting a teasing eyebrow. "And mess up that pretty face? What about your service to the state of Alabama? You wouldn't want to send all the women here packing, would you?"

I smirk down at her as she settles into her seat. Grabbing

the door, I prevent her from shutting it. "I don't care about all the women. Just a handful. As long as they stick around, that's all that matters."

She looks up at me, holding my stare through several deep breaths. Blinking away, she anxiously reaches for her belt. "I should go. Find out what's going on with my aunt and uncle."

She backs out of the driveway, hesitating to pull down the street when her eyes can't seem to leave mine. I don't look away when she finally manages to pull her attention to the road and drive away from the house.

She didn't want to leave.

If she hadn't gotten those phone calls, she'd still be here talking to me, smiling, getting comfortable with me again. That's what I want, and I'm going to get her there. Fuck CJ. That's my smile. Nobody's making her that happy but me.

I step up to the front door, hand on the knob, listening to the sounds of Nolan giggling somewhere in the house. Ben and Mia need this time together, just them and the boys. After all this shit, it should just be the four of them, healing with each other. I don't need to stick around for that.

I get in my truck and back out of the driveway.

Staying off the main roads, I take to the back ones I like to take when I'm not in a rush to get home. It's after six o'clock now, so there's no need for me to go back to the job site. Work's closed for the day.

Windows down, I inhale the cool night air as it blows against my face. Silence surrounds me, the only noise being the wind whipping around the bed of the truck. The tight coils of tension in my shoulders slowly unravel. I focus on the road in front of me, the quiet night, the faint smell of flowers nearby. My phone rings on the seat and I glance down at the name flashing on my screen.

I hit speaker phone, grinning like a fucking idiot.

"Miss me already?"

She laughs, but there's a nervousness to it. One I'd have to be fucking deaf to ignore.

"Yeah, I . . . okay, this sounds really crazy, and stupid, and you're probably going to laugh at how ridiculous I'm being right now, but is there any way you could talk to me for a little while? I know you hate talking on the phone, but I'm, I just . . . I would really, really love to talk to you right now."

I move the phone to my lap while my hand shifts gears. Her voice worries me.

"Beth, what's going on? Why do you sound like that?"

The squeak of a mattress comes through the phone. "My aunt and uncle had to go out of town. That's why they were trying to reach me, to let me know that they had to leave. I got home and found a note from them in the kitchen, and now I'm going to be in this house by myself for a few days and I'm freaking out a little. I just, I don't like being alone, Reed. I don't like not having someone to talk to."

I shift again, picking up speed while a pressure forms in my chest. She's not freaking out. She's fucking scared. Her breath is anxious against the phone, she keeps moving around on the bed, restless. Getting her to talk would be one approach, but she needs to hear my voice right now. She needs to know she's not alone.

Cue the most random shit I can think of.

"I had this dog when I was little that I rescued. He was so nervous all the time, like his fucking hair would fall out if you sneezed around him. Or if you made any sudden movements when he was near you he'd piss everywhere, and then he'd lay in it."

Beth laughs quietly as I turn onto another road.

"Oh, my God."

"We would've gotten rid of him, but we felt bad because his previous owners abused him, so it wasn't his fault he was like that. Those assholes kept him tied up outside all day, neglecting him, and they gave him the worst fucking name."

"What was it?"

"Butter."

"Butter?" she chokes on a giggle. "Why would you name a dog that? That's so weird."

"Yeah, I know. I tried changing it and calling him Hulk, 'cause I was obsessed with wrestling at the time, but he wouldn't respond to anything except Butter. I fucking hated that name. I wanted this bad-ass dog, you know? I didn't want to be hollering out the name Butter when he got off his leash."

"Did he look like a bad-ass dog?"

"Fuck no. He always had these stupid bows in his hair that Riley would put on him. She wanted him to be a girl." I pull into the driveway, taking the phone off speaker as I step down from my truck. "I caught him in my bed one day chewing on one of my shoes, and I yelled at him, and then I remembered that he always pees when you yell at him, and he was on my fucking bed."

Beth gasps. "Oh my God. Did he pee in your bed? Oh no, no, no." She starts laughing again.

"You want to know?"

"Yes!" she cries.

"Come let me in and I'll tell you."

Her laughing cuts off. "What? Let you in? Are you at my house?" Movement sounds through the phone, the mattress springs, hinges of a door swinging open, her footsteps on the stairs. "Reed, are you really here?" she asks breathlessly a second before the door opens.

I lean my shoulder against the frame. "That asshole peed all over my bed. I was so pissed," I say into the phone.

Eyes wide, she slowly lowers the phone from her ear, then lets go of it completely. It crashes against the floor, mine hits something when her tongue wets her lips. She lunges at me, wrapping her hands around my neck and presses her full, perfect, *fuck, I love this mouth*, against mine.

I moan, one hand in her hair, the other cupping her ass, grinding her against my cock.

Yes. Fuck, yes, please.

She slides her tongue along my bottom lip, then squeaks and quickly pulls back, looking startled as she backs away. "I'm sorry. Was it okay that I did that?"

I stare down at her, panting, my breathing all over the place, my cock harder than steel. "Are you fucking kidding me? I was worried I would never kiss you again."

She bites her lip, then grabs a handful of my shirt and pulls me inside. "Kiss me again now."

My hands are in her hair, my mouth moving over her lips, along her jaw, up to her cheek. She shudders in my arms when I bite her neck. "God, there's so much I want to do to you right now." I grip her ass, lifting her. "Legs, sweetheart."

She wraps them around my waist, moaning when my cock presses against her. "Reed," she gasps, tilting her head back as I lick the skin I've just marked. "What do you want to do? Tell me."

Her back hits the wall. "Everything," I say against her lips, dragging my teeth along her skin. "I want to put my mouth all over you. I want my fingers inside that tight little cunt while I suck on your clit." She moves her hips, grinding against me. I press my mouth to her ear as my hands knead her ass.

God, her ass.

"I want to watch those perfect fucking lips wrap around my cock, sucking me while you finger yourself. I want you bent over, spread out on the floor, tied to the bed while I'm fucking you raw."

I carry her up the stairs while her mouth devours mine. She sucks on my bottom lip, dropping me to my knees halfway up the stairs. My hands pull at her jeans.

"I want everything." She lifts her hips for me, her eager fingers pulling at my belt. "I want you to take me right here because you can't wait any longer."

I groan when she pumps my cock. "What does it look like I'm doing? You're lucky I didn't take you on the porch."

Her feet push my jeans down my thighs after I slide her panties off. She lays back, drops her knees to the side, and opens up that bare pussy for me. My cock slides between her legs, pushes against her clit, and the moan she gives me causes my balls to ache.

"Beth." I kiss her like I always kiss her, like I'm starved for everything this woman gives me. I slide in the first inch and moan into her mouth, fighting the urge to thrust my hips.

So wet. So warm and tight.

Tight. Wet. Warm. Perfect.

My legs shake. "God, you are fucking unreal."

She grabs my hips, her pelvis tilting up, seeking me. "Reed, please, move."

An inch more, slower this time.

She writhes against me like she's not loving this, but I know she is. Every tiny squeeze her pussy is giving me keeps my pace. I move my lips along her neck, sucking her skin as I grip the step above her head. She digs her heels into my back when I'm balls deep.

"Oh my God." Her hands pull down the straps of her

shirt, freeing her tits.

I run my tongue over a hard peak as I begin to move.

"Ow. Ow. Oh."

I freeze, raising my head. "What's wrong? Shit, am I hurting you?"

"Stairs." She winces, shifting her back.

I lift her, my cock sliding in and out as I get us to the top of the stairs. She moans in my ear as I lower her to the floor. "Better?" I ask, bracing my hands beside her head and driving into this perfection I don't deserve.

Her mouth falls open, her eyes roll closed. "Shit. Oh, God. Reed, that feels so good."

I wrap her legs higher on my waist, getting deeper, needing her deeper still. "I want all of me inside you. Every inch, Beth."

All of me. All of you.

You and me.

"Yes." Her hands claw at my shirt as her eyes flash open. She pulls my face down to hers, kissing me. "I want that too. That's all I want."

My muscles burn, the sweat beading up on my forehead, pooling around my neck. I fuck her slow until she's begging for faster. My mouth can't get enough of her skin. My fingers can't hold enough of her flesh. I'm all over her, taking everything and still telling her I need more. I whisper her name between her tits. I moan it when she pulls my hair. Her hips start circling underneath me, seeking more, needing . . .

"Reed," she breathes, her body shaking. "Oh shit. Ohshit, ohshit."

I push her knees against her chest and drive into her, faster, harder, giving her more when she clamps down on my cock. She's panting beneath me, cheeks flushed, her dark hair sticking to her skin. My spine tingles at the base, my balls draw up.

"Can I come in you?"

She nods through a moan, sucking on her lip, arching her back off the floor.

Arms flexed, thighs shaking, I lose my breath, my rhythm, my fucking mind as I release inside her, giving her all of me.

"Oh, fuck. Beth. Fuckkkk, I . . ."

"Harder," she demands.

I give her harder, deeper, every fucking inch. "God, you're perfect." With one final thrust, I collapse, burying my face in her neck, inhaling her sweet vanilla scent. "Beth," I whisper, brushing my lips against her skin. "Beth."

She moans, her hands moving beneath my shirt. "I love that. You always say my name at least twice after you come."

"Yeah?" I ask, leaning back to look at her.

I hate that she has to tell me that. I should fucking know what I do after I come inside this woman. Never again. I need every memory of her.

She stares up at me, her face breaking into that smile. My smile.

"Hi," she says through a laugh.

"Hi." I kiss her nose. "Beth Davis, from McGill's."

She purses her lips. I kiss them open.

I get her halfway down the hallway before she's on her knees and I'm taking her from behind.

beth

PUSH MY matted hair from my face and stretch my limbs
out against the sheet. A dull ache pulses between my legs.
My muscles feel worked, my lips sore and swollen.

I never want to stop feeling like this, from him, specifically. No one else.

Eyes closed, my hand reaches across the bed, seeking him,
eager for more even though my body needs recovery. I turn
my head when I discover I'm alone, then sit up, bunching the
sheet around my waist.

Sunlight streaks along the carpet, a few beams of light
shining through the break in the lavender curtains. I scowl at
the thought of a gorgeous day.

A gorgeous Thursday.

Damn it. Why didn't I think to pray for rain last night?
Reed probably slipped out early this morning to go to work,
and I missed him. I wasn't thinking before I passed out. I
wasn't doing much of anything besides letting him take me,
staring into those wild, blue eyes as he worshipped my body,
as he pushed my limits of pleasure again, and again. Exhaustion overwhelmed me, but I still begged for more. My sex
swollen, throbbing as he filled me, but I demanded harder.
Faster. Deeper.

"More," I whisper. "Please."

"All night," he promises.

My body hums at the memory of Reed's hands on my skin, his mouth against my ear, whispering his filth to me. Pinching my thighs together beneath the sheet, I stare across the room at the phone on my dresser. I want to call him, but I need to call someone else first.

Tomorrow can't happen. I don't want it to happen. I have no idea what's going on with Reed now that we've had sex and he was lucid for it. He told me things last night, sweet words between the dirty, but he was inside me when he said them. He also said things I didn't understand.

Something about magic pussy.

I was too delirious to ask him what that meant. We need to have a conversation with our clothes on, without the distraction of flesh.

Hard, wet, throbbing, aching flesh.

Right. Stay clothed around Reed. I'm sure that won't be a problem.

I slide out of bed and walk to the dresser, slipping on a fresh pair of panties and a long T-shirt. The faint sound of water running has my head whipping to my right, my feet moving me out into the hallway. I stop outside the closed bathroom door.

My heart batters around in my chest, my skin tingles.

He's still here. He didn't go to work?

The water cuts off. Scrambling back into the bedroom, I snatch the phone off the dresser and climb onto the bed. I have no idea if CJ will answer his phone right now, but I pray he does. I don't want to bail on him via voicemail. He's a nice guy. He deserves to hear this straight from me.

Three rings before the call connects

"Tully."

"Hi, CJ, it's Beth."

"Hey." His voice lightens, giving away that he's smiling. "Hold on one second for me."

I stare out the small opening in the curtain.

It's not raining, and he's here. Why is he here? Does his job close down for other reasons besides bad weather?

"Okay, I'm back."

I take in a deep breath. "Um, I'm sorry if this is a bad time, but I wanted to talk to you about tomorrow night."

"It's not a bad time. What's up?"

"I can't go out with you." I run my hand down the side of my face, shifting my weight on the bed. CJ remains silent. "I'm sorry. The other night when you asked me out, things were kind of complicated. I wasn't sure where I stood with someone, and now some other things have happened."

"With Reed?" he asks flatly.

"Yes."

"Yeah, I figured." He clears his throat. "Look, Beth, I wouldn't have asked you out if I'd realized something was going on with you and Reed. I'm not like that. He's a good friend of mine. Ben said something to me a couple days ago about it, and now all that shit that happened at game night makes a hell of a lot more sense. Reed's not an angry guy, but he was ready to rip my head off seeing me with you. I get it."

I wince at the memory. "I am really sorry about all that."

CJ's husky laugh comes through the phone. "It's okay. Like I said, I get it. Thanks for at least letting me know and not standing me up tomorrow. That would've sucked."

"Tully! Let's go!" another voice yells in the background. "I'll see you around, all right?"

"Yeah," I respond. "Thank you for understanding."

He pauses. "Yeah, no problem."

The call disconnects.

Standing from the bed, I turn around to set my phone back on the dresser. The sight of Reed in the doorway halts me mid-step, nearly causing me to face-plant on the carpet.

Holy fuck.

Wearing nothing but a white towel around his waist, he leans against the doorframe, his chest still damp from the shower, his hair wet and disheveled.

My eyes slowly move over his body.

Broad shoulders, well-defined arms, long, sculpted torso, he's built like an Olympic swimmer, and for sex. Mainly sex.

I look up into his face when he clears his throat. Cue knowing smirk.

"You're still here," I state, reaching up and sweeping a quick hand through my wild hair. *Tame, damn it!* "And you took a shower."

He rubs along his jaw. "I needed to shave. I always shower first."

"You shaved? With . . . did you use my razor?"

He smiles, crossing his arms over his chest. "No. I keep an electric razor in my truck for days when I'm running late, or for mornings when I don't wake up at my house and I have a sweet pussy to lick." He lifts an eyebrow. "I didn't want to burn you."

My mouth drops open. I stare up at him, speechless, watching his expression stiffen when he realizes how that came across.

Lips pressing into a thin line. Eyebrows pulling together. He tilts his head down. "I always wake up at my house, Beth. That razor has only ever been used when my ass is late for work."

"Oh," I reply, through a husky exhale. I run my hand down my neck, coaxing my throat to loosen. Everything suddenly feels restrictive. The T-shirt I'm wearing, the air in the room.

Reed has prepared his face to be between my legs. That's not hot at all.

His eyes slowly lower to my body. "Why did you put clothes on?"

"I thought you had gone to work." My hand gestures toward the window. "It's not raining, and it's Thursday. Shouldn't you be working?"

"I took a sick day."

"Are you sick?"

His mouth pulls up in the corner as he slowly shakes his head. He stalks toward me. "You broke it off with CJ?" He nods at the phone in my hand.

I look down. I had completely forgotten I was even holding my phone. Half-naked Reed is very distracting, which is why . . .

I push against his chest when he tries reaching for me. "I did. Maybe you should get dressed and then we can talk."

He frowns. "Or, you can get naked and ride my face." He grabs my waist and pulls me against him. Growling, he sucks on the skin of my neck. "I've never done this before," he whispers.

My body goes limp. I tilt my head, gasping when I feel teeth. "Never done what?"

"Taken a sick day to spend time with someone. I've never taken a day off, Beth. Ever, but I woke up next to you and I didn't want to leave." His lips brush against my ear. "Is this okay?"

The reservation in his voice has me pulling him closer. If I had any shred of resistance left in me, Reed would've stripped it away with what he's just confessed. And his question, I know he isn't asking if touching me is okay. He never has to ask that.

He's never done this before. Neither have I.

I grab his head, guiding him back to look at me. We're both panting, maybe him more than me, although I'm not sure how that's possible. I feel like I've just ran a hundred miles to get to him.

"Lay on the bed. I want to show you how okay this is."

His lips curl up in the corner. Keeping his eyes on me, he settles on his back between the pillows, crossing his feet at the ankles and tucking both hands behind his head. I kneel beside him.

"What are you going to do?" he asks, watching as I pull the towel back and let it fall to the bed. He groans when I slowly stroke him. Long, slow pulls.

"You gave me an idea last night." I lift one knee, then the other, sliding my panties off with my free hand. "Something about sucking your dick while I fingered myself."

His eyes fall closed when I wrap my lips around him. "Fuck, Beth," he groans, lifting his hips off the mattress, pushing more of him into my mouth.

I moan when my fingers press between my legs.

So wet. God, I'm so turned on by this.

"Look at you," he pants as I writhe against my hand, as I take him deeper. Sucking, licking, using my teeth when he throbs against my tongue. His hands thread through my hair. "Dirty girl, touching yourself while you suck my dick. You love this, don't you? You're making such a mess between your legs right now."

"Mm."

I rub my clit faster, my other hand pumping his dick, following the path of my mouth.

Yes, I do love this. I've sucked Reed off before, he just doesn't remember. I know what he likes. Pain mixed with pleasure, just enough to push him to the edge.

"Beth," he groans, thighs clenching, the delicious lines of his stomach forming deeper grooves as he sucks in quick breaths. "Fuck, take it. Take my dick. All of it. So good. God-damn, you suck my dick so good."

Oh, God. His filthy mouth. I love it.

"Is your pussy wet? God, how wet is it? Are you dripping on the mattress? Mm, fuck, I'm so hard. So hard it almost hurts."

It almost hurts.

I suck harder, faster, needing it. Needing him. I let him hit the back of my throat, tearing a growl from deep within his chest. His grip tightens on my hair, his dick pulses. "Gonna come," he warns, his voice strained. "*Beth.*" He floods my mouth, hips thrusting, my name rolling off his tongue between moans.

Wiping my lips against the back of my hand, I sit back, chest heaving, legs shaking as my fingers press against my clit.

"Reed," I gasp.

His eyes drop between my legs. "Get up here," he orders, pulling at my thigh, guiding me with greedy hands until I'm straddling his face.

I rip the shirt above my head and toss it. He moans, looking up at my breasts, then into my eyes as he lifts his head and slowly licks my slit.

"Oh my God." My hands grip the headboard. I've never done this before. I've never ridden someone's face, and Reed senses my hesitation, my embarrassment that has me tensing against his mouth.

"Take it, Beth. Fuck, just take it." His hands grip my thighs, urging me down until his voice is muffled. I gasp, tossing my head back when he slips his tongue inside me. My hips begin to move, hesitantly rocking. Faster, just a little faster.

"Reed, my God."

I stare down at him, looking into his eyes as he lets me coat his mouth, as my wetness drips down his chin. His tongue is everywhere, inside me, on my thighs, flicking my clit. He begins to moan, his hands falling away as I move with eagerness. I fist his hair, holding him still as I shamelessly grind against him, chasing my orgasm.

Faster. Almost. So wet. Oh, God.

My head falls back. My breath hitches. Reed slaps my ass, shoving me over the edge as a burst of colors explode behind my eyelids. I chant his name. I beg him to give me this.

I gasp when I feel his teeth sink into my thigh. My head snaps down.

His eyes are pinched shut as he moans against my wet skin. His arm is moving against my calf.

Looking over my shoulder, I catch the first spurt of cum shooting onto Reed's stomach, the next rolling onto his hand.

Oh my God. He got off on what I just did.

Shifting my weight, I kneel beside him.

He grabs the towel and wipes off his stomach, the top of his hand, then pulls me flat against his chest so we're nose to nose. I quickly wipe my hand over his mouth and chin, removing any trace of me before he bats my hand away.

We look intently at each other. I'm ready to ask what we're doing, what this is becoming, but he silences my words with a finger to my lips.

"I want this," he says, moving his finger along my cheek, tucking some of my hair behind my ear. "Whatever this is between us, I want it. I can't stop thinking about you. I haven't been with anyone else since you kissed me that first time. I don't want to be."

I smile, leaning into his hand as it caresses my face. "I want this too. So much."

He stares at me thoughtfully, looking all over my face. "Beth, I'll never hurt you, but you could very easily hurt me. I can't want you more than I want you right now. I can't. What we've been together when it's just been us, that's what I'm offering you." His other hand cups my face. He inches me closer. "You and me. You understand?"

I look back at this man, at the pain he's lived with that burns slow beneath the charming exterior I fell for. He loved that girl, and she made a fool out of him. He's worried I'll do the same thing.

God, I hate her. How could she hurt him?

I could never do that to Reed. He's everything I've ever wanted, even if he's scared to give it to me right now. He needs to see that I'll never hurt him, and it could take time, but I want time with him. I want this. I've never wanted anything as much as I want this. I can show him that I'm not like her, that he can love me without fear. He can love me.

No one will ever love you the way I do.

I shut out Rocco's voice and press my lips against Reed's. "You and me. Let's do it."

"Yeah?" He slides his hands down my back, cupping my ass, smiling when I nod vigorously. He kisses my chin. "I haven't been a boyfriend in nine years. I might suck at it."

"You were a good fake boyfriend."

He rolls his eyes, laughing. "I still can't believe you roped me into that shit. Jesus."

I punch his chest. "I didn't rope you into it! You agreed on your own, remember? At the pizza place? You came outside and dropped the whole 'you and me' line. That was all you. I was set on going to that party alone."

In one quick motion, I'm flipped onto my back and he's settled on top of me, his weight pressing me into the mattress.

"All me? Sweetheart, I had spent the past three days stroking my cock, thinking about nothing but you and that damn kiss. Then you walk in looking hot as shit, smiling at me like you do, reminding me how completely fucked I was over you already. You roped me in, Beth. You did it the second I looked at you that night at McGill's, and you did it again when I saw you that day at Sal's. I would've agreed to anything just to spend more time with you, but that was all you. Nobody else would've gotten to me like that."

Goodness. Filthy and sweet. I don't stand a chance here.

My face feels ready to split wide open with the smile I'm holding in, until I see the somber look wash over Reed's face. I brush his hair out of his eyes. "What's the matter?"

He opens his mouth, pinches it closed again, hesitating, then sighs.

"Reed, what?" I urge him.

"I want to know what happened after your mom died." His hand keeps my head from turning away, forcing me to look at him. "Don't. This might be hard for you to talk about, I get that, but it's going to be real fucking hard for me to hear it. I don't like thinking you were alone, Beth. I want to know what you went through, all of it, and I want you looking at me."

I nod against his hand, swallowing back my reluctance. He's shared things with me that weren't easy for him to talk about. Walking in on Molly with that other guy. The proposal. It's only right I do the same.

He settles on his side, tucking me close to his warm body, keeping his eyes on me as I roll over to face him. His hand strokes my arm, a fluid, soothing motion that calms my mind.

I wet my lips, staring into his eyes. "My momma was

a drug addict. That's how she died. It was sudden, and not something I could've prepared for. I didn't have enough money lying around to stay in the trailer we lived in, so I packed up everything I could fit into my car and I moved into that." I touch his hand on my arm that had gone still. "Can you keep doing that?"

He blinks several times, nods, then continues the path his hand was taking.

"I ran out of money pretty fast," I continue. "But it was the loneliness that scared me, not starving to death. I hated not having anyone to talk to. It's why I freaked out last night and begged you to stay on the phone with me. I got home, saw that note, and I panicked."

"You told me you didn't live in your car that long. What happened?"

Inhaling deeply, I shift my head closer to him on the pillow. "Please understand this, Reed, I hated being alone. I was terrified I'd never have anyone to talk to again. When someone finally did talk to me, and bought me food, and offered me a place to stay, I took it. I know it sounds crazy moving in with a stranger, but I did what I had to do." I drop my eyes to a spot between us. "I only lived with him for a couple months before I found out about my aunt. Then I moved here."

Reed tilts my head up. "Were you with this guy?" he sternly questions, holding my gaze.

I'm slow to answer. "In the beginning, yes. When the relationship changed, I stopped being with him."

With a heavy sigh, Reed drops his hand away from my face. "What do you mean, when it changed?"

I can't get into this. Not with Reed. I don't want him knowing this ugliness.

"Relationships change," I explain, keeping my voice even.

"We stopped being with each other, and strictly became room-mates. There's really nothing more to it."

This isn't a lie. I'm just leaving out a few details.

What good would telling Reed the whole truth do me? Or him? Rocco is a part of my past. He isn't in this future I want with Reed. I don't want even the memory of him in it.

Reed, seemingly satisfied with my response, leans close and buries his face in my neck. "You're fucking brave, you know that? My brave girl."

I close my eyes, moving my fingers through his hair.

We stay quiet for several minutes. Our hands explore each other, light touches that turn hungry with the more time that passes. Limbs tangling together, we get lost in the sheets as breathless promises are spoken against my ear.

"Never would've let that happen if you were here. You never would've been alone."

I hold him tighter, kissing his mouth, his jaw, scraping my teeth against his shoulder. He flips me underneath him and pulls against my hips, bringing me to my knees.

"I have to be inside you," he murmurs, squeezing my ass, running his finger along my slit. He moans when I shudder. "Mm. Do you like that?"

My head falls forward. "Yes," I breathe.

I should feel vulnerable like this. I'm completely exposed to him, and I know he's staring at the most intimate part of me, closely, his warm breath heating my flesh. But this is Reed. I've never felt more alive than when he touches me, when he stares at my body with that raw need burning in his eyes. The silent promise of wicked things.

"And this . . . do you like this?"

I bite my lip through a moan when he presses against the tight ring of my ass. "Mm."

God, who knew that could feel so amazing?

He laughs darkly. "I could fuck you right here and you'd love it, wouldn't you? You'd beg me for it."

"Reed." I squirm as one . . . no, two fingers slide into my pussy, a third pressing into my ass. Wetness sticks to the inside of my thighs as I rock back, taking more.

"Look at you. So greedy, Beth."

"I just . . ."

"Shh, I know. You want me to fuck you. This is what you want, right?" His fingers leave my body. His cock slips between my legs. A hand fists my hair as he teases my pussy, sliding along my slit. "Where do you want it? I have two very sexy options here."

My arms begin to tremble. I drop down to my elbows, closing my eyes, relishing in the feel of him. I'm so wet I should be embarrassed. I'm so horny I could take it anywhere.

He smacks my ass and I gasp. "Where?" he demands, tugging my hair.

"My pussy."

He makes a hungry growl in the back of his throat. His cock nudges against my slit.

"Wait." I look at him over my shoulder.

His wild eyes lift from between my legs and lock onto mine. His lips are parted. A light sheen of sweat beads across his brow.

God, he looks amazing.

"Do you have any rope in your truck?" I ask, wetting my lips as his slowly curl up. I've been bound twice by Reed, both on our first night together. There's something about giving up all control to him, watching him take his pleasure instead of delivering it.

I want that now. Even if I can't see the look on his face,

I'll be able to hear him.

He loosens his grip on my hair and runs his hand down my spine. "None I can use on you. You want me to tie you up?"

"Yes."

"Beth," he groans. His eyes shift around the room, then widen. "Hold that thought."

He scrambles off the bed, retrieving his jeans off the floor. He whips his belt out of the loops and prowls toward me like a predator.

A belt? Shit, how is this going to work? He's not going to hit me with it, is he?

More important question, would I be into that?

The mattress dips behind me as he climbs back onto the bed. I shift nervously on my knees.

"Put your hands behind your back. Keep your face down."

A shiver runs through my body as I lower my head to the mattress and offer him both my hands.

He grabs my wrists, pinning them together as the smooth leather of the belt slides under my arms, stopping just above my elbows. I gasp as the belt tightens, pulling my shoulders back.

Holy shit.

"This okay?" he asks softly, leaning over my body to brush the hair out of my face.

He's always so sweet in these moments before he takes me. Always making sure I'm on the same page as him. I know if I say I'm not, that this is too much he would rip that belt off me so fast I wouldn't even remember the feel of it.

"It's okay. I'm okay," I reassure him, linking my fingers together. I smile against his lips forming to my cheek. His hands run down my arms, over the belt, circling my wrists. I'm so ready my legs begin to tremble. "Are you going to fuck me now?"

The air leaves my lungs as he drives into me.

"Reed!"

"Fuck!" He grabs my shoulder, keeping me pinned as his firm thighs slap against my ass. "Fuck, Beth. Come on . . . come on."

"God, yes," I pant. "Reed . . . Oh shit."

He lifts my breasts and tugs on my nipples. He smacks them until I groan.

Over and over he fucks me. There's no teasing. There never is when Reed takes me like this, rough and wild, desperate and deprived. I writhe underneath him when he slaps my ass with enough force my eyes sting. I moan when he presses words against my back, telling me how hard he is for me, how much he needs this, and how he loves my sweet, tight pussy. How he wants to fuck it until I beg him to come. How he won't stop until I do.

He pulls out and runs his tongue up my slit, tasting my desire, making me wetter. I buck against his face. He moans as he consumes me, as he sucks and bites my lips. He slaps my ass and kisses the sting away. My arousal oozes from me. I don't know who loves this more. Him or me.

Me . . . no . . . him. No . . .

He fists my hair and tugs me upright until my hands press into his abs. His chest heaves against my arms. Sweat clings to his skin. He buries his cock inside me and thrusts deep.

God, so deep. So full. I'm so close.

"Goddamn, you're perfect. You're so swollen. So trusting, Beth. You know what that does to me?"

I tilt my head, granting his lips access to my neck. My palms form to his skin with each thrust.

"You feel so good," I tell him. "I . . . I'd trust you with

anything. Everything. I love what you do to me."

He growls against my skin. "Perfect," he whispers. "Do you want to come?"

"Yes."

He wraps his arm around my waist, his other hand glides down my stomach. One finger teases my clit. "Let me hear you."

"Please," I moan, letting my head roll back.

His thrusts become frenzied, hurried. I know he's close but he won't let either of us come until I beg him for my own release.

"Please, let me . . . come. I need to come. Touch me."

"Beth, yes." Two fingers pulse against my clit, circling. His hips pound against my ass. "Fuck, fuck, do it. Come on my cock. Come all over me. God, I fucking need this."

My orgasm builds between my hips, warming my body in that delicious heat, spreading down my spine and arching my back. His arm around my waist slides up my chest and his hand squeezes my throat.

"Oh, God, Reed," I moan, shaking violently. "Reed . . . Reed."

He makes filthy noises against my ear as he gives me his release. His pleasure spills into me, mine drips down my thighs. His hand around my neck loosens as he buries himself deep inside me and stills.

We're both gasping, swaying on our knees.

"Beth," he sighs, squeezing my breasts, kissing my shoulder. "Beth."

I smile as my head rolls forward, loving the sound of my name. Loving all his sounds, every note of his voice.

The belt loosens and disappears from my skin. It hits the floor with a clink. We both tumble down onto the bed and Reed pulls me against his body, rubbing my arms, kissing the flush of my skin.

My phone beeps across the room. Reed grumbles against my neck.

"Sorry?" I ask, giggling when he holds me down, preventing me from standing.

He bends his head and sucks on my nipple. "Nothing. I didn't want any interruptions, but if I don't eat something soon and replenish my body, I might not be much use to you the rest of the day." He releases me and rolls to his back. "My dick might also be broken."

Laughing, I swat at him and climb out of bed. Reed follows suit and reaches for his boxers, stepping into them.

"You like eggs?" he asks. "I'm fucking starving."

"I like eggs." I reply, pulling up the new text on my phone.

Mia: Hey! No lunch today. Ben took off the rest of the week and we're spending all day together. Xoxo

Good. That's exactly what they need after all they've been through.

I watch Reed move toward the door. Stopping himself when he's almost through it, he turns his head to look at me, bracing his hand on the wall.

"I just want to eat and fuck all day. You in?"

I don't need to say anything.

His eyes drop to my smile, lingering there a moment before he breaks away shaking his head. He exits the room, mumbling two words under his breath, over and over.

"So fucked."

reed

ON MY BACK in the middle of my bed, I absentmind-
edly move my fingers through the ends of Beth's hair
as she lays still, sleeping. Half her body is sprawled
on top of mine, while the other half is nestled against my
side, leaving no space between us. I stare up at the ceiling
as warm breath blows across my chest, as her heart knocks
against my ribs.

A lot of women have slept in this bed, but not like this.
They would stay on one side, and I'd stay on the other. I liked
it that way. I've never been a contact sleeper, until I slept with
Beth. She needs to have some part of her body touching mine
at all times. Even if it's just her hand on my hip, or her foot
pressed against my calf. She seeks me out in the darkness when
we unintentionally drift apart. It's as if her body knows I'm
here even when her mind is quiet. I'm a light sleeper. I always
have been. The second I feel her flesh, I'm stirred awake, pulling her against me, never satisfied with just a piece of Beth.
And fuck me, if she doesn't smile in her sleep when I do it.

Always giving me that smile.

Groaning, she shifts her body against mine, raising her
head to peer up at me through the dark strands hanging in
her eyes.

"Hey." I push her hair out of her face, my hand lingering
on her cheek. "Go back to sleep."

She looks at the clock on my night stand, her eyes widening. "Oh my God, Reed. It's almost three o'clock. We need to get up and do something."

"We've been doing a lot of something," I tease. Her cheek lifts against my hand. "If you'd like to change locations again, I think there's still a surface in this house I haven't pinned you up against. I'm willing to explore that."

She blushes instantly. I fucking love that I do that to her.

Wiggling out of my arms, she scoots to the end of the bed. "You're crazy."

I grab her waist, pulling her back down and pinning her underneath me. She squirms, laughing against my neck. I lock her wrists above her head with one of my hands while the other palms her breast. My lips brush against hers, my tongue wetting her skin.

"It's Saturday, and the only thing I plan on doing today is you. I'm making up for lost time."

"Oh," she moans, rolling her head to the side as I kiss along her neck. Her body tightens up again. "Wait, what lost time?"

I lean back, waiting until she looks up at me. "The ten hours I worked yesterday."

"Reed," she laughs. "We had sex all night!"

"So?"

She pinches her lips shut, shaking her head.

I rock my hips. "Like you don't want it."

"I'm beginning to forget what daylight looks like."

"I can fuck you outside."

Her phone rings somewhere in the bedroom. Gasping, she tries to throw me off her, bucking against the mattress. Her efforts are adorable.

I groan, dropping my head until our foreheads touch.

"Feels good. Keep doing that."

"It could be my aunt. Let me up," she demands, her face burning red from exertion.

I roll onto my back, laughing when she playfully glares at me before sliding off the bed. She searches through the pile of clothes on the floor, finally pulling her phone free.

"Oh, it's Mia."

"Call her back. I just realized I haven't fucked your tits yet."

Her mouth falls open as the phone stops midway to her ear. She stares at me, shocked, her neck rolling with a noisy swallow. Her eyes move down my body. "Hold that thought."

God, she's fucking perfect.

Beth steps out into the hallway to answer the call. I'm sure she's doing that so she'll pay attention to whatever it is Mia has to say, and not the hand on my dick.

She likes to watch, I know that now. She'll force my hand where she wants it while I'm bringing her pleasure. Those wild eyes lingering on my flesh as her body submits to me. I've explored every part of her over the past two days, taken her how we both needed, harder when she demanded it, slower when she begged. I've fucked Beth Davis until my body burned with exhaustion, and I'm nowhere near my fill. That's never happened to me, but it's her, it's fucking *her*, and it's not just the sex that's got me like this.

It's everything.

The moments in between when we're laughing in bed or on the couch, watching TV. When she's telling me every tiny detail of her life and asking me about mine. I've never enjoyed being around someone this much before. She's funny, she's constantly saying shit that makes me laugh. She's honest and sweet as hell, and she isn't ashamed to ask for what she wants.

Why the fuck would I want to do anything besides what we've been doing? The past couple days with her have been perfect.

She shrieks in the distance. "Oh my God! Yes! That sounds like so much fun!"

Shit. Why did I let her get up?

She runs into the room, the phone pressed to her ear. "Mia wants to go dancing tonight with everyone to celebrate her fantastic news. You wanna go?"

I watch, amused at her excitement, tucking my hands behind my head to prop myself up.

She slowly looks away, laying her other hand against her cheek while she listens to Mia. "Oh, um, Reed. I'm at Reed's house," she says quietly into the phone. "Yeah. Yeah, we are." Our eyes lock. She stares at me, sliding her hand down the side of her neck as a hint of a smile twists across her mouth. "Me too," she says into the phone.

I don't need to hear the other side of this conversation to know what Mia just asked. That sweet fucking face at the end of the bed is giving it away.

A strange stillness settles over me. My heart rate slows, my lungs taking in long, deep breaths, instead of the quick ones I'm used to taking whenever I look at her. There's something about listening to Beth tell someone else she's mine. Something so fucking right about it, like she's always been meant to say it. Like I've been waiting my whole life to hear it. I don't just want Mia to know, I want everyone to know. People I don't even give a shit about. My mind was made up five minutes ago that we weren't going anywhere today. I sure as hell wasn't in for going dancing, but hearing Beth's voice, watching that damn smile stretch across her face, I'm ready to agree to anything that'll get her out in public with me. I want her on my arm just as much as I want her in my bed.

Maybe even more.

"Yeah, definitely. Okay, great, we'll see you there." She walks back over to the pile of clothes and drops the phone on top. "We're meeting them at six. Some place called Heat. Do you know where that is?"

"Come here."

She scrapes her teeth along her lip, hesitantly crawling back on the bed. She kneels beside me. All dark hair, pale skin, and that sweet heart-shaped face.

"Was it okay what I just did? Telling Mia we're together?"

I run my knuckles against her cheek. She closes her eyes, leaning into my touch.

I spend the next two hours showing her just how okay it is.

"THIS PLACE IS packed!" Beth yells over the music, some Lil Jon, or Lil Wayne song. Lil somebody, I don't fucking know. She squeezes my hand as I lead her through the crowd of people on the dance floor.

Fucking right it's packed. It's Saturday night, though. I wasn't expecting the only nightclub in Ruxton to be dead, but I was hoping for it. If I have a hard time hearing Beth all night over this shit they're blaring through the speakers, I might drag her out of here before we have time to celebrate with anyone.

Through a break in the bodies, I spot Ben and Mia over by the bar. "Come on. They've got a table," I tell her over my shoulder.

As soon as Mia sees us, her face breaks into a huge, knowing smile. "Hey, you two."

She doesn't need to yell. The music isn't as deafening by the bar.

Beth takes the stool next to Mia, and they exchange a

brief hug before talking closely, looking over at me between every other word. I tip my chin at Ben as I take a seat.

"Hey, man. Sorry we're late."

Not really.

Taking Beth to her aunt's so she could get ready led to getting pulled into the shower, which led to returning to my house for another change of clothes, since mine were soaking wet. We were supposed to get here twenty minutes ago. Naked Beth and time management don't mix well, but I'll be late any damn time she wants to do that again.

Ben looks at Beth, smiling like he's just won the fucking lottery or something. Picking up his beer, he tips it at me. "I see you worked your shit out."

Nodding, I lean on my elbows, rubbing my hands together as he laughs behind his beer. "Yeah, it's good. Do me a favor and try not to bust my balls tonight. I know you're fucking ecstatic over this. You're practically glowing."

"Never thought I'd see the day."

"Here we go."

"I might start taking pictures. Commemorate the evening."

I glare at him, but fuck, I can't help smiling at the idiot. He's happy for me. I'm on cloud fucking nine right now myself. "You're such a dick," I joke. My eyes scan the bar. "Where's Luke and Tessa?"

He shrugs, setting his beer down. "I haven't talked to either of them since Wednesday. Luke's kept his phone off for some reason." He wraps his arm around Mia's body, drawing her attention up. She smiles at him. "Angel, where's my sister?"

Mia's face falls in concern as she looks around the table. Her shoulders drop. "I have no idea. I can't get Tessa on the phone to save my life. It's like her and Luke have gone into hiding or something. She texted me earlier after I left her another message. They're supposed to be here."

"Maybe they're both sick," Beth suggests, slipping her hand into my lap. I grab her stool and slide her closer to me. "Hi," she whispers against my arm.

I kiss her hair. "Hi."

Mia smiles at us. She's just as bad as Ben. Shaking her head, she drops her eyes to the table. "No, Tessa would've called if they weren't coming. She wouldn't just not show up."

"Angel, why don't you just say what you want to say to Beth and Reed. They're here. You might be waiting all night for the other two."

I'm fully focused on Mia now, as is Beth who goes stiff beside me. She's thinking the same thing I am, more bad news, or something else we have to worry about. I don't know if I can take hearing anything but positive shit from Mia right now. Not after Wednesday. But she doesn't look worried. Ben sure as hell isn't breaking shit and getting all of us thrown out of here.

What could she have to say to us?

Mia quickly kisses Ben, then turns back to Beth and I. "We just wanted to say," pausing, her eyes lock onto something over my shoulder. She slaps the table. "There they are."

Looking over my shoulder, I watch Tessa and Luke move through the crowd. Tessa reaches the table first, waving a dismissive hand in front of her.

"I know, I know, we're late. Blame Luke." She tugs her skirt down, looking around the table. Her eyes land on Beth, then me. She points a finger between the two of us, mouthing, "'bout time."

Christ. It's going to be the Beth and Reed show all night. Maybe we should've stayed home.

Luke steps up, wrapping his arms around Tessa and pulling her against his chest. "If she said it was my fault we're late, she's lying. I was ready an hour ago."

"Where have you been?" Mia asks Tessa, leaning forward. "I've been calling and texting you like crazy, and I get one response from you? What the hell?"

Tessa bites her lip, smiling up at Luke. He drops his mouth to her ear and whispers something to her. She giggles.

"Tessa!" Mia shouts.

"Babe, you better tell them," Luke says, kissing her temple.

Tessa looks around the table, smiling so big her one lonely dimple is on display. She takes a deep breath, clamps her eyes shut, then holds up her left hand. "We got married yesterday!"

Mia screams, clamping her hand over her mouth. Ben nearly spits out half his beer, choking on the rest he inhaled. My mouth falls open as I hear Beth utter, "holy shit," under her breath.

Holy shit is right. This is fucking awesome.

"You got married? And you didn't tell any of us?" Mia flies out of her chair and nearly tackles Tessa to the ground. "I can't believe you. Oh my God, I'm so happy right now, but I could seriously punch you in the face."

She wraps Tessa into a hug, and they both start doing this weird combination of laughing and crying. It's the strangest fucking sound I've ever heard.

I offer my hand to Luke, standing. "Congrats, man."

He shakes my hand, the biggest grin I've ever seen him have wiping across his face. His other hand runs over his buzzed hair. "Yeah, thanks. It's fucking crazy. I'm still waiting for this shit not to be real."

"Fucker. I laid into you about this and you were planning

on doing it all along? You should've said something." Ben pulls Luke into a hug as Beth brushes against my back. She joins the girls in their hysteria, hugging Tessa and admiring her ring.

Luke snorts, pulling back from Ben. "I should be thanking you. Saying all that shit to me and watching you with Mia. I don't know what the fuck I was waiting for. I kept thinking I'd do it when she wasn't expecting me to ask, but she was always looking at me, always ready. After all that shit on Wednesday, I looked at her and realized I didn't care if she was expecting it or not. If I went another day without asking, I was going to start ripping your deck apart and breaking boards myself."

I cross my arms over my chest, frowning, looking between the two of them. "If either one of you wants shit to break, fucking ask me. I got a ton of spare wood in the bed of my truck. There's no need to start pulling boards off the deck." I settle my gaze on Luke. "Did you guys go to the courthouse?"

He nods. "Yeah. I didn't want to wait. And I didn't care if anybody else was there." He shifts his eyes between Ben and myself. "No offense."

"Do my parents know?" Ben asks, his eyebrows lifting when Luke shakes his head. "Shit. My mom is going to kill you."

"She'll get over it," Tessa says, coming up and standing next to Luke.

He wraps his arm around her as Mia and Beth filter into the group.

"This is how we wanted to do it. We can have a party or something if the families want to get together." Tessa looks over at Ben. "Maybe if your deck ever gets finished, we can have it at your house."

I narrow my eyes at her. "It's almost finished."

Ben laughs, pulling Mia in front of him, staring at me over

the top of her head. "There's nothing left but the stairs, right?"

"Pretty much. I'll be over sometime tomorrow to get started on them. After five, probably. I'm going with Beth to volunteer at the soup kitchen first."

All heads snap in my direction, including Beth's. I ignore all but hers.

She touches my elbow, looking up at me with wide, curious eyes. "You want to go with me? Really?"

"Yeah. Can I?" I ask, suddenly feeling anxious about inviting myself to this.

Beth never asked me to go with her when she told me she was volunteering tomorrow. This could be something she doesn't want me to be a part of. Talking about being homeless was difficult enough for her. Maybe she doesn't want me to see what it looked like.

Shit. Why the fuck did I just blurt that out?

My arms fall to my side as I become very unsure. "If you don't want me there . . ."

She wraps her arms around my waist, squeezing me tight. Her chin hits my chest as she smiles up at me. "I want you there. So much."

"Quick. Someone take a picture of this."

I glare at Tessa as I pull Beth against me. Everyone else is smiling, staring at me and Beth, acting like we're some fucking exhibit at the museum they've all paid to look at.

Jesus Christ. What is the big deal?

The song changes overhead, something a little slower.

Mia spins and grabs Ben's shirt, pulling him. "Let's go dance, babe."

"Angel," he weakly protests.

Mia looks up at him with pleading eyes. "Dance with me."

Sighing, Ben rubs a hand down his face, but lets Mia lead

him out onto the floor. Tessa tugs against Luke's hand.

"No fucking way."

She puts her hand on her hip. "Really? Would you like me to go out there alone and let some sweaty creeper grind up against me? I'll let them, Luke. If you don't dance with me, I'll, ah!"

Luke picks her up and carries her through the crowd, mumbling something about Tessa driving him crazy.

Laughing, Beth lifts her head from my chest and looks up at me. Her nose wrinkles. "We don't have to dance if you don't want to."

I don't answer her. Not with words anyway.

Grabbing her hand, I lead her through the crowd out into the middle of the dance floor. She spins around, putting my front to her back, and starts moving her hips, grinding her ass against my dick. I splay my hands over her flat stomach, moving with her. I don't dance to shit like this, but I do know how to fuck, and that's basically what we're doing. She drops her head back against my chest, moaning when I dig my fingers into her hips. Her hands are in my hair, my lips are on her skin, kissing the line of her neck. No one is paying attention to us. I have no idea where Ben and Luke are with their women.

I want her. Right now. Right here.

My mouth presses against her ear as my hands move underneath her shirt. "Are you wet, sweetheart?"

She gasps. Her eyes roll closed. "Yes."

"Do you want me to finger you right here?" I slide my hand an inch lower, teasing the top of her shorts. Her stomach clenches against my hand. "I'll do it. I don't care if anyone sees us."

"No."

"No?" I kiss below her ear. She shudders. "I think you're

lying. I think you want my fingers inside your tight little pussy so bad you fucking ache right now."

She spins around and grabs my face, crashing her mouth against mine, devouring me. She bites my lip. "The only thing I want near my pussy is this dirty mouth." She palms my cock. "And this. Do you ache for me?"

I groan, pushing more of myself into her hand. *Fuck, Beth.* "You know I do."

Tearing through the crowd, I pull her down the dark hallway leading to the back exit. I could fuck her outside in the alley. Press her tight body against the brick and make her scream in the dark. Beth apparently has other ideas.

"Here." She pulls my hand, stopping in front of the men's room. "The women's room will be packed."

I swing the door open, only seeing one pair of feet.

Works for me.

Taking the farthest stall away from the occupied one, I lock the door and begin ripping Beth's shorts off.

"Why didn't you wear a dress?" I whisper.

She wiggles out of her panties and pops the button on my jeans. "Why didn't you?"

"Funny."

Lifting her, guiding her legs around my waist, I clamp my hand over her mouth, pull my dick out, and slide in the first inch.

So wet. Always so wet.

"Fuck, Beth. I need this."

Her eyes roll closed. Moaning against my hand, she digs her nails into my shoulders, tilts her hips, wanting more of me, until . . .

"Mm."

I freeze, not all the way inside her. Beth's eyes flash open as her head tilts up, looking above us. I lower my hand as another moan comes from the occupied stall.

"Oh my God," Beth whispers through a laugh. "Do you think he's jerking off?"

"Oh, oh, mm," a female voice softly cries.

My eyes widen. "Nope."

Shit. We should've gone for the back exit. I could be buried balls deep inside her right now without a fucking audience.

I begin to pull out, figuring we're done here. Beth tightens her legs around my waist and grabs my neck.

"Don't. Keep going," she urges breathlessly. Blush reddens her skin. Her eyes wander from my face.

Well, look at that.

I duck my head, forcing her to look at me as I slide my cock back inside her, as I give her exactly what she's asking for. "Dirty girl," I whisper against her hair. "You want to hear them while I fuck you? Are you gonna get off on that?"

Another moan has Beth clenching down on me. She lets out a ragged breath, drops her head back against the stall, and gasps when I thrust into her hard. "Yes, yes, I want it," she softly groans, squeezing me so damn tight I feel it in my spine.

More noises ring out around us, but nothing I'm hearing comes close to the filthy sounds Beth is giving me. She grabs my face, kissing me, sucking on my tongue as her legs begin to shake. I fuck her harder, slapping her back against the stall.

A strangled groan resonates in the air. "Ben, your dick, God, I love it. Give it to me. Give me that massive cock."

I suck in a sharp breath. *No. No no no no no. Please, God, let there be another Ben in this club. Don't let him say . . .*

"Mia," the dude groans. No, Ben fucking groans, like an asshole, getting off three stalls down from me. *You've got to be fucking . . .*

"God, you're fucking wet, baby. You want this dick? Huh? You want it right here? Fucking this sweet pussy?"

Mia gasps, moaning, "I want it everywhere."

Fuck my life.

I lean back to look at Beth, to see if she's reacting the same way I am, but she starts rocking her hips, clawing at my arms, riding my dick like she's never been this turned on before. She drops a hand between us and starts rubbing her clit. My dick swells, my brain shuts off.

Fuck everything. I'm not stopping. I can't stop.

"Beth," I whisper against her mouth, thrusting deeper, giving into this and blocking out everything that isn't her. "Beth, God . . . Beth."

She trembles, her body locks up. "Reed!" she cries out, jerking my dick with the hottest pussy I've ever had. "Yes, yes, yes, oh, God."

"Reed?" Mia's cautious voice cuts through one of Beth's noises. "Oh my God," she whispers.

I bury my face in Beth's neck, fucking her through her orgasm, feeling mine building at the base of my spine. *So close. God, Beth, give it to me.*

"Reed!" Ben yells, his voice echoing against the ceiling.

"One second."

"If your fucking dick is out right now," he threatens.

Blood rushes in my ears, drowning out every sound that isn't my own heartbeat. I squeeze her ass, grinding Beth against my dick as I come inside her, sucking her nipple into my mouth when she lifts her shirt. She pulls my hair, demands I bite her, whimpers when I kiss her marked skin. My legs nearly give out as I thrust into her one last time, pressing my face between her perfect tits.

"Beth," I whisper, licking up to her neck, sucking her lip,

savoring her sweet taste as it coats my mouth. "Beth."

She smiles against me.

A loud bang comes from the other stall, resembling a fist connecting with something. "Reed, get the fuck out of here before I beat the shit out of you," Ben growls.

I lower Beth to her feet, helping her get dressed.

"Sorry," she whispers, stepping into her shorts.

I look down at her wild, sexed-up hair, the glow in her cheeks, and the light sheen of sweat pooling in the dip between her collar bones. My eyebrows pinch together as I tuck myself away and button my jeans.

"Don't ever apologize for riding my dick like that. You just fucking owned me."

Beth blushes even more, staring up at me through those dark, long lashes.

"Reed," Ben warns, his anger tangible now.

"Ben, that was kinda hot though," Mia whispers. "Feel."

"Leaving. Wait a second before you feel." I pull Beth out of the stall after she fixes her cut-up Ramones T-shirt. The collar has been widened, allowing it to hang off her shoulder and reveal more of her flushed skin.

"Room's all yours," I tell them, opening the door that leads to the hallway. I turn back when I remember Mia's words before Luke and Tessa arrived. Beth halts with me. "Oh, what were you going to say to us earlier? Is everything all right?"

Ben mumbles something I can't make out. Mia laughs quietly, shushing him.

"We just wanted to thank you guys for being there for us. That's all. We love you both."

"Yeah, now get the fuck out."

Beth covers her mouth, laughing.

Leaving Ben and Mia moaning behind us, we head back

down the dark hallway toward the dance floor. The girl's bathroom door swings open and a woman runs out, her face pinched in disgust.

She hooks a thumb over her shoulder. "There's two people in there having sex! I can't pee when someone's yelling 'fuck me harder, Luke' a foot away! Can you?"

The woman stares at Beth, then looks up at me, waiting for an answer. She throws her hands up in the air and stalks away when the two of us start laughing hysterically. Falling against each other. Tears in our eyes.

I'm so fucking glad we went out tonight.

beth

THIS CAN'T BE real.

I'm going to wake up, and all of this will have been a dream.

Finding out about my aunt, moving to Alabama and getting away from Rocco, meeting Reed, falling for Reed, *really* falling for Reed. I'm too happy for this to be real. Happy doesn't even seem like an appropriate description of what I'm feeling anymore. I'm completely blissed out. I wake up like this. I go to bed like this. I'm smiling so much I'm waiting for my skin to crack open. I know Reed sees it, what he does to me, how he makes me feel. I can't hide my reaction to him. I don't even care that it's obvious. I want him to see it. I want him to see a lot of things.

I'll never hurt you. Ever. Please see that.

Please.

Please, God, don't let this be a dream.

I carry a large pot to the sink and ready it to be washed. Watching Reed help serve the homeless shouldn't be a turn-on. It shouldn't, but . . .

I think it's the fact that he's here, that he wanted to be here without me asking him to come that has me worked-up. Not the actual serving part. It could also be what he said to me before we walked inside Holy Cross an hour ago.

"If it means something to you, it means something to me."

I have never wanted to launch myself at someone in a church parking lot before. Reed takes me there.

Turning the water on, I wait for it to fill the pot as my hand agitates the soap at the bottom. My eyes wander across the kitchen, where they have continuously wandered since I volunteered to start on the dishes.

Reed is in the serving line, standing next to Riley. Getting incessantly bombarded with questions from Riley. I know this because every time Reed leans in and gives her a response, she turns around and gives me this look.

The, *he's not giving me enough details, I'll be asking you the same questions later*, look.

The, *I seriously can't believe you got him to volunteer*, look.

And my personal favorite, the, *I'm really, really happy for you two*, look.

Reed bends down, reaching for something on the shelf below the serving table. Bubbles lather against my skin as I move my hand in slower circles, as the bottom of Reed's T-shirt lifts on his back, revealing those two perfect dents at the base of his spine. His faded jeans pull taut against his ass. I begin breathing in and out through my mouth, doing more than admiring my amazing view. I'm staring. Blatantly, not paying attention to anything else. I wet my lips. The skin at the base of my neck grows hot. He straightens just as a warm burst of water spills down the front of my jeans.

I gasp, my stomach tensing. "Oh, great."

My hand wrenches the handle, turning off the tap. Stepping back, I grab a towel off the counter and press it against my jeans, absorbing some of the water.

"Everything okay?"

I look up at Reed, who's now standing a foot away.

Arms crossed over his chest, his light blonde hair tickling

his forehead, he smiles down at me as if he knows exactly why I overflowed the sink. It wouldn't surprise me. He catches me staring ninety percent of the time.

I fold the towel and press it against the bottom of my shirt. "Yes. Fine. I was just thinking about the text I got from my aunt. I kind of spaced out a little."

Good cover. That is what I should be thinking about. Not what Reed would look like serving the homeless naked. For sanitary reasons alone, I shouldn't go there.

He reaches into the sink and pulls the stopper out, draining the water. "What did it say again?"

"That they had something really exciting to talk to me about." I set the towel down after absorbing as much of the water as I can.

Reed picks up another towel and dries his arm off.

I lean my hip against the counter. "I have no idea what it could be. I mean, my idea of exciting is getting an Amazon gift card and buying a whole bunch of books. Something tells me that's not what they want to talk to me about."

Reed laughs softly, tossing the towel on the counter. "Are they home now?"

"They should be by the time I get back."

He nods, lowering his eyes to the front of me. A smirk tugs at his mouth.

"What?" I ask.

"You're still wet."

I drop my head, flattening a hand to my cheek. "Yeah, it's a perpetual problem."

We laugh together as I roll my eyes and step back up to the sink.

"Want some help?" Reed rounds the counter and comes to stand next to me. "We're finished serving, and I need a fucking break from Riley. If she asks me one more damn time how I asked you out . . ."

I tilt my head to look at him. "What did you tell her?"

"Nothing."

"Nothing?" I stab his side with my finger, glaring. "What do you mean, nothing?"

He snorts. "What was I supposed to say?" His voice drops to a hushed whisper as he ducks his head closer to me. "That you sucked my dick while fingering that sweet pussy? That you came all over my face, chantin` my name, makin` me so goddamn hard again I had to jack off while you did it?"

My neck warms with embarrassment. "Well, no, you'd obviously just skip to the part where you said you wanted this."

He grins, leaning back. "I'm all about the lead-up, though. It really adds to the story."

I slap his arm. "You're so dirty."

"You love it."

I do. God, I really, really do.

Laughing, he grabs the scrub brush and starts cleaning the pot. "I'll wash, you dry. I'd hate for you to get any wetter."

I grab a clean towel and hold it against my face, groaning. "I hate you."

"No, you don't."

My heart swells in my chest.

No, I definitely don't.

"AUNT HATTIE?" I call out, stepping inside the house with Reed close behind me. Their car is parked in the driveway, so I know they're home.

"In here, darlin`."

I follow her voice down the hallway and into the kitchen.

Her and Danny are standing at the island, both of them looking up and smiling at me as I step into the room. I run around the island and hug Danny first.

"I'm so, so sorry about your loss, Uncle Danny."

He squeezes me tight. "Oh, thank you, sweetheart. It's okay, though. My cousin has been sick for a long time. We've been ready for it." He releases me and looks across the room. His chest heaves with an inhale. "Reed, do I need to ask what you're doing in my house?"

He doesn't sound angry, which is a relief. Reed told me he knew Danny really well, but I'm sure seeing him walk in with me has to be a bit of a shock. I haven't mentioned anything about Reed to him. Something about him pacing outside with a shotgun kept my mouth shut.

Clearing his throat, Reed steps up to the island and extends his hand. "Sir."

"Sir?" Danny drops his arms and looks from me, to Hattie, back to Reed. Understanding washes across his face. He takes Reed's hand and firmly shakes it, keeping his expression stoic. "How long has this been going on?" He looks over at Hattie. "Did you know about this?"

"Danny, knock it off." She holds her arms out to me and wraps me into an embrace. Danny laughs quietly behind me, lightening the tension in the room. "You look happy," she whispers into my hair.

I nod against her. "I am. Very much."

She leans away, grinning, her dark hair falling past her shoulders, instead of tied back in it's usual clip. "Well, why don't you and Reed have a seat? I'm going to go grab something for you. I'll be right back."

I take one of the stools, Reed takes the other. Leaning on my elbow, I watch as Danny continuously glares at Reed, his arms crossed tightly over his chest while a deep frown settles in between his eyebrows.

"Really?" Reed speaks first, tilting his head. "You know me, Danny."

Danny lightly shrugs. "Hey, she's my niece. I don't give a shit who you are, or how long I've known you. I'm allowed to be protective over her. Deal with it."

Reed chuckles, holding his hands up in surrender. "All right. Fair enough."

Hattie's heels click on the hardwood behind us. She rounds the island and stands next to Danny, holding a piece of paper. Smiling gently, she looks at me.

"Beth, we didn't want to put this in the note we left for you the other day. We wanted to tell you, face-to-face, and after we got a little bit more information. We always want to be honest with you, darling`. Having said that, we have known about this since Wednesday, okay?"

I briefly look at Reed, who's watching me curiously. Turning back to Hattie, I nod. "Okay."

"Right before Danny got the call about his cousin, I was looking through the shoebox, pulling out pictures, and I found this at the bottom. Did you know your birth certificate was in there?" She slides it across the counter.

Leaning forward, I look down at the document I've never seen before, running my finger along the edge of the paper. "No, um, no, I had no idea. I've never really looked through the entire box."

Damn it. Why didn't I? This was in there the whole time?

Gasping, I stop on a name printed above mine. A name I figured I would never know. "Oh my God," I whisper.

Hattie's hand covers mine. "Beth, we found your dad."

I look up, my breathing erratic. My hands sweating,

sticking to the paper. "What? You found him? How?"

My dad. Oh my God. I can't believe this. I can't believe I have more family.

Danny steps to the edge of the counter. "I got in touch with a buddy of mine while we were gone. He's a private investigator. We gave him your dad's name, said he might be in Kentucky but we weren't sure. He got back to me late last night."

"He's in Tennessee now. We spoke to him on the phone as soon as we got home today." Hattie smiles, releasing my hand. "He said he would love to talk to you, if you wanted to call him."

I drop my hands to my lap, staring at the paper in front of me.

He wants to talk to me. My dad, actually wants to *know* me.

"He's in Tennessee?" Reed questions through a soft voice.

I look over at him, blinking quickly, almost forgetting who I've been sitting next to. His eyes are cast down at the counter, as if he's not focusing on anything. I shift on my stool and grab his hands.

"Reed, I can get to know my dad. Isn't this amazing?"

Hattie laughs quietly. "Yes, Reed, he's in Tennessee. He's lived there for a while, he said."

Reed briefly looks at Hattie, then turns his eyes on me. He smiles gently, running his thumb over the top of my hand. "Yeah, it's amazing. What's his name?"

"Jon . . . um." I look back at the paper. "Schilling. I could be Beth Schilling." I wrinkle my nose, and Hattie giggles. "Maybe not." I cover my cheeks with my hands, letting out a hurried breath. "Oh, my God, this is so crazy."

My dad, Jon Schilling, wants me to call him.

A stool scrapes along the hardwood. I glance up, watching as Reed gets to his feet.

"Where are you going?"

His lips pinch into a thin line. Blinking heavily, he scratches his head before pushing his stool in. "I really should head over and get started on those stairs for the deck. I'm going to lose daylight soon." He looks at Danny and Hattie, acknowledging them with a jerk of his head. He bends down and kisses my forehead. "I'll see you later."

Reed walks out of the kitchen, heading down the hallway.

I look up at Hattie and Danny. "I'll be right back." I rush out of the room and catch him at the front door. "Reed, wait."

He turns his head, keeping his hand on the knob. "Yeah?"

"Are you okay? You got really quiet in there."

Sighing, he lets go of the knob and faces me. He pushes his hair out of his one eye. "Yeah, sorry, I'm just tired, and I have a shit load of work to do tonight. I really want to get the deck done for Ben and Mia. Mia, especially. She's really excited about it."

I step closer, looking up at him, pushing the same strand of hair back again when it falls into his left eye.

A part of me thinks he's just saying this to satisfy me with an answer. But why would news about my dad affect him to the point of wanting to leave? Then again, he didn't seem tired five minutes ago.

Reed frowns. He must see my silent questions, the concern I know I'm doing a horrible job at hiding. Grabbing my face with both hands, he kisses my lips softly, then once more. "I'm really, really happy for you, sweetheart. I am. Okay? I'm just tired."

I close my eyes through a nod. "Okay."

Releasing me, he pulls the door open and walks the

distance to his truck, never once turning back. I close the door and lean my back against it.

Maybe he is tired. Ben said something at the club about not having any of the stairs built yet. I have no idea how long a project like that takes, or how much labor goes into it. Maybe Reed knows he has a lot of work to do, and he's anticipating a long night. That has to be it. What other reason is there for his sudden change of mood?

Nodding at my inner conclusion, I walk back down the hallway and into the kitchen. I reach for my phone in my back pocket. "Do you have his number handy?"

Hattie holds up a small piece of paper, as if she was anticipating my question. She hands it to me across the island as Danny pours himself a drink. I leave my phone in my pocket for now.

"Did you talk to him?" I ask her, reading the phone number.

"I did." Danny takes a quick drink of his tea. "Seemed like a nice guy. He said things just never worked out with your mom. She thought it was best if she raised you on her own."

A wave of frustration has me clenching my fist at my side, my lungs taking in slow drags of air. That wasn't her decision to make. I could've at least known about this man. She never once brought him up, never once shared his name with me when I asked about him. She acted like she didn't even know who he was, and all this time, she knew. How could she keep this from me? I've missed twenty-two years with someone.

No, not just someone. My own father.

I look between Hattie and Danny, swallowing down my irritation. "I'm going to go upstairs and call him. Thank you both so much for finding him for me. And for everything else. I really don't think I'll ever be able to repay either one of you."

"Beth." Hattie's mouth pulls down, the lines next to her eyes softening. "You never have to repay us for being your family. We will always be here for you. Our home is yours for as long as you want it to be, you have a job at the bar until you decide otherwise, and Danny will harass any boy you bring home, free of charge."

Hattie and I share a brief laugh as Danny finishes his tea, not disputing that last remark. I wave at them on my way out of the room. "I'll be upstairs if you need me."

Closing my bedroom door behind me, I sit on the edge of the bed, phone in one hand and paper in the other. I'm nervous as hell, but I want to do this. I want to know this man, and a little nervousness isn't going to stop me from making this phone call.

I dial the number, chewing on the pad of my thumb while I wait for the call to connect. I don't have to wait long.

"Hello?"

I smile at the deep voice that greets me. "Hi, is this Jon Schilling?"

"Depends on who's askin`. If you're selling shit, I ain't buying."

"Oh, no. No, I'm not selling anything. I'm . . . sorry, this is awkward." I shift uncomfortably on the bed. *Just tell him who you are. It's the whole reason you're calling.* "My name is Beth. I believe you spoke with my Uncle Danny earlier. I'm Annie Davis' daughter."

I'm your daughter.

My heart starts beating wildly in my chest as his response is delayed. I bite my thumb again, move around the bed so my back is resting against the headboard, then move back to the edge. I grab the piece of paper off the bed. "I'm sorry. Maybe I have the wrong number. Is this . . ."

"Beth," he interrupts with a kind voice. "Yeah, I'm sorry, I get those annoying telemarketer calls all damn day. How are you? How, shit, I don't even really know what to say. Um, how . . . how have you been?"

I laugh quietly, scooting further onto the bed. "I'm good. Great, now, actually. I never thought I would speak to my dad, so, I'm really, really good."

"Well, that's good to hear." His low laugh rumbles against my ear, followed by a few quick coughs. "Sorry to hear about your mom. Your uncle filled me in."

I pick at the tattered strings fraying from the bottom of my T-shirt. "Thank you. May I ask what happened between you two? My uncle mentioned something about her wanting to raise me alone. I'm just wondering why she would've wanted that."

"We didn't really get along too well. Except for that one time." A soft tapping noise comes through the phone. "One second, Beth."

He sniffs several times a short distance away from the phone. I tug hard at the string I'm twisting around my finger and pull it from the shirt, waiting for him to finish blowing his nose.

"Anyway, like I was saying," he continues, sniffing a few more times and clearing his throat again. "Your mom and me, well, let's just say we fought better than anything else. Honestly, Beth, I was only twenty-three when you were born. I wasn't ready for all that shit yet. Your mom taking care of you was the better thing at the time. I moved a few weeks after you were born to go live with a buddy of mine. Never told your mom I was leaving. Never called her after that. If you're looking for somebody to blame here, blame me."

"I'm not looking for somebody to blame. I just wanted

to know why she never told me about you. I asked who you were and she never would give me a name."

"I don't know about all that. I guess she could've been bitter after I left her. Maybe that's the reason."

"Yeah," I agree softly.

Maybe she was worried if I knew who he was, I'd get attached and he'd leave me too. Maybe she was only protecting me.

"We can get to know each other now," Jon suggests, cutting into my thoughts. "I only missed, what, twenty years? That's not that bad."

"Twenty-two," I correct him, smiling.

"Shit."

Laughing, I wrap another string around my finger. "How far away is Tennessee from Alabama?"

"'Bout eight hours, I'd say. Never driven it myself, though. Can't be positive."

Eight hours. That's too far to drive just for a quick, get to know you, visit. I wouldn't want to drive to his house anyway. I don't know him. I need to get to know him first before I make a house visit. An idea pops into my head.

"Would you be interesting in meeting halfway? Like at a place to eat or something? We can sit and talk. I'm free next weekend if you are."

"Yeah, yeah, all right. That sounds good. We can get a bite to eat and talk in person. I like that."

"Really?" I sit up straighter. "That's great. Do you want to do it Saturday? I can look online and pick a spot to meet up."

He wants to meet me. I'm going to meet my dad!

"Yeah, yeah, sounds good. You handle that and call me with the time and place," his voice is suddenly anxious, rattled with his abrupt energy.

I smile at his excitement. "Okay, great. I guess I'll talk to you later on this week."

"Yeah, yeah, perfect. Sounds good. All right, yeah."

I pull the phone away from my ear when the call disconnects, then quickly scroll through my contacts.

Wow. He might be more excited about this meet up than I am. His tone went from borderline sedated to fan girl status in five seconds. He's eager to meet me. He wants to make up for lost time.

I'm meeting my dad. In less than a week, I'm meeting him. This is crazy.

"Hey."

I smile at the sound of Reed's voice. It still carries the same tone he had when he left here so suddenly. Like something's weighing heavy on his mind.

Or, he's just tired, Beth. That is what he said.

I don't let my worry bother me. "Hey, I talked to my dad."

"Oh yeah?" The sound of a machine cutting wood dulls out in the distance. "What did he say?" he asks, his voice clearer.

"He said he wanted to get to know me. We made plans to meet halfway between Alabama and Tennessee on Saturday. Get a bite to eat and talk face-to-face."

"Really?" Reed asks harshly. "You're going to meet up with this guy, and you know nothing about him? You think that's a good idea?"

"He's my dad," I explain quietly. "And I was hoping you would come with me." I listen to him take in a deep breath, the soft sound of Nolan's laughter in the distance, and Ben's deep, muted voice, most likely directed at Nolan. Sighing, I find another string and wrap it around my finger. "I don't want to go by myself, but it's more than that. I want it to be you with me when I meet him. I'm really nervous, Reed, and I know if you're there, I won't be freaking out as much. Will you go with me? Please? You and me?"

"Beth." He says my name so softly, so gently, it's as if he's pressing it into my skin.

"Please?"

He exhales noisily. "Of course I'm going with you. You're not meeting this guy alone, and I'd go fucking crazy if anyone else drove you out there to meet him."

Grinning, I stretch out on the bed. "Thank you. I won't keep you. I know you're busy."

"Yeah, I'll be here for a while. I've only gotten one step done. Nolan keeps asking me shit and it's slowing me down. He's so damn cute about it though I have to answer him."

"He probably loves this time he gets to have with you. You get him so excited."

"Everything gets Nolan excited."

"Uncle Weed! You have to see dis!"

Reed laughs quietly. "He probably found a rock or something."

Hearing Nolan's anxious voice, I decide not to keep Reed. "Okay, I'll let you go."

"All right."

"Reed?"

"Yeah?"

"There's no one else I would rather be with. You know that, right?" I tell him.

"I'm not just referring to the plans on Saturday," I don't say.

He pauses, making me wait for his response.

After he gives it to me, I realize I would've waited more than nine seconds for what he tells me. Two words, that's all, but so, so much more than just two words.

"Me too."

reed

CHRIST, I'M NOT *ready for this.*

I fucking should be though. It's all I've thought about all week, an obsession that's taken over every corner of my mind. I haven't slept for shit. Work hasn't been the distraction I've needed it to be. Thank God for Beth's unreserved excitement keeping her sidetracked. She hasn't noticed how fucking tired I look. The dark circles under my eyes, the heaviness to my steps. My worry is consuming me.

I want to be happy for her.

Fuck, I am happy for her. How can I not be?

This is Beth. My Beth. I'd do just about anything to see that unfuckingbelievable smile light up her face, and it's been a permanent fixture all week. She can't stop talking about her dad, what he might look like, if she resembles him in any way. She even made a list of possible questions she could ask him if they run out things to talk about. She's so happy, so damn happy, and I want that for her. I want it more than my own happiness. Her dad is someone she should know. If they hit it off today and she chooses to pack up and leave Ruxton to go live with him in Tennessee, that's her choice, and I won't make her feel guilty for wanting it. I won't put my fear of losing her before something she deserves. This isn't about me.

This isn't about me.

It's about her.

Sitting in the passenger seat of my truck, wearing the same outfit she wore that day at Sal's. Clapton, tiny denim shorts, showing off those perfect fucking legs, and the boots I've felt digging into my back more times than I can count. If I haven't lived out every one of my fantasies of her wearing only those boots, I'm damn near close.

Beth picks at the polish on her thumb nail, her eyes staring blankly out the front window, her bottom lip caught between her teeth.

We're more than halfway into our trip and she's being unusually quiet.

I don't want her to be nervous about this. I don't want her to worry about anything, especially not whether this man will accept her, love her. Whether he'll want to know this amazing woman he's missed out on for twenty-two years. If he doesn't, if he has no interest in being her father after spending one second with her, he's a fucking idiot who doesn't deserve to live. I won't let anyone or anything else hurt Beth. Jesus fucking Christ, she's been through enough. I also won't let her sit next to me and worry herself sick over this shit.

I can worry enough for both of us. I can also hide it better. I've become a fucking master at it the past week.

Reaching across the bench seat, I grab her hand and give it a gentle squeeze. It's the pressure that does it, the stress of our hands together that breaks her concentration off whatever it is she's staring at right now.

"Come here," I demand gruffly. This isn't a request.

Her bottom lip, reddened from the bite of her teeth, presses against her slightly thinner top one as she thinks it over.

I tug her hand, urging her. "Beth."

"But I have to wear my seatbelt," she argues as her free hand unhooks the front clasp of the harness.

I look out the front window. "It's mostly back roads from here on out. I mapped it that way. We won't get pulled over, and I'm a damn good driver. You're fine." My eyes meet hers. "Slide over. I want you next to me."

She pushes the straps of the harness off her shoulders. "Um, what am I supposed to do with that?"

I look down at the gear shift she's eyeing up cautiously. Tilting my head, I grip her thigh and maneuver her across the seat. "Straddle it, sweetheart. I know how much you like having a big stick between your legs."

Her cheeks lift as she hooks one leg over the gear shift. "Speaking of big sticks . . ."

"The answer is yes."

"You don't even know what I'm going to say," she laughs, settling beside me.

God, I missed that sound. I don't want her to ever be quiet with me.

"Besides," she continues. "I doubt we have time for anything that filthy mind of yours is thinking up."

"Beth, if it has anything to do with my big stick and you, my answer will always be yes. And fuck time. It isn't an issue. As much as I hate to admit this, I can't last for shit when it comes to you. My only redeeming quality is that I can work that unfairly tight pussy of yours in a matter of minutes, sometimes seconds."

Her head falls against my shoulder with a soft giggle. "Okay, noted, but I wasn't thinking about doing anything with your big stick right now."

"No?" I ask, sighing heavily as I glance down at my lap. "You hear that? Are you as heartbroken as I am?"

"Your penis has feelings?"

"He does, and you've just crushed them."

Her lips brush against my neck. "I promise to kiss him all better later."

I shift to a higher gear after noticing the change in the speed limit, then rest my hand on Beth's thigh. "So, big sticks? What's on your mind, pervert?"

"I was just thinking about last weekend. The bathroom sex romp with Ben and Mia."

Our eyes lock as we both turn our heads at the same time. Her bold, brown ones, alight with mischief. Mine, broadened with discomfort.

I groan uncomfortably. "Please don't mention the words sex romp, and our friend's names in the same sentence," I beg through a shake of my head. "As hot as you were that night, I'm still trying to forget everything I heard that didn't come out of your mouth."

Making eye contact with Mia has been a challenge when I've seen her this week. Luckily, she hasn't seemed fazed by anything she heard in the bathroom.

Ben is a different story.

"See, that's what I wanted to talk about. Mia made a comment about Ben's massive . . . member," she pauses, smiling up at me. "And I feel bad about not giving yours a shout-out. He's massive too, and very thick. I could've said something about it."

I look down at her, briefly taking my eyes off the road. "Like?"

Talk about my dick. I fucking love when you do that.

"Like," she echoes, palming me. I groan, arching away from the seat.

"God, Beth."

She laughs wickedly at the desperation in my voice.

Her hand. God, her hand is a menace.

"How you're so big it almost hurts," she whispers, slowly stroking me. "So long, and thick. You fuck me so deep, I think sometimes you're hitting my spine. And your taste. I love the taste of your dick, Reed, especially after you've been inside me."

Jesus fuck.

I press my hand against hers when she goes for my zipper. "I'm worried we won't make it to the diner if you touch me."

"I thought you said time isn't an issue."

Raising an eyebrow, I remove her hand from my lap, put my arm around her, and tuck her against my side. Her hair tickles my mouth. "It isn't, but neither is my stamina. I'll pull over and fuck you into next week if you whip my dick out."

She shudders, then relaxes her body. Her nervousness forgotten as she melts against me.

I don't know how long we drive in silence, but it's different from before. It's the kind of quiet I'm used to sharing with Beth. The stillness that doesn't feel like it's missing anything. I'm still losing my shit on the inside, wondering how I'm going to take hearing her obvious choice if things go well today, but she's fearless next to me now.

My brave girl. So fucking brave. Does she know how amazing I think she is? Have I shown her? Told her enough?

Her head moves against my chest, and I glance down, meeting dark eyes brimming with tears.

What the . . .

My heart slams against my sternum, nearly rocking me forward. All words escape me. My fucking vocabulary reduced to a pained groan as I look to the road to make sure I'm still on it, then back down at her.

"Why did you stop?" she asks through a soft voice.

Stop? Stop what? What the fuck was I doing besides assuming my girl was fucking content next to me?

She laughs at my confusion, which only exaggerates at the sound of her amusement. "You were humming," she explains, running her finger below my bottom lip. "You do that when you're quiet sometimes. Did you know? I love hearing you, Reed. Your voice might be my favorite sound."

Humming? I was humming? And she's ready to burst into fucking tears because I stopped?

"You've hummed it before. I don't think I know that song."

Her hand falls away from my face.

What was I humming? Something she's heard from me before, but what?

I think back to the nights Beth has fallen asleep in my arms. When I've pressed my lips to the back of her neck and pulsed a melody against her skin.

Of course.

I take my hand briefly off the wheel to run it through my hair. "Yeah, I can't get it out of my head."

"It's beautiful. Will you sing it to me?"

"What?"

Sing it to her? Is she serious? I've never sung to anyone before. I do that shit when I'm alone, or when I can be drowned out by the radio.

Her full, red lip pouts as she looks up at me. "Please? I want to hear the words so bad."

"Your voice might be my favorite sound."

Sighing, my head hits the seat. I can do this. It's just singing.

Her finger traces lazy circles on my thigh, but she stops the second the words flow past my lips.

"I'm trying real hard not to shake. I'm biting my tongue,

but I'm feeling alive and with every breath that I take, I feel like I've won. You're my key to survival. And if it's a hero you want, I can save you. Just stay here. Your whispers are priceless. Your breath, it is dear. So please stay near."

I risk a glance down at her. Mouth dropped open, her eyes blazing with wonder as she stares up at me.

Well, at least she isn't crying.

"Reed," she murmurs, her gaze transfixed on my mouth. Her heartbeat thundering against my side. "Keep going."

I kiss her head, watching that smile grow, feeling it hit me in the center of my chest.

My eyes turn back to the road as I give her what she wants.

THE SILVER MOON Diner only has a few cars in the gravel lot surrounding it. None of them a black Monte Carlo, the vehicle Beth's dad told her he would be driving.

"We're early," I reassure her when she looks around the lot, then back at the road. I place my hand on her back as she turns her head, her eyes heavy with awareness.

Sighing, she tugs at the bottom of her shorts. "It's almost two o'clock. We're not *that* early."

I lead her toward the door, not responding, because fuck, she's right. We're meeting at two. It's less than five minutes 'til. We're not early. We're on time.

I take in a deep breath, calming my nerves.

The hostess inside the diner greets us with a smile. "Afternoon. Two today?"

"Three," Beth eagerly corrects her. "My dad's coming too."

I sit across from Beth in the booth, taking the menu from the hostess and flipping it open. Beth sets hers down and stares out the large window, keeping her hands in her lap.

An older woman in a bright teal apron walks up, smiling. "Afternoon. My name is Doris and I'll be your waitress today. Can I start you two off with something to drink?"

Beth doesn't respond. Doesn't turn her head or acknowledge our waitress is any way.

I look up at Doris. "Sweet tea for her. I'll take a root beer."

Doris walks away.

I tap my foot against Beth's under the table, setting my menu aside. She turns her head, the corner of her mouth lifting slightly. She looks sad and hopeful at the same time. How that's possible, I have no idea.

Our drinks are set in front of us. Doris pulls a notepad out of the front of her apron, ready to take down our order.

"Oh, we're waiting for someone," Beth tells her, holding up her hand. Her dark hair brushes against her cheek when she turns her head abruptly. "Can we wait until he gets here? I want us to eat together."

Doris tucks the notepad back away, winking at Beth. "Sure thing, darling. Let me know if you need anything in the meantime."

Beth settles back against the seat, setting her phone down in front of her as Doris walks away.

I glance at the clock on the wall above the door. Ten after two. The condensation building on my glass absorbs into my hand as I take a sip of the chilled soda.

"Did you tell your aunt and uncle where you were going today?" I ask Beth, wanting to keep her talking. Needing to keep her mind off the nearly vacant parking lot she's staring at.

Shit, I need to keep my mind off it. Where the fuck is he?

She nods, focusing on me, a hint of a smile touching her lips. "Danny lectured me for an hour when I told him what

I was doing. He seemed slightly less worried about it when I said you were going with me."

"Slightly," I repeat, laughing at Danny's protectiveness. *Bastard knows me well enough, but still gives me shit for dating his niece.*

I cross my arms over my chest and lean back. "Like I'd let you do this alone."

"I don't think I could've done this alone," she says quietly. Her eyes lower to the table, her finger moving along the edge of the black, floral phone case. "Especially if he doesn't show up."

A pressure builds in my chest. "Look at me," I demand. She raises her head. "Don't do that. He'll be here. He's probably just stuck in traffic."

Her eyes wander to the window.

I repeat the same words to her over the next hour, reassuring her, trying to keep myself convinced.

By three o'clock, I'm emphasizing how awful traffic must be coming from Tennessee. She dials her dad, frowning when he doesn't answer. Every time Doris begins to make her way to our table, I keep her back with a shake of my head.

By four o'clock, I'm ready to drive to wherever the fuck this dickhead is coming from and drag his ass here myself.

Beth tries to reach him again. And again, each time greeted with a voicemail. I try to engage her in conversation about anything, monotonous rantings spilling out of my mouth. Every thought that pops into my head I'm throwing at her, but it's as if I'm alone in the diner. The self-possessed woman across from me becomes a ghost of her former self. She stops smiling, stops flicking her eyes in my direction when I tap her foot. The sound of her name doesn't warrant the same reaction I'm used to getting from her. Each minute that passes drags her further away from me.

By ten after five, my body is rigid against the seat, my vision vibrating with anger. A single tear rolls down Beth's cheek, and I can't take this anymore. I'm ready to kill this man. I want to take his life away from him, and I want to do it slowly.

Drag it out over hours. Make him feel a fraction of the pain Beth is feeling. Then make him feel it again.

I lean over the table and grab Beth's elbow, pulling her hand into mine.

"He's not coming," she whispers through a shattered voice. She doesn't fight my hold. She allows me this, this one part of her to comfort. Her eyes fall to the phone on the table. "I don't understand. Do you think he could still be stuck in traffic?"

No.

"Maybe."

"Or he forgot? Do you think he forgot about me?"

I stare into her eyes when she lifts them, the unshed tears threatening to wet her cheeks. "When was the last time you spoke to him?" I ask, thinking maybe he did forget. Praying for that explanation, and not the one I fear kept him from showing up.

He doesn't want to know her.

My jaw clenches so tight, my teeth ache.

He doesn't deserve to live.

She swallows noisily. "Last night. He sounded really excited again, like he did when I first spoke to him. He was talking so fast. I reminded him where we were meeting and what time. He said he would be here. He promised. I tried calling him this morning before you picked me up but no one answered. I figured he left already."

"Beth." I squeeze her hand when her lip trembles. My

forearm shakes against the table. My whole body charged, ready to detonate at any second.

"He sounded so excited," she repeats, blinking heavily. Tears stream down her face. She pulls her hand out of mine and slips out of the booth, nearly stumbling, but righting herself quickly. She pushes against my shoulder when I lean to help her. "Don't. I'm fine. I just need to use the bathroom."

My back slams against the seat. I wipe both hands down my face, trying to keep myself from flipping over this table.

How could he does this to her? How could that fucker get her hopes up and then bail on her like this? He has her fucking number. He could've called if something came up. I'd still think he was a worthless piece of shit, but I'd be thinking it somewhere else with Beth. Not here. I wouldn't be watching her break down in the middle of a fucking diner.

I swipe her phone off the table and hit redial. A generic voicemail picks up. I disconnect the call and hit redial again. And again, the stress of the phone against my ear building to an unbearable pressure. If he's sleeping, if his ass is still home and he did forget, if he tries to give me one fucking excuse, I'm tearing into him. I press redial. Six attempts, seven, on eight I'm ready to give up, until . . .

"Hello? Yeah?" Two coughs, then the sound of bottles clinking together comes through the phone. "Shit," he mumbles, groaning. "My fucking head. Christ, what time . . . who is this?"

My breathing grows thick, scratching against the back of my throat.

His fucking head. Bottles. This asshole is hung over.

I turn toward the window, keeping my voice low, but unable to confine the rage to my tongue. It coats my words like fresh tar sticking to pavement.

"You fucking piece of shit. You're home? Do you have any idea how crushed your daughter is right now? She's fucking waiting for you, asshole, and you're just now waking up? Are you fucking kidding me with this shit?"

He moans. More bottles clank together. "Fuck, I . . ." Sighing, a mattress creaks through the phone before his bullshit excuse. "Look, I wanted to come. I was going to. I'm just . . . I can't be nobody's fuckin' dad, you know? It ain't me."

I angle more toward the window when two patrons walk into the diner. My mouth presses against the phone. "No, I don't fucking know. I don't know how you could act excited to meet your own daughter, get her fucking hopes up, and then tear them down like this. If you didn't want to be 'nobody's *fuckin'* dad', you shouldn't have arranged to meet her, motherfucker. She said you were excited and shit. What was that, huh? Was that all a lie?"

"Man," he mumbles. "Every time I talked to her, I was gettin' high. I don't remember half the shit I said. It was mainly her talkin' anyway."

I see red.

"You know what? It's fucking better this way. I'm glad you're not here. You don't deserve to know her. You never will. Don't ever call her, don't reach out to her, even if you're fucking sober, you hear me? I'll never let you anywhere near her. And if I ever fucking see you face-to-face, I'm going to cause you more pain then you've ever felt. You understand?"

He chuckles sardonically. "Threatening a druggie isn't going to do you much good. I'm slowly killing myself anyway."

"Not soon enough, asshole."

"Tell her I'm sorry."

"Go to Hell."

Click.

I stuff the phone into my pocket and push from the booth, heading toward the bathrooms. My fist connects firmly with the women's room door, rattling it.

"Beth?"

I step inside. I don't give a shit if there's other women in here. That's my last concern.

Beth turns her head as she stands in front of the sink, her fingers wiping underneath her reddened eyes. "Reed?" Her small voice echoes in the tightly spaced room. She takes a cautious step forward, taking the hand I'm holding out to her.

"Let's go home."

I leave a fifty on the table for Doris. She never got to bring us anything besides drinks, and I wasn't going to screw her out of a tip.

The clouds shift quickly overhead, darkening the sky as we walk across the lot, hand in hand. Thunder claps in the distance, the wind whips around us, blowing Beth's shirt up to reveal her flat stomach. The first few drops of rain pelt against my forearm as I open the passenger door.

"Storm's coming. A bad one, by the looks of the sky. Hurry, get in."

"My phone?" she asks, suddenly realizing she doesn't have it.

"It's here." I touch the pocket of my jeans.

She settles against the seat, allowing me to buckle her in. Her eyes are distant, losing focus on the dashboard as her body sags lifelessly, melting into the leather. If I could see her soul right now, it would look battered. Broken. On the exterior, she's still Beth, minus the spark. No smile, no surfaced excitement. Internally, she's a stranger to me. This isn't my Beth.

I need to get her home.

By the time I reach the driver's side door, the rain is steady, wetting my shirt, my hair, beading on my lashes. I wipe my hand over my face and start the truck. The gravel kicks up away from my tires. I get us onto a main road, avoiding the back ones because I know they'll flood first if the rain doesn't stop.

It doesn't.

It comes down harder, thicker, like sheets of fog blanketing my windshield. My visibility deteriorates with each passing minute. Lightening slices across the darkened sky, illuminating the road ahead. A car nearly clips my front end when the driver hydroplanes.

Beth gasps next to me. Her knuckles white as she grips the harness.

I take the nearest exit, pulling into the parking lot of a Holiday Inn. I turn to Beth after parking under the awning attached to the main entrance.

"Are you okay with us getting a room for the night? I don't think we should drive in this."

She nods, keeping her eyes on the dashboard.

I pay quickly for a room. Beth doesn't react when I climb back into the truck. Her head is still tilted back against the seat, her eyes still distant. Detached. After parking along the side of the building in front of our room, she allows me to help her down, burrowing against my side to shield herself from the rain.

We get inside the room.

I bolt the lock behind me, securing the door, wiping the rain off my arms as Beth moves toward the bed.

"I'm going to use the bathroom," I tell her, kicking my shoes off by the small table along the wall. My keys slide across the surface of the wood when I toss them.

Beth sits on the edge of the bed, her fingers tangling together in her lap, her head lowered.

I take her phone out of my pocket and place it on the quilted comforter. The bathroom door creaks as I pull it shut.

Cool water fills my hands from the tap. I splash it on my face, reaching back to squeeze the base of my neck. I stare at my reflection in the large, oval mirror above the sink. Dark smudges rim my eyes. My complexion washed out, paler than usual.

I need sleep.

After relieving myself and washing my hands, I open the door and find Beth standing next to the bed. Her hand clutching her phone. Her eyes narrowed, focused on the screen.

Fuck. Did that asshole call her?

I take a tentative step closer and she pins me with her stare. My feet stick to the carpet.

"I was texting my aunt to tell her I wouldn't be home tonight, and I saw the last call I made, but I didn't make it." She looks at the phone again, then back at me. "Did you speak to my dad?"

Shit. Shit shit shit. Didn't want her to know about that.

"Yeah." My eyes stray from her face. I wipe my clammy palms on my jeans, suddenly nervous as hell. "I did. I called him while you were in the restroom. A lot. I woke him up."

"He was asleep?"

"He was hung over, possibly high." My gaze meets hers. I move, tangling my hand in her damp hair. "Beth."

"What did you say to him?" A tear rolls down her cheek. She lowers the phone to her side, staring up at me.

I flatten my fingers against the back of her neck. "That he didn't deserve to know you. That I would beat the shit out of him if he ever came here. I don't know. I was pissed. I said a lot. I told him he would never hurt you again. I told him to stay away from you. To never call you. I said . . ."

Her mouth crashes against mine with an urgency I can taste. I moan as she clings to my body. Her lips are wet, damp from her tears. I suck them as we undress each other. Clothes fall to the floor, some hang off the side of the bed. We collapse into a tangled mess of limbs and fevered touches.

I lift her easily, sliding her further up the mattress.

She touches my cheek as I trap my cock between us.

"Beth." I press her name against her jaw. My breath hitches as I enter her slowly. Stretching her. Filling her.

Mine.

"God, Beth." I wet my lips, rocking into her. "Beth . . ."

If I could only say one word for the rest of my life . . .

She wiggles, presses her heavy tits against my chest, fists my hair and tugs it gently.

"Reed," she moans into my mouth. Her legs catch our bodies together. Greedy hands roam down my back.

I take her slowly. There's no rush to this. Digging my fingers into her hips, I lift her pelvis off the bed and drive into her. Deep, deeper, thrusting so goddamn slow she shakes as she stretches for me. Her hands flatten against the wooden headboard. Her eyes roll closed. My tongue swells in my mouth, preventing the filth I'm usually whispering against her skin from escaping. I drop my hands to the bed beside her head, flex my arms, and fill her. Again. Slower. We lock eyes. Our foreheads touch, damp with sweat.

"Oh my God," she says between ragged breaths. Her legs tremble against my hips.

This is different, and she knows it. I've never taken her this gently before. I've never been this quiet. My heart's never beaten like this.

Never. So many firsts. What is happening?

Is it because of today? It is because I've been a wreck all

week, worrying I'd lose her? I'm exhausted, my body drained of it's normal vigor during sex, but that's not it. That's not why I can't be rough right now.

This isn't fucking. Not this. I can't stop looking at her. I can't tell her how wet my dick is. I can't ask her to suck me while I finger her ass.

I don't want to stop.

I don't want to come.

I don't want anything but her.

I've never been this terrified.

She gasps, grabbing my face, biting my lip as she comes. "Reed," she whispers, moaning against my mouth. "I love you . . . I love you."

My body surges. I fill her, my control breaking as I bury my face into her neck. I groan against her skin, but I feel like I'm screaming. Words ring out in my ears, three simple words.

Her small body takes my weight as darkness pulls me under.

"It's okay," a soft voice murmurs. A hand strokes my hair.

I was wrong.

Now, right now, I've never been this terrified.

beth

HALF AWAKE, HALF floating in and out of a dream, my body slowly untangles itself from the sheet as I stir on the mattress. Warm skin against my shoulder peels my eyelids open. I turn my head, brushing the hair off my face.

Reed lies on his back, eyes closed, mouth slightly parted. Half his body covered in the gray sheet. He doesn't rouse from my hand ghosting over his chest. Normally, even the slightest touch has him pulling me closer.

"It's okay."

I stare up at the ceiling, trying to find comfort in the words I gave Reed last night. The words I whispered over and over into the dark. The words maybe I needed to hear more than him.

My heart thunders against my hand as I lay it flat between my breasts.

"It's okay."

"I love you . . . I love you."

Quick rushes of air burst past my lips. My mouth quickly growing dry with each passing second. My legs kick out, removing the rest of the sheet when my skin begins to burn beneath the surface.

People say things they don't mean when they're distressed. Having my dad bail on me could've loosened my tongue, leaking words of desperation from my mouth.

I was unraveling at the diner. I was breaking down in the hotel room. Reed was gentle, trying to hold me together. I almost sobbed when I came. I told him I loved him.

People say things they don't mean when they're distressed. I've never said one word to Reed I didn't mean. Last night was no exception.

"It's okay."

He didn't say it back. He didn't say anything. My heart slowly pulsed against his back as I held him, as he drifted to sleep turned away from me. As I waited and waited for that moment to hit him. Fear kept him silent, or maybe that wasn't it at all. Maybe he doesn't love me. Maybe he can't. Maybe . . .

"No one will ever love you the way I do. No one."

I squeeze my eyes shut. "No," I whisper, pushing the unwanted voice out of my head, but it grows louder, seeping into every crevice of my soul. Mocking me with the truth I'm too scared to admit.

"No one will want you."

I violently shake my head. Rocco's face materializes behind my eyes, his merciless smirk twisting across his mouth as he laughs at me. I can almost hear it above the rushing in my ears, above the cruel words. Above my doubt.

Throwing myself out of bed, I grab my clothes and quickly dress, my hands shaking as I step into the bathroom. Amber light flickers on above my head. The door shuts behind me and I want to collapse against it, but I don't. I dampen a washcloth and rub it over my face, underneath my hair, to the back of my neck. I rinse out my mouth. Bracing my hands on the sink, I stare at my reflection. Long minutes pass as I study my face.

I was unraveling at the diner. I was breaking down in the hotel room. But I don't believe I've ever looked this broken.

The chipped fragments of my heart are cutting me, slowly bleeding me out, draining the light from my eyes.

I chose to love a man who can't love me. Who will never love me.

Movement in the room pulls my gaze from the mirror. I step up to the door and listen.

He's dressing, the sound of fabric dragging across skin. I hear shuffling, then all too quickly the door opens and I'm facing Reed.

"Hey, hi," he quickly utters, startled. He looks half asleep. He clears his throat, looking past me. His eyes shifting nervously. "Need to use the bathroom. We gotta get going. It's almost ten."

Tears gather in my eyes and I blink them away. *What was I expecting? He can't do this. He warned me himself.*

"Yeah," I reply, padding out into the room. The door shuts behind me and I'm left alone.

I wait for Reed out by his truck.

It's no longer raining. The sky a kaleidoscope of blues and soft pinks. I stand in a shallow puddle, watching the mud squeeze out from under my boots. Growing impatient, and realizing I can't have Reed help me into his truck anymore, I test the handle to see if it's unlocked.

My hand falls to my side. I heave a deep breath just as a clicking sound pops the small tab up behind the window. Reed saunters purposely toward me over my shoulder. I tug the handle and climb inside, tumbling against the seat, quickly fastening the harness as he reaches my door.

His brow knits together as he stares up at me. "You good?"

God, how do I even answer that?

Nodding, I rest back against the seat, my eyes trained ahead. "Fine." Tension makes my stomach clench. I feel nauseous. I pray I don't puke all over the dark leather interior.

My vocabulary diminishes to one word responses the entire trip home, not that there's ample conversation flowing between us. Reed is deathly quiet for the most part, only asking me if I want to listen to music, if I'm hungry, and if I want him to stop. I can't eat. I wouldn't be able to stomach it. I give him my answers while I stare out the window, never turning my head.

Two and a half hours feels like a lifetime. I bite my cheek when I feel the threat of tears, the pain distracting me, harnessing my focus on the metallic taste coating my tongue. I can't cry. Not yet. Not when I still need to let go of him.

Reed pulls into the driveway and shifts into park. I have so much to say, but so little is needed.

He breaks the silence first as I'm shoving the harness off my shoulders.

"I'm going to head over to Ben's to finish up the deck. I'm fucking wiped, so, I'll probably just crash after."

Our eyes lock. My arms suddenly feel heavier, my limbs sticking to the seat.

That's all he has to say to me. Indeed, so little is needed.

I turn away and tug on the door handle. "Thank you for what you said to my dad, and for helping me through that. That meant a lot to me."

"Of course," he replies easily. No stammer to his words.

I turn around after climbing out of the truck.

His eyes search my face, so strange in color, then shift to the clock on the dash. "I should go. Get started so I'm not trying to hammer down shit at night. That didn't work out so well for me before."

His words are like a hand pushing me away. *This is it. Just go.*

"Okay. Yeah, sorry." My voice catches, but I hide it with a quick cough.

I step back after closing the door, my eyes following his truck as he backs out of the driveway. Dust hovers an inch above the dirt road behind him, settling after a few minutes.

Yeah, I stand there for minutes, thinking he'll actually come back. Believing he'll realize he forgot to tell me he loves me too.

Hope is a funny thing. Even when you think you have none, it refuses to lie down quietly. In the darkest moments of my life, I've always had hope. Why would I expect any different now?

The house is empty, the curtains pulled, keeping out the vibrant sky. Hattie and Danny are gone, most likely at the bar. I pack like a hurricane ripping through the house. Bed made, quilt neatly tucked in at the corners, leaving it just like I first saw it weeks ago.

With a heavy mind, I sit on the edge of the mattress and pull the cash I've made working at McGill's out of the drawer. I roughly flatten out the bills.

A little over three hundred dollars. That's a couple nights in a hotel, some food, not much. If I burn through that, I'll have nothing. I know where having nothing leads me. I can't live in my car again, but I can't stay here. I can't be this close to Reed and let him go.

I'll continue to love him in Ruxton. I might forget I ever met him somewhere else.

I have one option that keeps me from losing everything I have. One option I can at least build on until I find something else.

I grab a piece of paper and a pen out of the office and carry it into the kitchen. My duffle waits for me by the front door.

What do I say to people who gave me so much when I only wanted to know them?

Tears wet the paper as my hand moves with an energy I didn't think I had anymore. I tell them how grateful I am for everything, how I'll never forget them. I thank them for their kindness and love. Lifting my pen, I gather my explanation for my swift departure. I don't want them to worry. They have to understand, this has nothing to do with them.

Under my name, I ask them to tell Reed goodbye for me. To tell him I'm sorry and that I'll miss him, even when I don't want to. I leave my note for them on the table underneath the corner of a placement. Pulling my phone out of my pocket, I turn it off and set it on top of my goodbye.

Once again, time is my enemy. Eight hours in the car, two stops for gas, and one food break happens in a blur of headlights and highways. I'm back in front of that same house I left only weeks ago before my hands stop shaking. Or maybe I'm just now beginning to tremble.

The strap of my duffle digs into my shoulder as I walk up the stone steps. My fist hits the door, my head lowers when it opens. A familiar hand caresses my cheek.

"Knew you'd be back. Fuckin' knew it."

I wince at his voice, at the way his fingers linger on my skin as if he has any right to touch me. Leaning away from his hand, I wait for him to move out of the doorway. He takes great pleasure in this, me, needing him, crawling back so quickly.

I've survived this before. I can do it again until I find something else.

With an elaborate sweep of his hand, he gestures for me to walk inside.

"Thank you."

He takes great pleasure in that as well. My gratitude, lifting the corners of his mouth into the most deceiving smile

I've ever seen.

I'm sure the devil smiles too. I'm sure it's just as alluring.

He leans against the wall, picking at his teeth with a toothpick. "How'd the whole family thing turn out?" he asks behind me as I make my way toward the bedroom.

I stop almost to the door, my hand flattening against the wall. Slipping my fingers underneath the strap of the duffle, I pull my shoulders back and move with purpose.

Rocco finds my strength amusing, his cruel chuckle rumbling in the air like a storm in the distance, seeping into the bedroom after I collapse onto the bed.

I cry into the pillow, thinking about Reed and how sweet his laugh sounds.

reed

B ETH.

My hand reaches out, searching blinding for her warmth. Cool sheet fills my palm.

She's not here.

No, of course she isn't. Why would she be?

I did exactly what I told her I was going to do last night. What I needed to do. After finishing the last cosmetic details on Ben's deck, I came home and crashed. I needed time to process everything. She needed time too. She was obviously still reeling from the shit with her dad.

My brave girl. She looked so small sitting next to me.

My mind wouldn't go quiet, even at Ben's while I was focused. I figured a full night's sleep would help, but I was restless all night.

Beth.

At 11:30 p.m., I debated driving over to her aunt's to see her. At a little past two, I palmed my phone and stared at the picture she saved as my wallpaper. A selfie taken of her and I, our faces squeezed together.

God, I was in love with her.

I was in love, and I was terrified, but fuck, I was so lost in love I didn't want to be apart even while I came to terms with it. I forced myself to put my phone down and close my eyes. She didn't need me waking her up at odd hours in the night. I would let her sleep, I would hopefully get some myself. My soul missed her, my body craved her. Sleep evaded me.

"I love you . . . I love you."

She nearly sobbed those words. All I wanted to do was say them.

Turning my head, I watch the pale light from the window dance along the carpet. I don't need to look at the clock to know it's still too fucking early. My alarm hasn't sounded yet, but I can't lie here anymore. I can't ignore this strange loss settling over me any longer.

I shower and dress urgently after finally noting the time. Just enough to go see Beth, tell her everything I'm feeling, then bolt it to work. I'll probably wake her up at this hour. She'll look all sleep-rumpled and soft against the sheets. Leaving her might be a challenge.

As I'm grabbing a travel mug for my coffee, my phone rings from the bedroom. Puzzled, I run back up the stairs. It's barely after five. No one calls me this early.

Beth Davis, from McGill's flashes across my screen.

A familiar heat warms my chest, spreads down my spine. I'm suddenly wide awake.

"Hey, I was just coming over to see you. You're up early." My steps feel lighter as I advance back down the hallway. "God, Beth, I . . ."

"Reed, is she with you? P-Please tell me she's there."

I halt, not quite at the opening to the kitchen, recognizing the voice instantly. "Hattie? Hey, what's wrong? Are you okay?"

"Beth," she strains through a whimper. "Is she with you?"

I glance around me, confused, suddenly expecting Beth to jump out from behind something. "No," I answer curiously, brushing a wet strand of hair off my forehead. "Why?"

"Oh, no," she whispers. "Oh, no, no, no."

Her voice sounds miles away. Worry plagues me, spreading in my veins like an infection. Coffee forgotten, I swipe my keys off the counter and head outside to my truck. I'm sprinting, my boots kicking up gravel.

"Hattie, what's going on? Where's Beth?"

She mumbles something I can't understand, her voice breaking between fragile cries. Trapping the phone between my ear and shoulder, I start the truck and peel out onto the road.

"Hattie! Where is she?" I ask again when I don't get an answer, my voice more demanding. My skin growing hot at the base of my neck.

She cries harder, sobbing now, breaking down completely. "She l-left. She went b-back ," she wails, gasping for air.

Panic pollutes my mind. I break out in a cold sweat.

"What?" My response sticks to my tongue, struggling to roll past my lips as the world blurs in front of me. I blink heavily, solidly training on the road ahead. My hand violently shifts gears.

She went back? Why would she leave? What the fuck?

I search my memory for an explanation, something I obviously missed.

Images of Beth poison me with guilt. I looked at her yesterday, but did I really see her? Her sorrowed expression in the morning when I opened the bathroom door, the way she kept her head down, or turned away from me in the truck on the drive home. She was so small, so quiet.

How could I have been so blind?

"I love you . . . I love you."

Three words, three simple words. The ones she nearly sobbed the night before, the ones I couldn't seem to repeat. She wasn't dealing with the shit that happened with her dad.

She wouldn't leave because of him. He wasn't here.

It was me.

I told her I would never hurt her. I told her I could only give her so much of me, when in reality I never had a choice. I loved her, and I never said it. She left thinking I never will.

I blow through a red-light, heading for the nearest road that takes me to the highway. "Hattie, where was Beth before she moved here? Where in Louisville? Do you have an address?"

Hattie whimpers, quietly murmuring practiced words, as if she's reading them off something. She isn't hearing me. I can't make anything out over the noise of the engine.

"Hattie." I try for her attention again. Frustration flares to life in my veins. My blood runs hot. Realizing I'm wasting my time trying to get any information from her over the phone, I veer off onto a side road, heading to my original destination.

"I'm coming over, okay? I'm almost there," I tell her.

Her voice never pauses, never reacts to mine, but it does grow softer as the one in my head dominates for attention, reminding me over and over again why this has happened.

Why this is all my fault.

I feel sick when I don't see Beth's car parked in the driveway. I hate that fucking car, knowing she lived in it, but I would give anything to see it right now. I send a short text to my dad before I get out of the truck, telling him I won't be in today. Speaking to him would lead to being lectured about how reckless I'm being with my sick leave. The opinion of a man who's never missed a day's work.

The front door is unlocked, and I announce my presence quietly as I step inside. I don't have time to knock and wait to be let in. I'm hours away from Beth. This is about getting the information I need and getting on the road.

A soft light from the kitchen draws me down the hallway.

No voices.

Hattie looks up from the kitchen table when I enter, a piece of paper in her hand, her face flushed and wet with tears. The phone with the black floral case sits in front of her.

I disconnected our call shortly after I told Hattie I was on my way. I couldn't stand hearing and not understanding her at the same time. Knowing she was on Beth's phone, and that Beth was now without one.

I move further into the room, ready to ask for an address.

"I was hoping she was at your house. That she changed her mind," Hattie whispers, her eyes drifting to the paper. "We got home late from the bar last night. Her car was gone, but we figured she was still with you, so we went to bed. I didn't find her note telling us goodbye until this morning." Our eyes lock. She pushes away from the table, standing. "Reed, we can't let her go back to that man. I don't know what happened between you two, or if this is just because of the stuff with her dad, which I feel so horrible about, but she can't go back there. Not there. He was awful to her." Her face falls apart in tears. A hand covers her mouth, muffling her sobs.

He was awful to her? HE.

I stare at Hattie as every muscle in my body locks up at once. As the conversations with Beth about her life in Kentucky flood my mind with snapshots of information.

Her mom dying. Beth homeless, living in her car. Until . . .

I was so absorbed in her absence, in the address I needed to pry from Hattie, I didn't consider *who* Beth was going back to.

The guy she was with before me. The stranger who took her in. The one she didn't seem keen on discussing.

"Nobody. Just this guy I met. It doesn't matter."

She couldn't satisfy me with an answer quick enough on

the phone. Then a day later, in my arms, she was vague again.

"Relationships change. There's really nothing more to it."

Fuck. FUCK. What didn't she tell me? I understood her reserve as a sad moment in her life she didn't want to dwell on. I could tell she was uncomfortable discussing it. I didn't want to pry. I didn't want to sound desperate to know her.

This is all my fault.

And God, I *was* desperate, to anything involving her. I was sated and starved at the same time.

My nostrils flare in time with the heavy expansion of my chest. I begin to pace. "What did he do to her? Who is this guy? Fuck!" My hands tug my hair. "Fuck, Hattie! Did he hurt Beth? My Beth? Who the fuck is he?"

She lifts her hand. "Shh. Reed, please. You'll wake Danny. I don't want him to know about this yet. He'll drive up there and kill that man. I won't be able to talk him down."

I grip the back of a chair, leaning over it. My teeth clench. "What did he do to her?"

She stares at me for a long second, her eyes misting. "I think he was just very mean," she explains quickly, wiping her fingers across her cheek to catch the fresh tears. "She said he never touched her, nothing like that, but I could tell, Reed. She said she never would've stayed with him if she had anywhere else to go. Why would she have said that if he was a good guy?"

I take in several slow, deep breaths, relaxing my grip on the chair before I split the wood.

Beth.

"A name," I growl, pulling Hattie's eyes back up to mine. "I need a name, and an address. Please tell me you know where this shit-head lives."

Her shoulders drop. "I don't have an address. His name is

Rocco. That's all I know. I don't know his last name either. I'm sorry." She pinches her lips into a thin line when the bottom one begins to tremble.

I tug the phone out of my pocket.

"Who are you calling?"

Sliding the chair out, I slump down, leaning forward onto my elbows. I hold the phone in one hand while the other cradles my head. My throat constricts. I feel dizzy, sick with blame, with a number of other emotions I've rarely ever felt. Some entirely foreign to me.

Rage.

Fear.

Loss.

Love.

I press the phone to my ear as a chair moves along the floor behind me. Hattie's taken her seat. The call connects after the second ring.

"What's up?"

"I need you to find someone for me. I need an address, and it can't fucking wait, okay? Can you help me?"

"Hol-Hold on. Hey, turn that down a minute," Ben says away from the phone. The police scanner quiets. "What the hell is going on?"

"Who is that?" I recognize Luke's quick to annoy tone.

"It's Beth. She's gone. She went back to Louisville, to this guy. I need to go get her. I need to bring her back. She can't be with him. I need . . ."

"Whoa, slow down," Ben interrupts. "What about Beth?"

Swallowing, I cringe when I taste bile. I take in a shaky breath, blinking the room into focus.

"She left. It's my fault."

I try to speak slowly, to let the words settle in the air, but the longer they linger on my tongue, the sicker I feel.

I want them out. I want Beth back. I need to tell her so many things.

"I love you . . . I love you."

God, I was a fucking coward.

I stand and resume pacing. "She went back to this guy she lived with before she moved here. I need to find her, Ben. You need to fucking help me find her. This guy . . . he's mean to her. To my Beth, he's fucking mean to her, and I am losing it, okay? I have a first name. I know she's in Louisville. Please. I don't ask you for shit. I need this. Can you just . . ."

"Reed, fuck, man, calm down."

"I can't calm down! I love her! Can you help me or not?"

Hattie gasps from her seat.

I advance to the island and flatten my palm against the cold marble. My head hanging heavy between my shoulders. My legs threatening to give out.

"What's his name?" Luke's voice cuts through the line, a bit distant. I realize I've been put on speaker phone. Fingers tap hurriedly on a keyboard.

I sag against the corner of the island. "Rocco. I don't have a last name."

"Rocco? The fuck kind of a name is that? He sounds like a little bitch."

Luke's remark is fucking spot-on.

"I doubt there's a lot of Rocco's in Kentucky. Should help narrow the search. Where are you?" Ben asks.

"Beth's aunt and uncle's house. Where she was staying."

"Right . . . yeah, I know where that is. Mia mentioned how close Beth lived to us. What's the house number?"

"12," I blurt out, then question. "Why?"

"We'll pick you up. Be there in twenty."

"What? What do you mean you'll pick me up? Give me the address so I can get the hell out of here."

"And do what? Drive up there and beat the shit out of this guy for hurting Beth? Did you consider what might happen if he isn't so willing to let her go? You don't know anything about this guy. He could have fucking weapons in his house, Reed. What if he pulls a gun on you?"

"Don't be fucking stupid. We're going with you. We're getting ready to end our shift anyway," Luke adds.

I pinch my eyes shut. Fuck, I hadn't thought about how this could play out. Weapons? Could this asshole actually be dangerous?

Images of Beth cowering, scared and sad filter through my mind.

I'll kill him.

"Fine, whatever. Hurry up."

I disconnect the call, shoving my phone away.

"Reed?" Hattie's kind voice lifts my head. Our eyes meet across the room. "Bring her back. She loves you."

I wait for Ben and Luke by the front door, wiping the wetness from my eyes.

EIGHT HOURS, TWO state lines, and the impending obstacle of traffic stand between me and Beth.

The guys show up after ditching their patrol car, but staying in uniform. Ben insists on driving his truck, keeping his speed close to one hundred miles per hour for the bulk of the trip. I realize quickly how grateful I am to have them with me. If I had made this journey alone, I would've either gotten pulled over for speeding, or road rage. Most likely both. We're making great time, but I'm ready to crawl out of my skin. My stomach has twisted into an unforgiving knot. My leg won't stop bouncing restlessly against the seat.

"How you doing back there?"

"Mm. Fine," I answer Ben, or Luke, was it? My head shakes against my hand. Definitely not fine. I look up front. "I've never thrown a punch before. Ever, but I might actually kill this guy. There's a good chance I'll see him with Beth and lose my fucking mind. If that happens, am I looking at jail time?"

Wouldn't that be the perfect end to this nightmare. Telling Beth I love her behind a glass partition.

Luke turns his head. "You're not going to kill him. We'll let you hit him a little, but unless we see him doing shit to Beth, hurting her in some way or threatening us, there's not much we can do. We can't arrest him for being mean to her."

"He might not even be home. Most people work until five, six o'clock. If it's just Beth there, do you really want to stick around and wait for this prick to come home just so you can punch him?"

I glare at the rear-view mirror, meeting Ben's eyes.

Asshole. Like you wouldn't camp out on someone's lawn for a month if they looked at Mia wrong.

His gaze trains on the road. "Fair enough."

"If he has weapons and shit, that's different though. And we can make it pretty fucking clear that he needs to stay the hell away from Beth. You can drive that point home." Luke leans closer to the GPS. "We're close. Ten miles."

Ten miles. God, I can practically feel the warmth of Beth's skin.

"How do I," I clear my throat. My hand skims down my neck, tugs at my collar. *Fuck, I'm burning up.*

"What?" Ben probes in my silence.

"Tell her . . . I need to tell her I love her." My tongue thickens in my mouth.

Damn it. Is this how it's going to be?

I meet Ben's eyes again, gesturing at him. "You're so fucking upfront with your feelings. How can I be like that with her? Is it enough to just say it? Will she know how fucking lost I am?"

"You've said it before," he remarks evenly. "To that girl you proposed to. Was it hard then?"

"No, but this is Beth. I've never felt like this."

"You've never loved anyone but her."

"Right." I lean back against the seat. My eyes lower. *"Fuck,"* I whisper.

That's it. There it is, right there. How did I not see it until now?

I stirred all night in the absence of Beth. I've suffered through every separation from her, even in the beginning when we were only pretending.

Was I ever really pretending?

This, with her, has always been different. Molly could've been states away for years and I would've handled it. I never loved her. It's only ever been Beth.

"It'll be enough," Ben assures.

I lift my head and catch his gaze briefly before his eyes turn back to the road.

"Tell her everything. How much you love her, how long you've felt like that. Don't hold back. Don't keep shit from her she deserves to hear. I think she'll see how lost you are for her, Reed. It's fucking obvious to everyone else. Right now, she just needs to hear it."

"What if she doesn't believe me? What if she thinks I'm just saying it now because she left?"

"She'll believe you," Luke assures me. He jerks his chin. "Just don't say it while you're knocking out this fucker, yeah? Wait 'til you can grab her face and hold her and shit. Girls love that."

Ben laughs. "Really? Is that what you did with Tessa? Played the romance card?"

"Nah, that's your style. I just fucked her 'til she *knew* I loved her." Luke turns halfway in his seat. "That always works too. I . . . shit!" His body slams against the door. "Jesus! I was kidding!" he yells, prying Ben's fist off his shirt.

"I'll fucking bury you if you say shit like that again about my sister." He slaps the back of Luke's head. "Asshole."

"You mean, *my wife*? You can start calling her that, you know." Luke sits up, rubbing the back of his head. "And I was fucking kidding."

I lean back with a heavy sigh. My leg resumes bouncing. "How much longer?"

Luke looks at the GPS. "It's just up here on the right. 211 Willbank."

The truck slows to a stop. Ben grabs my shoulder and pulls me back when I make to sprint for the house.

"Wait a minute. You can't just go running in there, Reed."

I shrug his hand off. "Why the fuck not? You're both cops. Say you heard something suspicious. Kick the fucking door down."

"You see that?" Luke nods toward the driveway behind me. The sight of Beth's car makes my heart race.

And beside it, a black Lexus.

I crack my knuckles. "He's here. Good. I won't have to hunt his ass down to kill him."

The sound of snaps popping open draws my attention back to Luke, then Ben. They both pull the slides back on their

Glocks, then place them back into the holsters.

"Fuck," I mumble, my anxiety pitting in my chest.

"We probably won't need them. It's just in case." Ben jerks his chin. "Let's go."

The temperature in the air seems to drop as we climb the stone steps and collect on the porch. My eyes shift between the two of them. I'm expecting someone with an actual weapon to take charge.

"What do we do, knock? What the fuck is protocol here?" I ask curtly.

"Protocol? You realize we don't have any jurisdiction, right?" Ben motions toward the door. "I'm just hoping this asshole is too stupid to realize we aren't Kentucky cops."

A low, feminine moan pulls my shoulders back, whips my head around. *No. No no no she can't be. She's not . . .*

"Shit," Ben mumbles. "Reed, wait . . ."

Too fucking late.

I twist the knob and to my surprise and gratitude, the door swings open. I storm into the house. Grunts and wild, hungry growls muffle the commotion of our entrance. I cross the open room in four quick strides, barreling at the two bodies entangled on the couch. Long, dark hair spills over the edge of the leather. My stomach drops out. I grab the shoulders of the man thrusting into Beth and toss him onto the floor.

"What the fuck is this?" I shout, glaring down at Beth . . . only, it's not Beth. I stagger back.

Heavily lined green eyes blink up at me. Her mouth, too thin, with a piercing in the bottom lip, pinches together. Startled, she throws her arm over her breasts and scoots up the couch.

"Hey, what the fuck, man? Shit! I ain't breaking any laws!"

I turn my head.

Ben has Rocco easily pinned against the wall, face-first, one hand to his neck, the other securing his wrists behind his back.

"Don't fucking move. You fight me and you'll regret it," Ben warns against his ear.

The asshole snarls. "You can't just come into my house. Don't you need a fucking warrant or some shit?"

"We heard suspicious noises. A women in distress." Luke laughs. "You know, 'cause your dick's so fucking small. She sounded real upset about it." Bending down, he grabs a white dress off the floor and tosses it onto the couch. "Get dressed and get out of here," he orders briskly.

The woman quickly obeys. I step closer to Ben as a door closes in the distance.

My eyes flare with rage. "Where is she? Where's Beth?"

Rocco turns his face so it's flat against the wall. He laughs darkly. "Beth? Beth who?"

Ben grips Rocco's dark hair and cranes his head back. Rocco winces through a moan. "Answer him."

I step closer as Rocco shifts his eyes to me. He mouth twitches. "Ohhh, I get it. She came back 'cause of you, right? My girl's all sad and pathetic now. I should be thanking you. I like her better this way."

My fist connects with his jaw the second Ben jerks him back.

"She ain't your fucking girl!"

I get another hit in, this one to the nose. He groans as blood spills down his chin. Ben backs away and Rocco falls to his knees, cupping his face.

"Fuck!" he hisses. "You broke my nose!"

"You're lucky I don't fucking kill you!" A hand on my arm keeps me back when I try and lunge. I jerk my bicep out of Luke's grip and loom over the prick on the floor. My chest heaves against my shirt. "Where is she? I won't ask you again."

"The bedroom." Eyes watering over, he pinches them shut, still covering his nose. His head lowers with a strangled groan.

I make to turn and find a staircase, but I have more to say to this piece of shit. He looks up when I move closer.

"She's leaving with me, and you're to stay the fuck away from her. If I see you again, if you so much as think about *my girl,* I'll put you in the ground. I will fucking kill you, you understand?"

He huffs out a laugh, gesturing to Luke with a bloody palm. "Hello? You hear him threatening me? Ain't you gonna arrest him?"

Luke turns his head slowly. "Shut the fuck up. I didn't hear shit."

At that moment, Ben must kick against Rocco's back, because he face plants on the carpet, bellowing in pain like a little bitch. "Oww, fuucckk. My fuckin` nose. Christ!"

"Getting tired of seeing your pathetic excuse for a dick hanging out. Stay down." Ben lifts his head, nodding at me. "Go. We got him."

I find the stairs and take the steps two, three at a time. The upstairs is quiet. I pass a bathroom and an office before finally opening the last door at the end of the hallway.

The room is dark, compliments of the drawn curtains. My hand swipes along the wall in search of the light switch. A lamp in the corner sparks on, illuminating Beth's small body curled up on one side of the bed. I cross the room hastily.

Stopping when I see her, I stare down at my girl. I nearly fall to my knees beside her.

She's asleep in jeans and a faded concert tee, giant

noise-canceling head-phones covering her ears. I brush my fingers across her cheek and she stirs, her eyes fluttering open. A lazy smile pulls at her mouth.

"Mm. I don't want to wake up this time," she whispers, her voice thick with sleep, her eyes slowly moving over my face.

I sit beside her and slide the headphones off. *Does she think she's dreaming?*

"Beth."

She smiles again.

I fit her sweet face between both of my hands and kiss her soft mouth.

She inhales sharply, pulling back. "Reed?"

I move away an inch, nearly laughing at the shock blooming in her eyes. "Beth Davis. What are you doing to me?"

She touches my lips, moves her fingers over my jaw. "You're . . . you're here? How are you here? Why?"

"Why? That's a silly question. You're here."

"But . . ."

I slide my mouth over hers. "I should've said it." She goes perfectly still against me, her small hands circling my wrists as I hold her face.

Shaking her head, she sits up and pulls my hands away. Her touch suddenly feels cold. "No. No, Reed, it's fine. You told me you couldn't want me any more than you already did. I was stupid to forget that."

"You were stupid to love me?"

She stares at me for the longest second, her hands tangling together in her lap. "I was stupid to think you could love me back. That anyone could."

My stomach clenches as I look at her, as I reach for her again. "I want to get you out of here. I want to take you back to that hotel room and say everything I've always been meant to say to you. You weren't stupid, Beth. I was. I should've said it."

"Reed."

I move with her, refusing to let her slide off the bed. Her thigh tenses under my hand. "Just listen to me." Her eyes lift to mine. "I thought I couldn't love anyone again after all that shit with Molly. I hadn't done more than one night with a woman in nine years. I didn't want it. I didn't want to feel that helpless for someone again, just to have them break me. But you . . . God, Beth, I wanted all of you from the beginning, from that first night at the bar. I never wanted anything less. I never will. When I didn't say it back, it wasn't because I didn't love you. I was realizing I did. I was realizing that for the past nine years, it wouldn't have mattered if I was scared to love again or not. I could've dated those women, I could've kissed them, but nobody would've made me fall except you. It's only ever been you, Beth."

I shift on the bed. My other hand forms to her hip. I feel electric being this close to her.

"What do you mean, it's only ever been me?" she asks quietly, her tongue wetting her lips.

I duck my head and kiss her temple. "Only ever loved you, brave girl. No one else," I whisper against her skin, sliding my mouth to her ear. Her breath rushes hot against my neck as I close my eyes. "God, my heart's pounding."

She flattens her hand against the center of my chest, breathlessly murmuring, "Mine too."

"Come home with me."

Her chin lifts with guidance of my hand. I run my thumb over the flush in her cheek.

"Home. O-Okay." Her mouth lifts slightly. "To my aunt's? Or . . ."

I breathe a laugh. Only Beth can shove me in a direction

I didn't know I was ready for.

"I like 'or' better." I kiss her mouth quickly, then lean away, sighing, my hands refusing to leave her skin. "There's still so much I want to say to you, but I don't want to say it here, in this house. I don't want my words to be mixed with his."

After a slight hesitation, she nods, not questioning what I mean by that. She must understand that I know more than she's told me. If not, it'll be obvious the second she sees the state I've left Rocco in.

Fucker. He deserves worse, and he'll get it if he ever tries anything.

We pack up her things, which takes no longer than two minutes. Beth never really unpacked much of anything yesterday, except a few items. She pulls her Kindle against her chest, hugging it, then sets it on the dresser.

"You're not taking it?" I ask her, grabbing the duffle off the bed.

"It was from Rocco." She purses her lips. "It was the only thing I had before that I loved. But I have you now, I don't need it."

Shit. She loves that thing. She just fucking hugged it goodbye.

Grabbing the back of her neck, I drop a kiss to the top of her head. "I'll buy you a new one."

She smiles up at me, then lightly kisses my jaw.

I keep her against my side as we walk down the stairs. Rocco is sitting on the couch now, dressed, holding a bloody rag to his face. Ben and Luke standing in front of him like a pair of guard dogs on steroids. I take Beth immediately outside, expecting the questions to start, but she just snakes her arms around my waist and presses kisses to my chest.

She tries to lead me to her car.

"That's staying here. We'll get you another one."

I've never seen her look more confused. Her nose crinkles as she gazes up at me. "But, it's my car. I need a car."

"You don't need *that* car. I can't stand looking at it and knowing you lived in that thing. It bothers me. I don't want you driving it anymore."

She puts a hand on her hip, fighting a smile. "Reed."

"Forget it, woman. It stays here."

She narrows her eyes, laughing. Her arms snake around my neck, pressing her body into mine as she whispers kisses against my throat. "You love me," she murmurs.

"Mm." I trace my finger down the side of her face, gazing down at her. "I am scared though, Beth. If you leave me again I don't think . . ." I swallow hard. "No, I know, I know I won't survive that. You can't leave me, even when I fuck up, and I will fuck up. I've never done this. I might be bad at it."

My words hang in the air between us, different from the first time I said them to her. Before it was "I haven't done this in nine years". Now she knows she's my first.

"I've never done this either," she says. Her hands lightly squeeze my hips. "I'm scared too."

The front door opens. Ben and Luke walk down the stone steps.

"Let's go home." I wrap my arm around her waist, leading her to the truck.

I need to get my girl alone.

BETH CALLS HER aunt on the drive back. When Danny gets on the line and asks to speak to me, I hesitate bringing the phone up to my ear. It's my fault Beth left. She never would've gone back to some guy who made her feel anything less than perfect if it wasn't for me. I still don't know what all words Rocco used to break her down. I'm not sure I want to know. What would stop me from driving back to Kentucky and making good on my promise?

Nothing, that's fucking what.

Danny, to my surprise, doesn't tear into me for being the catalyst in all this. He simply thanks me for getting Beth back, in his own *I'm still going to give you shit for dating my niece* way. His tone can't be more critical. As always, I keep my reaction to his attitude silent.

I pull Beth into my arms after she disconnects the call, burying my face in her neck, letting my hands roam over her limbs, my fingers threading into her hair. I feel like I haven't touched her in years, or maybe never. There's a desperation to it I know she can feel.

Her warm hands cup my face. She brushes away the wetness brimming in my eyes. I don't want to be an emotional wreck but fuck!

"I'm so in love with you I feel like I can't breathe," I whisper against her neck, trying to somehow explain the reason behind my sudden discomposure.

Sudden. Right. She's been watching me unravel for weeks.

She leans back to gaze at me, staring at my mouth as if she wants to see my lips form those words.

"Love you, brave girl." I bring her hand to my mouth, kissing her fingers.

She strokes my face, kissing my mouth, my jaw, up to my ear where she whispers, "Thank you."

I tilt my head to see her. "For loving you?"

"For saying it."

I pull her into my lap, mumbling how crazy she is, how crazy I am for her.

AFTER THANKING THE guys, waiting impatiently for Beth to thank the guys, scowling at Ben when he won't stop fucking talking to Beth, I get her inside so she can see her aunt and uncle. Their exchange of hugs and quiet conversation is brief while I hang by the door. They need this time alone together.

I drive home with Beth tucked against my side, her hands clutching my shirt. Her duffle hits the hardwood as we stumble inside my house together. Grabbing her body and pinning her to me, I lower us to the floor just inside the doorway.

"Reed," she giggles against my throat. Her hands in my hair. "Here?"

I kiss her mouth. I bite her jaw. "Here, first. I can't . . . I need . . ."

"I know," she says. She understands my urgency.

Will it always be like this after any time apart?

I pull her boots and socks off, kissing her feet as she squirms. I cup her ass and tear her jeans down her legs. Her panties follow. Bunching her shirt above her full, perfect tits, I pull the shell of her bra down and tongue her nipple.

"Oh." She grabs my hand and forms it to her other breast, moaning when I squeeze.

"You taste so fucking good." I kiss her cleavage. I lick up to her neck, inhaling a lung full of her sweet scent. "God, Beth. Touch me. Please, I need to feel you."

She grabs a fistful of my shirt and pulls it over my head. My back hits the floor with the force of her hand. I yield easily to her assault. Straddling me, she fumbles with the button on my jeans, grinning.

"Hi," she murmurs in the softest voice, pulling her shirt the rest of the way off, discarding her bra.

"Hey." I press my thumb against her clit, moving in slow circles. Her fingers tremble against my zipper. "Come on. Pull it out, Beth. Get on my dick."

Her eyes flash with lust. She loves that. She loves when I talk filthy, when I order her to fuck me, suck me. My thumb coats with her desire.

She tugs my jeans down around my thighs and fists my cock, pumping my shaft, running her tongue over the head. I thrust my hips subtly. "Fuck, no, don't," I strain.

"No?"

"It's . . . it's a lot, right now. I won't last."

She bites her lip behind a smile, no doubt proud of her effect on me. "Help me," she whispers, splaying her hands over my lower abs.

Grabbing her hips, I sit up and shift us on the floor so my back is against the wall. She gasps as her nipples scratch against my chest. I take her weight, digging my fingers into her hips, slowly lowering her on my cock.

She squeezes my neck. "I love you," she murmurs.

"Beth." An inch more, she pulls me in, clamping down on me so goddamn tight my balls start to throb. "I love you. God, I love you so fucking much."

Her hips fully seat on mine. I lift and lower her, again and again, her smooth thighs tensing. When she starts to rock her hips, I drop my hand between her legs, sliding my fingers around my cock to feel where I enter her.

"Fuck, Beth . . . fuck, feel this. Here. Come here."

Grabbing her hand, I guide her fingers between us, my other hand rocking her so she slides up and down my shaft.

"Oh, God," she gasps. "How does it . . . tell me how it feels."

"Perfect." I slide her fingers to her clit, thrusting my hips off the floor. *God, it's so deep this way.* "It's never felt like this before . . . not with anyone else. I lose my mind every time you touch me."

"G-Go on," she stammers, her head rolling back, her swollen pussy soaking me.

I bounce her again and we moan together. "I'm . . . so hard, all the time, thinking about you. I love watching you take my dick like this. You like it deep?"

"Mm."

"You do, I know you do. Always telling me harder. *Harder, Reed. Do it.* You're so perfect, Beth. God, you're perfect." I push my jeans down further so I can feel her ass against my thighs. I slap one round cheek, again when she clamps down on me, again when she begs me for more. I lift her tits, circling her nipples with my tongue.

Beth rocks her hips faster. Her hands in my hair, she pulls my face away from her tits and takes my mouth. "I need to come. I n-need . . ."

"What do you need, sweetheart?" I manage, chasing my orgasm, my pace growing wild. I can't stop fucking her. She's here, Beth is here—my Beth. God, how long have I loved her? From the beginning? From that first kiss? Fuck, if it isn't the most cliché thing I've ever thought, but that's how long I've been hers.

She sucks on my lips, panting. "Oh, God, I need to feel you . . . come. Please come, Reed."

My hand grips her neck, the other holding her hip while I thrust frantically off the floor. With a cry, Beth shakes against me, bites my lip, claws her nails down my back. I bury my face in her neck and swear as I release inside her. Wetness sticks to my thighs.

"Beth . . . Beth . . . *fuck.*"

We collapse against the wall, sliding to the floor. I push her damp hair off her face and look into her eyes. She tucks her body next to me, still panting.

"I can't be apart from you," I say against her swollen lips, softly kissing her. "Not even for one night, Beth. Move in with me. Be here, with me. God, I want this so bad. I don't care how scary this is. I want all of you. Please, please say yes to me. To us. Just you and me, right?"

She stares at me for a second. Her warm hands touch my face, push through my hair.

"You and me," she murmurs, beaming up at me.

"Beth," I breathe, ducking my face under her head, kissing her neck, holding onto my girl so goddamn tight. Nothing else matters but this.

You and me.

beth

Three Weeks Later

REED LIKES TO say I've been his since that first kiss. McGill's will always be special to us for that reason, but here, at Swan Harbor, is where it feels like it all started. It's where we stopped pretending and lost ourselves to each other in a dimly lit room overlooking an engagement party. It might be where I fell in love with Reed, or when I knew I loved him. It's hard to pin-point that exact moment. Maybe it was that kiss at McGill's. Maybe neither one of us were ever really pretending.

This room . . . it wasn't just about those first touches, or the kiss Reed took that was all for him. I saw his pain in this room. I saw a man stuck in the past, held captive by his memories of this place and the woman who never deserved him. I wanted to be his distraction from all of it, but more than that, I wanted to be his only memory.

"I want to use my advantage now," I say, sounding hurried. Frantic. Desperate.

"I was picking up on that." He stares at my mouth, tilting his head down. "What do you want, sweetheart? You want to kiss me?"

My eyes flash open at the sound of the door creaking behind me. Reed sticks his head inside, smiling when he sees me by the window. The lamp in the corner casts streaks of soft amber light along the floor.

"Hey, there you are." He moves across the room after closing the door. "Hiding out? Luke and Tessa are about to cut the cake."

"I was just . . . having a moment."

He raises an eyebrow. "Déjà vu, you remember?"

"Of course. I practically molested you in here."

"Molested?" He snorts, gently squeezing my hips. He kisses my mouth. "I was a very willing participant, Beth. Best hand-job of my life." He leans back, smiling. "Best kiss too."

"Really? *That* kiss was the best one?" I bite my cheek to keep a straight face.

God, it's all I do anymore—smile around this man.

His lip twitches. "Second best."

"Mm" My hands tug at his belt. "I might be able to top that best hand-job, if you want." He groans when I slide his zipper down. Warm flesh fills my palm, quickly hardening.

"God, Beth."

"Reed?" I whisper against his neck, stroking him, moaning as his fingers dig into my flesh.

I knew he'd come find me. I knew exactly what I was going to do the second I stepped into this room, even before that. I've planned this out.

He tries to lift the hem of my dress. I bat his hand away, smiling at the frown he gives me.

"I can't touch you?"

I shake my head slowly, rubbing my thumb along the tip of his cock. Squeezing him from base to tip, I stroke him in the same spot we stood all those weeks ago. He makes hungry noises against my mouth, biting me, sucking my lips. He tugs on my hair to expose my neck, telling me how amazing my skin tastes, how wet he knows I am for him. His hands squeeze my breasts, pinching my nipples through the thin material of my dress.

I can't stop looking at him. At the light stubble dusting his jaw, the perfect line of his mouth.

"How long do you want this?" I ask as my back hits the wall.

He drops his forehead against mine, moaning. "This . . . hand-job? Until I come would be fantastic."

I wet my lips, my breathing all over the place, erratic along with his. "No. This. You and me, how long do you want it?"

He leans back slightly, staring down at me through hooded eyes.

"I want it forever," I whisper, fondling him roughly, squeezing his cock just how he likes it. "I'll never want anyone else."

"Beth," he groans, pinching his eyes shut. His hips rock into my hand. He's throbbing, swelling against my palm.

God, he gets so hard when I do this.

"How long do you want it, Reed?"

"Forever," he pants. He sounds tortured.

"Watch me. Watch me touch you."

His eyes spark open with desire, and something darker. It sends a violent shudder through my body. Tilting his head down, he watches my hand work his cock. His lips part, his hands on my waist tremble.

You and me.

"Fuck, Beth. I'm close."

I reach my other hand into his pants and cup his balls. He gasps through a moan. Sweat beads on his brow.

"Marry me. Marry me, Reed."

His eyes go round for a second, then flutter close as his orgasm takes him. "Yes," he moans. "Fuck . . . yes." He grabs my face, crashing our mouths together, moaning as his release coats my hand.

My body clings to him. I kiss him with everything I have, with every piece of my soul. Long, and deep, and full of all of my love for him. I swallow the soft murmurs of my name as he presses them against my lips.

He said yes! He said yes!

I want to scream. I want everyone to know that this beautiful man is mine. I want to run away tonight and make it official.

He reaches around my back and pulls me away from the wall, flattening my body against his.

"You said yes." I kiss his jaw as he cleans off my hand with a handkerchief. "I really didn't know if you would."

He tosses the cloth into the trash bin, zipping up his pants. His thumb moves over my cheek. "You get me a ring?"

Oh . . . well, shit.

Cringing, I shake my head. "No, I didn't even think . . ."

His hands fall away from my body, one disappears behind his back. "Thank God one of us came prepared," he says, his voice curling deliciously.

My mouth falls open when he produces a tiny black box out of his pocket. I don't know why I'm so stunned. I just proposed to him. He said yes. But the sight of him dropping to his knee in front of me has my heart racing so fast I fear it might break out of my chest.

I drop down onto the floor, grabbing his face.

"Beth," he laughs. "What are you doing? There's supposed to be a substantial height difference during this."

I shake my head. "No, like this, please."

I help him open the box. Tears well up in my eyes as he slips the ring on my finger, as he kisses the back of my hand.

It's perfect.

"You're perfect," he says matter-of-factly.

Oh, I said that out loud?

He cradles my face gently in his hands. "Beth Davis, from McGill's . . ."

We both laugh. He kisses me quickly.

"Brave girl, will you marry me?"

I throw myself at him, tackling him to the floor, planting sweet kisses all over his face.

"That a yes?"

"Yes!" I yell, giggling against his mouth.

He pins me beneath him, his eyes glowing like embers in the dark. "I can't believe you proposed to me with my dick in your hand. Jesus, Beth."

"It should've been in my mouth, right?" Sighing, I shake my head. "Such poor planning on my part."

"Mm." He traces my bottom lip with his finger, leaning closer. "This is for me. You understand?"

I melt against his mouth as he takes that kiss, again, and again, and again.

The End

acknowledgements

MR. DANIELS, YOU, YOU are my favorite. Thank you for loving me through all my craziness, for supporting my passion and keeping the kids in line while I hide out in my writing cave. You are the best assistant I could ever ask for. Let's run away together, just you and me . . . and the kids, I guess. I mean, I would miss them. They are adorable and could fetch us umbrella drinks. Just a thought.

Beth Cranford, thank you for being my Bethie, my boo, my beta, and my friend. I hope this story is everything you were hoping for. Reed is and will always be yours. Thank you for all the late night chats, the ramblings where we talk about absolutely nothing, the voicemails where I get to sigh over your dreamy Aussie voice, everything. EVERYTHING. I love your face, and I fucking miss it, so move up here already! (P.S. MINE)

Lisa Jayne, my sweet, sweet Brit! I love how you love this story. Your sweet messages, little snap shots of a passage, and purple hearts made me smile while I was stuck behind my laptop. I want to hop a plane and tackle you to the ground. I also want to drink tea and do proper things with you. Thank you for being my beta, and my friend.

Kellie Richardson, Pwincess Kellie, KG, CHLOE . . . I could keep going. What the hell can I say about my favorite Kinky Girl? Reese brought us together, but the entire world knows by now that Ben is your man. Although, you did try and give it to Reed in this book . . . shame on you. Thank you for loving my Bama Boys, for the amazing teasers you make me, for being my friend, and for responding right away when I text you . . . SIT DOWN. I have to wait hours sometimes! Thank you for your "hmmms", which ultimately made this story better. Okaaaay, Nolan woves you. Beth Davis from McGill's loves you. Big Ben loves you. #BitchesLoveIt

Kylie McDermott, thank you for EVERYTHING! Please come to the states so I can hug you! You bust your ass for me, and I don't know if you realize how much I appreciate you. Thank you. Thank you. THANK YOU.

J's Sweeties, my lovies! Thank you girls for getting my name out there. I love interacting with you in the Street Team. Your enthusiasm for this story has meant the world to me. I hope you love Reed as much as I do.

To all the amazing bloggers, thank you so much for helping me reach more readers, for adding my books to your TBRs, and for leaving me reviews. I wish I could meet each and every one of you and give you all massive hugs. LOVE you all.

To my readers, thank you so, so much for all of the love you have shown me, for the messages, emails, shout-outs, but most importantly, for wanting to read my words. I will never be able to express my gratitude to you.

A special thanks to Kinky Girls Book Obsessions.

xo,

J

books by
J. DANIELS

about the author

J DANIELS IS THE *New York Times* and *USA Today* bestselling author of the Sweet Addiction series, the Alabama Summer series, and the Dirty Deeds series.

She would rather bake than cook, she listens to music entirely too loud, and loves writing stories her children will never read. Her husband and children are her greatest loves, with cupcakes coming in at a close second.

J grew up in Baltimore and resides in Maryland with her family.

follow ᴊ at:

www.authorjdaniels.com

Facebook
www.facebook.com/jdanielsauthor

Twitter—@JDanielsbooks

Instagram—authorjdaniels

Goodreads
http://bit.ly/JDanielsGoodreads

Join her reader's group for the first look at upcoming projects, special giveaways, and loads of fun!

www.facebook.com/groups/JsSweeties

Sign up to receive her newsletter and get special offers and exclusive release info.

www.authorjdaniels.com/newsletter

playlist

Awake by Secondhand Serenade (Reed's song to Beth)

Pusher Love Girl by Justin Timberlake

Layla by Eric Clapton

Animals by Maroon 5

Wild Horses by The Rolling Stones

Work Song by Hozier

Hands Down by Dashboard Confessional

The Falling by Eli Young Band

Hold You In My Arms by Ray LaMontagne

CPSIA information can be obtained
at www.ICGtesting.com
Printed in the USA
LVOW11s0251030417
529387LV00001B/42/P